Anarchy

STEWART BINNS

PENGUIN BOOKS

PENGUIN BOOKS

Published by the Penguin Group
Penguin Books Ltd, 80 Strand, London WC2R 0RL, England
Penguin Group (USA) Inc., 375 Hudson Street, New York, New York 10014, USA
Penguin Group (Canada), 90 Eglinton Avenue East, Suite 700, Toronto, Ontario, Canada M4P 2Y3
(a division of Pearson Penguin Canada Inc.)
Penguin Ireland, 25 St Stephen's Green, Dublin 2, Ireland (a division of Penguin Books Ltd)
Penguin Group (Australia), 707 Collins Street, Melbourne, Victoria 3008,
Australia (a division of Pearson Australia Group Pty Ltd)
Penguin Books India Pvt Ltd, 11 Community Centre,
Panchsheel Park, New Delhi – 110 017, India
Penguin Group (NZ), 67 Apollo Drive, Rosedale, Auckland 0632, New Zealand
(a division of Pearson New Zealand Ltd)
Penguin Books (South Africa) (Pty) Ltd, Block D, Rosebank Office Park, 181 Jan Smuts Avenue,
Parktown North, Gauteng 2193, South Africa

Penguin Books Ltd, Registered Offices: 80 Strand, London WC2R 0RL, England

www.penguin.com

First published 2013
001

Set in 12.5/14.75 pt Garamond MT Std
Typeset by Palimpsest Book Production Limited, Falkirk, Stirlingshire
Printed in Great Britain by Clays Ltd, St Ives plc

ISBN: 978–0–718–19459–8

www.greenpenguin.co.uk

MIX
Paper from
responsible sources
FSC
www.fsc.org   FSC® C018179

Penguin Books is committed to a sustainable
future for our business, our readers and our planet.
This book is made from Forest Stewardship
Council™ certified paper.

ALWAYS LEARNING   **PEARSON**

To all those who fight for justice

Contents

Contents

Introduction

When Henry Beauclerc, King of England and Duke of Normandy, died in 1135, the powerful Norman dynasty that had conquered England in 1066 still held the English and its own Norman heartland in the iron gauntlet of its daunting rule. Henry was the fourth son of his formidable father, William the Bastard, Conqueror of the English. Henry had grabbed the English throne when his elder brother, William Rufus, was killed by an arrow while hunting in the New Forest in 1100. He then seized the Dukedom of Normandy from his eldest brother, Robert Curthose, who had been fighting in the First Crusade when Rufus died. Henry defeated Robert at the Battle of Tinchebrai in 1106 and imprisoned him for almost thirty years – until he died in Cardiff Castle, in 1134.

There was little room for brotherly love in the harsh world of Norman kings.

Henry Beauclerc ruled his domain as came to be expected of a Norman warlord: efficiently and harshly. The conquered English had been cowed into submission by their ruthless Norman masters, but bitter resentment lay not far beneath the surface.

Henry produced a huge brood of children by almost as many women, but only two of them were legitimate. His second child, William Adelin, was groomed to be his successor: he would be William II, his mighty grandfather's namesake. But William was drowned in the disaster of the White Ship in 1120. Carelessly, Henry was left without a male heir and, try as he might, he could not produce a replacement for William – even with a young and fertile second wife. He turned to his firstborn, his daughter, Matilda, who he had already married off to Henry V, the Holy Roman Emperor. But she was also childless.

Then fate played an unexpected card: Henry V died suddenly in 1125, making it possible for the Empress Matilda to marry again and give Henry his grandson and heir. Geoffrey, the son of the Count of Anjou, a handsome young man who would bring Normandy an important strategic alliance as well as the fruits of his loins, was chosen. Henry was delighted, but not so Matilda: Geoffrey was only fourteen years old, Matilda was twenty-five. The marriage was not happy and the King's anticipated heir did not appear. But Henry was patient and named Matilda as his successor in the hope that a grandson would eventually be conceived and that Matilda would act as Queen Regent until the boy was old enough to inherit.

Two years before his death, Henry Beauclerc's patience was rewarded when Matilda gave birth to a son. Dutifully, she called the boy Henry in her father's honour. All seemed well, but all was not well: what appeared to be a happy conclusion to a crisis of succession was just the beginning of a tragic tale. Matilda was not only the daughter of a Norman king, she was also the daughter of Edith, a Scottish princess. Edith not only carried Celtic royal blood but, through her mother, Margaret, was a direct descendent of the vanquished kings of England. Thus, the Empress Matilda and her baby son embodied the hopes not only of a Norman dynasty, but also of every Celt and Englishman.

When King Henry died in 1135, fate dealt another rogue card. Matilda's cousin, Stephen of Blois, the son of Adela – William the Conqueror's youngest daughter and the ninth child of his large brood – emulated his uncle Henry's audacious move in 1100 and dashed across the Channel to grab the English crown.

But fate had also played a third card: a wild one, a joker, which changed the game completely. It brought another family into the saga, an English family – not one of royal pedigree, but one that had already played a crucial role in England's destiny and could trace its lineage back to a man whose heroic deeds were almost lost in legend: the mighty Hereward of Bourne.

Chaos followed Stephen of Blois' impudent move in 1135, not just a short interlude of dynastic warfare, but a long and bitter feud that lasted almost twenty years and brought England and Normandy to their knees. So terrible were the times that the chroniclers called them 'The Anarchy'.

One such chronicler was Gilbert Foliot, one of the great minds of twelfth-century Europe. Born into an ecclesiastical family in Normandy in 1110, he entered the great Abbey of Cluny at the age of twenty. A typically ambitious and determined member of the Norman elite which ruled England after the Conquest of 1066, he became Abbot of Gloucester in 1139, Bishop of Hereford in 1148 and Bishop of London in 1163. He was thus witness to one of the most tumultuous periods in English history: the Anarchy of Stephen and Matilda, the troubled reign of the mighty Henry Plantagenet and the trauma of the murder of Thomas Becket. Fluent in French, English and Latin, he was the most prolific letter-writer of his age; almost 300 of his letters have survived into modern times.

As a young man at Cluny, Gilbert befriended Thibaud de Vermandois. It was an amity that would last a lifetime. Vermandois became Abbot of Cluny in 1180 and when Pope Lucius III named him Cardinal Bishop of Ostia e Velletri – the ancient port of Rome and a sub-diocese of the Bishopric of Rome – in 1184, he became one of the most powerful men in the Church and signatory of all Papal Bulls.

In 1186, Foliot, who was now almost blind, increasingly frail with old age and fearing his imminent death, felt compelled to begin a long series of letters to Vermandois.

This is the story of the turbulent events he chronicled.

Prologue

Fulham Palace, 1 September 1186

My Dearest Thibaud,

*Forgive me, perhaps I should not be so familiar now that you wear
the blue cape of a cardinal of Rome. I imagine it tempts one's
vanity to be addressed as 'Eminence'. I am accorded 'Lord
Bishop', which is quite enough for the son of a steward, although I
have been greeted as 'Beatitude' a few times and even 'Holiness'
on one famous occasion in front of the entire Chapter of St
Paul's, which found it difficult to contain itself for several minutes.*

*I am so pleased for you. Ostia is a very agreeable place to enjoy
your elevation to the most venerable College of them all. Perhaps
you will invite your humble friend to visit you one day. We have
both come a long way since our days together at Cluny: you, one of
the most powerful men in the Church, I, someone of at least
modest influence here in England. I am so proud of you and what
you have achieved; for my part, and I hope I do not appear to be
too conceited, I am content with my own modest success here in
London.*

*I am sure you have many crosses to bear, each probably far
greater than mine. But if I may, I would like to add a little to
your many duties. There is something I need to share with you
and, if you will indulge me, I would like this letter to introduce a
very important subject.*

But first, I have some news about me you may find interesting, although, sad to say, it is far from good news. Thankfully, contentment with my past and my modest contribution to the Holy Church are important to my peace of mind as age takes its toll on me. My eyesight is now very poor. I can see enough to get about in bright sunshine, but darkness is just that for me: candles are a mere flicker before my eyes, they illuminate neither face nor feature, unless the flame is held very close.

My monks write everything for me, so if my Latin is not what it was, do forgive me. To my immense regret, I am unable to read anything written in my name. Sad to say, I am becoming feeble and have to use a stick for my short perambulations around the palace gardens. Mercifully, there is always a young monk nearby to steady me if I falter, or gather me up if I fall — an embarrassing mishap that has happened more than once.

If my duties require me to go to London, I am transported to the quay in a litter like a prince and then rowed in my rather splendid barge up the river to the city. I often imagine I am your good friend Orio Mastropiero, the Venerable Doge himself, in his robes of gold, being rowed along the Grand Canal in his galley of state. I have never been to Venice, but your descriptions of it are so vivid, I can imagine it in detail. I know my false pride is a sin, but I'm sure you will forgive an old man a small flight of fancy.

You would be impressed by my parish church of St Paul's. It is not as grand as some in Normandy, nor as majestic as the great cathedrals of antiquity. But it is a towering edifice built, I am told, on a site that was originally consecrated in the time of Rome and a pagan place of worship before that.

In fact, London has a remarkable collection of churches and chapels. Many of the smaller ones are ancient Saxon in origin —

charming little buildings with timber frames and thatched roofs
– but, since the Conquest, they are gradually being rebuilt in
stone. Bishops from the provinces, powerful earls from the Marches
and the wealthy city merchants are also building in stone. This
creates an arresting visual contrast: the small beige and brown
thatched hovels of the lower classes, who are still almost
exclusively English, are cast into gloomy shadow by the
gleaming creams and greys of the palaces and churches of the
governing elite, who are of course predominantly Norman.

I feel sorry for the English. They have suffered greatly, and
many still do. But they have boundless resolve and preserve their
culture with a tenacity that verges on the fanatical. Most
Normans now speak English fluently, and many young Norman
knights find the English propensity for drinking and debauchery
very seductive. This is to the chagrin of the older generation, who
complain that our old Norman disciplines are being lost in a land
that is still so English in its ways. The Celts in the north and
west are similar: also often feckless like many of the English, they
are perhaps even more fierce and independent.

Overt resistance from the English is long gone, but an
undercurrent of sullen resentment remains – a glance, a deference
denied, an occasional outburst – for they are a proud lot. I admire
them, as do many of my kin. The Welsh are still troublesome,
even to the hardiest Marcher lords, and the Scots still raid the
north with impunity. I often think it must have been like this
when the Romans ruled here. It took them centuries to pacify the
natives; we Normans have only been here for two generations, and
we still look and sound like an alien presence.

We govern from our towering fortresses, build our glorious
cathedrals to celebrate the power granted to us by God and we have
sequestered all the land with ruthless efficiency. But we are still

foreigners – even the grandchildren of those who came with the Conqueror.

In the burghs, life seems normal and, on the whole, prosperous. But among the peasants, especially in the remote areas, the English seem untouched by us. There are still bands of outlaws, often leading squalid lives, and the families of dispossessed English landowners scratch an existence in the wild places. Occasionally there is an outbreak of violence among the English loyalists. This is dealt with by the torture and execution of the rebels, which only adds more heat to the cauldron of simmering discontent.

We Normans believe in a strict regime – often too strict, in my view – but when a miscreant's head is impaled on a spike above the gates of London, or his corpse is left to sway in the wind from a gibbet over the Thames, the mood of brooding hostility from many of the native population is palpable. Apparently, among themselves, we are called the 'Bastards' after the Conqueror – an epithet he deserved of course, both literally and metaphorically. Sadly, some of my kin have earned the appellation as well. I have seen them behave with a rare brutality, and usually without sanction from the King or the law.

Much of the story I would like to share with you centres on the continuing problem of our rule in this land and the reluctance of the English to accept its permanence. I will return to that, but let me tell you a little more about my circumstances here.

London continues to thrive, but with that comes an ever greater burden on the clerics in my diocese for, as you know, with wealth comes poverty and, in the wake of both, sin. London is a sinful place: alehouses and brothels multiply; disease is rife and villainy proliferates. I know this is yet another reference to Ancient Rome, but I often think that London must be a mirror of Rome in its

4

pomp and squalor. We do not have the Colosseum, but we have bear pits and cockfights, fisticuffs and wrestling — both of which usually result in death or maiming — brawls and murders daily, quite apart from various judicial executions and mutilations by the score. I had always assumed Rouen was a depraved city, but London makes it seem more like a monastery; though I confess, I've known a few of those to be a little decadent.

Amidst London's new buildings and on its streets and quays you see a menagerie of people from all over the world. In the port of London, one is just as likely to hear Greek or Arabic spoken as English or French. I am told there are men to be seen on the Venetian trading ships who are as black as soot.

King Henry's Lord High Treasurer, Richard FitzNeal, an odious little miser, who prays for my imminent demise and covets my bishopric with an unseemly passion, tells me that London is home to more than 25,000 souls. God help us all, no place on earth can hope to retain its civility and well-being with so many greedy ambitions to satisfy and ravenous mouths to feed. Sadly, the lovely Thames, once a more than adequate sewer for the city, is now overwhelmed and the stench downstream from St Paul's is unbearable. I thank my predecessors daily for choosing an upriver location and the clean water and fresh air of Fulham for our palace. I wake every morning to tranquil birdsong and gentle mist over the meadows of Putney and Barnes. Yesterday was the Sabbath and last night we had a full moon. The river danced, lit by moonbeams; it looked like a great lake of quicksilver and I sat and watched it for hours, listening to the quiet murmurings of the night.

My friend, we are both getting old, in fact, very old. Indeed, it would not surprise me if we were the last of our generation at Cluny. I am seventy-six now; you, I think, are seventy-three. God

5

has been good to us. But he has also smiled on a pompous fool who I am sure you know: Heraclius, Patriarch of Jerusalem.

I met him last year when he arrived in London to consecrate a new church for the Knights Templars, built on the ancient site of an old Saxon settlement in Holborn. It has a beautiful circular nave that, I am told, reflects the Church of the Holy Sepulchre, the Templars' mother church in Jerusalem. However, as much as Temple Church is charming, Heraclius is repellent. Self-serving, conniving and deceitful, he embodies all the ills that afflict our Church. It was his visit and the increasingly malign influence of the Templars in Church affairs that persuaded me to begin this lengthy correspondence with you. He was the final ingredient in a noxious concoction that has been under my nose for years. The stink has gone on long enough.

But there is another revealing story in what I will send you. It is a tale of two families: one high and mighty, but flawed; the other more lowly, but courageous and noble in sentiment. They have lived, and still do, parallel lives, each providing central characters in the dramas of England and Normandy.

I hesitated over the summer, but my declining health has finally prompted me to commit to record various accounts that you need to hear. Together, they represent a saga not only of England and Normandy, but also of Byzantium, the Holy Land and the Latin Princes. Needless to say, they tell us much about our human frailties, but also — thanks be to God — a little about our finer qualities.

My monks are now writing furiously, driven by my burgeoning desire to finish what I have begun. So, henceforth, these letters will arrive with you habitually; treat them with care, for they contain much that could be incendiary in the wrong hands. I will leave it to you to decide where they should ultimately rest; perhaps the

Vatican Library would be the appropriate place. I will also send you some important artefacts in due course. These should also find a safe haven, secure from those who would exploit their value, both tangible and spiritual.

I will try not to meander too much, but it is a long story, told to me by a man who you will find intriguing. I first came across him in late June 1139, shortly after I was elected Abbot of Gloucester — so long ago, my friend, when I was in my prime. At the time, this first meeting seemed likely to be the only encounter between us, for he was badly wounded and near to death. He had been brought to me to hear his confession and for me to confer the last rites. As you well know, it is not unusual for us to be called on to hear the confession of dying warriors who, as death approaches, find their dubious deeds suddenly bearing heavily upon them. But this one was different, very different.

I guessed his age to be thirty-five, perhaps a little older. He was dark of hair and olive-skinned, but with piercing blue eyes, and he had the handsome countenance of a courtier. He sported the usual scars of battle, most of which were hidden by a full beard, and carried an impressive array of the tools of his trade — an assemblage of lustrous weapons as fine as I had ever seen — but around his neck was a most remarkable object, unlike anything I have seen before or since. The size of a small bird's egg and not dissimilar in shape, it was a large piece of smooth amber, which glowed balefully in the candlelight. Astonishingly, when it was held to the light, it appeared to contain the image of Lucifer. He seemed to be surrounded by his familiars in the shape of small flies and insects. It also had a blood-red splash running through it, which at certain angles obscured the image of Satan.

I must confess it made me ill at ease. But I was determined to learn the identity of the man who wore what I feared was an evil

7

charm. 'Harold of Hereford' was the name he gave me. I had heard it before, although I was not certain from where. Only over the coming months and years did the name become more and more familiar to me as the turmoil about to envelop England began to emerge. It has been called 'The Anarchy'; the name is apt, because that is what soon came to pass. These were years of chaos and lawlessness, times I will never forget.

Miraculously, proving my physicians wrong, Harold of Hereford not only survived after leaving my cloisters at Gloucester, but went on to play a significant part in England's future affairs. Eventually, he returned – but not for almost forty years, in 1176 in fact – and when he did, it was to make his peace with God. By then, Harold of Hereford was an old man, in his late seventies, and almost everyone who had lived through the turbulent years of his life was dead. I suppose it was a confession of sorts, but perhaps more of a declaration: a testimony about his life and his fascinating family, and an avowal of his destiny and England's cause.

I remember the day well; it was a warm summer evening, the birds sang, and the insects hummed in the garden beneath my window. As I looked out, I saw him walk across the courtyard. My eyes were sharp then, a good ten years ago, and I could see that he stooped a little, but he still had the purposeful gait of a man of war. He had kept his hair and his beard was still full, but both were silver grey like a hoary frost on a winter's morning. His weapons were as brightly burnished as I remembered them all those years before. I knew it was him, even after the passage of many years. I always thought that if he survived his injuries, one day he would return.

He spoke of my reputation as an honest prelate and flattered my abilities as a meticulous chronicler. With that, and without ever receiving my agreement that I would act as his scribe – he was the kind of man who assumed that all his requests would be routinely granted and all his needs immediately fulfilled – Harold of Hereford began his story.

Long hours turned into long days; then weeks passed, as his remarkable story unfolded in vivid detail. I have waited ten years to commit this to vellum, but now my own advancing years mean I can't wait any longer. Fortunately, such is the drama of it, the story is as fresh in my memory now as it was then. I listened every day and he even accompanied me on my journeys to St Paul's so that he could maintain the thread of his discourse. As a houseguest, he was charming and I came to realize that beneath his warrior's gruff exterior, there was a man of great warmth and intellect. He began with his childhood and the astonishing circumstances of his birth and lineage. I sat to one side, as he stared out into my garden. His sun-burnished profile, deeply wrinkled but still handsome, broke into a smile. I smiled with him, sensing that what I was about to become privy to would be an illuminating and engaging revelation. I can still hear his melodious voice echoing in my memory.

My friend, forgive me for imposing this long correspondence on you, but I am too old to travel. It is now the dark of the moon here in Fulham. I fear that with the shorter days have come the first cold winds of the autumn. I am not looking forward to the winter; it can chill a man to his bones down here by the river, and the damp air's icy fingers make breathing troublesome. Still, to the matter in hand.

I have made arrangements with my good friend, Henry of Chichester. He is Abbot of Waverley, a Cistercian house at Farnham, not far from here, that operates an excellent ecclesiastical courier service. He has agreed to make sure my correspondence arrives at the Vatican in Rome, which I know you visit every week. His messengers leave London frequently, and I hope the letters will reach you in regular batches.

I trust this first letter has whetted your appetite. God forbid that I give you a sense that a chore is about to begin. Regardless, my course is set and I must go on. The story that I am about to tell you needs to be written down for posterity. Harold of Hereford's story unfolds below. Keep it safely in your care until the saga is complete.

Yours in God,
Gilbert

1. Birthright

When I think back to my arrival on this earth, I still smile at the convoluted circumstances of my birth. I was born surreptitiously, in Constantinople, in the most auspicious of surroundings, in the Blachernae, the private palace of Alexius I, the Emperor of Byzantium. Strangely, I had two 'mothers': Estrith, my real mother, and Adela, who briefly performed the ostensible role of my mother to all but a few who knew the truth of my conception and confinement. Even more bizarrely, when Adela, my surrogate mother, died only a few years later, Estrith, my birth mother, adopted me in a pretence designed to protect her status as a nun. It was a charade that survived until her death.

I arrived in the mid-summer of 1098, at the beginning of the Great Crusade. My two mothers were part of the English contingent to the Holy Land, led by Edgar the Atheling. Edgar was the rightful Cerdician heir to the English throne in 1066 – an inheritance first denied him in his tender years by Harold of Wessex and then by William the Conqueror and his Norman horde.

Edgar had finally become reconciled with the Conqueror and had befriended Robert Curthose, William's firstborn, who became Duke of Normandy when his father died. When the Great Crusade was called, Robert led the Norman contingent and asked his friend Edgar to join him as head of a small force of Englishmen.

My father, Sweyn of Bourne, was part of Edgar's contingent: a noble knight, of whom I have no real memory, only cherished stories passed on to me by my mother. He was killed when I was still a boy at the fateful Battle of Tinchebrai in 1106.

The secret that disguised my birth was contrived to protect my real mother, Estrith. She was only allowed to be present on the Great Crusade because of her status as Abbess of Fécamp and through her role tending the sick and wounded. The fanatical leaders of the crusade, most of whom were Christian zealots, would not have taken kindly to an abbess of the Church conceiving a child and giving birth in the middle of the holy crusade to liberate the sacred places of Palestine.

On the other hand, Adela was a warrior and an acknowledged Knight of Islam. But more importantly she was married to my father, Sweyn, and thus, as the spouse of a Latin knight, was allowed to accompany him on campaigns. Theirs was a marriage of convenience, never consummated, and agreed between them to allow Adela to fulfil her desire to fight as a warrior – a secret known only to those closest to them. They were more like brother and sister, and both hailed from my family's ancestral home: Bourne in Lincolnshire.

During a particularly treacherous skirmish with the Seljuk Turks in the Holy Land, Adela was badly wounded by an arrow, and Sweyn and Estrith became separated from the Christian army and had to hide in the desert. Estrith had also taken an arrow and had to be kept alive by Sweyn's skills as a battlefield physician. It was during these days alone, when both thought death was imminent, that a tender moment became a loving embrace and, against all the odds, I was conceived. Amazingly, thanks in large part to Sweyn's gifts as a soldier, both survived and made it back to the Christian camp.

Sadly, Adela's wounds were more severe, which ultimately led to her death. But she survived long enough to act out the role of being my mother and to make it back to England, before dying in desperate circumstances at Westminster. She was buried in Bourne; my real mother, Estrith, told me the whole story many years later, a beautifully poignant memory I will cherish forever.

When it became obvious that Estrith was pregnant with me, a devious plan was concocted to protect her and maintain the facade of the 'marriage' between Sweyn and Adela. Adela's wound was serious and would not heal, so it was agreed that both she and my mother would immediately return to Constantinople, long before her pregnancy could be noticed, where I could be born in secret in Emperor Alexius' private apartments. When the three of us returned twelve months later, to all but a select few it seemed perfectly plausible that Adela, wife of Sweyn, had given birth to me and had returned with her husband's child, both lovingly cared for by Estrith, whose nursing skills had led her to be christened the 'English Angel'.

Estrith, Sweyn and Adela were all part of a secret brotherhood, the Brethren of the Blood of the Talisman, formed in homage to all those who went before them and resisted the Normans in the final redoubt at Ely in 1071. The founding members of the Brethren were: Estrith of Melfi, Abbess of Fécamp; Adela of Bourne, Knight of

Islam; Sweyn of Bourne, Knight of Normandy; Edgar the Atheling, Prince of England; Edwin of Glastonbury, Knight of England and my grandfather's standard-bearer at Ely; and Robert, Sovereign Duke of Normandy.

My grandfather, Hereward of Bourne, and my grandmother, Torfida of the Wildwood, were guardians of the Talisman, an ancient and mysterious amulet that many believe possesses great powers. My grandmother died shortly before Ely, but my grandfather survived the siege and lived on for many years. Before he died, he shared the details of his life with the two Johns of Constantinople: Prince John Azoukh and Prince John Comnenus, who later became the Emperor of Byzantium.

For many years, no one knew what had happened to Hereward after Ely. It was only years later, when the Brethren travelled to Constantinople with the Great Crusade, that his whereabouts became clear. He had made a diabolical pact with William the Conqueror after the fall of Ely, which forced him to leave England forever. He had to assume a new identity as Godwin of Ely and served with the elite Varangian Guard of John Comnenus' father, the Emperor Alexius. After quickly rising through the ranks to become Captain of the Guard, he became the Emperor's close friend and confidant.

When he retired, he chose to live in his own remote eyrie, high in the mountains of the Peloponnese in Greece, his whereabouts unknown to anybody except the Emperor Alexius and his local governor – that is, until the Brethren arrived in Constantinople with the crusaders. The Latin Princes and the senior members of their entourage were summoned to the Blachernae to swear an oath of loyalty

14

to the Emperor, during which Estrith noticed that he was wearing the fabled Talisman, given to him many years before by its guardian, Hereward, a man he knew as Godwin of Ely. Later, in a private audience with Alexius, the link was made and a great circle of fate was closed. Alexius summoned Hereward back from his beloved eyrie and he was reunited with his family and the survivors of Ely.

Hereward became a member of the Brethren and accompanied them on their traumatic excursion to the Holy Land, after which he returned to his mountaintop. But to the immense joy of Estrith, she and I, still a babe in arms, returned with him, where we stayed for many months. Throughout my childhood, my mother passed on the minute details of our stay and the many stories of my grandfather's deeds and those of his followers. They are wonderful memories, many of which I now pass on to you.

After the Great Crusade and our time together with my grandfather, we returned to England, where my mother rekindled her passion for architecture by resuming her career as a churchwright – a skill she had to hide behind the pectoral cross of an abbess. She worked for the rest of her life as one of the senior churchwrights on the new cathedral at Norwich, where I grew up. The building is finished now, but my mother only saw it half built; she died in 1126, in an outbreak of scarlet fever. Nevertheless, she saw the completion of the presbytery and its magnificent vaulted roof, her pride and joy.

Although I was intrigued throughout my childhood by the inexorable rise of the mighty walls of the cathedral, and despite being in awe of the skills of its masons, carpenters and churchwrights, my yearnings soon turned to more martial pursuits, especially when I began to approach adulthood. I dreamed of emulating the deeds of my father and grandfather, both of whose exploits were well known – especially those of Hereward, who was by then a legendary figure, spoken about with hushed reverence.

No one in Norwich knew that we were related to Hereward and Sweyn; my mother preferred her anonymity, especially as she worked so closely with master masons and senior clerics, all of whom were Normans. Although the pain of the Conquest was becoming a thing of the past, resentment was never far beneath the surface within the English community and we had to be careful lest our lineage antagonize our Norman masters, or become a rallying call for our English friends. Still, my heritage resonated strongly in my heart.

I first made contact with young Englishmen who were determined to keep alive the dream of liberty from Norman rule through some of the masons working on the cathedral. Although the senior masons were Normans, most of the junior ones were English. They were intelligent and articulate, but were denied further progress because of rigid Norman control of the masons' hierarchy. This caused bitter resentment. Several of them would meet in Lion Wood on Sundays. Their women and sisters would prepare food, and they would share stories of the English resistance from the past, air their grievances and talk about how England could plot a way to freedom.

They were initially wary of me because my mother was one of the few prominent English people in Norwich and thus open to accusations of collaboration with the Normans. However, her deeds in the Holy Land with the English contingent nullified any suspicion and thus I was allowed to join the Sabbath gatherings. Sometimes I wished I could reveal my family history and so gain favour with them, but it would have put at risk my mother's relationship with the Normans, so I chose discretion.

Some of the men kept weapons in the wood and practised with them. They taught me many things about fighting, especially at close quarters, and how to survive in the wilderness – all of which was a useful supplement to my formal training to become a knight with Hugh Bigod, the Earl of Norwich.

My Sabbaths in Lion Wood continued blissfully for many weeks. My fellow renegades were older than I was – I had just turned fifteen – and keeping their company led me to pretend that I was older than my tender years. There were the thrills of clandestine rendezvous to be savoured and mock fights to be enjoyed. I learned that there was still a secret network of similar young men and women throughout the land, many of whom were descendants of those who fought the Normans on Senlac Ridge, or were part of my grandfather's resistance movement and the Brotherhood of Ely.

As time passed I was shocked to hear countless stories of brutality and oppression from Norman lords towards the English. Many Normans believed in firm rule, but acted with decency. Indeed, in Norwich we were fortunate that both the Earl and the Bishop were fair in their treatment of the local people. However, in many parts of the country, especially in the more remote areas and the border regions, Norman lords did just as they pleased, regardless of the law and even of human decency.

Their crimes went unrecorded: people disappeared, never to be seen again, and every imaginable cruelty was meted out to the local people, none of whom had any means to defend themselves. Retreat into the wildwood, or escape to the uplands and fenlands, was often the only recourse. Even then, they were ruthlessly hunted down, often for sport, their bodies brought back and displayed like hunting trophies. We were told that one particularly vicious lord in Northumbria kept a pack of wolves in a pit so that he could entertain his guests by throwing English captives into it after dinner. Another liked to disembowel anyone to whom he took a dislike.

In some places, huge tracts of land that had been sequestered by the new Norman lords from their old English landlords had been left to go wild and the villages that once were thriving homes lay derelict. Stories of tyranny and destitution were legion from every part of the country and strengthened our desire to find a way to resist – especially among the young, who knew that their English birthright meant they were unlikely ever to play a prominent role in the affairs of their own land.

I was the only member of the group without a female companion, but I tried to catch the eye of several of the unattached younger girls, sometimes with modest success. But then I could never be sure whether the smile or look returned was simply a gesture of kindness or the more enticing signal I hoped it would be.

Some of the older men began to make serious plans to disrupt the comfortable lives the Normans were leading:

poaching livestock to give to the peasants, stealing from granaries to redistribute the spoils to the poor, and there was even talk of mounting raids on small garrisons and linking up with bands of outlaws we knew lived in the remote parts of the wildwood. Not having any real sense of what the risks would be, I was a vociferous advocate of such plans and, to the credit of my companions, was humoured with gracious smiles and only the occasional look of disdain.

However, in September of 1113, the real world suddenly exposed the pretence of our Sundays of sedition. It was late in the afternoon, all the food had been eaten and the usual animated debate about future schemes and plots, fuelled by plentiful flasks of ale, had subsided. The rabble-rousing had been replaced by slumber for most, but a few of the more spirited ones had found discrete spots in the greensward for a little frolicking.

The distinct neighing of horses was the first sign of danger. Hunting was forbidden in the forest and farm horses would not be working on the Sabbath, so horses – especially several of them – signalled impending menace. Then came the animated cries of men-at-arms and the rumbling of hooves. They were Norman cries, and they were coming from all directions. Everyone was soon on their feet and running in panic in different directions.

All I could hear was the impassioned cry, '*Run!*'

I ran as I had never run before. My heart raced; I seemed to have the speed and agility of a stallion and leapt over brushwood and fallen tree trunks as if they were not there. I saw only two Normans, as I passed between them, each several yards from me. The late summer undergrowth was high and helped conceal my dash for safety and, to my immense relief, the two soldiers did not see me. They did not see the young couple who had been romping in the long grass either, but I did – I bowled over the lad as he was pulling up his leggings. His all-but-naked partner was still on the ground, screaming in terror. With shrieks and shouts ringing in my ears behind me, my impetus hardly stalled, I continued my desperate sprint, not really slowing until I saw Norwich's Eastgate ahead of me.

Then I stopped suddenly and dived for cover at the side of the road. The gate was barred by a patrol of mounted Normans, on guard, their distinctive conical helmets glinting in the setting sun. They had seen me, and three of them closed on me at a gallop. I ran again; my only chance was the deep forest, which would be too dense for the horses to pursue me at speed. But this time fatigue soon caught up with me and my lungs started to strain in panic and exhaustion. I stopped, in part to get my breath, but also to see if I could hear my pursuers.

I held my breath to confirm what I suspected, and heard the distinct sound of horses moving through the dense forest, the swish of their riders' swords slicing through the foliage. They were close, too close for me to attempt to run; they would surely hear my movements. Then I heard the barking of dogs in the distance. A new beast was hunting me – one I could not outrun.

I was agile and had no fear of heights – I had climbed the high scaffolding of the cathedral many times. My only hope was to scale the tallest tree I could find before the hunting dogs fixed on my scent. I disappeared into the heavy canopy of the towering elm just as the Normans appeared in view below. One of them dismounted to take a piss and they began to chat idly about 'English pigs, will they never learn . . .' and other such invective. Although I spoke their language fluently, as many Englishmen did, Norman always sounded guttural and threatening. These were harsh men, sons of an unforgiving race.

Then the dogs and their huntsmen arrived. The hounds yelped, barked and ran around in circles, desperate to be let off their leashes. I was certain they had already sensed my presence and I hunched on my perch, petrified, not daring to breathe. Then came the piercing scream.

Pursued by several riders, the couple I had fallen over as I made my escape stumbled into view. They were bedraggled and exhausted and were soon surrounded by more than a dozen horsemen, including those who had been about to discover me in my lofty refuge. My good fortune was a death warrant for the two lovers. I did not know the girl's name – she had only been to a couple of gatherings – but the boy was Wulfnoth, an excellent carpenter from Thetford, who had shown me much kindness when I first joined the group.

He was cut down without a moment's hesitation by a vicious blow from the sword of the first Norman to reach him. He cried out in agony as he hit the ground, blood spewing from a wound that ran from his shoulder to his midriff. More assailants speared him with their lances as he lay on the ground. He lived for what seemed like an eternity, squirming like a snake, trying to avoid the lethal blades. The hounds then bit and tugged at him before, mercifully, his life spent, he lay still. The dogs, rabid for their kill, then pulled him into the undergrowth and began to devour him.

The girl's demise was just as horrific. She was one of the pretty ones I had smiled at expectantly several times, until I realized she was enjoying Wulfnoth's amorous attentions. Hysterical after witnessing the slaughter of her lover, she ran around in a circle, her head in her hands, wailing. When the first Norman dismounted, she seemed to gather herself and tried to escape, but an ever-tightening circle of men and horses made that impossible. One by one they dismounted, their mood changing from animated ferocity to a more measured menace.

I suddenly felt ashamed that I did not know the girl's name; perhaps it was better that I did not, given what I was about to witness. She began to plead with them, in English and Norman, but they just sniggered. She said she worked in Bishop de Losinga's kitchen and that he would condemn them to Hell if they harmed her. It made no difference. As they circled her, leering and taunting, she tried to compose herself and took deep breaths, hoping to reason with them. It was all in vain.

They slowly stripped her and mauled her, flinging her from one to the other, before throwing her on to the ground and invading her body in every possible way. The humiliations lasted for at least an hour, at the end of which the girl was barely conscious. Perhaps that was a good thing because, having sated their lust, one of them knelt over her and sliced her throat from ear to ear, leaving her to die in a pool of blood.

I learned a lot about the savagery of men that day. I

turned away from the spectacle many times, but kept looking back, callously fascinated by their cruelty. I realized how terrifying it must be to live as a woman in a world where women could be treated so brutally. Now I understood why my parents and grandparents had fought so courageously against evil and lawlessness. I vowed to espouse their cause with all my heart and soul, and to fight for freedom and justice for all men and women, wherever they are denied.

It was all but dark when the Normans moved off towards Norwich, allowing me to clamber down from my sanctuary. I did not dare look for the grisly remains of Wulfnoth, but I felt compelled to pull the girl into the undergrowth. I turned her on to her side and tried to arrange her hair around her face in a token gesture to restore her modesty. She was at peace, her ordeal over. I gently pushed a strand of hair behind her ear, revealing a now serene profile that gave no hint of what had just happened to her. I vowed to remember her like that – not as I had seen her, contorted by the torment of the assault. I retrieved her clothes and covered her with them, before finally spreading a cloak of leaves over her. It was all I could do.

For what seemed like half the night, I hid in the undergrowth, trying to come to terms with what had just happened. It must have been near to dawn when I ran to our modest abode in the shadow of the mighty cathedral. Thankfully, the sentries had gone and the old gatekeeper let me in at the burgh's Eastgate. He looked distressed and pleaded with me to get off the streets.

My mother was waiting for me, slumped at her churchwright's table, a nearly exhausted candle barely flickering.

I rushed into her welcoming arms, feeling more like a frightened child than a confident young man hoping soon to become a knight of the realm.

'Thank God you're safe. I have been sick with fear, thinking you had been caught. Or worse . . .'

I told her what had happened, laying the blame at Hugh Bigod's door.

'There has been mayhem here too, but they were not the Earl of Norwich's men. They came from London on the King's orders. Somebody had sent word about treason among the masons, and the King sent a squadron of his cut-throats to deal with it.'

'We only talked . . . it was only bluster. Why would anybody tell the King?'

'To gain favour, for money, out of jealousy – there are many temptations to seduce the feeble.'

'It must have been an Englishman.'

'Or an Englishwoman! Earlier, there were four masons' bodies swinging from the scaffolding of the nave. They had been dragged from Lion Wood and hanged on sanctified ground. I hear that there are many more bodies in the wood. Most of the surviving masons are in hiding. There has been trouble on the streets all day – even usually calm people who avoid trouble are incensed. The houses of some of the Norman merchants have been burned and also the houses of the Jewish goldsmiths.'

'The Earl must have been involved.'

'I don't think so. He is furious and has had the bodies cut down. He called out his retinue and ran the King's squadron out of the burgh. The Bishop has already left for London to protest to the King. I know that the Bishop and the Earl are both Normans, but they are better men than that and would not commit such brutality.'

It was then that my mother told me what had happened to my second mother, Adela, at Bourne all those years ago, when she was abused by King William's henchmen in an act of vengeance following the Siege of Ely.

'My poor boy, I'm so sorry that you saw what you saw today. Adela was scarred for life by her experience, but it also made her determined to fight for what is right. I hope the same thing happens to you.'

'Don't doubt that, mother. You have told me about evil many times and now I've seen it for myself. I will never forget.'

I never did forget. And while I did not blame the many Normans I knew in Norwich – who were not the kind of men who would commit such atrocities – I knew then with an unwavering certainty and a renewed passion that the English cause my family had defended over forty years would also be my cause.

My mother had recognized my warrior ambitions from an early age – after all, she was her mother's daughter, both of whom had lived adventurous lives in the company of warriors – and had sent me to be trained as a knight as soon as I was old enough. I continued my training with Hugh of Bigod, until a year had passed since the trauma of Lion Wood and calm had returned to Norwich.

Paradoxically, although I was still determined to challenge our Norman masters one day, the only way I could acquire the skills to become a warrior was by undergoing the training regime of our Norman lords and become a knight of their realm. So, in 1114, at the age of sixteen, I accompanied King Henry Beauclerc on a punitive expedition against the Welsh, who had been causing mayhem in the Marches.

I was spoiling for a fight, and soon found one. But it was not the breath-taking adventure I had imagined.

2. Atrocity in the Marches

King Henry's major concern in 1114 was the situation in Wales. Both during the period of Norman rule and under the English kings before them, the Welsh princes were a thorn in the side of English magnates – especially those on the western borders, and those who had built fortifications within Wales to try to pacify them. Norman lords had been murdered, their families abducted and tortured, their women raped and mutilated. The Welsh also fought amongst themselves, and there were hostile feuds between those princes who had made alliances with the English kings and those who had not.

In Mid Wales, Madog, son of Rhirid ap Bleddyn, had been blinded and mutilated by his cousin Owain ap Cadwgan, who was the most notorious of the Welshmen that King Henry was determined to subdue. This act of revenge between cousins led to an outbreak of tribal bloodletting. In the north, the King of Gwynedd, Gruffudd ap Cynan, had been raiding the lands of the Norman Marcher Lord Richard, Earl of Chester, who had complained to the King, as had Gilbert FitzRichard, Lord of Ceredigion.

Henry Beauclerc had had enough and decided to teach the Welsh a lesson. With himself at its head, a large force advanced deep into Wales. He split his soldiers into three main armies, each over 2,000 strong, including archers and heavy cavalry. In the south, Gilbert FitzRichard commanded an army from Cornwall and South Wales. In the north, Richard of Chester advanced to Penant Bachwy, while the King led the third group into Merionethshire. Alexander, King of the Scots was with the King, in large part to demonstrate to the Welsh that the Scots had succumbed to the power of the Norman King of England and had accepted Henry as their overlord.

I had been taken to Wales in the King's retinue as a favour to my mother, granted by Hugh Bigod, Earl of Norfolk, one of the main benefactors of the new cathedral at Norwich. I was put under the care of Olaf Godredsson, heir to the Kingdom of the Isles and Mann, who had lived at Henry's court since he was a boy, as part of the King's treaty with Olaf's father, Godred Crovan.

Olaf had been made constable of the King's cavalry for the expedition into Wales, an assignment that filled him with pride. A man in his mid thirties, nicknamed 'The Red' or 'Bites your Leg' based on his bright red hair and diminutive stature, he was, despite first impressions, a kind and thoughtful man and an excellent soldier. He did tend to bellow his orders and to intimidate those around him, but those close to him knew him to be loyal and generous to all who served him. He was also a brilliant horseman and cavalry officer, particularly fond of mass charges in close formation.

I joined the army at Oxford and my status as a junior knight of the realm meant that Olaf made me a messenger in his personal troop. He seemed to like me – especially after I was able to stumble through a conversation in Norse with him, and I explained my Norse ancestry on my mother's side. It was Olaf who told me about Owain ap Cadwgan on our long march to Wales.

'Is this your first expedition?'

'It is, sir.'

'How old are you?'

'Sixteen, sir.'

'That's about right, let's hope you learn from it. Do you want to join the King when you are of age?'

'I'm not sure, my Lord. I just know that I must find what awaits me in the world.'

'So, you believe in destiny?'

'I do, sir. My mother taught me that we each have a destiny, but that most people don't find theirs and live their lives unfulfilled and resentful.'

'Your mother is very wise. Perhaps you can win your colours chasing this rogue, Owain ap Cadwgan?'

'Sir, what has he done to annoy the King so much?'

'Well, the King wants to teach several of the Welsh princes a lesson, but this one is a particular villain. A long time ago, when William Rufus was King, a young Welsh princess, Nest, daughter of Rhys ap Tewdwr, King of Deheubarth, was captured by Arnulf of Montgomery – one of the King's most ferocious warriors – and brought to the King's court. She is still very beautiful, but as a young woman she caught the eye of everyone at court – especially young Henry, now our Lord King, Henry Beauclerc. She bore him a child, rumoured to be the renowned Robert, Earl of Gloucester, before he tired of her and married her off to Gerald of Windsor, Lord of Cenarth Bychan. Five years ago, Owain ap Cadwgan heard about the beautiful Nest at a drunken feast and became obsessed by her, particularly given that she had become a concubine of the Normans. He convinced himself that Henry Beauclerc had raped her and that she was now trapped in a remote castle by her equally rapacious Norman husband.'

'Could that be true, my Lord?'

'Who knows? The King has so many mistresses . . . I'm sure most are willing partners. Perhaps she wasn't. That's certainly what Owain got into his head. Shortly after the feast, Owain summoned a dozen or so of his followers and rode to Cenarth Bychan. The keep was barred to them, so they dug under the walls – an exercise that took half the night – before slaughtering the garrison and bursting in on Nest and her captor, with whom she had had three children. Like a coward, Gerald of Windsor escaped down the chute of the garderobe and into the pile of shit his shameful behaviour deserved, leaving his wife and children at the mercy of Owain and his men. In a fury fuelled by his killing spree, Owain ripped Nest's clothes from her and while his men held her down viciously raped her in front of her children. He repeated the humiliation at dawn and again a few hours later, before carrying her off with her children to a remote hunting lodge at Eglwyseg Rocks north of the Vale of Llangollen.'

'Sir, it's easy to understand why he's a hunted man –'

'Wait, there's more to the story. Nest agreed to stay with Owain if he let her children return to their father, which he did. She was true to her word and bore him two children. It is hard to believe, but some say she grew to be fond of him. But, regardless of that, when he was finally tracked down in Llangollen by a Norman expedition,

Owain escaped to Ireland to avoid the King's wrath. Nest was reunited with Gerald of Windsor, a man who had been doing penance ever since abandoning his wife.'

'But, sir, if Owain is in Ireland, why this expedition?'

'He is not in Ireland. Three years ago, Owain returned to Wales to claim his father's title as Prince of Powys, his father having been killed by a man he thought was his friend, Madog ap Rhirid. Owain captured Madog, tied him to a stake, blinded him with a hot iron and castrated him with a seax. Owain then declared his loyalty to King Henry and began to attack the other Welsh princes.'

'So, my Lord, did the King accept Owain's submission?'

'On the surface, yes, but the King is shrewd. Let's just say that Gerald of Windsor is with the King on this expedition. He has his wife back and has done his penance, but he still wants his revenge.'

Olaf's inference was all too obvious: Owain ap Cadwgan was walking into a trap.

In the early weeks of the expedition, the King was as astute as he was belligerent and systematically bought off the Welsh with land and favours. But not before he hanged a few troublemakers, blinded some miscreants caught hunting in royal forests and tortured a couple of local firebrands to show that he meant business. A large English army and cartloads of English silver were enough to convince even the hardiest of Welsh princes to bow to the great king from the east and retreat to their remote fortresses.

I was witness to these punishments and found the proceedings repugnant. I was not opposed to violence if it was the result of a fair fight – or in pursuit of a just cause – but the almost indiscriminate use of force against those unable to resist was simply an act of cruelty. Nevertheless, the brutality and bribery worked and the King prevailed.

Owain had been told to rendezvous with Henry's army at Abergavenny to celebrate the success of the expedition. Owain duly arrived with only his personal retinue of about a dozen men, vastly outnumbered by our force. The King had already departed for Winchester, leaving Olaf in charge of three squadrons of his elite cavalry, about seventy-five men.

Olaf greeted Owain ap Cadwgan when he arrived at Abergavenny.

'Prince Owain. I am Olaf Godredsson, Prince of the Isles and Mann.'

Cadwgan realized that all was not what it should be, and he was ill at ease.

'Prince Olaf, it is an honour to meet you. I know your father, we met on Anglesey Isle many years ago. I thought I was to meet King Henry?'

'I'm afraid the King has had to return to Winchester. Affairs of the realm . . . you understand.'

'Of course.' Owain was looking around agitatedly. 'But what of our celebration and the new arrangement we were going to –?'

Prince Olaf interrupted him before he could finish.

'Owain ap Cadwgan, Prince of Powys, you are under arrest. Your men may go, but you are now a prisoner of King Henry, held under his authority by Gerald Fitz-Walter, Constable of Pembroke.'

Owain did not recognize Gerald's Norman name, nor

his new title as Constable of Pembroke. But as soon as the new constable rode forward, he saw that his captor was Gerald of Windsor, Nest's wronged husband. As Owain's men began to melt away, Gerald of Windsor issued his orders. He did so calmly and without apparent menace, disguising years of seething hatred.

The Welsh Prince, now alone and defenceless, was stripped of his weapons, armour and clothes before being hoisted on to a pair of crossed timbers usually used for floggings. In his case, his torso faced forwards – the opposite way to that used in a whipping. A large fire was lit nearby while he was bound tightly at the ankles, wrists, neck and forehead. He was asked if he had anything to say, to which he responded by shaking his head as much as his bindings would allow. Then he set his jaw to face what was to come.

Gerald of Windsor nodded to the executioners before issuing his proclamation.

'For the heinous crimes you have committed against the people of your own land and against the people of England, you are to be executed so that you can face the judgement of God to atone for your sins.'

One of the executioners then cupped Owain's chin firmly in the palm of his hand and, without a moment's hesitation, took out one of his eyes with the sharp point of his seax. Gerald, now less in control of his emotions, spat in Owain's face and hissed at his prisoner.

'We will let you keep one eye for now, so that you can see what we are going to do next.'

Owain, screaming in pain, blood trickling down his face from an empty eye socket, shouted back at his tormentor.

'Yes, and so that I can still see your wife writhing beneath me. She hated me at first, but soon couldn't get enough of it!'

Enraged by that, Gerald took his seax and thrust it through Owain's cheek until it exited on the other side.

'Do you have anything more to say, you filthy pig?'

Owain tried to speak, but it was impossible. Blood was filling his mouth and cascading down his chest. The executioners then tied lead weights to their victim's testicles before, like a slaughterer preparing sweetbreads, slicing them off with a slow and deliberate sawing motion. They then did the same to his manhood, before throwing his excised genitals on to the fire.

I had to look away, as did many around me.

Gerald then leaned forward and slowly pulled his seax from Owain's face. The man was still conscious but was now convulsing in pain, hardly able to focus on his captor just inches from his face.

'This is for Nest, the Helen of Wales.'

With that, Gerald thrust his seax deep into Owain's remaining eye and continued to thrust until it met the wooden post behind the back of his head. Owain's ordeal was over but, as a final indignity, his body was cut down, covered in goose grease and cast on to the fire, where it roared and crackled as it was immolated by the flames.

It was a gruesome end. What beasts we are to one another.

Our journey back to England was a sombre occasion. Olaf was helpful to me as I came to terms with what I had seen.

'It is a kind of justice. Not, I grant you, what Christ teaches, but cruel punishments are as old as history. My great-grandfather was the first in my family to convert to Christianity, but he only did so because he had to make an alliance with the English. He would have had no hesitation in killing a man or having him maimed. Not much has changed today. If kings didn't act firmly, there would be anarchy.'

I hesitated, knowing that my family had always believed there was another way.

'I know, my Lord, but I wish it could be different.'

3. Waking the Dead

After the expedition to Wales, I realized that there was much I had to learn about the world and myself. I still had some way to go before winning my knight's pennon, but I was not happy at continuing to serve under our Norman masters. So, I decided that just as both my parents and grandparents had undertaken great journeys in search of their destinies, I should venture to the counties of the Christian princes in the Holy Land to find what fate would make of me. After much debate and still with reluctance, my mother eventually succumbed to my pleadings, but at a price I found hard to accept.

'You may not go before your eighteenth birthday.'

'But that's almost two years away – an eternity for someone of my age.'

'You'll just have to bear it.'

She was blunt and to the point. The terms of her hard-struck bargain continued.

'In the meantime, you will return to Hugh Bigod, Earl of Norfolk, to train with his men. He'll toughen you up – he's a hard taskmaster.'

And thus, just over eighteen months later, with my side of the bargain completed, I was ready to embark on my own personal crusade to the Holy Land. My training with the Earl's men had indeed toughened me up, and I had made full use of the intervening months to find a local sweetheart. In fact, I had found several and felt that my education in the art of love was as complete as my schooling in the art of war.

I was soon to be proved wrong in both respects.

I had been born blessed with much good fortune. Not only had I been born into an illustrious family, I had also been left a significant sum of money. The Emperor Alexius had endowed me with ten gold Byzantine bezants to celebrate my birth and Edgar the Atheling had left me some carucates of land, sufficient to provide a good annual income. All in all, I was a man of some substance. I was able to recruit for my expedition a sergeant-at-arms, two men-at-arms and a groom. All were good men, vetted by my mother as entirely trustworthy and each sworn to keep me safe.

Eadmer was my sergeant: a man in his thirties, a local lad from Norwich, fair-haired, broad and strong of arm. He had served in the Earl of Norfolk's retinue all his life, was an excellent all-round soldier, honest and loyal, and had fought with the Earl on several campaigns against the marauding Scots and on the Marches against the Welsh princes.

His two men were Toste and Wulfric, brothers from Lincoln, men from my ancestral county and very much in Eadmer's image and trained by him. Both were short, lean and had the look of a dark Celt about them – the result, they said, of a maternal grandparent from the wilds of Cumbria. They too were experienced soldiers in the service of the Earl.

My groom, Alric, was not a soldier but wished he were and acted like a veteran of countless campaigns. He was a kindly soul, attentive and considerate and a good companion. His girth was prodigious, but so too was his humour; he could cook, tend a steed and find food and provisions where none seemed available. He was an ideal quartermaster for a troop of soldiers.

All my many advantages in life came with equal burdens. I had to live with many expectations, both real and imagined. The more my dearest mother told me about the heroic deeds of my father and grandfather, the more I realized how great a responsibility I carried. Could I emulate what they had achieved? Would I make them proud?

Often, I had my own private doubts and anxieties. But regardless of whether or not I could live up to my own expectations, my own journey was about to begin. Both my grandparents and my parents had done remarkable things, some of which had changed the course of history. They had fought and died for freedom; they had bound themselves together for the greater good; and they had set an example of how lives should be lived and justice should be served.

I suddenly felt overwhelmed by the burden of responsibility I carried.

Two days before I was due to leave Norwich, I went to the presbytery of the cathedral that my mother had helped design. Desperate for inspiration, I sat and stared at the huge vaulted ceiling way above me. The ribs of its arches were covered in gold leaf; its bosses were elaborately carved and beautifully painted with the faces of gargoyles, Satan's familiars and a host of mythical beasts and sundry saints and martyrs. It was a thing of wonder. I sat there for several hours, craving a steadfastness that did not materialize.

Sometime later, with darkness almost obscuring the architectural wonders and the cathedral falling silent from the bustle of the day, my mother appeared and eased herself on to the bench beside me.

'What troubles you, Harold?'

'Nothing, I'm fine –'

'You don't mean that. What is it?'

I hesitated, embarrassed that private doubts were bearing down on me. My mother did not probe, but simply joined me in staring upwards as her masterpiece began to disappear in the gloom of the advancing evening.

She stood and offered her hand.

'Come, let me show you something.'

My mother then took a lantern and led me high up through the passageways of the huge walls of the presbytery until we were at roof level, close to the decorated bosses of the vaulted ceiling.

'There . . . the third and fourth ones along on the right.'

She pointed with her mason's dividers, a tool that always hung from her belt, at the brightly painted images.

'The nearest one is Wodewose, the Green Man of legend – a mythical figure your grandfather talked about a lot – and the next one is your great-grandfather, Torfida's father, the Old Man of the Wildwood. They look alike, don't they? That's my doing; I designed them as a tribute. Torfida is over there with my twin sister, Gunnhild.'

'And my father?'

'Yes, he's the handsome knight further along.'

'And you?'

'Yes, I'm there as well, but I'm not telling you which one. It's a little rude.'

'It's not like you to be bashful.'

She smiled mischievously. Although I was her son, and she always behaved discreetly, she had never hidden from me her healthy appetite for the pleasures of the flesh.

'I suppose you're right. Well, I'm the naked strumpet over there, cavorting with the Devil.'

'Very appropriate! I hope you haven't got me up here?'

'Of course I have – you're the babe in arms, over there in the corner, being offered up to God by the handsome knight. Do you see? It's Hereward, based on my memory of you being sworn into the Brethren in the Holy Land by my father.'

As she led me down through the walls again, she continued the story of my heritage.

'I think your great-grandfather was the embodiment of all that the Green Man represents: our links to our ancient heritage and beliefs, and to the importance of the natural world and our place in it. He was a seer, and my father always believed that my mother inherited many of his gifts.'

'What about the Talisman? Do you think it carries mystical powers?'

'I don't know for certain. I first saw it around the neck of an emperor, and he wasn't the first great ruler to wear it. But it's not a trinket or a charm – for good or evil – more a stone of destiny.'

'I know it's supposed to carry eternal truths, and I'm supposed to go and collect it from the Emperor himself one day. But first I have to deal with my fears ... I'm hardly a worthy inheritor as the guardian of such an important amulet –'

'Harry, it's your birthright, your responsibility. I can help you, but you have to come to terms with it in your own way.'

'I know, but after years of yearning to begin my own adventure, I'm suddenly overawed by the prospect.'

'That's understandable ...' She paused to gather her thoughts. 'But listen, this is what I think you should do. Travel via Bourne, visit the grave of dearest Adela and reflect on what happened to her and the horror that took place in that village all those years ago. When you do, think about what happened to those young people in Lion Wood. An experience like that gave Adela great strength and courage.

'Then move on, take your companions to Glastonbury and lodge them in the burgh. Go off on your own to where my mother and sister are buried. Spend some time there. It will allow you to think. It is a beautiful place. I can draw you a map to help you find it. Try to absorb some of your grandmother Torfida's empathy and wisdom, and think of what Gunnhild and I lived through with your grandfather at Ely. Then go to Cirencester and leave your men there. Seek the humble forest home of the Old Man of the Wildwood, where Torfida was raised. Its exact location is unknown, but I think I can give you some clues, based on what my mother and father told me. It is where our story begins, deep in the wildwood of the Wodewose. Hereward discovered his destiny there, you might find yours.'

I liked her plan. Leaving Norwich would not be easy,

and parting from my mother would be even more painful. But her advice had offered me the chance to undertake a spiritual journey and meet a personal challenge that would help me come to terms with my fears.

Thus, in the summer of 1116, I rode off westwards with my four retainers towards Bourne. I had lived my life in the shadow of my mother's marvellous achievement at Norwich and overawed by the doughty deeds of the rest of my grandfather's clan. Now it was time for me to write my own chapter in the family history.

Bourne was a hive of activity. Its fields were verdant with crops, fruits and vegetables; its artisans and retailers were busy servicing the needs of its farmers and those travellers who chose to visit the village on their way along the ancient road to the north, which ran nearby.

To my dismay, the old Saxon church was being pulled down when we arrived. The new lord, Baldwin FitzGilbert de Clare, a descendent of one of the Conqueror's most trusted henchmen, had decided to build a new abbey church in grand Norman style to accommodate a community of Arrouaisian monks he wanted to bring from Flanders. Such was the intended scale of the new abbey, FitzGilbert had ordered that all the old Saxon graves be ploughed over. Thankfully, the local villagers, horrified by the thought, had removed all the human remains from the cemetery in the dead of night and reburied them deep in Bourne Wood.

Delighted to meet a descendant of Hereward, several of the locals were happy to escort me to the hidden burial ground, where they left me to pay my respects. They had built a small pile of stones, a shrine to the memory of Adela of Bourne and all the villagers who had been slaughtered at the hands of Ogier the Breton – murders that had been ordered by William the Conqueror in an act of vengeance for Hereward's continuing opposition to his rule. Almost the entire village had perished – except the young boy Sweyn, later to become my father, who escaped to hide in the forest, and a young Adela and two companions. They had been raped and abused by the Normans for several days until my grandfather rescued them. The dead included my great-grandparents: Leofric, Thegn of Bourne, and his wife, Aediva.

I spent over an hour there reflecting on my heritage. It was an eerie place for me. Norwich was one of the largest burghs in the realm and I had lived right in its heart in the cathedral precincts. Alone, deep in an almost impenetrable wildwood, surrounded by the ghosts of my ancestors, I began to realize why my mother had suggested my itinerary. There was something unsettling about the wildwood – it seemed challenging, putting me on my guard – but it was an emotion to draw strength from, to meet the challenge, not a feeling of which I should be afraid. Many people thought that when the wind blew, making the trees groan and their leaves shrill, it was the Green Man talking to them. I listened hard. It was not a threatening voice, though certainly primordial, but soothing, reminding me that it was ageless, like nature itself.

Our next port of call was Pennard Hill near Glastonbury. I left my men in the burgh and rode east. My mother's map was easy to follow and precisely accurate, as I had known it would be. The glade was also just as she had

43

described it: an idyllic natural dene flanked by tall oaks, limes and elms. From its edge it was just possible to glimpse the ancient Tor of Glastonbury.

The two oaks in the centre marked the resting places of my grandmother Torfida and my mother's twin sister, Gunnhild. The older tree, planted fifty years ago, was already over seventy feet tall, the smaller one at least fifty feet in height. It was a chastening thought to imagine that the two trees had once been tiny saplings. I spent two nights camped in the glade between the pair of oak trees, thinking about the two women and drawing strength from what they had endured and achieved. Like the people of Bourne, both women had died in pain, but their resting place was strikingly tranquil. They were now far removed from their suffering, and I found that calmed my anxieties.

Hereward had always said that Torfida was a seer like her father. I hoped it was true and that, from her grave, she would be able to imbue me with some of her wisdom. I carved my own personal tribute into the two trunks of the trees, in honour of Torfida's precious memory. I wrote in Latin, something I knew my grandmother would appreciate – my mother had taught me Latin, just as Torfida had taught her. On Gunnhild's I carved: *Aeternum vale* (Farewell Forever), and on Torfida's: *Non est ad astra mollis e terris via* (There is no easy way from the earth to the stars).

My next task was more of a challenge. My mother had always wondered where the remote home of the Old Man of the Wildwood might have been. After assimilating everything she had been told by both Hereward and Torfida, she calculated that the spot was two miles due north-west of a milestone on the Fosse Way, sixteen miles from Cirencester, in an area known as Chedworth Wood. Even with this precision, it was a very large area of forest to search. So when I left my men in Cirencester, I told them not to expect me for some time.

When he was banished by King Edward, my grandfather had to forage in the wildwood with no tools, weapons or provisions. So, following in his footsteps, when I arrived in Chedworth I tethered my horse and sallied forth in the clothes I stood up in with just a seax in my belt.

The first few days were full of activity, as I made a camp, built some shelter and found food and water. My military training with the Earl of Norfolk was invaluable; without it, I would not have survived. Once I became settled and felt secure, I began to plan my search.

Drawing on my mother's inestimable wisdom, I found elevated ground and climbed high into its tallest trees so that I could begin to plot the lie of the land. That took me several days. I then began my search by pacing the large plots of ground I had organized into squares on my ground plan. Despite all my diligence, the exercise was tedious. I had to put my faith in my mother's research and instincts. But two weeks into my quest, just when my enthusiasm was waning rapidly, I found what I was looking for.

It was as it had been described to me: a small, natural meadow with a fast-flowing stream running through it. At the edge of the meadow, hard against a stony outcrop, were the unmistakable remains of a man-made stone hearth. Little else was visible, other than a few bits of rotting timber that had once supported a lean-to and a few rusty old iron implements half hidden in the ground, more of which emerged as I trampled the undergrowth over the following days.

I stayed in the Old Man of the Wildwood's lea for over a week. I set traps and strung rabbits, just like he must have done. I lit fires and roasted my game, as he would have. At night I listened to the wind and the noises of the forest. I tried to imagine the violent storm when he first appeared just yards from Hereward, a fateful meeting that my grandfather had described to my mother in vivid flashes of memory. I thought about their long and profound conversations together, enfolded in the heart of the wildwood. It was a calming and reflective experience, one that I will never forget.

Did my pilgrimage to my family's burial grounds fundamentally change me? Did I feel the presence of the Green Man, or understand what he represents? Did I absorb any of the wisdom of the Old Man himself? The answer to all of those questions is probably, 'Yes, a little.'

But what I certainly found was a strong sense of humility. I felt meek in the face of the power and complexity of the natural world that surrounds us, and humbled by the memories of the deeds of my family. Most importantly, I understood that from humility comes strength – something that now dawned on me for the first time in my life. I realized that trying not to be overawed by things that we ought to find daunting is an arrogance that leads to weakness. Having a real sense of one's own frailties and anxieties, and knowing how to deal with them, is the solid foundation of courage and strength.

I was reminded of the five abiding truths embodied by

the Talisman, truths that my mother had repeated to me over and over again but which I was only now beginning to understand: the need for discipline, to control the darkness within us; the value of humility, to know that only God can work miracles: the basis of courage, to overcome our fears and anxieties; the purpose of sacrifice, to forfeit ourselves for God and for one another; and the power of wisdom, to understand the Talisman itself and not to fear it.

My passion for my homeland also became stronger through my vigils at the graves of my family in their resting places. Even though I admired the great cathedral of Norwich, and all the other Norman architectural triumphs being built all over England, they were not part of my heritage. My heritage was the fens, heaths and forests of old Saxon England and the uplands of our Celtic cousins.

In the Old Man of the Wildwood's glade, time stood still; not even mighty cathedrals and colossal mottes and baileys will stand the test of time like nature itself. As I reflected on that, my ambition to preserve our folk heritage and protect our ancient liberties, just as my family had done, was made steadfast.

Conscious that I alone was the inheritor of that tradition, I had found the responsibility overwhelming just a few weeks ago in Norwich, but now I was reinvigorated to realize that I could find a way to make my contribution to England's future.

I was now ready to collect my men from Cirencester and begin the search for my own destiny.

Dear Friend,

*Thank you for your letter, which arrived yesterday. The politics
of Rome leave a lot to be desired – I don't envy you. I'm glad my
packages offer some welcome distraction; I hope your life continues
to prosper and the politics of Mother Church are not too
distressing. All is calm here, except for the usual tensions
between York and Canterbury. The Bishop of Rouen often asks
me to act as intermediary – not easy, as I'm sure you know.*

*The days are getting shorter and the wind colder. The Thames
has taken on that brooding look it gets through the dark days of
winter. Today my journey back from St Paul's was agonizingly
cold. The wind on the river sprayed water over me for the entire
journey and the oarsmen struggled against the wind and the flow so
much that they had to rest at Chelsea Reach for twenty minutes to
get their breath.*

*Perhaps foolishly, but it is a cold evening, I have let the young
monks light a small fire in the cloister to roast some chestnuts. It
is a jovial way to spend a cold evening, but I don't think my Dean
will approve. Even so, it warms the bones and the soul a little.*

*My scribes are already complaining about their workload, and
yet we are only at the beginning of Harold's story. He is now
heading towards your homeland; unlike me, at least he will soon be
in warmer climes.*

*Yours in God,
Gilbert*

4. Arsenale

We soon found passage on a Breton trader from Bristol to Fécamp. It was a long and difficult journey with some fierce weather to contend with off the Cornish coast, especially around Lizard Point, where we had to take shelter for several days. We made better time after that with a good westerly behind us in the Channel. We got our land legs back in Fécamp, where Eadmer and Toste were both able to eat properly again after days being as sick as dogs during the crossing.

We were in Rouen within days – the seat of government of our Norman masters, and a place that had figured prominently in my family's history. Normandy was everything I had expected it to be. My mother could speak several languages and had taught me the language of our lords and masters from an early age. An upbringing among Norman craftsmen and clerics had shown me their many virtues as builders of fine monuments and as devout Christians. But I had also been witness to their proclivity for violence and cruelty, and to the ruthless behaviour of their soldiers and lords. Their homeland reflected my experience of their presence in England, studded by towering testaments to their pride; it was an unyielding place, unforgiving of its enemies and of any of its own miscreants who broke the law or slighted its hierarchy.

We spent some time in Rouen observing the ordered

and disciplined city, and I also made another excursion. This time not to a family shrine, but many miles to the west of Normandy, to Tinchebrai, a remote, heavily wooded valley, to see the site of the battleground where, ten years earlier, my father had fallen in the service of Robert Curthose, Duke of Normandy, on that fateful day when Robert lost everything to Henry Beauclerc.

My father had no known grave, but I knew from those who witnessed his demise on the field that he had been mortally wounded by a lance through his chest. Sadly, no one knew what became of his body, so I walked around the site looking for the remnants of the mass graves that had been dug for the dead. The local people helped me identify several mounds of earth, and I used my instincts to select a spot that might be his final resting place.

I had brought a small silver crucifix with me from Norwich, which the old Bishop, Herbert de Losinga, had blessed for me. I dug a small hole on the top of the mound for the cross and said a prayer in memory of the noble Sweyn of Bourne, the father I never knew. I had been a boy of eight when he died, and there had been times in my childhood when I resented the fact that my father had never visited us in Norwich. But my mother always reassured me that he loved me very much. She emphasized that personal sacrifice was at the heart of our family's legacy. My grandfather's generation was prepared to sacrifice everything for England's just cause, and my father had given his life to protect his brother-in-arms, Robert Curthose.

She would always remind me how part of that sacrifice often involved the denial of the normal pleasures of life, how she was denied the presence of her father for many years and had no idea of his fate or whereabouts, and how my father's loyalty to Robert Curthose consumed his entire life.

I thought about how loneliness must be one of the greatest trials of a life devoted to a cause. Was I prepared for such a burden? Would I be prepared to die for a cause, or to save the life of another, like my illustrious predecessors?

These were questions I could not yet answer with any certainty. But I knew that my chosen path meant that, one day, I would be able to.

My duties in honour of my family done, and in a much better frame of mind than when I left Norwich, we began our long journey to the Holy Land.

Our first port of call was Paris. Like London, an ancient Roman city of fine buildings, it was bursting with merchants and artisans, busy with their trade and products. The lord of Paris and the French was King Louis VI, 'Louis the Fat' to his subjects. Perennial enemies of the Normans – their neighbours just a few miles to the north – we joined one of the King's squadrons as mercenaries to see how they trained and fought. After several weeks of slack and ill-disciplined training, with no military adventures in the offing, we decided to move on. But not until after an incident had occurred that would sound an ominous echo much later in my journey.

We were drinking in a hostelry by the banks of the Seine, a fine river not unlike the Thames in London, when two knights walked in with the swagger of men of some importance. They were fearsome-looking characters who had the aura of seasoned warriors – indeed, so much so that the loud noise of animated conversation and banter among the drinkers dropped noticeably as they sat down.

For a few minutes, we paid them no more attention until sudden shouts made us turn round. As we did so, one of the knights, the larger of the two, got to his feet and raised his sword to deflect a blow from the sword of an assailant bearing down on him. In the same instant, he raised his Norman mace high above his head and brought it crashing down on to the helmet of his attacker. It was a mighty blow; the helmet all but disintegrated and blood spewed down the face of its hapless wearer, who collapsed to the ground in a heap. The victim did not move. I suspect he was dead before he hit the floor.

Blood had splashed across our table and our instincts made us jump to our feet and draw our swords. As we did so, the imposing knight turned to face us, quickly followed by his companion. I held my sword at arm's length, no more than a yard from the knight. I will never forget the look on his face. He was totally calm – as if he had just got up to leave, rather than having brutally crushed the skull of an opponent. He looked at me carefully before speaking in perfect Norman.

'Your name, Sir Knight?'

'Harold of Hereford.'

'I have no argument with you. You may sheath your weapon.'

He smiled at me benignly – like a priest comforting one of his flock – and, with his companion in his wake, walked away before I could reply. As the landlord carried away the body of the stricken man, I asked him the name of the knight who had killed him.

His answer was blunt.

'If you want to know his name, go and ask him. But if I were you, I'd leave well alone.'

'I'm only asking you for his name.'

'I don't know his name; he's a knight from Champagne, and the other one is from further north. They are veterans from the Great Crusade and have been causing trouble for months. They say they are God's avenging angels, sent to punish evil-doers.'

Eadmer and I helped the landlord haul the body into the alleyway. After he had sent a young boy to alert the city's garrison to the killing, the landlord turned to me.

'Thank you. They say this knight has the blessing of Galo, the Bishop of Paris, and that he flogs himself in the crypt of Notre Dame three times a day. If you ask me, he's just a killer. Stay away from him.'

Although I did not know his name, the knight's rugged face was etched in my memory. I would meet him again – but not for almost three years.

Disenchanted with service for the King of the French, we left Paris a few days later and continued along the ancient route to the south via the fine cities of Dijon, Geneva and Montreux. The journey was uneventful – except for the marvels of the almost never-ending diversity of dukedoms, principalities, languages and customs.

We stayed longer than expected at Martigny, an important fortified town in the Alps, just to admire the remarkable scenery – both in terms of its mountainous vistas and its more venal attractions. All five of us found bounteous female companionship in the thriving Alpine burgh. It was a temporary home to many travellers from all parts of Europe, including scores of unattached young women on their way to famous nunneries in the dukedoms of Italy. For many families in northern Europe unable to provide a sufficient dowry for their daughters, a prestigious convent in Tuscany or the Papal States was an ideal home for a surplus daughter. They usually travelled in groups, nominally guarded by a small retinue of ageing warriors, and were often allowed far more liberty than they would have been accorded as individuals. To our delight, more than a few looked forward to an ascetic life of devotion and toil with some reluctance and were keen to partake of the pleasures of the flesh before such joys were forever denied them by the confines of the nunnery.

I learned several things about women in Martigny, the most lasting of which was the simple observation that, shorn of their badges of identity – their distinct languages, their forms of dress and their local mores – girls from all over Europe were no different from the girls I had known in Norwich. We were using them and they were using us; it was a shallow exchange, but not a transaction between equals. A life of adventure still awaited us, but for them it was an interlude that was unlikely ever to be repeated.

After a life under the strict control of their parents, they would soon enter a regime of devotion and servitude where temporal pleasures would be forbidden under pain of damnation. Like the young women of Norwich, most of whom could look forward to nothing more than an impoverished life of drudgery, the young girls we met had been given no choice in determining their future.

Although I felt sorry that their lot was not as propitious as mine, it did not of course prevent me from helping them enjoy their brief respite of freedom.

We would have tarried longer before traversing the Great Pass of St Bernard, down into Aosta, capital city of the lands of Amadeus III, Count of Savoy, but the snows of the winter of 1116 were almost upon us. I decided that we would make the crossing, then replenish our supplies in Aosta before seeing out the winter in Venice, from where we could board a ship to Constantinople in the spring.

Venice was a sight to behold: its palaces, churches and marketplaces seemed to float on the sea, most of its thoroughfares were waterways, and transport was undertaken by barge or small flat-bottomed paddleboat. The few areas of dry land that had not been built on formed small markets in front of churches, or narrow walkways between buildings. Despite its unusual architecture, Venice was a mighty power. It controlled the Adriatic and much of the Mediterranean beyond, and its income from commerce and trade made it as rich a city as any in the world.

Venice was not ruled by a sovereign but by the Doge, the military leader of the city, who was elected for life by its elders. When we arrived in January 1117, the Doge was a fascinating man called Ordelafo Faliero – a warrior of some repute who I decided was a man worth meeting. I set about trying to find a way of gaining an audience.

The key to Venice's power was its Arsenale, a huge fortified shipyard dedicated to building its enormous navy.

All the finest maritime craftsmen in the Mediterranean flocked to the Arsenale to perfect their skills. Although the five of us possessed not an iota of naval skill between us, the Arsenale seemed like the best place to make a name for ourselves. Language was also a problem. Venetians spoke Veneto, a tongue hard to fathom, while educated men used Greek rather than Latin in sophisticated circles, so communication was difficult. All the same, I was determined to meet the esteemed Doge and learn as much as I could from the enterprising Venetians.

We found lodgings close to the Arsenale and it took me a couple of days to devise a plan. I put it to my companions over a flask of the dark red wine favoured by the locals.

'Gentlemen, we are going to present ourselves as aspiring marines for the Doge's navy.'

I had recently decided to drop formalities within our close-knit band of brothers and allowed them to call me by my Christian name, which soon became abbreviated to 'Hal'.

Eadmer made the obvious point in response to my bold suggestion.

'Hal, you are not yet a dubbed knight and not yet nineteen. How will we get accepted?'

'Leave that to me. We English have a good reputation as warriors, Wulfric and Toste are excellent shots with the bow, and my sword arm is strong. Eadmer, you are a very experienced soldier, I will rely on you a lot.'

'I can fight too.'

As always, Alric was keen to fight rather than be a cook and groom.

'Of course you can.' I looked at the four of them. I knew they were not convinced. 'I've decided that I will win my knight's pennon here, rather than with the Normans. I want to be made a Knight of Venice and be dubbed by the Doge. I'm impressed by what I hear of him; I think he would be a good man to serve.'

Eadmer's unease was escalating.

'But we have no experience at sea. And besides that, I get seasick – and so does Toste.'

'You'll get over it.'

Eadmer was beginning to lose his self-control.

'Look, Hal, you could get us all killed. I made a promise to your mother to keep you safe. The plan was to go to one of the Latin Princes in the Holy Land, where you could continue your training as a knight. Not to join an army, and certainly not one that fights on water!'

I decided it was time for me to assert my authority. This was something I had rarely done with my amiable companions before.

'Firstly, my mother is not here, you are in service to me. Secondly, I've made my decision. And I expect you to respect it.'

I looked Eadmer in the eye. I tried not to blink or waver in any way; he had to know that I meant what I said. With that, I walked away, leaving my companions to ponder my words. I had only made three steps when Eadmer called after me.

'Hal, you are right, we are in your service and paid to do as we're bid. But don't get us killed.'

I hesitated for barely a moment, but decided not to answer and walked on. I had made a big decision, based on my instinct that, despite the fact that almost everything about Venice was alien to me, the city and its Doge would be part of my destiny. The question was: did I have the stomach to meet that destiny?

The man I needed to convince about our credentials was Raphael of Pesaro, Master of the Arsenale of Venice. A large man with a neatly trimmed black beard, flecked with grey, he was responsible for the daily running of the Arsenale, as well as the recruitment of men to guard Venice's trading vessels. I left my companions in our lodgings, cleaned up my weapons and clothes, trimmed my somewhat youthful beard and made my way to the Arsenale, the most powerful military establishment in the Mediterranean.

I felt I looked the part. I was fortunate that I could afford quality weapons: my knight's sword and battle-axe gleamed in the sunlight, and both were tooled with the elaborate designs of a man of substance. Battle-axes, the main weapon of my English kith and kin, had been abandoned since the Conquest, the Normans believing the sword a more chivalrous weapon for a knight. Nevertheless, I carried mine with pride, in tribute to my grandfather's legendary weapon, the Great Axe of Göteborg. Mine was a single-bladed one-handed axe, not the double-headed mammoth that Hereward had wielded. I also carried my family colours on my shield: the gules, sable and gold of my grandfather and the English revolt of 1069.

My mother had described my grandfather's helmet to me many times. I had made sure that, when it came time for me to have my own helmet made, it matched her description of it as closely as possible: made in quarter-plates of iron, joined by reinforced bronze bands, it had a domed top with nose and eyepieces shaped to fit tightly to the face. On its front, from the tip of the nose guard to the dome, ran a piece of highly polished bronze, elegantly chased with runic swirls.

I also wore fine leather knee-high boots, another legacy passed on by family tradition from my grandfather's days in Sicily. Made for me by a cordwainer in Norwich from a design supplied by my mother, they made a distinctive clatter on the sett stone approach to the gates of the Arsenale.

My knightly garb and weaponry made it relatively easy for me to pass the guards to the great Venetian dockyard and I was soon striding purposefully across what seemed like an infinite expanse of moorings, timber, rigging and sail. There were all manner of pulleys, hoists, blocks and capstans hauling weights; myriad artisans and craftsmen toiled at their tasks, and the incessant squawk of gulls conflicted with the rhythmic din of the labour of thousands of men.

The Venetian galley was not just a vessel for trade; it was also a fearsome man-o'-war. The larger vessels had upper and lower decks of oarsmen, as well as a mainsail and sails fore and aft. They also had a body of professional marines to keep the pirates at bay. These larger ships usually acted as escorts to fleets of smaller cargo ships that were similar in design but smaller and lighter and with only one deck of oars. It was service on the larger war triremes that seemed to offer me the best chance for adventure and military experience.

After finding a Norman shipwright who was fluent in Veneto to act as interpreter, I made my approach to Raphael of Pesaro. I thought I sounded convincing about my suitability to mount a marine escort to a Venetian galley, but the Master of the Arsenale took a different view.

'Young sir, you are not much more than a boy. Come back in five years when that bum-fluff on your face has grown into a beard!'

He laughed as he spoke, and the artisans and stevedores around him sniggered with him.

'But, Magister, I have fought with King Henry Beauclerc in Wales. And my men are fine soldiers. Do not insult me or my noble family.'

My challenge made Raphael change his tone to one that was even more disparaging.

'Henry Beauclerc – who's he? And Wales? Never heard of it. A land of woodchoppers and sheep-shaggers by the look of that peasant's axe you're carrying.'

'My axe is a family tradition. My grandfather was Godwin of Ely, Captain of the Varangian Guard of the Emperor Alexius.'

Although I was reluctant to use my grandfather's reputation to gain favour, I had little choice but to use it to persuade Raphael to take me seriously.

'Do you expect me to believe that? I saw this man once, many years ago in Bari. He was a huge blond man, and his axe was the biggest weapon I'd ever seen. And it was double-bladed.'

'He was the only one who could use it effectively. My axe is the more typical single-blade design, but I am very proficient with it. As for my appearance, my grandmother,

mother and father were all dark; they had the ancient Celtic blood of Old Britain.'

Raphael moved closer and stared at me. He was taller than I was, and broader at the shoulders, but I remained resolute.

'How many men do you have?'

'Three and a groom.'

'Is that all? Not much of a retinue for such an important knight!'

He started to smirk again.

'Magister, I travel light. I am going to serve the Latin Princes in the Holy Land, which is not a place to try to provision a large force of men.'

'What do you know of the Holy Land?'

'My father and mother fought there, at Antioch and Jerusalem, with Robert Curthose, Duke of Normandy, and Edgar the Atheling, Prince of the English.'

'Your mother was a knight? That's not possible, boy.'

'It is in Islam. My mother was knighted by Ibn Hamed, Emir of Calatafimi, when she and my father fought for him and Roger of Sicily at the Battle of Mazara. I am Harold of Hereford, Knight of England. I stopped being called "boy" when I won my knight's pennon on my eighteenth birthday.'

I had told a blatant lie about my knight's pennon, but I was beyond the point of no return and threw caution to the wind. Raphael stared at me even more intently.

'That is impressive; you certainly talk the talk of a knight. Do you have a testimonial from your lord?'

'No, Magister. I had to leave in a hurry.'

'Tell me more.'

'Well, I had a dalliance with someone in my lord's household.'

Another lie of course, but one born of desperation. By his demeanour, Raphael of Pesaro looked like the kind of man who was rather too fond of female company and I gambled that an infidelity at court might win me some esteem in his eyes.

'Was she worth it?'

'Yes, she was. But it got me into murky waters.'

'Your lord's daughter?'

'No, his mistress.'

The belligerent expression on his face softened as he thought about what I had told him.

'Why do women go for skinny dogs like you? Can't understand it.'

He smiled. My gambit had worked; there is nothing like male vanity.

'Can you and your men use a bow? All our marine cohorts have to be experts in the bow. It is most effective against pirates.'

'Yes, of course. Archery is a great tradition in my country.'

'Ah, yes, the land of the woodchoppers! Where is your bow now?'

'With my men at our lodgings.'

'Very well, come back tomorrow with your men and your weapons and we will see how well you measure up to your boasts and the pedigree of your family.'

'Thank you, Magister.'

As I walked back to give the news to the others, I was delighted that I had got as far as I had. But when I told the others, they were less than enthusiastic. Eadmer had a look of horror on his face, but it was Toste who spoke first.

'So you told them you are already a knight?'

'I did. It was only a small lie.'

Wulfric spoke next.

'It sounds like a big one to me. What could be bigger?'

'I also told him that we had to leave Norwich because I had been tupping the Earl's mistress.'

All four of them looked at me incredulously. Alric tried to make light of it.

'Well, that's not too bad. You could have told him that you were an earl and had been humping the Queen.'

None of them smiled at his attempt at whimsy. Eadmer was still frowning.

'Hal, you know it is an offence to pass yourself off as a knight. The punishment would be severe in England, I'm sure it is the same here.'

'I know. But when the Doge makes me a knight, it won't matter.'

'I thought you followed the Mos Militum and its code of honour: truth and justice, in all things?'

'I do! But needs must. My family found its destiny beyond England's shores, and that's what I intend to do.'

'Hal, the Master is obviously going to put us to the test tomorrow, but how?'

'I don't know. Archery for sure. He didn't mention anything else.'

'So we're in a foreign land being tested as marines – something entirely alien to us – by people who think we're barbarians. Is there any good news?'

'Yes, of course! We'll pass with flying colours and be on a galley to the Levant on the next tide.'

My glibness did not seem to impress them. Eadmer just stood up and walked away sullenly, leaving the others to stare at me wide-eyed.

The next day, in a perfect example of Eadmer's loyalty and professionalism, the men were ready in excellent order for their ordeal. Their discipline also helped fortify me. I had not spent the most comfortable of nights coming to terms with what I had let my companions and myself in for.

Raphael of Pesaro was in a more generous mood when we arrived. He had gathered a small group of marines and men, who he introduced to us as his training officers. I could sense that these men had been told that the morning might be entertaining, with an adolescent English knight making a fool of himself in a futile attempt to join Venice's renowned corps of marines. Our Norman interpreter looked uncomfortable, which only added to my apprehension.

'So, Harold of Hereford, to the bow. First, six arrows each from your quivers. Your target is over there on the other side of the dock – the large mooring post in the middle.'

The post was about seventy yards away, so demanded a flatter trajectory than our usual aerial tactic. But, at about a foot wide, it was relatively easy to hit. The wind was light and our aim good: from our twenty-four arrows, we had thirteen hits and most of the rest were very close. There were nods of approval from the Master's retinue.

The arrows were brought back to us and Raphael issued another challenge.

'The four of you shooting together, four volleys. Your target is that patch of dry ground in the empty dock area beyond the furthest quay.'

The area was almost 200 yards away, a target distance much more like the one we would use in battle. Using our English stance, we launched our volleys high into the air at an acute angle. The Master and his men seemed impressed as each volley landed in unison with increasing accuracy, all within a few yards of one another.

'I can see you prefer to shoot at distance. That is good – we have crossbowmen for close-quarters battle. Now let us see what you are like in combat.'

We were then led to a large open courtyard, which was immediately recognizable as a military training area. There were stacks of weapons all around the perimeter, and in the middle various combat mannequins were being vigorously assaulted by trainees with swords and maces. The rhythmic clamour of orders being barked, the war cries of the trainees, the clash of steel on steel and the thud of metal on wood created a strange sort of bellicose harmony. It fell silent as soon as the Duel Master shouted the order, '*Cease!*'

After a few stern commands in Veneto were given, four swordsmen appeared. They were clearly seasoned veterans.

Raphael turned to me.

'Your men first, one at a time, then you.'

Wulfric, never shy of a fight, stepped forward. His Venetian opponent bowed politely before launching a ferocious assault with his shield and sword. Wulfric did well, parried everything, and even managed a few heavy blows to his adversary's shield. After about two minutes, the Duel Master called a halt and nodded his approval to Raphael of Pesaro. Toste and Eadmer also acquitted themselves well.

Then it was my turn. My comrades were experienced soldiers, but I was not. This was my moment of truth. I had been through many training routines, but I anticipated that my opponent would have been told to give me the sternest possible examination. So it proved.

After the perfunctory bow, he came at me like a man flailing wheat. The speed of his blows was such that I found it difficult enough to follow the arc of his blows, let alone parry them. I was in almost constant retreat until my flight was halted by one of the large stone columns holding up the colonnade around the training area. I ducked under the next blow, hearing the piercing crack of a sword blade striking stone. My sudden move, born of desperation, gave me confidence. I was more nimble than my opponent, and I began to move more adroitly and get on to the balls of my feet.

My opponent, a short stocky man at least in his late thirties, began to sweat. I still felt fresh and slowly started to take the initiative and launch my own attacks. Then I must have become overconfident because, in an instant, my sword was knocked clean out of my hand with a vicious swipe from my opponent's shield. I reached for my axe, which was slung across my back, and used its haft to parry several more lunges and blows.

Again, my adversary began to tire and I was able to start swinging my axe in wide arcs, giving me an advantage and allowing me to advance. But my rival was too clever for me. He swung away from one of my strikes, and as my blade hit the dirt floor of the arena he managed to trap it with his foot, leaving me exposed. To my relief, the Duel Master then cried, '*Subsisto!*' and brought the contest to an end.

I was mortified, thinking I had failed, but Raphael of Pesaro stepped forward with a broad smile and held out his hand.

'Congratulations, Harold of Hereford, you and your men will serve the navy of Venice well.'

He could see that I was puzzled.

'Vitale is one of the finest swordsmen we have. You did well to keep him at bay for almost three minutes, not many have achieved that. You fight well and I can see that your axe can be useful. There are only five of you, so you will have to join a larger squad of marines, probably on one of the battlefleet's men-o'-war. Your groom will join the mess crew. Your pay will be twenty denari per month, to be shared as you see fit. Come back in two days, when we will assign you to a ship's captain.'

We celebrated well that night and drank far too much Passum, the local sweet dark wine, which after a while had a kick like a mule. I woke in the morning, still drunk on the excesses of the previous night. Fortunately, the extra day we had been granted by the Master of the Arsenale gave us all time to recover from our revelries.

5. Dalmatian Pirates

Eadmer found his sea legs quite quickly. Toste took a little longer, but within a few weeks our service on the *Domenico Contarini*, named after a revered doge from the past, became routine. Apart from the privations one would imagine on a vessel that was home to over 120 men, time passed quickly. Discipline at sea was strict: watches had to be meticulously observed, and we had to be vigilant and prepared for attack at a moment's notice.

What little time we had to ourselves was spent trying to master the rudiments of the many languages spoken by the crew and the marines, so that we could exchange stories and good humour. All orders were issued in Veneto, and it was vital to recognize these quickly.

I was made third in command – the junior knight of three – at the head of a body of twenty-two marines. My superiors were Pietro and Vitale, the former a courteous Venetian, the latter a surly brute from Taranto. Both treated me with some disdain, doubting my worthiness and being patently dismissive of the abilities of my men. In contrast, the ship's captain, Enrico Selvo, a Venetian from a long line of seafarers, was friendlier and keen to hear about England and its Norman rulers. He had sailed as far as Toulon and knew a little of the history of northern Europe. He had also heard of the exploits of Godwin of Ely and Hereward of Bourne – but of course did not know that they were one and the same man.

For many weeks, all was peaceful on board the *Domenico*. Life on our long voyages up and down the Adriatic became tedious. It was a monotony that was only enlivened by loading and unloading at Venice and at our destinations, including Tripoli and Alexandria – cities full of fascinating buildings and teeming with exotic life.

The cities of North Africa were even more cosmopolitan than Venice. Some were ruled by Latin Princes and had Norman, German and Norse mercenaries serving there, whose pale faces and fair hair were in stark contrast to the dusky skin of the Arabs and Berbers and the pitch-black faces of the nomads from the deserts of the south. The markets were full of fruits and spices, the like of which we had not seen before, and their animals were of a species unknown to us. Their beasts of burden were tall ugly creatures called 'camello', and they had small hairy monkeys for sale as pets that resembled little men, which they called 'simia'.

At sea, there were storms and squalls to endure and periods of calm when the oarsmen earned their meagre keep. Most of these men were slaves, bonded to Venice for life. Some more fortunate ones could serve ten years on the galleys to win their freedom; a few were thieves and men of violence being punished for their crimes.

The only real threat to our heavily armed galleys were the equally powerful pirate ships. We had seen them in the distance several times off the coast of Dalmatia, stalking our progress, but had suffered no attacks. That all changed in the late summer of 1117.

We were making good progress, homeward bound for Venice, with a strong south-westerly wind in our sails pushing us up the Dalmatian coast, close to the island of Vis. We were especially vigilant: these were the most treacherous waters in the Adriatic, where numerous small and craggy islands offered perfect hidden moorings for pirates. The *Domenico* was one of Venice's new and much larger galleys, with powerful oarsmen capable of outrunning most vessels and sufficient marines on board to repel boarders. But we were heavily laden with Sicilian wine and spices from North Africa, and we sat low in the water.

It was late in the afternoon and we could see from the black sky to the east that Vis was experiencing the kind of heavy storm typical of that time of day in the hot summer. Captain Selvo stood aft watching the eastern horizon; he looked calm enough, occasionally ordering small trims to the sails and checking that the oarsmen were ready to row if needed. He then issued the orders that I knew meant we were going to the first level of preparedness for battle.

'Get the marines on deck and issue water to the oarsmen.'

He spoke quietly. The *Domenico* became silent, and men began to peer to the east. But the attack did not come from the east.

The Captain had stationed a lookout at the stern, facing south, and he was the first to see the three muddy-brown sails to the south-west.

'Pirates off the port stern!'

They had obviously tacked round behind us in the

night and were now bearing down on us at a rate of knots. They knew that the setting sun would freshen the wind and give them the advantage of speed to our stern.

The Captain ordered the oarsmen to row, and the war drum began to beat its steady rhythm.

The pirate ships were sleeker than our galley and stripped bare to accommodate Venetian booty. Their holds would be empty of cargo and lighter to row. Their oarsmen were free men, happy to row and fight in return for a share of the spoils. Commanded by buccaneer captains who owned their vessels, and sponsored by rich merchants who traded in contraband, every one of their ship's company would share in the booty. Such men were hard to beat in a fight.

Their strategies were subtle, based on excellent seamanship, but their tactics were brutal, based on the ferocity of greed. If they managed to ensnare their prey, they would fill their hold to the brim and discard what they could not carry. They would kill all survivors on board their stricken victim, then hole its hull, consigning it to the murky depths, and sail for home laden with their ill-gotten gains.

The pulse of the war drum began to increase as Captain Selvo realized that the pirate sails were looming larger and larger on the horizon.

'Increase to pursuit speed, but hold there. This could be a long haul.'

He began to look at the sun dropping towards the horizon and then back at the encroaching sails. He did this several times, calculating whether darkness might come to our aid.

'Trim the sails. We need every cubit out of them.' He then turned to his helmsman. 'Hold her hard.'

Again, he spoke calmly; the crew followed suit. These were hardy seafarers. There was no need to panic – at least, not yet. We sailed like this for over an hour. Every five minutes, the oarsmen would rest to get their breath. The Captain looked at the sun again to repeat his mental arithmetic, relating the speed of the setting sun against the pace of our pursuers. Satisfied that he knew the grim answer to the equation, he ordered barrels of pitch to be brought on deck and torches lit. That meant only one thing: there would be a fight and fire-arrows would be critical to its outcome.

The pirates arrived within range with the sun low in the sky behind them. The wind was by then gusting and tossing plumes of foam from the tops of the waves. Two of the bandit ships began to move to either side of the *Domenico*, while one continued to close directly to our stern. The Captain ordered his corps of marines to divide into three to cover the port, starboard and stern. I was assigned to the port side and I summoned Eadmer and the men close to me.

Our bows were at a disadvantage. We were upwind of our hunters; the pirates had made a clever approach. The order came to light our first volley of arrows. We plunged their hemp-covered tips into the barrels of burning pitch and took aim.

As we loosed our volleys, we could see the pirates in their rigging ready to douse any flames with pails of water. Several of our arrows hit their targets, but shooting was extremely difficult into the strong wind and many of our missiles fizzled harmlessly into the sea. Not so the pirates' arrows. Aided by a following wind, their volleys came straight and true. Soon our mainsail was ablaze and losing shape, without which we were easy prey.

The long slim arrows from the pirates' Kipchak bows soon began to ricochet into our deck like hailstones. Men fell all around us and I ordered my men to cover themselves with their shields. I could see grappling hooks and ropes being prepared for boarding less than a hundred yards away. The Captain had disappeared from deck – not to desert us, but to prepare a desperate counter-attack.

The pirate oarsmen stopped rowing to arm themselves, ready to board us. Below deck, Captain Selvo used the hiatus to prepare our oarsmen for a fast and furious onslaught. With a huge cascade of water, our oars were plunged deep into the sea and, with a mighty pull, the ship lurched forward. He then shouted his orders.

'Hard a-port, ramming speed!'

The *Domenico* swung to the left and the war drum's cadence increased, making the oarsmen strike faster than I had ever seen them row before.

Half our company of marines were dead or dying on the deck – including my superiors, Pietro and Vitale – and our ship was alight fore and aft. All three sails were in shreds. We were doomed, but Enrico Selvo was determined to take at least one of the pirate vessels to the bottom with us. We were going to hit the scavenger vessel amidships, and I looked around to see how we might survive the impact.

The captain bellowed at his men.

'Pull for your lives! *Pull!*'

The impact was like nothing I had ever felt before. The buccaneers' man-o'-war heaved backwards, forcing a huge swell of water with it, as our bull-nose prow smashed through the side of its hull. We rose in the air, like a dolphin leaping over a wave. There was a cacophony of sounds: the splintering and creaking of oak planks and heavy beams; the shrieks and cries of stricken men; and the roars and growls of a boiling sea.

Most of the men on the pirate ship were already floundering in the water. Their ship, breached almost in half with its belly and keel exposed to us, was taking on water rapidly and sinking fast. I mustered our remaining marines and we formed up behind the helm, gathering together whatever quivers of arrows we could find. We managed to get away several volleys before the two remaining pirate ships were upon us.

As the grappling hooks clattered into the deck and started pulling us towards the pirates, I noticed that the *Domenico* had been holed in the impact and had already started to list. Eadmer was standing next to me. I felt a rising panic as I began to look around frantically for a means of escape. Thankfully, Eadmer grabbed me by the shoulders and turned me towards him.

'Hal, think clearly! You need your wits about you.'

It was a timely piece of advice that helped me maintain control. I began to look around again, but this time with a level head. Captain Selvo was lying on the deck; it looked like he had been hit by a grappling iron and was unconscious. I was suddenly in command of the ship at the very moment the first pirates swarmed over our decks. We numbered no more than two dozen fit men: some sailors, and a few marines. Most of the oarsmen had already abandoned ship.

I told Eadmer and Wulfric to drag Captain Selvo towards us, and we formed a redoubt by the helm. The fighting was intense, but we held a confined space, surrounded on three sides by water, so we were able to form a solid wall of shields and swords, not unlike the English shield wall of legend. More importantly, knowing that the fight was won, most of the pirates were preoccupied collecting weapons and armour from the dead and emptying the hold of whatever wine and spices were still above the waterline.

We had one advantage amidst our dire circumstances: our position at the helm meant we could only be attacked from the front, a space of no more than three yards. But in that confined area, it was like a whirlwind of flashing blades accompanied by the thunder of clashing shields. I have no idea how long we held the pirates off. Time seemed to stand still. I took some blows, but they did not seem to hurt. My blood was up. I just kept flailing with my sword, trying to hit whatever was in front of me.

Inevitably, our small band of defenders started to diminish in number as arrows found their targets and swords and lances struck home. Toste and Wulfric were at my feet. It was hard to tell if they were still alive, but neither moved.

We were within minutes of being wiped out altogether when our assailants realized that they had taken all the cargo that was still above the waterline and that the *Domenico*'s demise was imminent. The pirates started to leave for their ships, taking care to cut the ropes holding the three vessels together. To hasten our doom, they tipped over the barrels of flaming pitch on to the deck and rowed away, leaving us to our fate.

I took a deep breath and looked around, not noticing the blood flowing down my legs. I had been slashed across the midriff by a sword, had puncture wounds in both arms, and had been hit on the side of the head – a blow that had creased my helmet and made me bleed from a badly mangled ear. The frenzy of battle had rendered me momentarily immune from pain. But as soon as Eadmer steadied me, I started to stagger, convulsed by searing agony.

Alric had taken up arms, as he always said he would, and was trying to help Toste and Wulfric. Both began to move, but they had been badly wounded. Toste had a deep gouge to the top of his shoulder, while Wulfric – the more seriously wounded of the two – had taken a sword deep into the abdomen.

I could stand only with the support of Eadmer, but I still had sufficient wits about me to issue orders. I asked the four remaining fit and able marines to get Captain Selvo to his feet. We were almost engulfed by flames and the heat was beginning to scorch our faces. I told every-one to discard their weapons and armour, save their seax and belt, and made them get into the water that was now lapping at our ankles.

I heard myself shout over and over again, 'Rope! Cut some rope!'

Eventually, Eadmer shouted back, 'Hal, I have rope, enough to hang fifty men!'

He helped me into the water, but it was only as we

moved away from the flames that I realized darkness had fallen. The water appeared black and threatening, but its cold lick energized me and I shouted to everyone to find floating timbers that we could lash together as a raft.

It was a makeshift affair, on to which we hauled the injured. We were fortunate: the impact when we had rammed the pirate ship had produced enough flotsam to make a flotilla of rafts, so we added more and more timber to give enough space for everyone. Our first priority was to get away from the remains of the stricken ships. Sails that could snag us were drifting on the surface of the water and patches of burning pitch were still alight, creating eerie halos of light in the gloom. We used whatever we could as paddles to pull away, until the glow of the pitch was on the distant horizon.

Captain Selvo came round within the hour, not long after we had managed to stem the bleeding from Wulfric's wound. Eadmer had taken off his undershirt and bound it tightly around Wulfric's midriff, using rigging rope as a binding. He had lost a lot of blood, but was calm and breathing normally. My wounds were weeping a little and I felt some pain from my stomach wound, but not as much as from my head, which throbbed as though someone was holding it in a carpenter's vice. Eadmer, composed as always, checked my wounds regularly to make sure the bleeding was only minor. He used seawater to cleanse them, the sharp stinging confirming its medicinal qualities.

Enrico Selvo had roused himself sufficiently to speak. The Captain was anxious about his crew.

'How many survivors?'

'Just us, Captain. I'm sorry.'

'The *Domenico Contarini* and her cargo?'

'Gone to the bottom, sir.'

'Do you know where we are?'

'We should be drifting towards Vis. The wind is still to the south-west.'

'You had better leave me there. There is no future for me in Venice, now that I've lost one of the navy's finest galleys. I should have died on board with my men. Or gone down with my ship.'

Selvo, looking distraught, then turned to peer in the direction of his sunken vessel. Only a few hours earlier he had been resolute and strong, now he looked like a broken man.

After a while, we all fell asleep, to be woken an hour or so later by the rolling of a rising swell and the whistle of an ever stronger wind. Where Captain Selvo had lain was just an empty space. He must have slid off the raft while we were sleeping, unable to face the shame of having lost his crew, his ship and his cargo. I felt stricken by his demise. He was a noble man and had shown me great kindness.

The elements did not allow me to contemplate his passing for long. There was the rumble of thunder in the distance and flashes of lightning beyond the clouds on the horizon. Carried on the wind, another storm was coming our way. I was already beginning to feel very cold, and I could see that Wulfric was shaking uncontrollably. We needed to make landfall as soon as possible.

Within thirty minutes, our makeshift raft was lashed by torrents of rain and tossed by a rolling sea and howling wind. Eadmer and Alric held on to Wulfric while Toste and I held each other tightly, all desperately trying to stay on the raft. For several long minutes, I found it impossible to see beyond a hand in front of my face, until the storm slowly began to abate. It was then that I realized that Alric and one of the Venetian marines were no longer with us.

We scoured the sea as far as we could see and shouted incessantly in every direction, but we saw and heard nothing. They had been washed away.

Eadmer was distraught. I had never before seen him shed a tear, but now he struggled to speak.

'I thought he was still there . . . I was holding Wulfric as tight as I could, concentrating on him . . . Alric was on the other side . . . he must have let go.'

The black sky of the storm was replaced by a clear night, sparkling with stars. But the temperature dropped significantly and the wind still blew. Wulfric shook even more; I was very cold, shivering, my teeth chattering. I just wanted to close my eyes, and drift off to sleep, but Eadmer forced me to stay awake and shouted at all of us.

'Everyone get close together! We must keep one another warm, otherwise the cold will draw the life out of us. I've seen it happen. Men go to sleep and never wake up!'

We then spent what was left of the night curled up together like pups in a litter. We recited prayers, sang songs, repeated old tales and legends and counted the stars to stay awake. Although we were far from safe, and faced an uncomfortable night, at least we would see the sunrise in the morning – unlike our ill-fated companions whose remains would serve only to feed the creatures of the deep.

By morning, when the first rays of the sun began to warm us, there were only seven survivors of the *Domenico Contarini* – and two of those were not in good condition.

With the low sun behind it, we then got the first glimpse of the small island of Bisevo that would offer us salvation. Just three miles west of Vis, the strong south-westerly wind had propelled us within touching distance of its shore. Despite my fragile condition, I roused myself sufficiently to get Eadmer and the men to use their hands as oars to get us on to the beach.

It was like arriving in paradise: the beach glistened with golden sand, the hillsides were swathed in abundant pine trees, and a gentle breeze moderated the heat of the hot sun. Home to a colony of Benedictine monks, the island's twelve resident brothers rushed to help us within minutes of spotting our raft on the beach. Realizing that we were not the pirates who infest their shore, but rather their hapless victims, they soon fed and watered us, dressed our wounds and placed us in the shade to sleep and recover from our ordeal.

Over the ensuing weeks, we learned a good deal about the pastoral charms and exacting rigours of being a Benedictine monk, especially when scratching a self-sufficient existence on a remote Adriatic island surrounded by ruthless pirates. We also discovered a good deal about the pirates who had ambushed us. Paganians by name, a Slavic tribe, they had lived on the islands off the coast of Dalmatia for centuries, supplementing with piracy the meagre agricultural existence offered by the harsh limestone islands. They would trade their loot with any passing merchants who dared to enter their waters. Any rich prisoners they snared were ransomed, while the less valuable ones were sold into slavery.

The monks had to buy their trouble-free life with butts of olive oil, which the pirates came to collect twice a year. The Benedictines had few other visitors and kept only a small skiff for rowing to Vis in an emergency. They helped us build a good shelter and fed us until we were able to fend for ourselves. The island of Bisevo had fresh water, a little game in the interior and plenty of fresh fish teeming in its waters. Within a few weeks, we were all recovered from our various injuries and fit and eager to return to Venice.

As leader of our small band, I took the decision not to use the monks' skiff to row us to Vis, as the island was controlled by the Paganians. However, that meant that we had to wait for sight of a friendly trader – a rare occurrence that had not happened since the turn of the year. It was a long wait, and I questioned the wisdom of my decision more than once.

We did not see a passing trader until the bitterly cold days of November 1117, by which time Bisevo had lost much of its idyllic charm to monotonous boredom. The tranquil life of monks was not for us. When we eventually caught sight of a ship, it turned out to be part of a large flotilla of Venetian traders, guarded by three large war galleys. We said our grateful goodbyes to the monks who had helped us and left for Venice, feeling hugely relieved.

There was amazement on board our rescue ship that they had stumbled across seven fellow-Venetians and that we had survived the demise of the *Domenico Contarini*. It had been assumed in Venice that she had gone down and that all had perished with her. Our rescuers' amazement slowly turned to admiration as the details of the battle circulated across the flotilla.

Within days of our arrival at the Arsenale, we were lauded for our courage and resolve, especially for our final redoubt on the burning deck, a story that became embellished in the telling as 'The *Domenico*'s English Shield Wall'.

I hoped of course that news of our redoubt and survival might reach the ear of the Doge, and a few days later I received the news I wanted from Raphael Pesaro, Master of the Arsenale.

'You have been summoned to the palace to see Ordelafo Faliero. It is a great honour.'

'Thank you, Magister.'

'Word has gone around the Arsenale about the young Englishman. You did well to get the men home; you won their respect.'

'I appreciate your kind words.'

'But remember, the Doge is a difficult man. Mind what you say. He's going to war against the Hungarians again, and he may want you to go with him. Be clear in your mind what you want to do if he offers you the option. He won't like it if you're indecisive.'

'I thank you for the advice.'

I then talked to some of the senior knights commanding the Doge's marines about the campaigns against the
Hungarians, and later that evening I discussed the situation with my men.

'Raphael of Pesaro thinks the Doge may ask us to join
his campaign against the Hungarians. Are you happy with
that?'

As usual, Eadmer spoke first.

'Do we have to fight the Hungarians at sea?'

'No, the Doge's knights have told me that the Hungarian king, Colomon, became ruler of Venice's rival city,
Zadar, a few years ago. But he has just died and the Doge
thinks King Stephen, his son, is weak and that it's a good
time to strike at the city. He believes the Hungarians have
made a secret pact with the Paganian pirates and he wants
to punish them for it. We will embark as a fleet, but make
a landing north of Zadar. It is on the Dalmatian coast, not
far from our sanctuary on Bisevo, but we will attack by
land.'

'As long as we don't have to fight with fire and water
around our ankles, as we did on the *Domenico*, we're in.'

We all smiled ruefully at one another.

'We will fight in the name of Alric.'

Wulfric bowed his head.

'He died trying to keep me alive. I will never forget
that.'

I reached out and put my hand on Wulfric's shoulder.

'He got his wish in the end. He always wanted to fight.'

My gesture towards Wulfric seemed to meet with Eadmer's approval. He gave me a short nod and a warm smile

of endorsement before also putting his hand on our friend's shoulder. I then reached out to Toste and placed my other hand on his arm.

'We are just four now. Let's keep it that way.'

The Doge's palace was even more remarkable than I had imagined. Built by the side of the Canalazzo, the Grand Canal of the city, it towered over the waterfront as a symbol of the power of Venice. Flying high from its roof was the crimson flag of the Republic, with its golden winged lion emblazoned at its centre.

Entrance to the palace was gained by gondola through arches at the water's edge, which opened to a dock beneath a grand staircase leading to the receiving rooms. There plaintiffs and their lawyers waited for hours for an audience with the Grand Council or the Doge himself. I took Eadmer with me for the audience. We had washed ourselves and cleaned our clothes. But as we had lost our weapons and armour at sea, we were unarmed and looked a little impoverished amidst the splendour that surrounded us.

When we arrived at the Great Council Chamber, it was as big as a city market. Its walls were adorned with frescoes and tapestries, and its floors were covered in carpets the size of a yeoman's house. My mother had told me many times about the wonders of Constantinople and the splendours of the Emperor's palace, the Blachernae, but what we saw here made us gawp in wonder.

As well as being the elected leader of the Most Serene Republic of Venice, the Doge was also a soldier. The present incumbent, Ordelafo Faliero, had personally commanded a Venetian fleet of a hundred ships to assist Baldwin I, King of Jerusalem, and Sigurd I, King of Norway, in capturing the city of Sidon in the Holy Land in 1110.

The Doge sat on a gilded throne in the middle of the long rear wall of the chamber, from where he could see the Canalazzo crammed full of the trading galleys that brought Venice its vast wealth and power. Beyond it was the open sea, the lifeblood of the city. The Council members sat and stood around him, listening to the pleadings of the wronged, the disgruntled and the distraught. Everyone wanted justice – or perhaps his or her version of it – while many wanted loans or bills paid, and some wanted revenge.

A pair of Republican Guards dressed in dark-blue tunics flanked him. Tall and standing rigidly to attention, they wore highly polished swords on their belts and carried long pikes, at least the length of two men, at the top of which were tied the Doge's pennons in red and gold. Their conical helmets were topped by plumes of feathers, which added considerably to their already prodigious height.

The Doge himself wore the famous Corno Ducale, a circular crown made of cloth of gold decorated with precious gems, which sat over the Camauro, a fine linen Phrygian cap with a horn-like peak, a classical symbol of liberty. He had a pure white ermine cape over his shoulders and robes of imperial purple, trimmed at the hems with elaborate gold embroidery. His sword was even shinier than those of his guards. It had intricate scrolls chased on to its blade, and gleaming rubies and emeralds decorated the cross-guard and pommel of its hilt. I was very envious and wondered if it had ever been wielded in earnest.

Although he was sitting, it was obvious that here was a man of significant dimensions. His long dark beard, streaked with grey, resembled the mane of the winged lion embroidered on to the tapestry above his head. He had a hawk-like nose and piercing amber eyes, as intelligent as any I had seen, which were sharply focused on us as we approached him.

His chamberlain leaned towards him and read my name from the appointments' list. The Doge raised his hand slightly from the arm of his throne. Silence reigned immediately, allowing him to speak to me in a deep but soft voice.

'You are younger than I thought you would be.'

He had the grandest of titles: Serenissimo Principe. But it was one that seemed to match his power and presence.

'Most Serene Prince, I am tender in my years, but I have learned much in your service, for which I am humbly grateful.'

'I have read the account of your courage against the Paganian pirates and how you managed to survive. You did well.'

'Thank you, Serenity. But my sergeant here, Eadmer, was the prop I leaned on.'

Eadmer looked down at his feet and shuffled a little, embarrassed by the praise.

'You chose him well. He will be granted five pieces of silver, and two pieces each for your men.'

'Serenity, that is very generous.'

Eadmer shifted again, but this time with a smile on his face, followed by a deep bow to the Doge.

'And how may I reward you, Harold of Hereford?'

'My service to you and to Venice is sufficient recompense for me, Most Serene Prince.'

The Doge smiled benignly.

'The answer of a worthy knight. I would expect nothing less from a man of your pedigree.'

'Serenity, I am not of the nobility. My grandfather was born to be an English thegn, a minor lord of a small village, but was banished and became an outlaw. My father earned his knighthood as a warrior.'

'You make my point for me, young knight. Your pedigree speaks for itself. Venice is a republic, built by warriors and merchants; like your family, we are all self-made men.'

It was my turn to smile and look down a little self-consciously. My instincts had told me that it would be worth meeting Ordelafo Faliero. Now I knew my intuition had been right.

'I believe your grandfather was called Hereward Great Axe, when he served with the Guiscard family in Sicily.'

'Indeed, Serenity. He is known as Hereward of Bourne in England and led the English revolt against the Normans after the Conquest. My father was Sweyn of Bourne, who fought with Edgar the Atheling and the English contingent in the Great Crusade.'

'It is a fine lineage. You should be very proud.'

The Doge then reached out towards his steward. The man handed him a rolled and sealed parchment.

'I would like to offer you a commission as a captain in

my service. I am mounting a campaign against the Hungarians, who continue to be a nuisance on the Dalmatian coast. Will you accept?'

'Most Serene Prince, I will, without hesitation.'

'Good. Report for duty in two days. We depart on the neap tide.'

When I later told Raphael of Pesaro about the commission from the Doge, I reminded him of his words of caution.

'I thought you said the Doge was a difficult man?'

'Wait until you fail him, or raise his ire.'

6. Burning of Zadar

We were soon on the Dalmatian coast, anchored in the sheltered port of Senj, a city under Venetian control for many years, situated about a hundred miles north of Zadar. The Doge had brought over fifty war galleys, all with a full complement of Venetian marines, reinforced by a large contingent of Swiss archers and infantry. He had sent a baggage train overland from Venice, including sappers and catapult and ballista engineers, supported by all the skills and resources necessary to sustain a significant army in the field for an extended period.

After leaving a small force to guard the ships at anchor, he armed his oarsmen to act as an infantry reserve and we began our march to the stronghold of Zadar. With 1,500 regular marines and almost 3,000 auxiliary infantry, we were a significant army. The Doge meant to put an end to Hungarian interference in the Adriatic and to King Stephen's support for the Paganian pirates, once and for all.

As we progressed down the coast, I began to understand why the Doge had developed his reputation for military prowess and firm discipline – and also his notoriety for possessing a fiery and irascible temperament.

'Stay in line!'

'Your men are too slow, get them moving!'

'Tell that sergeant he and his men are to report to me at dusk to learn how to march in step!'

These were just some of the more moderate orders he would bellow as he rode along the ranks on his huge black Norman destrier.

I was assigned to Ordelafo's general staff, as a junior officer, and soon learned to keep my head down and speak only when spoken to – usually in the peremptory style of, 'Englishman!' I would be expected to be at his side in moments.

We had been assigned small but fleet-footed Arabian horses and spent most of our time scouting and carrying messages. Our new weapons and armour had been allocated by the quartermaster of the Arsenale. We carried circular shields of crimson, with Venice's winged lion in the centre, and the standard marine's weaponry: lance, sword and bow. In addition, as Englishmen fond of the short seax, I had bought us short daggers from a Venetian merchant. He called them a 'pugio' and told me they were what Roman soldiers would have used as a side-arm. They were shorter and thinner than our beloved seax, but they sufficed and gave us the comfort of having a weapon of last resort in our belts.

We wore leather tunics, which we covered with chainmail corselets and conical helmets. There were plumes of ostrich feathers for knights and officers, which the Doge had brought from Egypt in vast quantities. I had lost my fine leather boots in the pirate attack, but had found a Venetian cordwainer to make new pairs for me and my companions. It did not take the Doge long to change my name from 'Englishman' to 'Grosso Stivali'

– Veneto for 'Big Boots'. I heard it more times than I care to count.

'Grosso Stivali!'

'Yes, Serenity.'

'You should be able to see Zadar from the top of the pass ahead. It is about fifteen miles beyond the summit. Ride to the top and, under cover of darkness, approach the city. I want a full report first thing in the morning.'

'Yes, my Prince.'

As I rode away from the column with my companions, we could hear, slowly receding behind us, the distinctive commotion of an army making camp.

Soon there was peace.

It had been some time since we had enjoyed the comforts of the open spaces and the tranquillity of nature. For months we had lived amidst the bustle of Venice, a confined environment surrounded by water. The *Domenico* was even more cramped and oppressive, with over a hundred men in a space the size of a village longhouse. Even our island refuge of Bisevo was small and restricted, bounded by leagues of open sea. Now, for the first time in a long while, we could ride through open country with far horizons of flora and fauna. Eadmer and Wulfric in particular – neither of whom was happy in a maritime world – felt particularly invigorated.

The scenery along the coast was spectacular: tall jagged peaks of white limestone and, lower down, large forests fringed by rich farmland. It seemed like good land to cultivate, with cold winters and hot summers, but plenty of moisture from the stormy Adriatic, which lapped its shores.

When we reached the crest of a long ridge of hills to the east of Zadar, we could see the city in silhouette against the low setting sun. Although it was winter, the sun was warm and the Adriatic glistened on the horizon. All seemed calm, with the city about to settle down for a peaceful night. It would be the last such night for many poor souls.

We paused for darkness and rode as far towards the city as we thought was safe. The ground sloped gently, but steadily, to the sea. Soon the rough stony terrain turned into fertile soil in which vines, olive groves and citrus trees grew. We avoided any sign of farmhouses and kept off the roads and tracks. Toste tethered the horses in a small gorge, hidden by undergrowth, and each was given a nosebag to keep him quiet. It was an almost full moon; we had to be careful. We took off our armour and boots and put on the kind of small leather slippers preferred by ladies at court – a tactic my mother had told me was favoured by my grandfather, who was renowned for his prowess at war-by-stealth.

As we got close to the city, it became clear that news had reached the citizens that the army of the Doge was approaching. It was not unusual for a city's gates to be barred so late at night, but the number of sentries patrolling the walls and the fact that the farmsteads of the hinterland and the peasants' hovels under the shadow of the walls were deserted meant only one thing: Zadar was ready for a fight. The harbour was empty of ships – they had been sailed away, probably lashed together and manned by skeleton crews safely out at sea.

We could see that Zadar sat on a small peninsular of

land which had the shape of a thumb projected into the sea. Its walls surrounded the entire city but on three sides rose out of the sea, so a land-based assault was only possible from the base of the 'thumb', a narrow strip of land only 200 yards wide. It would be a very treacherous assault.

Eadmer was very blunt with his assessment.

'Assuming the defenders have good archers and plenty of stones and hot oil, a frontal attack will be suicidal.'

I looked at Toste and Wulfric, who clearly agreed.

'Let's hope the Doge has a plan.'

Our return journey was uneventful. By the time we returned, we found a flurry of early-morning activity. The Doge had ordered the camp to be struck ready for the march to the city. The weather had changed overnight. A cold wind was blowing from the sea and rain was beginning to fall.

For once, Ordelafo addressed me by my name.

'Sit, Harold of Hereford. What have you seen?'

I gave my report in as much detail as I could.

'Good. You have done an excellent night's work. Now go and get some rest. You have a few hours. We will leave soon, but you can catch us up later. We won't attack until tomorrow.'

'Serenity, may I offer a view?'

'As long as it's helpful.'

There was a look of surprise and even concern on the faces of those close to the Doge. I had come to realize that his general staff was run strictly from the top, with little or no opportunity for debate – and certainly not for dissension. But I thought it was important that I express what I assumed was obvious.

'Serene Prince, if you intend to attack rather than besiege the city, it will be hazardous. The walls are thirty feet high, we are not sure how many men are behind them and how good they are and, although considerable, we don't have a huge force.'

Ordelafo stood up and stretched himself to his full height. He looked at me sternly, then seemed to relent.

'The walls are thirty-two and a half feet high, and behind them are five hundred and twenty Hungarian archers, and three hundred and ten infantry. There are also at least twelve hundred and fifty assorted pirates and cut-throats. The civilian population is around seven thousand. They will have stones and oil to hurl. The hinterland will have been stripped bare of food, the wells poisoned. They will almost certainly have provisioned themselves for a siege of many months. That's why we're going to attack.'

The Doge had made his point. He was well prepared, but I still thought he had not answered my main point: we didn't have enough men to cover the losses that would inevitably be sustained in an attack on a fortification of the strength of Zadar. Even so, I knew it was wise not to pursue it.

'Forgive me, Serenity, but I thought it worth raising my concerns with you.'

'I understand. It would have been wrong for you not to mention it – especially as, when we are ready, you will lead one of the scaling teams.'

Ordelafo grinned at me, and the others around him sniggered. I bowed and turned to go, but the Doge had another barb to deliver.

'Grosso Stivali, why are you wearing ladies' slippers?'

There were roars of laughter from everyone. I had forgotten to change back into my boots!

'Serenity, they were for the approach to the city – a ruse my grandfather used to use.'

'You English are very strange. The legendary Hereward Great Axe – in court slippers! From now on, we will call you "Dama Stivali" – "Lady Boots".'

The hoots of laughter intensified, leaving me with no choice but to bow and skulk away with my tail between my legs.

When I rejoined Eadmer and the men, I barked my orders with some venom.

'Get some rest! Tomorrow, we lead one of the attacks.'

'That's a death warrant,' was Eadmer's blunt response.

It took the entire day for the army to reach Zadar, where it immediately started to make camp. Working at an astonishing pace, the sappers and engineers began to assemble the catapults and build the siege towers and ladders. The Doge's army preparing for war was a sight to behold. Everyone knew his task: pegs were driven into timber, leather thongs were lashed around cross-beams, marines sharpened and oiled their weapons, and cooks skewered carcasses on to spits. The noise was overwhelming, the mood jovial, both helping everyone to keep their minds off the battle to come.

The curfew bell in Zadar sounded loudly about two hours after dark, which prompted the Doge to order that work should cease and that the army should eat. Most armies would be given copious amounts of alcohol on the eve of battle, to help steady the nerves of the men. But not the Doge's army. He insisted on nothing other than water, believing that men fight better with a clear head.

There was no contact with the city, and no offer of parlay. The assault began at noon the next day. The rain continued to fall and mists rolled in from the sea; the ground was sodden, making it difficult to manoeuvre the catapults and siege towers.

We took our position, just out of range of Zadar's archers, and watched as huge stones were hurled into the city. Most volleys were followed by the sound of crashing masonry and the terrified shrieks and cries of people hit by the missiles. The city soon responded in kind. Stones and rocks of all sizes landed all around us. Some small ones were stitched into leather bags, which exploded on impact, sending their deadly contents in all directions.

We stood our ground. When men were hit, they were carried from the field and we closed ranks to maintain our shape and discipline. Some were killed instantly, heads taken clean off, torsos mangled beyond recognition, while others lost limbs. Blood and body parts cascaded all around, splattering almost everyone in gore. We stood in stoical silence, save for the brief yelps of men who had been struck and the cries and moans of the injured.

The captains and sergeants steadied the men.

'Stand your ground!'

'Eyes to the front!'

'We'll soon be over those walls!'

Our passive vigil was suddenly interrupted by shouts

going through the ranks and gestures being made towards the sea. Emerging out of the mist were countless red sails bearing down on Zadar's shore. Within moments, huge balls of fire began to spew from the ships, their trajectory targeting the city.

'Greek fire!' cried the men. 'It's the Genoese!'

I looked at Eadmer. He looked as bewildered as I did. It was something I had never seen before. But whatever it was, it was causing mayhem inside Zadar. The heavy smoke and the glow of fires burning inside the walls grew stronger and stronger; the cries of anguish from the citizens became more and more voluble. Then came the smell – the dense acrid smell of burning pitch and thatch – mingling with the sweet smell of burning flesh. The city was an inferno.

At last the order came to attack the walls. The siege towers began to be rolled forward, and we followed in their wake. The tower squads were divided into two groups: a small group at the top of the tower, whose job it was to launch an initial attack as soon as the tower reached the walls, followed by the bulk of the men beneath, whose role it was to push the tower to the walls before climbing its stairways to join their comrades in the assault.

The ground shook as the mighty mobile barbicans trundled onwards. The defenders shot flaming arrows into the flanks of the towers, but they had been covered with hides soaked in brine and did not easily catch fire. By the time we reached the bottom of Zadar's walls, we could hear the roar of flames and the crackle of burning buildings on the other side, as yet more fire rained down from the ships offshore. The screams intensified, the smoke grew thicker, the smells became stronger. Then the towers hit the walls and the assault platforms were lowered. Venetian marines streamed over the ramparts to confront the defenders in vicious hand-to-hand fighting.

It was time for our scaling ladder to be hurled against the wall by the sappers, and we sprinted to its bottom rung. I was about to make my leap to begin my ascent when Eadmer pushed me to one side.

'I'm the sergeant-at-arms! Let me go first!'

He put his shield above his head and raced upwards, with me close behind and Toste and Wulfric following. I could see men falling from ladders all along the wall, some hit by rocks, some pierced by arrows. Hot oil was being poured over some of the towers; others were being drenched in burning pitch. Men were jumping off covered in flames or had their faces blistered and blackened by the oil. Now the screams of anguish from outside the walls were matching those from inside. This was war – and I was in the thick of it.

As we reached above halfway, our ladder began to bow towards the wall from the weight of men it was carrying.

'Keep going!' was the cry from below us.

Eadmer's shield had several arrows in it by the time we reached the top. It had deflected several rocks, one of which smashed his shield into his shoulder, forcing him backwards on to my shield. I thought he was about to go, but he held on and, with a heave from my shoulder, I managed to help him straighten himself.

When we jumped on to the ramparts, to our immense relief our section was relatively clear of defenders, but many more reinforcements were streaming up the ramparts' stairways. Some of our marines had already cleared a few of the stairs and were fighting down at ground level. I looked around to see if there was a quick way down.

The city was ablaze. Every building seemed to be on fire, with people running around in panic, some trying to douse the flames with pails of water, a clearly futile exercise. Women and children screamed. The heat scorched our faces – even up on the battlements – and lower down it must have been like a furnace.

Wulfric grabbed me by the shoulder and turned me round. Several defenders, looking very similar to the Paganian pirates we had fought on the *Domenico*, were running towards us. I rushed forward to lead our challenge, with Eadmer at my right shoulder. We slashed and cut, just as we had done so many times in training.

My instincts took over, the elixir of battle replacing the cold blood of fear. I swung wildly, bounding forward with big strides. One man got my blade through his stomach, another plummeted from the ramparts, felled by a blow from my shield, and a third was sliced at the top of his shoulder as I hacked at him. His lamellar hauberk took a lot of the impact, but blood oozed from the gash all the same.

My next opponent began to back away, colliding with his comrades behind him, who stiffened his resolve. They stood firm as I moved forward. But as I raised my sword, a huge ball of fire hit the ramparts beneath their feet and exploded, consuming them in flames. Two men seemed to disappear, incinerated before my eyes. Two more were thrown over the wall into our oncoming army, and several more fell back into the city. The heat was intense as I stepped back and covered my eyes. When I looked back to the place where, moments earlier, several men had been standing on the sturdy wooden ramparts, there was just an empty space with the remnants of charred and burning material scattered over the ground below.

The others were at my side, and I could feel them holding me. I looked at them and could see the concern on their faces.

Eadmer shouted at the men, 'Get water!' before helping me to the ground.

My face started to sting and then the feeling escalated into pain. I reached towards my face, but Eadmer grabbed my hand.

'No, your face is burned.'

The battle noises were subsiding; the city would soon be under the Doge's control.

'Hal, lean back.'

Wulfric and Toste had returned with water. Eadmer took off my helmet, pushed me backwards and began pouring water on to my face.

'You're lucky. You have lost your eyebrows and most of your moustache, but your helmet and ventail protected most of your face. Your lips are singed and your cheeks look like baked apples, but you'll be fine in a couple of weeks. Not a pretty sight for the girls, though – you might need to find an old hag who's not so fussy for a while.'

I tried to smile, but it was painful. The rain that had persisted all day was still falling, and every drop bit into my swollen face. Eadmer looked to Wulfric and Toste.

'See if you can find some cloth. We must cover his face

to stop any infection. Be careful down there – the fight's not over yet.'

I looked down at Zadar below. The Doge's marines were moving down its narrow streets, putting an end to whatever resistance they found at the end of a sword. The old, women and children were being corralled into small groups, surrounded by guards. Some were already being led out of the city. The few buildings that were not alight were being torched. Soon, Zadar would be no more.

Word began to circulate that the Genoese navy had found the pirate fleet far out in the Adriatic and sent it to the bottom in flames. Not only had Ordelafo destroyed the pirates' safe haven, he had also wrecked the tools of their trade.

The Doge had had a plan all along: it later transpired that he had struck a deal with the Doge of Genoa many weeks earlier. He had paid the Genoese a huge geld for their services and had agreed to keep out of their trading area west of Sicily. The amphibious strategy was a master-stroke; his victory was complete.

I spent the night in the field infirmary. Fortunately, it was several hundred yards away from the camp, far removed from the revelries of a victorious army. The no-alcohol policy the Doge had insisted upon before battle did not apply afterwards, and the celebrations were as expected – raucous and exhaustive. Even so, Ordelafo still imposed rigid discipline: no looting and no rape. Both were punishable by execution.

Although the merriment was a long way off, I did not sleep well. My faced burned, and hot blood still coursed through my veins from the day's battle. I had fought well.

But more importantly, I had learned how to deal with fear and had memorized a little catechism that would serve me well.

'Control fear before the fight; harness it during the fight and let it give you strength.'

It was what my grandfather had always said. And he was right.

The next day, the surviving civilian population of the city was led away in a long column. The wretched souls were escorted north for several miles, given carts of flour and a small herd of goats, then left to fend for themselves. It was a generous offering by the Doge, contrary to the usual practice of selling prisoners into slavery or worse.

Two days later, despite my burns, I was able to ride and left Zadar with the rest of the army. It took a long time to obliterate the odour of the ruined city from my memory. The smell of charred timbers and burned flesh seemed to hang on me like a woollen cloak. I could taste the bitter tang of ash on my tongue, and every time I ruffled my clothes a pungent dust stung my eyes.

I also evoked the memory of the sounds repeatedly. For many days afterwards, whenever I heard a horse neigh or someone shout loudly, the screams and cries of the dying of Zadar flooded into my head. It was difficult to sleep, and I had vivid dreams – especially one that repeated the moment when my foes were incinerated before my eyes on the ramparts of the city.

Eadmer said that what I was experiencing was normal and that the dreams and memories would soon fade. But he stressed fade, rather than pass, and told me that he still had vivid recollections of the battles he had fought. As always, he was a great comfort to me.

When we reached the ships at Senj, we made camp. It took several days to load the ships; most of the sappers were still at Zadar dismantling the catapults. The rain had relented and there was bright sunshine to illuminate the beautiful crescent-shaped harbour and the wooded hillsides above it. What a contrast it made to the scene we had left further down the coast. Both Senj and Zadar were small picturesque trading ports, of ancient pedigree. One remained so; the other was a vision from Hell.

I was hoping to be summoned by the Doge and that he would have heard of our exploits in the battle. I was proud of our role in the attack and prayed that it would be another step towards the recognition I sought. I had not seen him after we scaled the walls of the city. I had been in the infirmary, and he had ridden on ahead to supervise the embarkation of the army at Senj before I rejoined the column.

Sadly, the summons never came. When the stewards went to the Doge's tent the next morning, he was lying cold in his bed. He had died in the night. He was fit and strong, so poison was suspected at first. But he had no enemies in Venice, and it was difficult to imagine how the defeated pirates could have got a deadly potion into his food or drink. The physicians said that almost all poisons would have woken him in pain, and that he had eaten several hours before retiring. The water and wine in his tent were checked and both were found to be untainted.

The physicians decided that the Most Serene Prince, Ordelafo Faliero, the 34th Doge of Venice, had died from a sudden and severe apoplexy in the night. What a paradox it was: a soldier all his life and about to receive the accolade of having masterminded a famous victory for Venice, and he dies in his bed. On the other hand, he could have met a worse fate – perhaps as grisly as those who died in Zadar.

There was a huge victory procession along the Canalazzo to welcome home the conquering fleet, but the city's joy was tempered by the loss of the Doge, one of the city's most respected leaders. The Grand Council decided on a clever reflection of the contrasting emotions: half the city's flags were flown in celebration, and alternate flags were flown at half mast. Similarly, the crowds on the left bank of the Grand Canal were encouraged to cheer loudly, while those on the right were asked to bow their heads. It made for a very poignant homecoming.

The four of us got very merry that night in one of the city's many waterside hostelries and took full advantage of the affections offered by the young women of Venice, eager to reward the heroics of its warriors. My swollen and blistered face did not prove to be too much of an obstacle to at least one willing young lady, who thought my quaint English voice adequate compensation for a less than handsome countenance.

The following weeks passed slowly. It was a time for reflection. It was hard to deal with the disappointment after Zadar. We had fought well and survived, but my hoped-for reward in recognition from the Doge and the possibility of a knight's pennon seemed doomed by his sudden death.

I had a decision to make. Should I move on to the Holy Land and seek a new adventure, or stay in Venice to consolidate what we had achieved as marines?

Dear Thibaud,

I pray that life is comfortable for you. There are some ecclesiastical issues that I would welcome your advice on, but I will write separately about them.

The fascinating story of Harold of Hereford continues below. It is a sad story, in part, my friend. When the old knight recounted some of the details, his eyes were filled with tears. He was telling a story from almost sixty years earlier, but it was obvious it was as fresh in his memory as the events of yesterday.

When he had finished the last instalment, he told me he needed to take a break for a few days. I didn't see him again for almost a week. It was a fortunate coincidence because my scribes were in much need of rest and refreshment before I could continue my account. I find I must remind them daily that it is a privilege to be made privy to the details of such a remarkable life.

Winter now has London in its icy grip. There are no boats on the Thames, but there is much traffic. I went to St Paul's today by carriage and we were able to travel the whole way on the frozen waters. The boatmen tell me that the ice is a foot thick at London Bridge.

I had another fall yesterday. I couldn't get up. It took three of them to get me into a chair. Ah well, so be it; it is the will of God.

Yours in God,
Gilbert

7. La Serenissima

The new Doge was appointed in February 1118, after what was said to be a very fractious meeting of the Grand Council. The Old Families were split and so a compromise candidate emerged who was from a wealthy new mercantile family but with a strong military background, in the tradition of Ordelafo Faliero. My ears pricked up when I heard the news.

Domenico Michele was installed as the 35th Doge in a dazzling ceremony in March of 1118. The spring tides were in full bore and the Canalazzo's waters lapped halfway up the steps of the great palaces along its banks as the bucentaur, the Doge's beautiful state galley, was rowed past the cheering crowds. He sat on the throne in the stern, and the prow bore a figurehead representing Justice with sword and scales.

As the bucentaur passed each of the city's quarters and districts, the State Herald announced to the crowd, 'This is your Doge, if it please you!' This was to remind the people that their new Doge was chosen on merit by his peers, not as a ruler by birthright. It was a way of ruling a domain not unlike Ancient Greece and Rome, a system that I have always thought had many merits – especially given what happened to me later in my life.

Barely a week later, when I was beginning to think it

was time for me to try to get an appointment with Michele, I was summoned to see Raphael of Pesaro.

'Well, it seems that your courage at Zadar has reached the ear of the new Doge. Congratulations.'

'Thank you, Magister. You have been good to me and my men. I will always be grateful for that.'

'You have served Venice well. I hope that Domenico Michele has something interesting for you. He's a good man and a good soldier.'

I walked a lot taller and felt much more assured when Eadmer and I strode into the Great Council Chamber of the Doge's palace for the second time. The generous bonus we had earned by the victory had allowed us to commission our own armour and weapons and buy the sort of fine-quality clothes worn by the elegant young men of Venice. My beard was fuller, and the Mediterranean sun had turned my skin the colour of almonds and put pale streaks in my dark-brown hair. My face was fully healed and my beard had filled out into a thick auburn sward. I began to think that I was passably handsome.

Domenico Michele was not as tall as his predecessor, nor as heavily set. He was a much younger man, his hair and beard still black with not a hint of grey, and he had the air of a man who inspired confidence in those around him. His court seemed more relaxed than that of the previous Doge. There were laughter and broad smiles, whereas Faliero's court was more like an austere military high command.

For this audience, the Chamberlain did not need to prompt the Doge with my name.

'Harold of Hereford, you are welcome. I have been reading the account of the taking of Zadar. You fought with great courage.'

He nodded at the Chamberlain, who began to read from a page of a bound vellum book.

'"The English knight, Harold of Hereford, acquitted himself with great distinction on the walls of Zadar. He led his squad in a perilous assault on a scaling ladder, before despatching several of the enemy in single combat on the city ramparts to secure a vital piece of ground."'

As I bowed to the Doge, Eadmer smiled at me and nodded his approval, and applause broke out in the chamber. It was a moment to cherish.

The Chamberlain then raised his hand and addressed the assembled audience.

'Harold of Hereford, Knight of England, you are to be installed as a Knight of the Serene Republic of Venice. Please kneel.'

The Doge stood, his ermine cape gleaming in the rays of the sun that were streaming through the windows of the Great Council Chamber. He drew his sword to place it against my cheek.

'Stand as a Cavaliero of Venice, Harold of Hereford.'

The Doge then gestured to one of his stewards, who stepped forward with a scarlet cushion from which he took a small circular medal embossed with the winged lion of the city. It shone with the buttery glimmer of gold as he tied it around my neck with a crimson ribbon.

'You have been awarded the Order of San Marco for your gallantry at Zadar. The Order is restricted to forty living knights and you will join four other men who, following their bravery in Dalmatia, have also entered the Order today.'

'I am deeply humbled, Most Serene Prince. And proud to have served Venice and its Doge.'

'Ordelafo Faliero thought very highly of you, as does the whole city.'

The Doge turned to his steward.

'A chair for the Cavaliero.'

He beckoned me to sit.

'I have a commission for you. Raphael, Master of the Arsenale, has told me about your family's pedigree and of your desire to go to the Holy Land.'

'I am proud of my lineage, Serenity. The Holy Land and the Great Crusade are an important part of my background. I was there as a child, but was too young to remember. One day soon, I want to go back.'

'Then you shall. My sister, the Lady Livia Michele, is betrothed to Roger of Salerno, Regent of Antioch. I have asked Raphael of Pesaro to take a sabbatical as Master of the Arsenale to command a squadron of marines to escort Lady Livia to Antioch. He has chosen you as his third-in-command.'

'That is a great honour, Serenity. I am indebted to you and to Raphael of Pesaro.'

'You have deserved the commission. Bring Lady Livia there safely. You sail in a week. Go well, Cavaliero.'

I bowed and backed away, hardly able to contain my excitement. Then, as Eadmer and I left the Great Council Chamber, gliding towards us, accompanied by several ladies-in-waiting and two Republican Guards, materialized a vision more beautiful than Venice itself: La Serenissima's most serene being.

'Is that who I think it is?'

Eadmer did not answer; he was too busy observing the apparition walking away from us.

Tied at the waist by a dark-blue tasselled cord, she wore a figure-fitting pale-blue kirtle of fine silk covered by a flowing mantle of cobalt-blue velvet that trailed at least a yard behind her. A wimple of fine white silk, which perfectly framed the symmetry of her face, covered her hair. Her lips glowed deep red with the ruby wax favoured by Arab women, and her pale-grey eyes contrasted sharply with her flawless ochre skin. She did not smile. She did not need to; her face was the essence of her city's legendary name – serenity.

'She nodded at me!' I whispered to Eadmer.

'She did not.'

'I'm telling you –'

'Wishful thinking, Hal.'

'We'll see . . .'

I was certain that the girl, perhaps fifteen or sixteen, saw my Order of San Marco around my neck and acknowledged me with the slightest nod of her head. I was also certain that she was the Lady Livia, the treasure we were to deliver to Roger of Salerno.

My heart raced – I felt like a young boy casting his eyes on his first true love.

My next encounter with Lady Livia was when she boarded the *Candiano*, our galley for the crossing to the coast of the Holy Land at Seleucia Pieria at the mouth of River

Orontes, south-west of Antioch. It would be a difficult journey of many days, along the east coast of the Adriatic and the entire length of the south coast of Anatolia. At least the menace of the Paganian pirates had been eradicated in Dalmatia. However, the Anatolian coast was also perilous. Although nominally under Byzantine control, its rule was fragile, with many hostile Seljuk Turks operating in the hinterland and many buccaneers hiding in its remote coves and inlets. Anchoring close to the shore for water and supplies, or when in need of shelter, would require vigilance.

A small private cabin had been built behind the helm on the galley's quarterdeck to allow Lady Livia some privacy. It had its own commode, as well as bunks for her and her two ladies-in-waiting.

The presence of ladies on board meant that pissing over the rail was banned for the duration of the voyage, and everyone but the ladies had to use the communal privy at the bow. The arrangements were a source of great mirth among the ship's company. Forward latrines were always called 'the heads' in naval parlance – because of their position on the ship – and it did not take long for the ladies' commode to be christened 'the arses'!

Lady Livia came on board with all the ceremony appropriate for a woman who was about to be the instrument of an alliance between the Republic of Venice and the Christian Princes of the Holy Land. Besides her ladies-in-waiting and Republican Guards, she was accompanied by two members of Venice's Grand Council, who each had their own entourage.

Raphael of Pesaro made the introductions.

'My Lady, Rufio of Ferrara is my second-in-command.'

Rufio bowed as Lady Livia smiled sweetly at him. Now that I had time to study her more closely, she was even more stunning than before. She had dispensed with her wimple but had covered her head with the hood of a flawless black sable cloak, the most beautiful fur robe I had ever seen. Although it was almost Easter, it was a wise choice for the turbulent weather of the Adriatic.

At the edge of her hood, I could see chestnut ringlets cascading over her cheeks and the satin shimmer of her powdered features. I was close enough to smell her perfume, the beguiling scent of attar of rose, which drifted on the breeze in glaring contrast to the earthy smell of ship's timbers and flax rope – and the even more spicy odour of its crew.

'My third-in-command is Harold of Hereford, now a Knight of Venice.'

I smiled and bowed deeply, but I could still see that she noticed the medal around my throat.

'I see that my brother, the Doge, has awarded you the Order of San Marco in recognition of your courage at Zadar.'

'Indeed, my Lady. I am honoured.'

'I hear that English knights follow a strict code of chivalry.'

'They do, my Lady. I also adhere to the Mos Militum, an old code from ancient Rome, not unlike the Futuwwa of the Knights of Islam.'

'Do you know much about Islam?'

'A little, my Lady. As a young man, my father was betrothed to a Muslim girl who died in tragic circumstances.

Later, he and my mother went to the Holy Land on the Great Crusade.'

'I would like to hear more. Perhaps we can talk on the voyage.'

'It would be a pleasure, my Lady.'

I could sense the eyes of every man on board boring into me in jealous fury. For my part, I could barely contain myself and for the next few days could think of nothing else except her smile. Every time she appeared on deck, my eyes followed her like a hawk spying its prey.

'Hal, you could go to Hell, for thinking those kinds of thoughts.'

'Eadmer, you are blunt as always. But how do you know what I'm thinking?'

'Because I'm thinking exactly the same.'

The fourth evening of the voyage was warm and tranquil; summer was on its way and I was thinking about England and its sweet meadows. Soon, they would be bursting into life with all their lush colours and raucous birdsong. I was also thinking of my mother; I could see her with her dividers and rule, marking up a beam for the carpenters, or drawing a sketch of a huge arch. I missed her: her humour, sometimes crude, sometimes very ingenious; her deep well of knowledge; and her constant thirst for new ideas and information. I prayed she was well. She was now in her fifty-ninth year. Although I did not like to dwell on it, and despite being fit and sprightly, she was an old woman and I had left her to fend for herself.

There had not been a man in her life for many years, and I knew that she was lonely. She had always confided in me and been open about her past. I knew about her liking for men, her honesty and her passions, and of course her tryst in the desert with my father — which produced me — all of which were in denial of her status as an Abbess of the Church. To those close to her, she made no secret of the fact that her nun's habit was little more than a disguise that allowed her to pursue her burning ambition to build churches. Now she was paying the price: loneliness in old age, and a son far away in a foreign land, who she may never see again. It was her sacrifice, a part of our family's sacrifice.

Soon we were under way, out beyond Venice's lagoon into the open sea. Because there was no wind, the oarsmen were straining their sinews to keep up with the pace drum — a less strident drum than the war drum, but after several hours of rowing a demanding beat all the same. Those were the only sounds: the thud of the drum, then the cut, draw and release of the oars.

The cadence of the sounds was making me drowsy and I began to close my eyes as the sun approached the horizon and lit the sea with the rich colours of flame and fire. Then I heard her tender voice again.

'Are you thinking of home, Harold of Hereford?'

I jumped to my feet and clasped the hilt of my sword in salute.

'I am, my Lady. But how did you know?'

'You had that look on your face . . . you were either thinking of your home or your sweetheart. Please sit. May I join you?'

'Please.'

I gestured to a space a polite distance from me. I could

see her guards and one of her ladies-in-waiting staring at us intently. She was wearing her blue velvet cloak and her chestnut hair was uncovered, but no longer in tight ringlets; it flowed over her shoulders in scrolls like polished walnut. The cords that bound the top of her dress strained against her breasts. I glanced – I couldn't help myself – to see their form and scale; they seemed ample enough. I thought, if only I could see more of them ... By God, Roger of Salerno was a lucky man!

Then, in what I convinced myself was a rather coquettish way, she asked me a question.

'If you don't mind me saying so, aren't you a little dark for an Englishman? I thought all Englishmen were fair.'

'Well, my Lady, many of us are fair, but not all. There is a lot of Celtic blood on our islands and many Celts are dark. My mother is very dark, as were my father and grandmother. Only my grandfather, Hereward of Bourne, was fair. He had Saxon and Norse blood – northern peoples well known for being blond and fair-skinned.'

'Magister Raphael has told me about your famous family. You should be very proud. And now you are becoming famous too.'

'Oh no, ma'am, I am far from famous. I have a long way to go.'

'I am told that my betrothed, Roger of Salerno, is very fair.'

'That is not surprising, my Lady. Lord Roger is of Norman stock, descendants of Norse warriors who conquered that part of Old Gaul. Indeed, their name is a derivation of "Norsemen".

'You seem to be very knowledgeable.'

'Not really, ma'am, but my mother is a very learned woman. She taught me many things.'

'So you do not have a wife or sweetheart?'

'No, my Lady. I have many things to do before I think about a wife and a family.'

'I hope you find what you are looking for.'

'Thank you, my Lady.'

'I must go now. Dinner, or at least what passes for dinner, will soon be ready. Good night.'

I stood and bowed as she turned and walked to her cabin, her cloak gliding over the deck, leaving me to savour the sweet scent of roses in the air and relish her intoxicating aura.

I was smitten, utterly besotted.

8. Shipwreck

Several days of good progress ensued as we sailed down the Greek coast on our journey to Seleucia Pieria. We anchored off Messene to replenish our water and supplies and allow the ladies to go ashore to bathe in fresh water.

Little of note happened as we passed by the islands of the Cyclades and the Dodecanese, and we made another stop at Rhodes for supplies and female ablutions. There, the local Byzantine Governor, Theseus, a tubby little man from Crete, was very hospitable and insisted that the entire ship's company disembark to rest for a few days. Clearly captivated by the Lady Livia, he organized a grand feast every night, at the end of which he would invariably whisper some sort of drunken proposal in Livia's ear that made her recoil in revulsion and me stiffen in anger.

Master Raphael thought it wise to humour Theseus for a while as Byzantium was a very powerful neighbour of Venice. But after Lady Livia discreetly indicated to him that she had had enough of the Governor's 'hospitality', he agreed that we could move on.

Again, our journey after Rhodes was uneventful until we reached the Anatolian coast, east of Kalonoros. The sailors on board told me that the sea is very deep off this coast. Cold currents rise up only a mile or so from the shore, bringing up huge sea serpents and other monsters from the abyss, which create violent storms, especially in summer.

We did not see any serpents, but we did run into one of the storms. It was late in the afternoon and we were in full sail with a good westerly astern. We were some way offshore from a rugged coastline with heavily wooded hills running down to the water's edge. There were no settlements and very little ground level enough for farming. As we passed a large headland, we suddenly saw a huge column of black clouds rising in front of us.

Master Raphael ordered that our sails be lowered and stowed and that the oarsmen row to find a sheltered cove to anchor in. But the storm was on us in minutes, raising a swell that tossed the *Candiano* around as if it were no more than a cork. The crew had not got the sails down in time and several men were flung from the rigging into the sea. The oarsmen also found it difficult to row against such a violent sea; oars started to clash and splinter.

The Master ordered Rufio to prepare the ship for possible capsizing or grounding. Then he bellowed instructions at me.

'Take your men and make sure Lady Livia is safe. If we go aground, get her on to dry land at any price.'

He then rushed over to the helmsmen and tried to stop the ship coming broadside into the wind. The storm was now so fierce it was almost impossible to see anything other than walls of black water all around the ship. It was hard to hear even the loudest orders, and the rain was so intense it was like standing under a waterfall. The crew looked terrified and were convinced that a huge serpent was about to devour us. Master Raphael shouted at Rufio to calm the men, but many were beyond reason.

Then came a shudder from the hull and a sound like a huge axe striking a tree. We were still some distance from shore but had hit submerged rocks, and not a glancing blow, but a collision that had ripped open the hull. The oarsmen started to pour on to the deck, creating a melee of frightened men in a confined space. They reported that water was coming up from the cargo hold beneath them, which was already completely flooded. I looked at the Master, and from his expression it was clear that the *Candiano* was within moments of sinking.

He beckoned me over to him.

'Get Lady Livia ready to abandon ship now. She has a dowry in her cabin: a large chest of silver and a jewellery box. Give those to your most trusted men. You take care of her. She must take nothing else. Let's pray to God she can swim. I'm going to make a run for the shore – at least some of us will have a chance if we're close to land.'

I gathered Eadmer and the men, ran to Livia's cabin and banged hard on the door.

'Lady Livia! I'm coming in with my men!'

I burst in and found the three women cowering in the corner, shrieking hysterically. I pulled the two ladies-in-waiting to their feet and shook them.

'Ladies, control yourselves! You have to help Lady Livia. Give the dowry and jewels to my men. Your guards and I will help you, but you must take off your shoes. And no capes either. Take off your dresses, or tear them above the knee and elbow.'

They started to protest.

'You may have to swim. Do as I order you to!'

Lady Livia started to remove her dress and spoke firmly to her ladies.

'Do as he says. You've still got your underwear on!'

She then looked at me with an expression of abject terror on her face.

'I can't swim –'

'Don't worry, I'll take care of you. Quickly, we haven't got much time.'

I could see the rapidly approaching cliffs of the shore, perhaps no more than fifty yards away.

'Everyone out on deck. *Now!*'

I almost pushed them on to the deck, even though they had barely got their long kirtles off. I gestured to the guards to hold on to a lady-in-waiting each and I clasped my arms tightly around Lady Livia – something I had been dreaming about night after night, but not in these circumstances. We braced ourselves hard against the rail of the stern.

The crash came almost immediately, followed by the cracking and squealing of splintered timbers, the anguished cries of men being hurled into the water, and the rumble of the keel scraping itself along the rocks. We were all thrown forward as the *Candiano* lurched to the side. She let out a cry like a wounded animal and we were in the water in an instant.

I held on to Livia with all my might and looked around. Eadmer was at my side, and I could see Toste and Wulfric close by. It looked like we had gone over the port side of the ship, while the majority of the crew had been cast out on the starboard side. The waves were still mountainous and the rain continued to lash down like a torrent.

'Let's get away. She's going down!'

Eadmer helped pull Livia clear. I peered into the gloom, hoping to find something to use as a raft. I grabbed the *Candiano*'s war drum and made Livia hold on to it.

Toste then produced some rope, which he had tied around his waist.

'Good man, lash it to the drum. What about the chest?'

'Gone, I'm sorry. It was too heavy when we hit the water.'

I looked at Wulfric. He shook his head; the jewels had gone as well.

Only one guard appeared with his charge, both of whom could swim well, and we all gathered around the drum. We were being pulled towards the remnants of the ship, which was tearing herself apart on the jagged rocks.

'We should make for the shore. Ladies, hold on to the rope and the drum. Let's go!'

It was very difficult to swim and pull the rope at the same time, but the wind that had dashed the *Candiano* on to the rocks now helped propel us to the shore. To our immense relief, we were ashore in about ten minutes and all collapsed on to the sand in utter exhaustion.

The storm started to abate and the sky began to clear. I guessed that we had at least two hours of daylight and I started to issue orders.

'Eadmer, take Wulfric and Toste. Have a look around,

check for habitation, any kind of shelter. Then find water and firewood. If there's a stream, take the wood there and we'll try to make a camp.'

I turned to the Republican Guard.

'Your name, soldier?'

'Sandro, sir.'

'Do you have a weapon?'

'Only my knife, sir.'

'That will do. Guard the ladies with your life. I'm going to look down the beach.'

'Lady Livia, are you comfortable for now? I must assess our predicament.'

'Well, other than the fact that I'm on a deserted beach in my chemise, with all my worldly possessions at the bottom of the sea, I'm fine.'

I smiled at her. The Lady Livia had a sharp wit. She was also brave and mature beyond her years. Her lady-in-waiting, who was easily ten years her senior and there to protect her, just sat at her feet in paroxysms of woe.

'Is she hurt?'

'She's lost her sister.'

'I'm sorry. But there is still hope. I'm sure others will come ashore.'

I walked up and down the beach several times. Bodies were being washed up on the beach in greater numbers than survivors. Most men had gone into the water on the other side of the rocks, where the current would have taken any survivors further round the headland. I sent the few who had made it ashore alive over to Sandro and the ladies. There was no sign of Rufio or Master Raphael, and only about a dozen oarsmen and the same number of marines were gathered ashore. Both members of the Grand Council and their entourages appeared lost. It had been a devastating disaster. I calculated that more than three-quarters of the *Candiano*'s complement had perished.

I rejoined the others and checked the sun. It was low in the sky; we had perhaps thirty minutes of daylight. I started talking to the men, checking names and beginning to get them organized.

Eadmer returned with his report.

'There is no sign of human settlement, either now or in the past. It's deserted. There is plenty of firewood and a small stream in that gorge over there. The water seems fresh.'

'Food?'

'Nothing big to hunt nearby. Some roots, a few berries, and lots of snakes and scorpions.'

'Good, we can eat the snakes.'

'Can we? How do you know?'

'My mother told me the Seljuks did, on the First Crusade.'

Eadmer did not look convinced.

'I'm going hunting for boar in the morning!'

Without further discussion, I made plans for the night.

'We need two fires: one for the ladies out of sight from the men, further up the gulley; another one at the entrance, for the men. Same for latrines. A separate one for the ladies. Let's get everyone dry and get some water into them. We'll think about food in the morning. Eadmer, you take charge of the marines, Sandro, the oarsmen. Wulfric, Toste, a shelter for the ladies, please. A lean-to of branches will do for tonight. Move, all of you, there's not much daylight left. Let's get on with it!'

I asked for sentries at both ends of the beach, which Sandro organized into a watch from among the marines. Then I went to check on Livia and her lady-in-waiting. Sandro had informed me that the Lady Alice's sister was still missing.

'Ladies, how are you feeling?'

'We've dried our clothes and the fire is warm, but we're hungry.'

'I'm sorry, we have no food until tomorrow. There is nothing nearby, but I'm sure we can rectify that in the morning. Lady Alice, I'm so sorry about your sister. There's still a chance she may have drifted down the coast.'

My futile attempt at offering a glimmer of hope only made matters worse and intensified the woman's whimpers.

'She couldn't swim. She's lying at the bottom of the sea somewhere!'

I thought it best not to say any more, but to let them rest.

'Good night, Ladies.'

Lady Livia smiled at me.

'Thank you for saving us. We would have drowned without you.'

It was a long night, and I did not sleep much. We were in some difficulty and I spent hours going over our various options, before finally falling asleep.

Eadmer shook me awake shortly after dawn.

'Hal, it's light. There is much to do.'

'Thank you, Eadmer. I'll check the ladies. Get the men up and organized.'

Both women were asleep in their shelter. Alice's face looked strained, even in her sleep, but Livia was a picture of innocent beauty. Her white cotton chemise covered her down to her waist and her leggings hid her modesty from her midriff down to her knees. But I could see the gentle curves of her form in all their symmetry, especially the ascending mound of her backside as she nestled one thigh in front of the other. How innocent she looked . . . and how much I wanted to take that innocence from her.

She stirred and woke with a jolt. She looked shocked, aware that I had been enjoying the sight of her vulnerability. She pulled her legs up to her chin, the most modest pose she could adopt.

'Please announce yourself in future.'

It was a rebuke I deserved.

'Forgive me, Lady Livia, I was checking that you are well.'

'I am better for some sleep. But Lady Alice and I can't wander around in our underwear. What are we to do?'

'My Lady, I had to make you take off your outer garments and shoes. You may well have drowned if you had been weighed down by heavy clothes.'

'I understand, but there is no danger of us drowning at the moment. Please find us something to wear.'

Lady Alice now stirred, and Livia motioned to me to sit down. After considering my words, I decided to give a blunt assessment of our predicament.

'Noble Ladies, we are in a precarious position: we are a long way from home; we appear to be in a very remote place; we have neither weapons nor tools and only a meagre prospect of food.'

Livia had relaxed a little from the surprise of waking to find me staring at her, and her humour returned.

'Not exactly the outcome I had in mind when we left Venice.'

'No, my Lady. I'm sorry for being blunt, but I can't hide the facts from you. I only wish I could. But you are in the company of trained marines, Venice's finest. We are a reasonable number and can defend ourselves. Give me a few hours to gather my thoughts and develop a plan. Why don't you bathe in the stream? I'll make sure you're not disturbed. When you are ready, come and join the men.'

'We can't join them dressed like this.'

'Give me an hour or so. I'll see what can be done.'

I walked back to the men's camp.

'Eadmer, Sandro, get the men together in a group. How many are there?'

Eadmer's response was swift and precise.

'Twenty-six: two are slightly injured, and one may have a broken arm. There are twelve marines and fourteen oarsmen.'

'So with the three of us, Wulfric and Toste, and the two ladies, thirty-three souls in all. No sign of other survivors?'

'None so far.'

'The *Candiano*?'

'Broken on the rocks, just a few timbers showing, some rigging and sail.'

'How far out?'

'Fifty yards, maybe a bit more.'

As soon as all the men were assembled, I went through our immediate priorities.

'Gentlemen, we are fortunate to have survived a major tragedy. We have lost close friends, and some of Venice's most important citizens have perished. We are the lucky ones. Thankfully, the Lady Livia is alive and so our duty to her continues. We are not in the best circumstances, but we are professional soldiers and we will find a way out of this dilemma. We start right now. I want the following done immediately.

'Food – twelve men to split into pairs to go hunting. Use your knives and daggers, make wooden spears, set traps, collect what you can and don't forget fish and crabs. Supplies – I want six men to make a raft and go out to the wreck. Find what you can. We need the strongest swimmers for this. Dive as deep as you can and see what's lying on the bottom. Be careful, the currents are strong and the rocks sharp. You may also come across a few bodies; take their daggers and anything else useful. Burial party – four men to begin burying the bodies. As far up the beach as you can. Strip them of whatever we can use. Reconnaissance – two men need to get up this hillside and survey the whole area as far as they can. I don't want them back until nightfall. Firewood – the last two men to collect firewood. I want a pile as big as a house, enough to keep us warm at night and to signal to a passing ship when we see one.

'Finally, the chain of command. Eadmer, you will be sergeant of the marines. Sandro, you will command the oarsmen. Wulfric and Toste, you are assigned to guard the ladies. They need clothes. Find the best leather leggings and jerkins you can retrieve from the bodies. Find the smaller men, and cut the leggings down if you need to. They'll need shoes as well, and belts, cord for their hair, anything that could be useful to a lady. And wash everything in the sea – we don't want them smelling like deckhands. Any questions? Good, let's get on with it!'

I took Sandro and my men to one side.

'Sandro, there may be discontent about we English taking command. But I am in command, whether the men like it or not. Nip it in the bud if you hear anything. If it persists, tell me about it.'

'Do not worry, sir. You wear the Order of San Marco. That is enough for them. The men respect you.'

'Fine, but it may get a lot worse before it gets better. I'm relying on you.'

By mid-morning, our situation began to improve. The ladies were drying their new clothes, not that they were thrilled by the cut of their leather jerkins, nor the elegance of their cotton leggings, but at least they had something to cover their fine but flimsy underwear. A simple wooden comb had been found on one of the bodies and the shoes of some of the young deckhands had been trimmed to fit their small feet.

The salvage teams were starting to bring in weapons and a few tools and utensils, and they had found some flagons of wine. By the end of the day we had a stock of rabbits and fish, some herbs and a few berries. The shelters were habitable, the latrines usable, and we had an adequate pile of firewood. No other survivors had been found, even though we scoured the beach for several miles, and we held a simple interment ceremony at dusk.

Sandro said a few words in Veneto, as a mark of respect, and we all reflected on how lucky we had been to survive. Enough weapons had been found to arm each man with at least one means of inflicting damage, and several shields had floated to the surface after the shipwreck. Unfortunately, the caskets of silver and jewellery were nowhere to be seen.

By nightfall, we were sitting around a roaring fire eating grey mullet and sea bream stuffed with herbs, followed by roasted hare and rabbit garnished with whatever edible leaves we could find, all washed down with good North African wine. For most of us, famished from a day and a night without food, it was as good as a Doge's banquet. However, the ladies appeared to find negotiating a whole fish or rabbit impaled on a skewer fashioned from a twig a little challenging – especially without the aid of a fork. They did not comment, but had to concentrate hard on their task.

By the time our bellies were full, the scouts had returned with their report. As they ate, we listened anxiously to what they had to say.

'Sir, the nearest settlement is about fifteen miles to the north-west. We could see its smoke from a high point about five miles up the coast, but did not get closer than that. It's a small settlement and unlikely to offer any threats; it's almost certainly a fishing village with no garrison. All we could see inland were more and more hills of pine, with higher peaks in the distance. There are probably roads in the far valleys, but none nearby. There will be deer and boar in the forests, for sure, but also leopards. This coast is famous for them.'

Our position was a lot bleaker than I had hoped. No farms and no settlements meant no horses. At least there would be boats at the fishing village.

'Thank you for your report. How far is to Kalonoros?'

'At least forty miles, sir. Perhaps fifty.'

I turned to Sandro.

'What will we find there?'

'There will be a Byzantine garrison. Not a big one, but this land is under the rule of Constantinople, so there will be a fortification and a governor. From memory, and it is from a few years ago, there is a strong fortress on a hill that extends into the sea with a small harbour and village beneath it. The hinterland may be peaceful, but there may also be hostile Seljuk Turks – Muslims who raid the coastal cities all the time.'

I stood up to talk to the assembly.

'We have two choices. We either send a small group to the nearby fishing village to find a boat to sail to Kalonoros to bring help. Or we set off overland as a group.'

I looked towards the ladies, who seemed bemused by the options in front of them.

'If we decide to walk overland, it will be difficult and we will have to sleep where we can. If we find horses, we will have to steal them as we have nothing to buy them with.'

'Will these help?'

Lady Livia handed me five freshly struck silver coins, Venetian ducati, bearing the mark of Ordelafo Faliero. It was sought-after currency anywhere in the Mediterranean.

She smiled at me mischievously.

'You would be amazed at what a woman can have sown into her underwear.'

'Thank you, my Lady, how very resourceful of you. What would be your preference? To sit it out here and wait for help, or try to go overland?'

'I am happy to go along with your advice. You are in command.'

'Thank you, Lady Livia. I will think about it overnight.'

As everyone started to settle down for the night, I asked Sandro and Eadmer to walk down the beach with me.

'What are your thoughts, Gentlemen?'

Eadmer was the first to answer.

'We will be safe here. There is food and fresh water, and we can protect Lady Livia. I think we should send a small party to the Byzantine Governor at Kalonoros and ask him to send a ship to collect us.'

'Sandro?'

'I'm not sure. Even though we have a few weapons, if someone sees our smoke and word gets back to the Seljuks in the hills, they could come in numbers and we'd be practically defenceless.'

'You both make good points. Let me think more about it.'

I walked further along the beach, deep in thought. After five minutes or so, I saw a dark figure coming towards me. I put my hand on my dagger and called out.

'Name yourself!'

'Livia Michele, Princess of Venice.'

'I'm sorry, my Lady. You startled me. You shouldn't stray too far from the camp. Did the sentry not warn you?'

'He was relieving himself, so I just walked past. I was only taking some air. Have you decided what we should do?'

'I think so, my Lady. I am going to send Sandro with some marines on foot overland, to bring a ship from Kalonoros.'

'Very good, then we will find things to do to occupy our time. Perhaps you can teach me the languages of the north?'

'It would be a pleasure, ma'am. Perhaps you will help me improve my Veneto and my Greek?'

'It is a bargain. But you will have to start calling me Livia. May I call you Hal?'

'Of course. But I must continue to address you formally in front of the others.'

'Agreed. And so we have another bargain.'

She turned and walked off down the beach, a little jauntily, and I tried to convince myself that she had been flirting with me. I also wondered whether my decision to sit and wait for help had been influenced by a hidden yearning to spend as much time as possible with her in our remote refuge.

Sandro and seven marines left the next day to make the long journey to bring help. I estimated that a ship could be back to us within a week.

As agreed, Livia and I spent each evening before dinner helping one another learn our various languages. She spoke four – Veneto, Greek, Lombardian and Genoese – and I spoke English, Norman and Latin. Lady Alice was very wary of me and always stayed within earshot, which inhibited our conversations a little. Then, one night after supper – yet more fish, but this time with a main dish of venison – Livia asked me to stroll along the beach with her. She made a point of telling Lady Alice to go to bed.

It was a beautiful summer night. The day had been hot, but the temperature had fallen to a very pleasant level, helped by a cooling breeze from the sea. There was a half-moon casting silvery ripples on the sea, and the gently lapping waters to our left contrasted sharply with the incessant buzz from the creatures of the forest to our right. We had gone some way before Livia spoke. I could sense that she was tense.

'Are we going to survive this?'

'Yes, of course. Sandro will be back with a ship any day now.'

'If you say so. I'll try to stop worrying . . .'

She paused.

'May I confess something to you?'

'Well, I am not a priest, but I will help if I can.'

'It is not a sin – or, at least, I don't think so. It's just that I am frightened about meeting my betrothed. I know it is what I must do . . . but he is much older than I am . . . and I don't know what he's like. Also, Antioch is surrounded by Muslims who would slit a Christian throat in the blink of an eye.'

'I'm sure Roger of Salerno is a fine man and a good soldier. As for the Muslims, you will be safe in Antioch. I am told that the city is practically impregnable from attack. Besides, I don't think Muslims are better or worse than any other men.'

'You have a very reassuring way about you, Hal. I hope my future husband is like you.'

'You are very kind. I am but a humble knight.'

'Why do you not have a sweetheart?'

'It is not easy to have a sweetheart when serving as a soldier. Perhaps there will be time for that one day.'

'Have you had many lovers?'

I was shocked by her bold question. And yet, I felt excited by her lack of restraint.

'Livia! I am your escort. You shouldn't ask me such things.'

'I know, but I have asked. So . . . what's your answer?'

'A few.'

'I envy men, it is understood that they can take a woman when they want to. But I am a virgin. It is a condition of the marriage . . .'

Again, she paused. I sensed her fragility and loneliness as she began to confess her most intimate fears to me. She spoke hesitantly, trying to gauge my reaction to her words.

'That's something else I'm scared of . . . losing my virginity. Alice says it's a lot of fuss about nothing. But my mother said it was very special . . . something to cherish. I don't know who to believe.'

'Your mother is right, it is very special.'

I began to feel very uncomfortable. I wanted her so much – she was so trusting and beautiful – but if I took advantage of her, it could ruin her future and mine.

'I should get you back. You need to get some rest.'

'No, I don't. I'm fine, Hal. I want to talk more.'

'Sleep, I insist. Let's go.'

She smiled at me like a naughty child, then turned and

started to run down the beach. I heard her laughter as her words drifted back to me.

'Yes, sir! Whatever you say, sir! You're in charge!'

I desperately wanted to chase after her, pull her down on to the sand and take her there and then on the beach. I could have shown her that her mother was right – it is very special, something to cherish, something she would remember for the rest of her life. I had no idea what Roger of Salerno was like, but I was beginning to envy him with an intensity bordering on malice.

Was he a good man? Or was he an arrogant and spoiled son of a noble crusader who coveted a beautiful Venetian wife like a hunting trophy?

When twelve days had passed since Sandro's departure, my impatience turned to anxiety. Something had gone wrong: even with unforeseen delays, procrastination by the Byzantine Governor, or bad weather, they should have been back within twelve days.

I called everyone together that evening.

'We must make a new plan. Something is amiss. Sandro and his men should be back by now. We will all walk out to the north-west the day after tomorrow. In the meantime, we must prepare for the journey. Eadmer will assign scouts to move ahead of us and I will organize teams to be responsible for food, water and shelter on the journey. We will go steadily. Are there any questions?'

There were none from the men.

'My Lady?'

She shook her head.

'Good. Let's all get some rest.'

Two days later, we set out to follow Sandro's route. I warned the scouts to be doubly vigilant. Although I felt much more comfortable on dry land than at sea, there was no doubting the difficulty we faced.

Whatever fate had befallen Sandro and his men was almost certainly a real threat to us as well. And we were walking directly towards it.

9. Horned Vipers

We avoided the heat of the middle of the day as much as possible and made good progress on our route to Kalonoros. The coastal scenery soon became flatter and we began to see the ruins of abandoned farms, the remnants of neglected fields and endless olive and citrus groves gone wild. It was a sad sight, but there was still no sign of life, except for the unwelcome attentions of snakes and scorpions. One of the marines, an Anatolian by birth, had given us a quick guide to the creatures we should avoid. It was useful information, but the lurid details he offered were perhaps less than helpful.

The most dangerous beasts were the horned viper – a sand-coloured brute with brown spots on its back – and a black scorpion the size of a man's hand, which bears the Greek name *Androctonus Crassicauda*, which Livia told me means 'Fat-tailed Man-killer'. We saw neither at first, but certainly checked our camp's undergrowth very carefully at night. Then, when we reached the desolated farmlands, they littered the ground. Two of the oarsmen were bitten by scorpions that crept into their clothing at night.

Drawing out the painful venom and allowing the men to rest cost us anxious time in the infested area trying to avoid any more mishaps. When we were ready to move off, things deteriorated rapidly and Eadmer came to me with a disconsolate look on his face.

'Most of the men are in the bushes because the latrine is fully occupied. Everyone seems to have the shits. A few are in a bad way.'

'What about you?'

'Yes, but not as bad as some.'

'And what about the ladies?'

'I think they have a problem too. When I went to tell them we were about to leave, neither was there. I just heard a voice from the undergrowth asking for a few minutes' grace before we moved off.'

'Was it the water?'

'Probably. We filled our skins with water from an old well last night. It seemed fine but, with hindsight, it obviously wasn't. How are you, Hal?'

'I'm fine, but I had enough left from yesterday. I didn't fill my skin with the fresh water last night.'

'You're lucky – everyone else is as sick as a dog.'

'Then we must stay here. Tell the men to make themselves as comfortable as possible. How many men are fit?'

'Five or six.'

'Are you well enough to get a few things organized?'

'I think so. I didn't drink too much water last night.'

'Right, let's get started. Empty all existing flagons and skins of water and rinse them in the sea. Find us a fresh stream, make sure it's clean, and check it as far as you can upstream for animal carcasses. Everyone must drink, and they must keep drinking. See if you can find any or all of the following: yarrow, honey, garlic. And if any of these groves have limes, collect them.'

'How do you know all this?'

'My grandmother was an apothecary and a healer. Now,

let's get on with it. Everyone's going to get a high fever in this heat. I'll check the ladies.'

There was still no sign of the ladies where they slept, so I shouted into the bushes.

'Lady Livia! Lady Alice! How are you feeling?'

A thin voice called back.

'We are not well this morning. I don't think we're going to be able to travel.'

'Most of the men are the same. Find somewhere in the shade and rest. I will bring you fresh water as soon as I can.'

'Alice is not good. She has a fever and a lot of pain in her belly.'

'Try to get her into the shade. I will bring something to help.'

I joined Eadmer and the fit men and left two of them to guard the ladies. Eadmer took two men in search of a stream, while I took the rest to scour the countryside looking for remedies among the wild vegetation. Apart from me getting a nasty bite from one of those fat-arsed scorpions, we found what we needed without too much trouble. The pain from the sting was excruciating, but Eadmer helped me draw out the venom and after a couple of hours I was able to carry on, if a little incoherently. The limes were a bit lean, but there were plenty of them, and I found what looked like yarrow. It had red flowers, where I was used to seeing white or yellow, but it looked and tasted the same.

By late morning, we had replenished our water and I had mixed my remedy and distributed it to the men. Even so, some of them were in a bad way. So was Lady Alice.

'Livia, give her this and take some yourself. How are you feeling?'

'Better, but I'm worried about Alice.'

'Make her drink. It's important. I'll be back in a while.'

When I returned to the men, I greeted the return of the two scouts we had sent out the previous afternoon. Eadmer's face foretold bad news. I looked at the scouts.

'Sir, you should come with us. We've been waiting for you about three miles ahead.'

'What is it?'

'You should come.'

I asked Eadmer to stay while I followed the scouts through a narrow track just off the beach. After a few miles they stopped and beckoned to me to turn right into a small clearing. What I then saw made me shudder in revulsion.

Sandro and his men were naked and had been hung upside down by their ankles, their heads no more than a foot off the ground. Their bodies were covered in flies and had started to decompose. Their faces were badly disfigured and their torsos covered in blood. Beneath them were large dark patches in the earth, the residue from hours of heavy bleeding. They had been castrated and emasculated. I looked at the scouts, one of whom was an Anatolian Christian.

'Seljuks. It is a common punishment for any Christians they capture. They learned it from us. We do it to them; they do it to us. They use the whip and then they kick their victims' faces like a pig's bladder. They make it into a competition.'

'How long ago?'

'At least a week.'

'Will they still be around?'

'In the hills somewhere. They may have moved on, but they may have seen the smoke from the camp last night.'

'How many?'

'Thirty at least. They usually move around in large raiding parties.'

'Cut them down. I will bring back some men. We don't have tools to dig a proper grave, but a shallow resting place in the sand is better than this charnel house.'

By the following evening, when the full impact of our circumstances became clear, we had lost six men to what Eadmer was sure was the bloody flux, caught from the dirty water, and Lady Alice was close to her end. The rest of the men were recovering but were in no fit state to move. All the while, we were still at risk from attack by the Seljuks who had murdered Sandro and his men.

We were now just eighteen survivors from the great entourage that had left Venice. We were still in grave danger, and Livia was a long way from her destination. I needed a new plan.

Lady Alice died later that night. Livia was inconsolable and immediately said she did not want to go on to Antioch – yet another issue for me to wrestle with. I tried to help her, but she just wept and wept, uttering the odd semi-coherent sentence in between the tears. She spent the night curled in a ball at my feet, crying for at least an hour before she eventually fell asleep.

My only priority was the safety of Livia. Despite her pleas, my commission had come from her brother, the

Doge. Therefore, my duty was to get her to Antioch. Our greatest threat was from the Seljuks lurking in the hinterland. I decided that we should make for the small village that had been Sandro's destination. My only fear was that rather than it being a small fishing village, able to provide us with a boat to get to Kalonoros, it may be a nest of Seljuk Turks – a species with a bite far worse than the horned vipers of the undergrowth.

When Livia woke early the next morning, I told her that I planned to make for the fishing village to find a boat.

'Thank you for staying with me last night.'

'It was the least I could do. How are you feeling this morning?'

'I have felt better ... I just want to go home now, to Venice.'

I decided not to pursue the issue of which direction we would take when we got to Kalonoros.

'Today we will bury the dead and after a few days' recovery for the men, we will move on. When we do, I need to ask you to do something important.'

She looked very apprehensive.

'I want you to crop your hair short, like a boy. I'm going to pass you off as a boy servant.'

To my surprise, she did not baulk in the slightest at my request.

'I understand. It will grow again. I suppose you will be my master?'

'Yes, I'm afraid so.'

'Don't be concerned. From now on, I will address you as "sir".'

143

I was relieved that she had acquiesced so readily to the more eccentric details of my plan.

For the rest of the day, Livia stayed at Lady Alice's graveside. When she came to the fire for food that evening, she had cropped her hair as tightly as a sharp blade would allow. She had dirtied her face like a street urchin, stuck a dagger in her belt and tried to adapt the elegant bearing of a lady to the ungainly gait of a young boy.

I had to smile.

'Why are you laughing at me, sir?'

'I'm not! I'm admiring you.'

'You're not supposed to admire me. I'm your servant boy, remember . . . sir?'

'Quite so, sorry.'

She was playing a game with me, and I was enjoying it. Despite her new appearance, she was still a goddess and my urge to have her had not diminished in the slightest. I was sure she knew my feelings and was also enjoying the frisson of the game.

Four days later, we were on our way. I had told the men to treat Livia as a boy servant, stressing to them how imperative it was for her safety. As we walked, I thought about our good fortune in avoiding contact with the band that had killed Sandro and the marines. I then wondered whether the Seljuks had asked them where they had come from and why they were there. I realized that it was probable that Sandro and the others had been tortured in order to get them to talk. I would never know for sure, but I imagined we must all owe a great debt to Sandro and his brave marines.

When we reached the point where we thought the village was located, we turned to our right, through the trees, to find high ground so that we could put the surroundings under observation. After choosing a place where we could see the smoke from the settlement and a few boats in its small harbour, I sent Toste and Wulfric and two marines to make a thorough reconnaissance.

We waited for over two hours, but there was no sign of their return. I took Eadmer to one side.

'What do you think?'

'It's not good. They are four good men, no noise, nothing. I suspect a trap.'

'So do I. Scratch "ddwyrain" in the ground.'

Eadmer looked puzzled.

'It's Celtic for "east". Wulfric and Toste will understand it. The Seljuks will expect us to go north or south, and there's no chance of them being able to read Celtic.'

'Shouldn't we try to find Wulfric and Toste?'

'We can't risk it. We must get Livia away. The boys can take care of themselves.'

'I doubt it, with that lot of murdering bastards! Have you forgotten they're our comrades?'

'No! But we must get her away.'

'Bugger that, you're obsessed with that bloody girl. Our friends are more important than her.'

'Eadmer, they're professional soldiers. And so are you. We're moving east, now! Let's go.'

As usual, Eadmer had spoken his mind and then got on with it. I called to the other men and beckoned to them to move east, further up the hillside away from the beach. There was a small path, slightly overgrown, but manageable in single file. Livia came to stand by me, and I looked back to see Eadmer scratching our signal in the dirt.

'Hal, I could hear you arguing with Eadmer. I couldn't understand everything you were saying in English, but I think you were arguing over me.'

'No, we were arguing about which direction to take.'

'But you can't leave your friends! Not for my sake.'

'I can and I must –'

At that moment, two minutes of mayhem began. Arrows came cutting through the air, swords clashed and men shrieked and shouted. I looked up the path to see a melee of men fighting furiously. Eadmer had drawn his sword and was running towards us. I grabbed Livia and ran to meet him.

'Go south, it's a trap!'

We three ran and ran, until the sound of the ambush subsided. As soon as it did, we turned left and followed a path eastwards into the hills.

'Let's make for high ground – the higher the better.'

We ran for at least an hour, at which point Livia could run no more. The ground was getting steeper and Eadmer and I took it in turns to carry her over our shoulder. We climbed higher and higher. When the slope became too steep to run, Livia was able to walk.

We walked the rest of that day, until the coast became a distant ribbon of sand against the blue of the sea far below us. The air was much cooler now, and the trees started to disappear in exchange for barren crags and mountain meadows.

We made camp and gathered our thoughts. Eadmer was still brooding, as he had been all day.

'Why have we come so high?'

'I spoke to Andros, the Anatolian-born marine, about our position. We needed a reserve plan should it prove too difficult to reach Kalonoros, and he described the hinterland behind us. He also said that there could be more Seljuk bands further up the coast. We are heading into the Taurus Mountains. They rise thousands of feet, but there are several routes through them –'

Eadmer interrupted me.

'You mean we're leaving Wulfric and Toste and the others?'

'Do you really think we have a choice?'

It was one of the most difficult decisions in my life – one that I thought about for many years afterwards – but Livia was my priority, and a soldier's duty was what it was. Eadmer went quiet; he looked more disappointed than angry. It was Livia who asked the next question.

'But where do the mountains lead us to? Anatolia is a huge place.'

'Andros said that it was about sixty miles across this first range, but then there is a valley where we will find the main route from Iconium to Tarsus. He was certain that the road would be garrisoned and under Byzantine control, as would be the two cities. We will be able to find horses when we reach the road.'

'So we're going to walk the sixty miles across the mountains in the middle of summer?'

'There's no better time, it's nice and cool up here.'

Livia looked at me as if I had lost my sense of reason. Perhaps she was right. Eadmer stirred himself and got to his feet.

'Hal is right. There'll be no Seljuks up here. If we stay high, we'll be safe.'

Livia looked at Eadmer with the same expression of incredulity.

'How long will it take?'

'Five days, perhaps six. It depends how quickly you can walk, my Lady.'

Eadmer then set off at a fast pace, leaving Livia to stare after him.

'You English are very strange. Only a minute ago, he wanted to go back.'

I just nodded and followed Eadmer.

A few moments later, Livia started to follow us.

It was unlikely we would ever see Wulfric and Toste or any of our Venetian comrades again. As we trudged across the rugged Anatolian landscape, I thought about the demise of our friends – two likely lads from Norwich, as honest as the day is long, meeting their end in a far off land. They had done their duty, and I had done mine. But their deaths were my responsibility, and my conscience would have to live with it for the rest of my life.

Andros had been very specific about a possible escape route: climb until you see a high limestone plateau, on the right of which will be a craggy peak, the Caga Tepesi. Keep it on your right, cross the plateau eastwards until you descend towards a valley where you will see a broad river below, the Göksu Nehri. Stay high, keeping the river on your left. Eventually you will come to Mut, a settlement above the valley where two broad rivers meet. There will be a Byzantine garrison there. There is also a ruined monastery at Alahan, which all the locals will know about, now the home to some famous mystics and hermits.

Andros was a good man and I had every confidence that his route was accurate and reliable. Besides which, it was the only viable option we had.

The following two days would prove to be a major challenge for Livia. Her life had been one of comfort and privilege, with every conceivable luxury to hand, lived within inches of the cool lapping waters of the Lagoon of Venice. Now she was high in the deserted Taurus Mountains, shorn of any feminine accoutrement, with a few berries and strips of dried meat to eat and only a meagre ration of water. She endured by sheer willpower, which was a great testament to her courage.

When we reached the top of the plateau, it was just as Andros had described it, a wide barren landscape with almost no shade. The winter's snowfall had long since trickled away through the limestone; where occasional small pockets of water were to be found, they were green and brackish. We made most of our progress in the early morning and in the late afternoon. We walked slowly, resting in the middle of the day when the sun bounced off the white limestone like the blast from a blacksmith's furnace. Little was said between us. Thankfully, Livia did not mention returning to Venice again, which was an issue I was relieved not to have to confront.

When we reached the eastern edge, late on the fourth day of our trek, we prepared to spend our last night on the plateau. The valley below was already in deep shadow, but we could see the murky green of acres of thick forest and the swirling shape of a wide river snaking its way along the valley bottom. By now we had run out of water and the last of our dried meat and berries had gone. Livia was looking quite frail, her lips were cracked and swollen, and her skin had lost its sheen. I wanted to make her well again. The first step was to get her down the valley to fresh water and food.

'Fresh water by midday tomorrow,' was Eadmer's relieved comment.

Livia simply said, 'And a cool bathe in fresh mountain water.'

The next day, we made good progress and reached a small stream in the middle of an open clearing amid the pine trees long before midday. I decided it was better to give Livia a chance to recover there before moving on to the unknown challenges of Mut.

We stayed for a week. In some ways it was idyllic. It seemed to be too high for snakes and scorpions, the game was plentiful and the water clean and refreshing. Livia would bathe in the stream in the heat of the day and then dry herself in the sun. I was so tempted to join her and relish the inevitable consequences.

Eadmer constantly goaded me to do so.

'When are you going to take her and have done with it?'

'I'd love to. But our duty is to deliver her to Roger of Salerno, at Antioch . . . and intact.'

'Don't let that stop you. You can still deliver her. Not quite as a virgin – but no one would know.'

'She would. And besides, she would never allow –'

'She's desperate for you to forget about your "duty". Why do you think she goes to the stream every day and then lies in the sun, naked?'

'To get dry!'

It was difficult enough to keep my hands off Livia, even without Eadmer's encouragement to act on my desires, so I moved away to spend some time alone. I chose a part of the stream further up the hillside, where I bathed in private and lay down to relax and close my eyes for a while. I fell soundly asleep. Sometime later, I woke with a jump. Livia was tugging my arm. I reached for my clothes.

'I've hidden them!'

Livia was grinning at me like a naughty child. She was dressed, but only in her underwear, and her chemise was unbuttoned almost down to her waist. I covered myself with both hands and appealed to her.

'Where are my clothes?'

'I've told you . . . they're hidden.'

I tried to ignore the playful tone in her voice.

'Livia, this is not right.'

'Don't be cross. You never came to watch me bathe, so I came to watch you.'

She lay down on the grass beside me. I pulled up my legs to hide my manhood, trying to conceal the effect she was having on me.

'How long have you been here?'

'Long enough to see you get out of the water. You have a fine body, Hal.'

When she said my name, I struggled to maintain my self-control.

'Oh God, Livia, behave yourself. I'm not made of stone!'

She leaned over and mischievously tried to prise my fingers apart.

'So I see.'

'Livia, please!'

'I am not a child.'

'You are not a woman either.'

'But you could make me one . . .'

Her words hung tantalizingly in the air as she rested her hand on my stomach and started to move it towards my fully swollen prick. At the same time, she pushed her chemise open so that I could see her breasts, beautifully symmetrical with pert, dark-brown nipples.

I do not know how, but I forced myself to get to my feet and walk towards the nearby bushes, hoping that I would find my clothes.

As I dressed, the silence of the hillside surrounded me, broken only by the sound of Livia's muffled sobs.

Livia did not speak to me for the next two days. My rejection had humiliated her of course, and she must have felt very embarrassed. I was in turmoil. I knew I had done the right thing – my conscience and all reason kept telling me that – but every sinew of my body craved for me to do otherwise.

When we later started to walk down the valley towards Mut, I tried to broach the subject delicately with Livia.

'I'm sorry if I have caused you offence. I hope you understand that I have a duty to your brother and to your future husband.'

Her face was set like stone; she did not blink, but turned to look at me, white with anger.

'I hope *you* understand what you did. You humiliated me. We could have returned to Venice as a married couple; my brother would have had no choice but to accept it.

You would be rich and powerful. Circumstances threw together a young English knight and a princess of Venice on a mountain in Anatolia.'

Her stony face softened. She shook her head and grimaced.

'And you turned her down. You're a fool, Harold of Hereford. Anyway, I'm sure Roger of Salerno will be more than adequate in making a woman out of me.'

I turned away and moved quickly ahead. I had never imagined she would contemplate marrying me. Could it be true? If it was, I really was a fool. Was this the kind of sacrifice that I would have to endure? If it was, it was unbearable.

I continued to look ahead. I walked briskly, trying to separate myself from what had just happened. There was no turning back, nothing I could say to Livia that would repair the damage. After a cosseted young life, which demanded that she remain chaste and precious for her future husband, she had chosen to risk everything, to follow her heart and give herself to a young English knight with few prospects. It was a choice made out of young love. But the man she had chosen had made a choice born of duty.

The two positions were irreconcilable. Even if I changed my mind, it would do no good; the damage had been done. Truly, I was a fool.

We found all that we needed at the Byzantine fortress at Mut. With Livia's silver ducati, which I had kept safe throughout our ordeal, we bought horses, provisions and a string of mules. We travelled south through the fabled Cilician Gates, a narrow pass to the coast through which armies had marched to the Levant for hundreds of years. We were told in Mut that Alexander the Great had taken his army through the Gates, as had Darius and his Persian horde, and Mark Antony and his Roman legions on his way to meet Queen Cleopatra in the ancient city of Tarsus.

The journey should have been a fascinating one, following in the footsteps of mighty warriors from the past, but our mood was sombre. Apart from the tension between Livia and myself, we had to come to terms with the loss of Wulfric and Toste and all our other comrades. Their eventual fate outside the lair of the Seljuks was a mystery to us, and so it would remain, leaving us to reflect on their demise for the rest of our lives. The one grain of comfort I had was that Eadmer eventually acknowledged that I had done the right thing in making sure Livia was safe when we were ambushed by the Seljuks. It was our duty to protect her, and Wulfric and Toste had almost certainly already been killed.

Within the month we were in Tarsus, before moving on to the coast, to the impressive Byzantine fortress at Mamure, from where we could send a message back to Venice. Livia insisted that we stay in Mamure for the winter, so that her hair could grow and she could prepare herself for her wedding in Antioch. The boy-servant pretence was over and such was the rift between us that she insisted our informalities must end. Once again, she became Lady Livia, to be addressed as 'ma'am' or 'my Lady' at all times.

She stayed at the residence of the Byzantine Governor of Mamure, while Eadmer and I were quartered with his garrison, a Greek theme from Thrace. We saw very little of Livia and, when we did, she hardly acknowledged us. At the end of the year, a Venetian war galley arrived with a new dowry for Livia and a new escort of marines. The commander of the galley brought a message from the Doge.

Noble Knight, Harold of Hereford,

My gratitude to you knows no bounds. You have done a great service to me and to Venice. Please continue your mission to deliver the Lady Livia to Antioch and stay with her until her safety and happiness are assured by Roger of Salerno.

I have ordered that you be elevated to the status of Knight Commander of Venice, a position that includes a gift of land and an annual gratuity from my Exchequer.

I look forward to thanking you in person when you return.

Congratulations,
Domenico Michele

Although it was gratifying to receive such a commendation from the Doge, it did little to assuage the loss I felt in being ostracized by Livia.

I was in despair and beyond help.

10. Battle of Sarmada

The Doge had sent new weapons and armour for Eadmer and me. Livia had been sent a new lady-in-waiting, Constance, and with her a trunk of fine new clothes. I should have been proud and excited as I stood on deck next to the Captain to welcome Livia aboard. I was in command of the ship and the Captain reported to me. But I felt empty inside, a feeling made even worse by the perfunctory greeting I received from Livia, who went straight to her private cabin and seemed determined to shun any contact with me.

Her disdain towards me lasted for the entire voyage: she favoured me with a few caustic remarks and a generally sullen appearance, which quickly got the crew gossiping about what had happened between us in the Taurus Mountains.

We finally arrived in Seleucia Pieria in May 1119. Our journey had taken over a year, but we were fortunate to be there at all. We disembarked with an immense sense of relief. The sea voyage had brought me a numb sense of acceptance, and now all I wanted to do was to complete the final leg of our journey to Antioch and deliver Livia to her betrothed. Perhaps then I could find some peace and resume my search for my own destiny.

However, our docking in Seleucia Pieria signalled more disconcerting news. Antioch was only a day's ride away and we were making our final preparations to leave for the city when disturbing rumours began to circulate among the marines. The Captain – a dour, thin-faced man called Giovanni – called me over to tell me that it was common knowledge that Count Roger, Prince of Antioch, had recently married Hodierna of Rethel, the very rich widow of Heribrand III of Hierges, one of the leading knights of the Great Crusade. She was considerably older than Roger, but very wealthy.

As Captain Giovanni was at pains to make clear to me, it was my duty, as commander of Lady Livia's escort, to tell her the news. It would have been an onerous task at the best of times but, in the circumstances, it was a task I would have given the earth to avoid.

Livia was making her final preparations for the journey when I approached her. Lady Constance was scurrying around, checking that everything was in order.

'My Lady, may I have a word in private?'

'You can speak in front of Lady Constance.'

'Ma'am, in this instance, we should speak alone.'

She looked annoyed and inconvenienced, but she grudgingly acquiesced to my request.

'Very well.'

We walked a little way down the quayside. Livia would still not look me in the eye.

'May I call you Livia?'

'No, you certainly may not!'

'I need to talk to you as a friend –'

'Don't be impertinent!'

'Livia, please listen to me. I have some news you are not going to like.'

She suddenly turned and looked at me, something she had not done in weeks. Although she tried to appear forthright, I could see that she was anxious.

'Well, spit it out, *friend*.'

'Count Roger already has a wife: Hodierna of Rethel, widow of Heribrand III of Hierges.'

Livia's face froze in horror, and her eyes widened; she did not speak for some time. I could see her trying to compose herself. Her hands started to shake and I stepped towards her, in an attempt to comfort her, but she waved me aside in a gesture that obviously said no. She dropped her chin on to her chest and took a deep breath.

'I'm ready to leave. I would like to go immediately.'

'To Antioch?'

'Yes, to Antioch.'

'Very well, my Lady.'

I left four marines with the galley and, using horses provided by Roger's stables in Seleucia, we rode off as a column. The ladies and their baggage were transported in a small carriage, and I placed six pairs of riders to the front and six to the rear. Eadmer led the rear platoon while I took the lead. The road to Antioch was in excellent condition and we made good progress.

Late in the afternoon, the huge walls of the most impressive citadel in the Holy Land towered above us. It was just as my mother had described it; her stories of the crusaders' long siege and my father's part in the eventual fall of the city came flooding back to me.

The Holy Land had been under the control of the

Christian Princes ever since the fall of Antioch in 1098 and, a year later, the capture of Jerusalem. Since then, the Christian counties of Edessa and Tripoli, the principality of Antioch and the Kingdom of Jerusalem had held at bay a great encirclement of Muslim armies – and even, in some cases, formed alliances with them.

In the recent past, the old generation of conquering Christian Princes had gradually been replaced by their equally ambitious offspring. The last of them had just died, King Baldwin I of Jerusalem. Having already secured the vital route to the Red Sea at Aqaba, he had been leading a dramatic incursion deep into Egypt with an army of only 1,000 knights and 3,000 infantry.

He was sixty years old, a veteran of countless battles, but an old wound opened in his abdomen and he became desperately ill. He died en route back to his kingdom at the remote desert outpost of al-Arish. Determined that his body should not be left behind in Egypt, he had ordered his cook, a resourceful man called Addo, to prepare his corpse for the long caravan to Jerusalem. Addo was required to open his belly, discard his entrails and salt the rest inside and out. His eyes, mouth, nostrils and ears were pickled in spices and balm and placed inside his body, which was then sewn up, rolled in a carpet and carried back to Jerusalem on the back of his horse. He was buried next to his brother, Godfrey de Bouillon, another legendary figure from the Great Crusade, and another name whose exploits resonated with me from stories my mother had told me as a boy.

I mention the account of King Baldwin's death and

embalming because it was related to me by two knights who were serving with the King and witnessed the events. They were Hugh de Payens and Godfrey de Saint-Omer – two men who would soon play a significant role in my life.

We were escorted through Antioch's famous Dog Gate and greeted outside the keep by Prince Roger's surprisingly aged wife, Princess Hodierna, who ushered us into the Great Hall. The whole city seemed deserted, the garrison almost empty and there were only a few servants in the hall. The iciness between the two women was palpable – their jaws set, they resembled two animals stalking one another before a fight. The princess had a chair brought forward for Livia, but she declined the offer.

Livia introduced us, her voice and demeanour betraying no sign of the precariousness of her situation.

'I am Livia Michelle, Princess of Venice. This is my escort, Harold of Hereford, Knight Commander of Venice. I am here to marry my betrothed, Prince Roger of Salerno.'

Princess Hodierna's reply was outwardly civil, but her words held a barely disguised hint of condescension.

'My dear, I think you may have heard by now, Prince Roger and I were married three months ago.'

'Yes, I have heard. But the fact remains, there is a marriage agreement between Venice and Antioch, an arrangement made in person by my brother, Domenico.'

'That's as maybe, my dear, but we thought you were dead or enslaved. There was no word of you for months.

And Venice could only tell us that you had left them a year ago.'

'I need to see Prince Roger.'

'I'm afraid that will not be possible. He left a week ago with the army. The Muslims are wreaking havoc in the east.'

'If you will provide us with a guide, we will go after him.'

'My dear, this is Palestine, it is the middle of June. You cannot go riding off into the desert.'

Livia's patience finally snapped.

'I am not your "dear". I am Lady Livia. If you will not provide a guide, we will find our own way.'

Livia turned to me for confirmation. I was sorely tempted to say no: it was a venture into the unknown with only two dozen marines as escort, and into what appeared to be an impending battle. But I did not want to embarrass Livia in front of her betrothed's wife. I simply nodded my assent.

Princess Hodierna, no doubt relieved to be rid of her inconvenient visitor, drew the conversation to a close.

'Very well, Lady Livia, I will give you a guide. But on your own head be it.'

Livia bowed slightly, turned haughtily and departed with her cape flowing behind her.

As soon as we had left the Great Hall, I confronted my mistress.

'My Lady, this is not wise. I have no experience of the desert, my men are marines; they fight at sea. There is clearly a battle looming and we would be riding into the middle of it. My advice is to wait for the Prince's return.'

'You mean sit in that old keep with that hag of his? It could be months.'

'Going to see Prince Roger is not going to change anything. They are married. Let us go home to Venice. Your brother will know what to do about the marriage settlement.'

'You are my escort, not the Venetian Ambassador. I will go to Prince Roger and demand an explanation. He should not have taken a wife without talking to Domenico. There was an important trade agreement in the marriage settlement. If an alliance is not created through marriage between Venice and Antioch, it leaves the door open for Genoa to walk in with a new offer. I need to ensure that Prince Roger confirms the agreement.'

I was impressed with Livia's calculated summary of the predicament we faced, and her willingness to play her role in it.

'But, ma'am, I am responsible for your safety and I answer to the Doge. I cannot guarantee your safety if you insist on riding into a battle zone.'

'You don't have to. I will take responsibility for my own safety. While you're here with me, you answer to me. Now, let that be the end of it.'

I could see her mind was made up and that she was unlikely to be dissuaded. But before she dismissed me, I was determined to impose my terms.

'There are conditions, my Lady.'

'What are they?'

'You travel light; your dowry and jewels stay here in

Antioch's treasury. You and Lady Constance must take simple lightweight clothes, with an emergency contingency of soldier's dress if something goes wrong – you cannot ride side-saddle if we have to outrun a Muslim army.'

'Agreed.'

'We leave at first light tomorrow, my Lady.'

'Very good, I'll be ready.'

When I told Eadmer of the plan, he was, as usual, philosophical about it.

'It's madness! So far, we've been ambushed by pirates, shipwrecked, nearly killed by the bloody flux, waylaid by the Seljuks, and now we're marching off into the desert in the middle of a battle . . .'

He paused, but only to grin at me.

'The men will be ready at dawn. I'll make sure we have good horses for the ladies and each man will carry two skins of water.'

Roger and his army, slowed by a full baggage train, could not have gone far in a week. We had no wagons or pack animals, so I calculated that we could travel between a third and a half as quickly again as he could. I estimated four days before we would catch up with him. I had only two concerns: running into reconnaissance troops from the Muslim army, and the pressure on Livia and Constance from long days in the saddle.

Livia had regained all her radiance; the lustre of her hair and skin had returned. Even with the stern demeanour she had adopted towards me recently, the beguiling serenity of her face was still irresistible. Her body was still a captivating mystery, and I longed to see if it matched my imagination. I fantasized about it, both in my sleep and in my daydreams. I had seen the arresting curves of her slim and girlish form while she slept, and had peered through her open chemise during our disastrous encounter in the Taurus Mountains. But these were only tempting morsels. What I desperately desired was to feast on her without inhibition and to reveal every part of her. I struggled to make such thoughts stop; they made me breathless, and my heart raced like a galloping warhorse. But I had to contain them – where we were going would require a calm body and a clear head.

We rode as a highly disciplined group: three hours at dawn, then food; two more hours, then food and rest in the shade until the late afternoon; three more hours, then food and sleep. All the time it was canter, then trot; canter, then trot. Men continually peeled off to look for water for the horses – without that, we would have had to walk. Thankfully, Constance was a lot younger than Livia's earlier companions and kept the pace well. Livia never gave a hint of discomfort. Her mind was on only one thing: confronting her erstwhile fiancé. And that opportunity arrived a little sooner than I had anticipated.

We had just reached the end of the third day when a pathfinder I had sent ahead with the guide returned at a gallop, pursued by several Christian knights and a squadron of cavalry. I rode ahead to meet them, to be confronted by an agitated knight who, without any of the usual courtesies, demanded to know what our business was on the frontier of Christendom. Although the Christians of the Holy Land had come to be known as 'Franks', most of them were either Norman or from Normandy's neighbours. The Norman tongue had thus become the common language.

'Good evening, Sir Knight. I am Harold of Hereford and I am escorting the Lady Livia, Princess of Venice, to meet her betrothed, Prince Roger of Salerno.'

'You have brought a woman out here?'

'Perhaps you would give me your name, sir?'

Irritated at my insistence on formality, he spat his answer at me.

'Guy of Amiens. I ask you again, you've brought a woman out here?'

'Yes – two, in fact. They are back there with my marines.'

He turned to his fellow knights, smirking.

'Marines . . . and two women . . . out here? You must be a madman!'

He started to laugh out loud, causing his comrades to do the same. While they did so, Livia, pursued by Constance, rode at speed to join us. She hesitated for just a moment, gave the Christian knight a withering look, and rode straight past him.

The knight was dumbfounded.

'Where is she going? There's a Muslim fanatic out there, Il-Ghazi, the Atabeg of Aleppo, with an Artuqid army ten thousand strong!'

I ignored him and waved to my squadron to follow me in pursuit of Livia. It was a long chase. She did not let up her pace, leaving Constance fifty yards in her wake, and was in danger of exhausting her horse. I caught her after about ten minutes and bellowed at her to stop, which she eventually did, harshly pulling up her mount.

'Livia, for God's sake! You'll kill your horse, he's been ridden all day.'

'I want to see Prince Roger tonight. If there's going to be a battle, I want to challenge him before he gets himself killed.'

'Fine, we'll get you there. Just wait for the military escort. Let's make our entrance in a way befitting the arrival of the Princess of the Serenissima.'

She relented and, with Guy of Amiens and his squadron leading us, we rode into Prince Roger's camp in a highly disciplined fashion. Venetian marines are not trained cavalry, but they looked splendid in their red tunics and carrying their shields decorated with the city's golden lion. The squadron horn-blower sounded our arrival, making the whole camp stop and stare at the unexpected visitors.

I helped Livia down from her horse and she marched over to the Prince's tent with long, deliberate strides, more like the gait of a military equerry than that of a gentle lady of a royal household. Prince Roger was already on his feet. He was surrounded by his entourage and senior knights. They were relaxed and had already started eating and drinking. The Prince was very tall and thin with red hair, scorched blond by the hot sun of the Levant, but with long streaks of grey at the temples. He looked mean-faced and calculating, but had all the superficial charm of a nobleman.

'My Lady, I am honoured. Welcome to my camp. I am Roger of Salerno, Prince of Antioch.'

'I know your name, my Lord. I am Livia Michele, Princess of Venice.'

The Prince visibly blanched.

'Madam, please sit. I am overwhelmed. I thought you were lost. I . . .'

He hesitated, not knowing what to say next.

Livia seized the advantage.

'May we go inside and talk privately?'

The Prince nodded his assent.

'Of course, madam. My constable will take care of your men and horses.'

She turned to me.

'Please wait here.'

I did not want her to leave my sight. But there was nothing I could say to justify being privy to the conversation she was about to have.

After about half an hour, Livia emerged looking much more relaxed. With a large goblet of wine in his hand, the Prince was smiling broadly; it looked like an amicable deal had been struck. Livia spoke to me a little less sternly than she had of late.

'Would you ask Lady Constance to join me? We are going to eat with Prince Roger.'

'Very well, ma'am. Do you want me to stay with you?'

'That will not be necessary. You can stay with the men.'

'And what about you?'

'Prince Roger is arranging a tent for me.'

'Then we will guard it.'

'You will not! That would be an insult to the Prince. I am his guest.'

'And yet, thirty minutes ago you were ready to roast him alive. So what has changed?'

'He is charming. He explained that he was certain our

ship had been lost and that his marriage to Hodierna was vital to Antioch's future prosperity. More importantly, he has agreed to all the terms of the agreement with the Doge. We have an exclusive trade arrangement for five years.'

'So is he going to marry you both? I think that's called bigamy in the eyes of the Church.'

'Of course not! We leave for Antioch in the morning.'

'Meanwhile you are still my responsibility. I would feel better posting a guard to protect you tonight.'

'No, I am surrounded by the Prince's bodyguards and his army. I am perfectly safe.'

I could do nothing other than bow and leave. I was anxious: I did not like the Prince, but I assumed that it was mainly jealousy. Even so, there was something fabricated about his manners. Chivalry required that he should welcome a fellow knight – even a relatively lowly one – but he had ignored me. Although, since Livia had failed to introduce me, perhaps he had taken his lead from her discourtesy. I forced myself to accept that I was being too protective – and, indeed, too covetous of Livia's attentions – and returned to Eadmer to ask him about the men.

'So what do you make of Roger's army, my friend?'

'There are some seasoned knights by the look of them. I'm not too sure about the infantry – they look like a lazy ill-disciplined bunch. Only about half of them are Christians. That lot over there are Turcopoles, according to that officious bugger who came to greet us – Anatolian mercenaries. Muslims, he said. It seems strange to me to pay Muslims to fight Muslims. I wouldn't trust any of them in a fight.'

I looked over at them. Eadmer was right: they seemed impressive enough in their red tunics and conical helmets, but they had an aura of indifference about them.

'How many men do you think the Prince has?'

'I count seven hundred knights and three thousand infantry, half of which are Turcopoles and half made up of a Christian rabble that looks like the dregs of Europe.'

'I thought Guy of Amiens said the Muslim army is ten thousand strong?'

'I know, but he said the Muslims flee as soon as the battle gets fierce and that seven hundred battle-hardened Christian knights would have them on the run within an hour.'

'Do they anticipate joining battle soon?'

'He wasn't sure. He didn't seem to know where the enemy was camped either.'

'None of this inspires me with any confidence. Livia says she has done a deal with Prince Roger and that we will leave in the morning, but I'm going to keep an eye on her. They're eating and drinking without a care in the world, and I don't see anyone planning for a battle. Get the men camped near the perimeter, where we came in, then have a look round. I'm going to check on the ladies.'

All I could hear outside the Prince's tent was laughter and animated conversation. All seemed well. However, when I met Eadmer again he was looking anxious.

'This camp is in a steep valley. The far end, over there, is the top of it. There is only one way in – the way we came.'

'The Prince is either very confident that the Muslims are miles away, or he's a fool.'

'The men will be ready at dawn.'

'Good! I'll go and speak to Livia.'

It took Livia several minutes to emerge from the tent when I asked to see her. She was furious with me for disturbing her.

'Well?'

'We should leave at dawn. Eadmer and I are very concerned about the safety of this camp. And it appears that the Prince's army is outnumbered at least three to one.'

Livia smirked. I could see that she had been drinking and was merry.

'Don't fuss. These are men whose fathers conquered this land and now they hold it against an enemy that is both a savage and a coward. We will leave when I see fit. But I can tell you it will not be before the sun has warmed the ground.'

I had no choice but to obey my mistress's orders, and I left her without another word. It was a long night; I found it difficult to sleep and checked on Livia several times. At first there were the same sounds of revelry and then, at a very late hour, all was quiet. With the Prince's tent in darkness, I returned to my tent and must finally have fallen asleep.

I woke with a jolt. I could hear a cacophony of sounds: men were shouting orders, armour was clanging and there were horns in the distance that I had not heard before. I knew immediately they were Muslims battle horns.

I shouted at Eadmer to get the men mounted and meet me at Prince Roger's tent. I ran to check on the ladies. When I arrived at the Prince's tent, he and his senior commanders were already in their saddles and starting to ride out. They looked a lot more animated than they had been last night, but also very bedraggled from what must have been a long night of revelry. When I pulled open Livia's tent, Constance screamed; she was barely dressed and close to hysterical. Livia was not there.

'Where is Livia?'

Her reply was incoherent. I shook her and repeated the question.

'It was late ... I left her with the Prince. They were enjoying themselves ... I was too tired.'

I shouted at her, furious at her carelessness.

'Get dressed! *Quickly!*'

I rushed to the Prince's tent and barged the two sentries aside. The remnants of the night before were all over the floor and several stewards were collecting the debris of discarded food, plates, goblets and cutlery. I pushed past them and threw back the curtain of the Prince's sleeping quarters. At first, all I could see was a heap of rugs and pillows, but then I heard sobbing from beneath the pile.

'Livia!'

A small head, covered in matted hair, peered out from underneath the rugs, but then pulled itself back out of sight. The sobs became more pitiful. I sat down beside her, but she still buried her face in the pillows and curled herself into a ball.

'Livia, the battle has begun, and the camp is under attack. We must go!'

'Leave me to the Muslims ... that is all I am good for.'

I grabbed the many layers that covered her and wrestled them from her. She was naked, and I could see welts

171

on her arms and thighs. Her face was swollen, as were her lips, and her left eye was bloodshot and bruised. She collapsed into my arms in convulsions of anguish. A battle had begun outside and I was desperate to get her away, but I knew that she needed time.

After a few moments, she started to speak.

'He hurt me so much, Hal. I had too much to drink and stayed too long. Suddenly, everyone had gone. He was drunk . . . and he started to take his clothes off. I said no, but he hit me. He hit me so hard. He did horrible things to me . . . I couldn't escape. Why did I send you away? You would have protected me.'

'Livia, the only important thing now is to get you away from here.'

'No, please leave me. I am as good as dead already.'

Her pitiful words galvanized me. Nothing was more important than Livia. My only duty was to her; anything else could go to Hell.

'My love, we can still have a life together. You will always be safe with me. You were right, I was a fool to put my duty before you in the mountains. It will never happen again.'

I looked around for her clothes, but couldn't see them. Then Eadmer and Constance appeared and I issued my orders as calmly as I could.

'Constance, get Livia dressed. Eadmer, we're leaving, get the men ready. I want this tent surrounded until we're ready to leave. Everyone is an enemy, including the Prince's men. We're on our own.'

Livia had become lifeless, as if in a trance. Constance had brought clothes, but could only wrap her mistress in a cloak. Eadmer helped me to lift Livia's still form and place her over my saddle. He suggested an escape through the dead end of the valley, rather than the way we had come in, where a ferocious battle was already joined. I would have done anything to go the other way – so that I could challenge Prince Roger and make him pay for what he had done to Livia – but I knew my priority was to get her away safely.

As soon as the ground started to rise steeply, we dismounted and continued our climb in silence. I tied a cord around the cloak at Livia's waist and started to pull her up the slope, but she kept stumbling and I had to carry her. Looking up towards the crest of the valley, we could see Muslims on all sides around us. But their focus was on the mayhem at the mouth of the valley, where wave upon wave of Muslim cavalry were hurling themselves at a thin line of Christian defenders. It was not yet entirely daylight and the head of the valley was facing east, so we were in shadow.

As we cleared the crest, I took one look back before we resumed our mounts. The Christian army was by then entirely encircled and vastly outnumbered. It resembled a fallen fruit being devoured by ants; a pitiless massacre was happening before our eyes.

As soon as the sun's rays caught us, our position was revealed to the Artuqid reserves waiting to join the slaughter. Horns sounded and squadrons of cavalry started to gallop in our direction. We had perhaps a 1,000-yard advantage. I knew it would not be enough.

After a chase of a mile or so, the countryside became less barren and trees started to appear. I immediately ordered that we separate into three groups, thus dividing our pursuers, and I led my group south-east, towards a small outcrop of rock about two miles away. With Eadmer taking responsibility for leading Constance and her mount, we galloped as hard as we could. But with Livia across my saddle, it was obvious that we could not outrun our pursuers. She did not complain, but I could see the discomfort etched on her face. A redoubt of some sort at the rocks was our only option.

We pulled up behind the outcrop and took up positions giving us as much cover as possible. Eadmer assigned one of the men to hold the horses and guard the women, and we prepared to stand our ground. I counted six remaining marines, besides Eadmer and myself. Our pursuers were shrouded in dust, but numbered at least fifteen.

'Raise your bows, make every arrow count.'

I calculated that we had time for two volleys.

'*Release!*'

I ordered the second volley immediately. The Venetian marines' excellence with the bow was telling. At least six of our pursuers fell before they were upon us. The odds were still not good, but if we could disable a few more they might well think better of it and return to their comrades, where easier pickings were available among Prince Roger's beleaguered army. I glanced back to make sure Livia was safe. It was a pitiable sight: she was sitting wide-eyed and motionless on the ground, wrapped in Constance's arms, with no focus, like someone mesmerized.

In the next moment, the Artuqid horsemen were upon

us, lances couched underarm. Knowing that marines are not used to fighting cavalry, I bellowed my orders.

'Bring down the horses! Strike at the legs!'

We managed to unseat several of them, but it was not enough. I ordered Eadmer to use the man holding the horses to help Livia on to a mount and to make a run for it with her and Constance. He hesitated for a moment. But when he saw that I meant it with all my heart and soul, he did as I bid him to.

The remaining marines and I then formed a loose circle and a fierce fight ensued. Some of the Artuqids were on foot, but several more were still on horseback. Thankfully, they got in one another's way and the melee was not as one-sided as it might have been. We fought for our lives, a cause more exhilarating than that of our opponents, who were fighting for the scant reward of the execution of a few Christian stragglers. Perhaps if they had known that the valuable prize of a princess of Venice was among us, it would have made a difference. But they were not to know.

Two brave men were cut down next to me and another was on his knees with a lance through his shoulder. But our adversaries had lost even more men: the four of us still standing were facing only six opponents. They looked at one another briefly and one of them spat on the ground at our feet, before they turned and rode away towards their army. They would surely send out more men to pursue us, so we were far from safe, but we had bought ourselves some time and a fair chance of escape.

My arm had been sliced above the elbow by a lance, and my face was bloodied after being struck by my own shield after a blow from a horse's shoulder. But I had survived another bloody encounter.

We mounted quickly and rode off in the direction taken by Eadmer. I knew that he would not have ridden as the crow flies and would instead have used every opportunity to deceive any pursuers. I also knew that he would be aware that he was riding away from Antioch and deeper and deeper into Artuqid territory. We would have to have our wits about us to avoid losing him altogether. I took a calculated gamble: assuming that leaving a trail of dust would not be wise, I guessed he would not gallop his horses and might even trot them. Given that, I also surmised he would veer south rather than north. Heading north was easier ground and closer to Antioch's domain, whereas south was inhospitable desert. Therefore, I decided he would choose the opposite direction to the one the Muslims would predict. I prayed my conjecture would prove to be right.

After only an hour of riding, we saw tiny specks in the distance to the south-east. The specks were four in number. My guesswork had been right, and within a few minutes we were reunited. We saw no sign of any of the marines who had peeled off in different directions during the chase. This meant that, of our original contingent, Eadmer and I now commanded just five men.

Constance looked petrified and was of little help to Livia, who continued to stare vacuously into the distance. It was as if she had closed a door on the world and was locking herself away behind it. I tried to talk to her, but I could elicit no response.

Further to the south-east, the ground rose rapidly to

meet a long ridge that ran diagonally across our path. It was our lifeline. We crossed the ridge and rode down the other side for about a mile and then followed a route back towards the coast, out of sight of the Artuqid army.

Thankfully, after three days, we finally arrived in Antioch.

11. Desolation

Antioch was in a state of panic. Since the fall of Jerusalem and the establishment of the Christian states in the Holy Land twenty years earlier, no Latin army had lost to a Muslim foe in a major battle. A mythology had been created on both sides that a large force of Christian knights was invincible. It was a view founded partly on the military prowess of the Christian warrior, but mainly on the power of the Almighty himself – who was clearly a Christian divinity, rather than a Muslim one.

We took Livia and Constance to Prince Roger's rooms in the keep. Princess Hodierna had already left for the safety of her brother, the new King of Jerusalem, Baldwin II, taking most of her entourage with her. A junior chamberlain found a chamber for Livia and Constance and gave them a young maid, who tried to make them as comfortable as she could. Eadmer posted two men outside their room. He and I then went to what remained of the city's garrison to find out what had happened to Prince Roger's army on the battlefield and to assess the current state of the city's defences.

What we heard was a very chastening account.

Of the men who had ridden out of Antioch on 28 June – a force just less than 4,000 strong – fewer than 150 had made it back alive. Foolishly, Roger of Salerno had decided not to wait for the arrival of King Baldwin's army from

Jerusalem, but chose to confront the Muslims with only his Antiochene forces. Prince Roger's camp was in an area called the Belus Hills, close to a settlement called Sarmada. His scouts had told him that the valley he had chosen would conceal them from Il-Ghazi's Artuqid army and that from there he would be able to launch a surprise attack. However, the Artuqids had infiltrated Prince Roger's corps of scouts and he had been led into a trap. By first light, the Muslim army was poised to attack from three sides.

Prince Roger tried to muster his army and called on his priests to carry aloft the relic he always carried into battle, the True Cross of Christ, discovered by Arnulf of Chocques in Jerusalem on the Great Crusade. Although the defenders tried to form into defensive formations, the position was hopeless. They attempted to create a line commanded by Robert of Saint Lo, Prince Roger himself, Guy de Frenelle, Geoffrey the Monk and Renaud Mansoer.

With the Muslim army poised, a fabled qaadi, Abu al-Fadl Ibn al-Khashshab, wearing his lawyer's turban but brandishing a lance, rode out in front of the troopers and gave a passionate evocation of the duties of a jihadi warrior. Il-Ghazi's men were in a frenzy by the time he had finished and rode into battle baying for Christian blood. It had the reverse effect on Prince Roger's army: already doomed, they knew they faced men bent on merciless revenge for a generation of Christian occupation of their land and desecration of their holy places.

The crusader army fought for their lives with some success on the right flank from the men of Geoffrey the

Monk. Guy de Frenelle also held some ground, but the battle was soon decided on the left flank. Robert of Saint Lo and the Turcopoles were driven back into Roger's division, disrupting it. A north wind blew dust in the faces of the Antiochene knights and footmen, confusing them further. Soon, Il-Ghazi's forces enveloped the crusaders.

As most of Roger's senior knights fell around him, he was soon left isolated amidst the mayhem. Standing next to the priests carrying the jewel-encrusted True Cross, he fought off several assailants before he was killed instantly by the point of a sword which entered through his eye socket and exited through the back of his skull. The priests were cut down and the holy relic was desecrated in a mock crucifixion as the Artuqids tied Prince Roger's body to the cross and hoisted it high in the air to symbolize their victory over the infidels.

Walter the Chancellor, who was the only senior knight to escape the slaughter, said the earth could not be seen for the bodies of men and horses, so densely impaled with arrows that they resembled hedgehogs. He said that the battlefield was an *Ager Sanguinis*, a Field of Blood.

Fortunately for Antioch itself, Il-Ghazi had since indulged in a mammoth drunken celebration, following which he had turned for home, pursued by King Baldwin's army from Jerusalem, bent on revenge. I decided to use this good fortune to get Livia out of the city and back to the ship at Seleucia Pieria, planning a return to Venice as quickly as possible.

We retrieved Livia's dowry and jewels from the Treasury and, once again, the journey to the sea passed quickly. We made preparations to sail on the next tide and tried to make Livia as comfortable as possible in her cabin. I tried several times to comfort her – but for the time being, at least, she was lost to the world.

As we had only a handful of marines for the return journey, I made it clear to the Captain that he was to avoid the Anatolian coast and make the more difficult crossing via Cyprus and Crete, where Byzantium had much more control. My intention was to follow the coastline once we had passed the Greek mainland. Soon we were in the open sea, and for the first time in many months I started to relax. As soon as I did so, I started to reflect on what had happened on our tragic adventure to the Holy Land.

Apart from my personal regrets about my aborted relationship with Livia, my professional failure in not protecting her preyed on my mind more and more. Facing the Doge would not be easy. As for Livia, I felt powerless. She felt she had no future and was clearly living a private hell from which recovery would be difficult. I was determined to help her, no matter what it took – even if it involved taking her away from Venice. Perhaps then we could eventually start a new life together. This resolve helped me cope with the melancholy of the voyage.

The third night of the journey was cool and fresh. It was the middle of July, and the day had been hot, but the night sky was clear and the scorching heat had subsided. It was the dark of the moon and the stars glistened against the black of the night. I began to fall asleep listening to the ship creak and groan in the choppy waters, enjoying the sensation of drifting into a peaceful oblivion.

I was woken abruptly by a woman's shriek. It had Constance's unmistakable pitch. I rushed to the ladies' cabin, where I was met by an appalling sight.

Constance was distraught, drenched in spray and pulling at the helmsman's arm, imploring him to bring the ship about. When she saw me, she started to shout hysterically.

'Livia's gone! I can't find her!'

We were soon joined by Eadmer and the Captain. All hands were called on deck to scour the horizon, as the ship began to turn back in a big arc. Lanterns were lit and a search party was organized to scour every inch of the ship. I grasped Constance and tried to calm her down.

'When did you last see her?'

Constance gasped out her answer between racking sobs.

'I'm not sure ... it was late ... she was in her bunk, with her back to me. I'm not sure if she was asleep ... I fell asleep and woke with a fright ... Livia wasn't there any more.'

'You've no idea how long?'

'It could have been a while ... I think I was asleep for some time.'

She was now sobbing uncontrollably, and I asked one of the stewards to put her in her cabin.

When I joined Eadmer and the Captain, they both looked forlorn and shook their heads. There was no sign of Livia on board. Clouds had come in and the sea was an infinity of inky black waves.

It was Eadmer who said what everyone was thinking.

'She could have gone overboard more than an hour ago.'

I asked the Captain if the helmsman had seen anything, or if the men on watch had been aware of a disturbance.

'If she left her cabin at the stern, she would have been behind the helmsman. With the noises on board from the fresh winds, it would have been difficult to hear her.'

I sat on the deck and put my head on my hands. It was the lowest point in my life. Not only had I not been able to protect her from Roger of Salerno, I had now failed to prevent Livia from throwing herself to her doom. I supposed that she had waited for the familiarity of the sea – an environment that had always been part of her life – and chose to end her agony in the anonymity of the deep, rather than face the public shame of returning to Venice.

So many things could have been different, and I vowed there and then never to make the same mistakes again.

We continued to search for several hours after dawn, but daylight only served to add to the desolation of the vast and empty sea.

Livia was lost to me, consigned to a watery grave.

Eadmer and I had long conversations on the remainder of the journey to Cyprus. Most of our discussions focused on whether to return to Venice, or to find a ship in Cyprus that would take us back to the Holy Land.

Eventually, we decided to return to seek a new beginning with the Latin Princes of the Holy Land. However, as soon as the decision was made, I realized that there was an element of cowardice in choosing not to return to Venice. I decided that I must come to terms with my demons and face the Doge.

When we arrived in Venice, I saw it with different

eyes. Its splendour was tainted by my regrets. I had lost my Serenissima, and the beautiful city would never again beguile me as it had before. I was haunted by the thought that Livia must have imagined that we would share a life together amidst its elegant palazzi and fabled canali. But I had shattered her dream. To travel now along the waterways she loved so much, but to which she could not bear to return, was a torture almost impossible to bear.

Domenico Michele had already heard that Lady Livia was not aboard our ship. He declined to see us, asking instead to see Lady Constance and the Captain alone. I gave them a full account of our mission before they joined us at Mamure, which they rehearsed and conveyed to the Doge.

I then waited to hear the Doge's reaction.

About an hour later, Constance appeared, looking sombre. She spoke to me in a voice that was formal and devoid of emotion.

'His Serenity thanks you for your duty in trying to protect Lady Livia. On behalf of Venice, he wishes you well in your future endeavours. However, he asks that you do not repeat the circumstances of the voyage, or of her demise.'

She then turned and left without another word.

It was an abrupt end to our Venetian adventure. But under the circumstances, it was perhaps not surprising. The Doge had lost a sister in the most tragic of ways and obviously wanted to bring the matter to a close as quickly as possible.

I hoped that he felt no malice towards me, nor attached

any blame to my conduct. I liked to think that his perfunctory dismissal of us from his service was simply his way of bringing to an end an episode on which he did not wish to dwell in any more detail. I wished that I could have shared with him my affection for Livia and my respect for the courage she had shown.

But that was out of the question.

Within the month, we were back in Antioch. The city was under the guardianship of King Baldwin II, who had become its regent and made Antioch a vassal state of his kingdom in Jerusalem. Order had been imposed on the city and a semblance of normality had returned. We took lodgings close to St George's Gate and that evening Eadmer and I discussed our options.

I began by summing up our situation.

'Our biggest problem in the short term is that our funds are exhausted. We need to find work in the service of one of the Latin lords – perhaps King Baldwin himself.'

Eadmer smiled at me before asking for the unpalatable truth.

'How much do we have?'

'I'm afraid we have just two pieces of silver, our weapons and armour, and the clothes we stand up in.'

'You'd better have this then.'

Eadmer pushed a purse across the table. In it were at least two handfuls of pristine Venetian ducati and four gold bezants – enough to live on for a very long time.

'Where did you get that?'

'I requisitioned it from Livia's dowry chest. I estimate

the silver is what we're owed for our service to the Doge. The bezants are a bonus.'

'Eadmer, that's a lot more than we're entitled to.'

'I don't think so! Without you, none of us would have made it to Antioch. The Doge owes you far more than is in that purse.'

'I'm not sure he'll see it that way.'

'Hal, there was nothing you could do to save Livia. She chose to end her life. And Prince Roger has already suffered the fate he deserves. None of it was your fault.'

In many ways, he was right. I tried not to think too much about the callousness of taking money from Livia's dowry, and hid behind Eadmer's estimable pragmatism.

What haunted me, as it would for years to come, was what had happened between Livia and me in the Taurus Mountains and all the horrors that had occurred afterwards. Had I known that Roger was already married and a cruel abuser of women, I would never have agreed to deliver the innocent Livia to him.

But that was all in the past; I now had to find my destiny elsewhere.

Dear Thibaud,

Winter has got much worse here in London. I haven't left the Palace for ten days. I have caught some sort of chill and several of my scribes are ill. Bodies are found on the roads on a daily basis – people are frozen to death, the beasts are dying in their stables. We have had several blizzards and all roads to the north are closed.

I don't want to go to St Paul's today, but I've missed two services already, I can't miss a third. I think of all the poor souls who have to venture out by necessity and pray to the Good Lord to help us survive this weather.

But enough of my tribulations. Today another year begins – a day that young people look forward to with relish, but one that older people dread. Another year on the tally stick, and not many more to go.

It is a new beginning for Harold of Hereford too: we are about to open a new chapter in his absorbing story. When you read it, my friend, you will understand why I have been so keen to get this story on to vellum. Here is a man who was a founding member of the Knights Templars and took the oath with Hugh de Payens in Jerusalem in 1119. Given all that has happened since, I think you will agree that his story is a vital part of the history of our Church.

Yours in God,
Gilbert

12. Initiation

Eadmer's unwavering support was vital over the coming months in the Holy Land. Always loyal, he had a quiet strength that I drew on constantly. He missed England but, as he often said, his sworn duty was to me; as long as I wanted to continue my adventures, he would be at my side. His was the life of a warrior, a life of dedication and resolve based on discipline and duty. He was a constant source of inspiration to me. Sometimes he would find himself a woman, but they were only temporary assignations and he never seemed to be interested in long-term companionship and the pleasures of a family. His loyalty was to me, and to me alone, and every day I tried to remind myself how fortunate I was.

The mood among the Christians of the Holy Land after the Battle of the Field of Blood was very sombre. Defeat at the hands of the Muslims was inexplicable: were they not inferior and worshippers of a false god? Therefore, ought not the Christian cause in the name of the One True God be invincible? Word began to spread that the defeat could only have been caused by Christian sin against the Almighty. Roger of Salerno became the culprit. His blatant adulterous relationships with any woman he chose was his greatest stain, but then stories about his brutal rape of Livia started to circulate. Some of his household had survived the Field of Blood and one in particular, a steward, could be found any night of the week in the taverns of Antioch relating the lurid details.

The reaction to defeat and the sins of arrogant Christians such as Prince Roger created a wave of support for a return to the valour of the Great Crusade. It was said that twenty years after their exploits, the crusaders' courage, sacrifice and devotion had been forgotten and that those virtues needed to be reaffirmed.

I was not a particularly religious man, but the fundamental principles of the Great Crusade appealed to me. They were the values central to the Mos Militum and the other codes of chivalry that my family had always believed in. Although the crusaders had committed many sins and behaved with unbridled barbarity on many occasions, their original cause had been laudable and their virtues admirable. It was in this context that a group of men appeared in my life who would have a profound influence on my story.

Their leader was a man called Hugh de Payens, a knight from Champagne in France, and the others were his life-long companions. They were Godfrey de Saint-Omer – who had served with Hugh in the contingent of Geoffrey of Bouillon in the Great Crusade – Andre of Montbard, Payen of Montdidier, Archambaud of St Amand, Geoffrey Bisol and two monks: Gondemere and Rosal.

Eadmer and I were sitting drinking fresh lemon juice in the shade of Antioch's huge walls when the group of knights appeared. They were a formidable array of warriors. Hugh and Godfrey were perhaps fifty years old, battle-scared and bronzed by the hot son of the Levant. The others were younger, in their forties, and equally

intimidating. Eadmer and I tensed when they approached
– such was their bearing, they could easily have been mistaken for brigands – but we were reassured by the smiles
on their faces. We noticed that they were all dressed in the
same way: each wore a black ankle-length hooded cape,
and under it a long white cappa robe tied at the waist.
Both the cape and the cappa had the insignia of a red
crusader cross over the left breast. Their weapons were
humble: a lance of plain ash, a simple yeoman's sword, an
undecorated dagger, a heavy Norman mace and a triangu-
lar white shield with a black band at the top. Their helmets
resembled the Norman design – except they were domed,
not conical – and they too were decorated with the
crusader cross.

We stood when they reached our table. Hugh introduced himself and his companions, and I responded and
asked them to sit. Their hair was cropped short and their
beards closely trimmed. Most noticeably, their eyes shone
with a solemn intensity that was fascinating. They were
clearly men with a purpose.

'Your name goes before you, Harold of Hereford.'

It was when he spoke again, with his deep harmonious
voice, that I remembered who he was. His shorter hair
and beard had changed his appearance a little and he was
wearing different clothes, but it was suddenly clear to me
that he was the knight who had killed his opponent with a
single blow from his mace in Paris three years previously.

'I am honoured that you know my name, Sir Hugh.'

'No such formalities, my friend, my name is simply
Hugh.'

'And mine is Hal. This is my sergeant, Eadmer. We have

met before, in Paris. I was in service to King Louis and we were enjoying a drink by the Seine.'

Hugh looked a little disconcerted, and he hesitated before replying.

'Ah, yes . . . I remember. He was a man who had a score to settle with me from many years before – an evil individual – the world is a better place without him.'

'Well, you made sure of that.'

Hugh de Payens smiled, just as he had done when we met him before, and then returned to his purpose.

'Your exploits in escaping from Anatolia are well known here, as is your survival at Sarmada. You and your sergeant are brave men indeed.'

'Thank you, but our deeds are modest compared to some.'

'On the contrary, your reputation is what led us to approach you.'

This total stranger then did something unexpected. Immediately followed by his companions, he fell to his knees and bowed his head in prayer.

'We give thanks for the life of Lady Livia Michele, Princess of Venice, who, driven by despair, took her own life. Now she is at peace, restored to her beauty and dignity, thanks be to God.'

Hugh then took my hand and pulled me down to kneel next to him. He put his left arm around me and his right around his friend Godfrey de Saint-Omer, prompting the others to form a circle of brotherhood.

'We humbly ask, Lord, that you permit us to share the pain of Harold of Hereford, thus making his burden easier to bear. Amen.'

We all responded in unison, after which Hugh pulled me to my feet and embraced me like a long-lost brother – as did each of his companions, in turn.

Feeling somewhat overwhelmed, I ordered some wine.

'Not for us, Hal; we do not take alcohol. Some lemon juice would be more to our liking.'

I noticed that Hugh did all the talking. His companions were hanging on his every word, like disciples.

'Hal, we are eight in number, men who have recently come together devoted to a cause: the cause of the Great Crusade and the protection of Christians everywhere. We are a militia, Christ's Militia, bound by our own code of chivalry. The defeat at the Battle of the Field of Blood at Sarmada was the final straw for us. Enough is enough. Men like Roger of Salerno have no place in the Holy Land, especially as princes. We heard that he raped and sodomized the Lady Livia and beat her like a dog. That is the kind of evil that we aim to drive out of the Latin Principalities. King Baldwin has given us lodgings and stables on that most holy of places, Temple Mount in Jerusalem, the Temple of Solomon, so we will call ourselves the Poor Fellow-Soldiers of Christ of the Temple of Solomon – in short, the Knights Templar.'

'It is a worthy cause, Hugh. I wish you well.'

'You can do more than that. You can join us. Eight is not a good number; we want to model ourselves on the Nine Worthies of Chivalry.'

'Forgive me, but who are the Nine Worthies of Chivalry?'

'They have been identified by scholars and sanctified by his Eminence, Garmond of Picquigny, the Patriarch of Jerusalem. They are three noble pagans: Hector, Alexander the Great and Julius Caesar. Three honourable Jews: Joshua, David and Judas Maccabeus. And three gallant Christians: King Arthur of England, Charlemagne of the Franks and the mighty crusader, Godfrey de Bouillon. We revere them as men whose deeds we try to emulate.'

'Great men indeed, and a noble cause. But why would you want me to join your group? I am not a crusader . . . and I am not sure that I am all that worthy.'

'On the contrary, you are as worthy as any of us. You are young – we need young recruits, and you can help us find them. You are English – we are Franks, and so we need someone to help us find good Englishmen. Most importantly, you are brave – that is evident from your deeds. Men of courage and integrity are rare in the Holy Land. Greed and cowardice have replaced the values we fought for in the Great Crusade. We would rather let the Holy Places revert to the Muslims – many of whom still hold to a code of honour – than let them rest in the hands of men who are not worthy of the name Christian.'

'Well, I am flattered. Tell me more about your mission here in Antioch.'

I looked at Eadmer – I could tell he was suspicious, as always. He was scrutinizing these strange men with his usual intensity. I brought my attention back to Hugh's words.

'I understand from the stories in the taverns that you follow the code of chivalry called the Mos Militum?'

'I do.'

'Well, our Order has the same principles. We apply them to bring Christian justice and honour to all. We are going to build a military order of devout men all over Christendom which will be an army of Christ. King Baldwin has given us an allowance to recruit enough men to protect the route between Antioch and Jerusalem; each of us will be responsible for a squadron of cavalry along the way. That is our first commission. But one day, we will be a colossal army to match the mighty host that came here from Europe to liberate this land.'

'That is an ambitious plan.'

'Indeed it is. But don't have any doubts, it will be done.'

Hugh de Payens spoke with passionate conviction, his pale blue eyes mesmeric and piercing. He had a ready smile, and his tanned face was etched by wrinkles of happiness. He was a beguiling man – a man I wanted to believe in. My mother had described such men when talking about the leaders of the Great Crusade, many of whom had turned out to be immoral hypocrites. Were Hugh and his Templars the same: zealots with feet of clay?

I needed to find out more.

'So you are in the service of King Baldwin?'

'No, my friend, we are a brotherhood; we serve only our God, our mission and one another. The King provides us with lodgings, stables and horses and a small stipend. We live under strict discipline by our own rules, which include modesty, chastity and frugality. As soon as our Order is well established here, I will return to Europe where I will seek the blessing of His Holiness, after which I will found communities in all Christian domains and kingdoms to provide the resources to support our cause.'

I was intrigued. There was such a plausible certainty about Hugh de Payens. Then Godfrey de Saint-Omer spoke. He had a more moderated tone than Hugh, but still possessed the same look of unwavering conviction.

'Hugh is Grand Master of our Order. We follow him in strict obedience. You will be required to do the same.'

These Knights Templar sounded very similar to my grandfather's Brotherhood of St Etheldreda at Ely, and my father's Brethren of the Blood of the Talisman – except their cause extended beyond the borders of a single domain. I needed time to think.

'Hugh, I would like to reflect on everything you have said. May we discuss this tomorrow?'

'Of course, my friend. We leave for Jerusalem in two days' time. There we will take our oath together on Temple Mount in the eyes of God, and our mission will begin. Let us meet here tomorrow evening.'

As the Templars left, I noticed the expressions on the faces of those around us in the tavern. It was plain to see that these men had a charismatic effect on all who met them. I turned to Eadmer, who was ready with a question.

'You are tempted to join them, aren't you?'

'Intrigued, for sure. What do you think?'

'They certainly look like they can fight – confirmed by the way their leader despatched that man in Paris – but I'm not sure about the frugality and the chastity!'

I couldn't help a wry smile at Eadmer's blunt assessment.

'I'm sure that the chastity part only applies to the knights. Sergeants will be exempt.'

'You are tempted, I can tell. Do you really think you could live on bread and water and give up women on a permanent basis?'

'Nothing is forever, Eadmer. Besides, after what happened with Livia, I have decided to avoid the fairer sex for a while.'

'Well, I suppose it means we can travel to Jerusalem and have the chance to meet King Baldwin.'

'Quite right! But let's sleep on it and decide in the morning.'

At breakfast the next day, Eadmer and I agreed that we would join this strange group of men. There was no doubt that the Templars – and in particular, Hugh de Payens – had an aura about them. So I decided that, for the time being, their journey was worth following. Eadmer also had one shrewd suggestion to make before we departed for Jerusalem.

'If, God help us, we are to commit to a life of "frugality", let's leave our money with one of the Jewish moneylenders here. They offer good rates for a sum as large as ours.'

'Always thinking, Eadmer – what would I do without you? When you get the promissory note, add it to this one.'

I gave him a note written in Latin twenty years earlier by a Lombardian usurer in Toulouse.

'This is the balance of the sale of my family's home in the Lot, in Aquitaine. It is an idyllic place, but tragedy struck. My father's first love, a beautiful Muslim girl called Mahnoor, was murdered there by assassins sent by her own father. Later, my grandfather's extended family died in an outbreak of the putrid fever, and so it was sold before my mother and father left on the Great Crusade.'

Eadmer looked at the note closely.

'I can't read the Latin words, but I can count the numbers. This is a lot of geld. We must make sure that if we ever travel back to England, God willing, we go via Toulouse to retrieve this promise.'

'It has been a long time. Perhaps the lender is long dead. But it would be good to see the place that I know was very important to my family. There is a small plot on the land where several precious people are buried. We kept ownership of the plot; it would be good to pay my respects there. Let's agree that we will return via Aquitaine when we travel back to England.'

Eadmer smiled at me with the mischievous grin he reserved for moments of mockery.

'Agreed! Assuming you haven't become a religious fanatic in the meantime . . .'

When we met Hugh and the Templars later that day, there was a genuine sense of brotherly comradeship between us as I confirmed my willingness to become the ninth and final founding member of the Knights Templar.

Before we left for Jerusalem the next morning, Rosal – a Cistercian monk and the least fearsome of the Templars – cut my hair and trimmed my beard. He gave me my new white cappa robe, and my cape and shield. Eadmer got the same haircut, but as a sergeant-at-arms wore a black cappa under his cape.

Rosal did not say much, but he gave me a reminder of the strong code of discipline to which I must now submit.

'Remember, Harold of Hereford, Hugh is our Master. You must be sure always to address him as such.'

*

Jerusalem was over three hundred miles from Antioch. It was a long and exhausting journey in conditions Eadmer and I had never experienced before. Although it was mid-October, when the sun reached its zenith it was unbearably hot. The summer had been unusually dry and the autumn had brought little rain to soften the ground. Around the middle of that first day, I surveyed the barren and remote environment of our route and asked Hugh the most obvious of questions.

'Master, how do just nine knights and their squadrons protect a road as long and isolated as this?'

He gave me an answer that was equally evident to him. 'With faith, my friend.'

We passed many pilgrims on the road, mingling with myriad caravans of traders and merchants whose predecessors had trodden the route for centuries. The names of the ancient cities we visited prompted many memories for me. They were placenames I remembered from the Gospels, and cities that my mother had described in such detail: the magisterial Phoenician port of Tripoli, home to countless tribes and tongues; Sidon, with its many Roman buildings still in daily use, its bustling markets selling everything from silks and spices to swords and slaves; and Acre, the greatest port in the Holy Land, richer, it was said, than any European kingdom.

Everything that my mother had passed on to me, as told to her by my grandmother, about the wisdom of the ancient world and the great achievements of Egypt, Greece and Rome, seemed to be there before my eyes: towering domes, triumphal arches, circuses, theatres and hippodromes. I was utterly captivated by the journey.

The whole experience was enhanced by being with Hugh de Payens and the Templars. Wherever we went, Muslims looked on in awe. Christians bowed their heads; some even fell to their knees and crossed themselves. The Templars seemed to epitomize the indomitable knights of the First Crusade. I felt invigorated in their presence, knowing that I was travelling in my family's footsteps, and I saw them in my mind's eye: my grandfather, mother and father, and the fearless Adela.

When we reached Jerusalem, the feeling of euphoria was multiplied. After enduring the pain and hardship of an almost impossible journey from Europe, here was the Holy City that thousands of Christians had fought and died for. I remembered, word for word, my mother's description of Jerusalem: 'It was a thing of wonder. From the top of the Mount of Olives you could see the holiest places in the world for the three religions of Abraham. There before us, beyond its lofty walls, were the Dome of the Rock, the Temple of Solomon, the al-Aksa Mosque and the Holy Sepulchre – the most revered buildings in the world. They glowed in the sun, their walls bleached white, their domes, minarets and crosses gleaming symbols of man's devotion to his maker.'

On cold nights in Norwich, with snow swirling around the massive walls of her cathedral, I would imagine the sights she described to me. When I finally saw Jerusalem, it was as if I had been there before.

I began to regard my own trials and tribulations at sea, and in Anatolia, as my personal crusade; Livia's death was part of the sacrifice that so many others had to endure. I came to the conclusion that Hugh de Payens was right:

what had been fought for a generation ago was worth protecting from the non-believing Muslims and from those Christians who had lost the vision and rigour of the Great Crusade.

After spending the night in our new lodgings beneath the vaulted arches of the Temple of Solomon, we rose early the next morning to take the oath of our new Order. With our sergeants-at-arms standing behind us, the nine of us stood in a small circle beneath the twelve tall arches of the Temple of Solomon. We drew our swords and held them with the tip down, resting on the floor in salute, and bowed our heads.

Hugh de Payens, Grand Master of our new Order, then read our vows, which we repeated in unison.

The Cord around our waists signifies our chastity, thus making us pure in the eyes of God. We shall speak little and be courteous when we do. We shall avoid the company of women and the temptations of their flesh. We shall eat bread and water and wear simple robes and bear without complaint much hardship and labour. We do this in God's name, answerable only to Him and our Master.

When the vows had been spoken, the Master addressed us in turn, concluding this solemn initiation.

Be a truly fearless knight, secure in every way, for your soul is protected by the armour of faith, just as your body is protected by the armour of steel. You are thus doubly armed and need fear neither demons nor men. Be at one with your Maker, for He will make you worthy men.

So, in a simple ceremony, I had become a founding knight of the Poor Fellow-Soldiers of Christ of the Temple of Solomon. Little did I know then how powerful our Order would become in the affairs of the Holy Land, how influential it would be in the affairs of the Church of Rome, and how far it would reach into communities across the whole of Europe.

13. Succubae and Sodomites

Life as a Templar passed quickly. The daily routine was like that of a monk, but also similar to the discipline of a professional soldier, so neither Eadmer nor I found it too demanding. The constant liturgy of mass and prayers was tedious, but it gave me time to reflect on recent events and to come to terms with Livia's death. I came to think of it as a time of cleansing.

By the turn of the year, we had recruited over 150 knights and had more than 500 men in various squadrons and specialist militias. There were occasional skirmishes with Muslim raiding parties, but we dealt with them effectively, adding considerably to our reputation. By January of 1120, knights began to arrive from all over Europe, swelling our numbers to the scale of a significant army.

The mood within the Order remained brotherly, but Master Hugh was becoming an increasingly potent force within the Christian states. Some of the brothers thought his authority was beginning to be autocratic and even cruel. Disobedience was punished severely, as was dissent. Solitary confinement for days on end within our headquarters was one of the milder penalties. Floggings were commonplace, as were public humiliations – such as being required to do multiple Stations of the Cross around the Temple walls in the heat of the day, wearing no more than a loincloth.

Master Hugh continued to smile benignly, but some younger recruits began to say that the fixed smile disguised a troubled man.

My own serious reservations emerged after Godfrey de Saint-Omer began to give impassioned sermons about the temptation of women. He said that one of the new recruits had come to him to confess that he had been seduced by a succubus in his sleep and that she visited him every night to repeat the torture. 'Lucky boy' was Eadmer's sardonic reaction, a sentiment I shared. But two days later, Godfrey declared that he had been unable to cleanse the demon from the young knight's soul and that he would have to have it flogged out of him.

He was given thirty brutal lashes, which was a punishment so severe that he had to be taken to the monks at the nearby Hospital of St John of Jerusalem. Sadly, his wounds became infected and he died of a fever a week later.

Although the disquiet in the Order grew, most brothers accepted that the Christian States had been made weak through sin and that rigid discipline and the cleansing of the soul was the only way to redemption. Thus Hugh's authority remained largely unchallenged.

Nevertheless, after a couple of days of thought, I decided to talk to our leader.

'Master, may I raise an issue with you?'

'Of course, Brother Hal.'

'Brother Godfrey is preaching about the temptations of women, which is all well and good. But on the matter of the young monk who said he was visited by a succubus, is it not to be expected that young men bound by vows of chastity should dream of women?'

For a moment, Hugh's smiled wavered. There was a sudden flash of anger across his face, before he resumed his benign grin.

'My son, his dream was not about a woman. It was the Devil defiling him in his masquerade as a woman.'

'But, Master, what sin did the boy commit that led to him being flogged?'

'His sin was obvious; he let the Devil into his soul.'

I realized that our Master had a totally closed view on the matter and that further discussion would only provoke his anger. He looked at me imploringly with his piercing eyes.

'Are you troubled, my son? If you are, you can talk to me or to Brother Godfrey. Because of his wisdom and total devotion to God, I am going to appoint Godfrey as Grand Chaplain of the Order, to be responsible for our spiritual well-being. You know, succubae can be very persistent – having been driven out of one member, they can easily attack another.'

There was something unnerving, even threatening, in Hugh's question.

'Master, I am only troubled by the death of a young Brother who had dreams about women.'

This time, Hugh de Payens' mask of benevolent charm disappeared for more than a moment.

'Do you question my absolute authority on all matters, spiritual or temporal?'

'No, Master.'

I had no choice but to back down, although I did not

like to be bullied and despised his blatant abuse of power. Hugh's compassionate countenance returned, and I took my leave of him.

I had realized two things: those who thought that Hugh's charm was superficial were right; and in the long term, my future did not belong with the Knights Templar. However, it soon became clear that once the Oath of the Templars had been taken, there was no turning back. Leaving the Order was not permitted. This was clearly a concern that Eadmer and I would have to address when the time was right.

In the middle of January 1120, our Master led the nine founding members of the Order to Nablus, a Samaritan city forty miles north of Jerusalem. A Great Council had been called for all the Christian States of the Holy Land to discuss their existing problems and produce an agreement for the future. Hugh intended to speak to the Council about his vision for the security and prosperity of the 'Outremer' – the name the Franks gave to the Holy Land.

The Council of Nablus was a sight to behold. The entire Christian ecclesiastical and secular nobility of the Holy Land was there, supported by their military and personal entourages. The fields around the city were covered in row after row of tents and pavilions, each topped by the pennon of a knight or gonfalon of a lord. Hundreds of horses were tethered in long picket-lines, their bay coats glistening in the sun, lending straight lines to the patchwork of colourful canvas.

Long trestle tables had been made to feed the hordes,

and food and drink were being consumed on a scale reminiscent of the baronial banquets of our European homelands. In fact, had it not been for the arid surroundings of Palestine, the scene could easily have been in Normandy or England. There were hawkers and minstrels, jugglers and jesters, artisans of every trade and merchants selling any product you could wish for.

The serious business of the Council began the next day – on 15 January 1120, a day that changed the history of the Holy Land – presided over by Garmond, Patriarch of Jerusalem, and Baldwin II, King of Jerusalem. The great and the good of the Holy Land were assembled: Ehremar, Archbishop of Caesarea; Bernard, Bishop of Nazareth; Ansquitinus, Bishop of Bethlehem; Roger, Bishop of Ramla; Achardus, Prior of the Temple; Arnaldus, Prior of Mount Sion; Girardus, Prior of the Holy Sepulchre; Pagan, Chancellor of Jerusalem; Eustace Grenier, Lord of Caesarea and Sidon; and Baldwin, Lord of Ramla. I had never seen so many fine robes and glittering insignia of office.

They met in the an-Nasr, an ancient Byzantine church which the Muslims had converted into a mosque and which, in turn, King Baldwin was in the throes of transforming into a Christian church once again. Reputedly built on the exact spot where Jacob, son of Isaac and grandson of Abraham, was brought the bloody and tattered coat of Joseph by his sons, it was one of the holiest of all places for Jews, Christians and Muslims. Its scale reminded me of Norwich and the stories my mother had told me about how she and my grandmother had been inspired by the wonders of antiquity.

Garmond opened proceedings by outlining what he thought was the extent of the decline in Christian values and behaviour.

'My Lords, the sins of our people are reaping a bitter harvest. Our cities are plagued by mice and rats, our granaries are diseased, our wells foul. Locusts come every year and strip our fields bare. The infidels attack us on our roads and storm the gates of our citadels. Like beasts, they smell our weakness. Our domains are only twenty years old; if they are to survive for our children and grandchildren, we must act now, or the Almighty will turn his face against us and we will be cast into the wilderness. Remember, the Lord said he will "give us as meat to the beasts of the field and to the fowls of the heaven".'

The Patriarch's impassioned words brought a rapturous response from the audience. Many knights thumped their shields with their swords and maces. All the speakers at the Council kept to the same theme: wholesale sin in the Christian community was turning God against the Christian States, and their punishment was nigh. Immorality and adultery were the worst crimes. Many spoke about the increasing fetish for young Arab boys, claiming that sodomy was widespread in the garrisons of soldiers – and even among knights and priests.

When it was time for Hugh de Payens to speak, he rose deliberately and paused to look slowly around the entire gathering before uttering a word. He was greeted by total silence; although his station as a mere knight from a modest region of Champagne was far below the status enjoyed by most of his audience, his reputation and bearing stilled the gathering.

'Your Majesty, Eminence, Lords, fellow knights, we all know what ails us. But I want to talk to you about redemption.'

His voice rose and rose as his oratory blossomed, until he had the entire gathering on the edge of their seats.

'My order of brothers, the Knights Templar, will drive sin from our domains. No stone will be left unturned, no dark hiding place of evil will remain in shadow. All sinners will be exposed and face the wrath of God.'

He then turned to the theme of safety and security.

'As you all have been witness to, our roads are now much more secure since the patrols of my Knights Templar began. We will maintain our vigilance on behalf of all Christians in the Holy Land and will show no mercy to any infidel who dares harm even a single hair of our Christian brothers and sisters.'

More cheers and cries ensued as the Grand Master reached his crescendo.

'But I want to rekindle the flame of the Great Crusade, a flame that burned in the hearts of our fathers and grandfathers with an intensity that swept all before it. As you know, the city of Tyre is still in the hands of the Fatimid Caliph of Cairo, al-Amir, and is the only Muslim port in the Holy Land. From there, the Muslims who harass our cities and roads get their weapons and supplies. Now that His Majesty King Baldwin has control of Sinai as far as Aqaba, if we can capture Tyre, we will cut the umbilical cord of the Muslim brigands. Give me an army and I will give you Tyre!'

The roars from the audience meant that there was little doubt about the answer to the Grand Master's request. I looked at Eadmer, who was standing right behind me. He nodded his head; he knew as well as I did that we would soon be preparing an army for war. It had been a charismatic performance from Hugh de Payens, who had caught the mood of the Christians of the Holy Land perfectly and in a massive leap had elevated himself to the front rank of the hierarchy of the Latin Princes.

The rest of the Council's business involved setting new laws for the Holy Land in a series of canons – something that had been neglected since the Great Crusade – the tone of which was as severe as any I had ever heard. Canon 23 referred to theft and decreed that any theft of a value more than one bezant would cost the perpetrator an eye or a hand. Canon 4 dealt with adultery, which was punishable by branding with a hot iron and repeat offences by emasculation, while adulterous women would have their noses removed. Canon 12 required the same fate for any man who had sexual intercourse with a Muslim woman. Canons 8 to 11 addressed the growing problem of sodomites. 'An abomination that is desecrating God's most beautiful creation' declared Arnaldus, Prior of Sidon. But whether he was referring to the whole of the human body, or just one part of it, was a source of amusing conjecture between Eadmer and myself when we reflected on the proceedings that evening. More importantly, for those indulging in sodomy Canon 8 stated that they 'be burned at the stake, so that their evil be extinguished as in the fires of Hell'.

Two days later, we joined our Grand Master in a council of war with King Baldwin, to begin the planning for an attack on Tyre.

The King had his senior commanders with him, all of whom were visibly furious that Hugh de Payens had been given command of the attacking forces. Baldwin was a man of medium build, with a thick head of hair and dark beard. He had only been King for eighteen months but already had an air of easy authority about him. He had restored the security of Antioch and defeated Il-Ghazi's army decisively.

'Tyre is a mighty fortress with a high, easily defended position and with its back to the sea. It will be a long siege.'

Hugh de Payens then went through the tactics he intended to use in detail. It was an impressive plan, which partly won over the King's senior men. The King, who was clearly in awe of Hugh, as were many people, then put in a word of caution.

'In order to have the money and resources required for success, we're going to need help. I am told that an agreement was struck between Roger, Prince of Antioch, and the Venetians immediately before he was killed at the Battle of Sarmada.'

'That is true, Your Majesty –'

I had spoken without thinking, forgetting that I should not have spoken without being invited to. Hugh made to speak, but the King raised his hand to stop him.

'How do you know this?'

'Forgive me, Your Majesty; I am Harold of Hereford, an English knight and a Knight Commander of Venice before I joined Master Hugh's Templars. I was there at Sarmada, as escort to her Serenity, Princess Livia of Venice. She told me on the eve of the battle that Prince Roger had agreed to the pact with Venice.'

'It is true. I remember the knight.'

The voice came from a dark corner of the King's tent, from Hodierna – his sister, and wife of Prince Roger – the woman I had met in Antioch with Livia. I had not noticed she was there.

'So you are the knight who managed to get her away during the battle. Is it true that the Prince had raped her?'

'Yes, sire.'

'You see, Gentlemen, such is the evil that besets this realm . . .'

He paused and looked at Hugh. My words had added weight to the plan that had already formed in his mind.

'This man could be very useful to our cause.'

He then turned to me.

'Do you speak their language?'

'Yes, Your Majesty, well enough.'

'Hugh, I am going to send Eustace Grenier – Lord of Caesarea and Sidon, and my Constable of Jerusalem – to the Venetians. He is an excellent soldier and wise counsel. We need the Venetian navy and a mountain of silver for the siege. I want your young Templar, Harold here, to go with him to help him negotiate with the Doge.'

For obvious reasons, I was worried about accepting such a commission.

'Sire, forgive me, but when I returned to Venice, the Doge declined to see me. I fear he believes I should have done more to protect the Lady Livia.'

'He will have had time to reflect on that, I'm sure it will be different when you return. You did all you could – to get her away from the slaughter at Sarmada was a miracle. Besides, you will be in Venice with a very lucrative proposal from me. Venetians never miss an opportunity to strike a profitable deal.'

And so, in a turn of events that I could never have foreseen, by the middle of 1120, we were back in Venice. Only a day after our arrival, we had an audience with Domenico Michele, the Doge of Venice. It was a meeting I was not looking forward to. The last time I had been in the Doge's palace was on the day when I first saw Livia – a moment of rapture still vivid in my memory.

When we were introduced, the Doge acknowledged me with only a perfunctory nod. But at least he had not refused to allow me to accompany Eustace Grenier. The Constable had brought a very generous offer from the King, which made the negotiations go well.

The trading agreement with Antioch was confirmed by Baldwin as Regent and extended to the whole of the Kingdom of Jerusalem. Venice would be granted one third of the Lordship of Tyre upon its capture and an annual payment of 300 gold bezants from the royal treasury at Acre. The Venetians would also be exempt from all taxation on their holdings in the Holy Land and be granted a parcel of land in every town or city in the realm, which would be made up of one street, one market square, one church, a bakery and a bathhouse. It was an offering that made the Doge's eyes visibly widen as he heard it.

In exchange, he promised to build a navy of eighty ships, fully manned by newly recruited and trained marines, which would remain in Tyre as a standing navy to protect Venice's interests in perpetuity. Although it would take two years to build, he was true to his word. The fleet would be ready by the end of 1122, and we planned to sail for the Levant at the beginning of January 1123.

Eadmer and I spent the long months while the ships were being built helping with the training of the new marines. In the company of earnest young men from all over the Mediterranean, we enjoyed our time in the familiar surroundings of the Arsenale watching the Holy Land's Grand Fleet being built.

I did not expect to see the Doge again, but just before we left for the Holy Land, I was summoned to the palace. The Doge was walking along his private terrace overlooking the Grand Canal as I was ushered in.

He was alone and appeared pensive.

'Walk with me, Harold of Hereford.'

I bowed and began following him, a polite distance in his wake.

'Lady Constance has told me a good deal about the circumstances of Lady Livia's death and what preceded it.'

He stopped and looked me in the eye.

'Were you in love with my sister?'

I hesitated and looked away, across the Canalazzo towards the east.

'You can answer honestly. I bear you no grudge.'

'Yes, Serenity. I regret Lady Livia's passing with every breath I take.'

'And yet Constance tells me that you never wavered from your duty to deliver my sister to her intended bridegroom.'

'That is so, Serenity.'

I wanted to tell him how much I regretted the choices I had made, and the pain I had caused my beloved, but knew I could not; it would have been unkind to add more detail to his burden.

'Thank you for doing what you did to try to save her. I know my sister was strong-willed and impetuous; you must have been a great comfort to her.'

Domenico Michele had tears in his eyes. He took a deep breath.

'They say Roger of Salerno died a painful death at Sarmada.'

'I believe so, Serenity.'

He nodded in approval and held out his hand for me to kiss his Doge's ring, which I did willingly.

As I turned to leave, I was gratified to see that his tears had been replaced by a faint smile. It was a comforting end to a painful chapter in my life.

14. Siege of Tyre

As we prepared for the Siege of Tyre, I was told by one of the King's advisers, a learned man called Barisan of Ibelin, that Alexander the Great had laid siege to Tyre many hundreds of years earlier. I made sure word of that was spread among the men, for those who had heard of the exploits of the mighty Macedonian would surely be inspired by his deeds.

The Venetians had brought timber from the forests of the Alps and we began to construct siege towers, catapults and scaling ladders. Most importantly, the Venetian navy blockaded the port, while King Baldwin's men closed the roads to the south, thus isolating the Fatimid defenders of Tyre from the outside world.

Barisan's description of Alexander's siege offered King Baldwin a model for how to conduct his assault and acted as inspiration for all the sappers and engineers. Because the city's citadel was located on a small craggy island just off the coast, Alexander had built a stone causeway, almost 1,000 yards in length, stretching out to the island. This allowed him to position his siege artillery within range of the walls. As the causeway approached the walls, however, the water became much deeper, so Alexander had constructed two huge towers with catapults on the top, to clear defenders off the walls, and ballista below to hurl rocks at the walls.

After many months of bitter fighting and countless attempts to breach the walls, Alexander finally prevailed. Unfortunately for the Tyrian defenders, they had made the mistake of executing several captured Macedonians on the walls of the city in full view of their comrades before hurling their bodies back into the Macedonian camp. So when the citadel fell, at the cost of over 6,000 Tyrian defenders, Alexander ordered that 2,000 more be crucified on the beach. The rest of Tyre's population, over 30,000 souls, were sold into slavery.

The great Macedonian's causeway was still intact. It had later been completed up to the city's gates by the Romans, making our task a lot easier than it might otherwise have been.

King Baldwin's opening gambit was a generous one: he offered safe passage to Egypt for the Fatimid garrison and the entire population, if they relinquished the city peacefully. The offer was refused, but with a grisly message. A small population of Armenian Christians – at least 200 men, women and children – lived in the city, and had done so for many years. The Emir of the city, al-Malik, ordered them to be rounded up, blinded by hot irons, placed in carts and wheeled out of the city. Baldwin took pity on them and had them escorted to Jerusalem, but his anger at the Fatimid Emir knew no bounds and he swore to exact an appropriate revenge.

After several months of careful preparation, the King was forced to reduce the scale of the siege when he heard news of an approaching Fatimid army from the south. He was only able to leave a skeleton force outside the walls, under the command of Hugh de Payens. This allowed the Emir of Tyre to get fresh water and supplies into the city.

For me, the King's foray to the south to halt the approaching Fatimids provided invaluable military experience. Master Hugh granted me permission to join the King's staff, which not only removed me from day-to-day contact with the rigours of Templar life, but also allowed me to observe the skills of one of the Levant's most accomplished soldiers at close quarters. Never happier than living a soldier's life, Eadmer was also much more content away from the rigid strictures of our Order.

I grew to like King Baldwin. He had an aura of calm, but a strong personality, and I understood very quickly that he expected rigid discipline and the utmost professionalism from his men. He rode his cavalry in well-ordered squadrons and expected a brisk pace from his infantry, even in the heat of the Holy Land. Their reward was excellent food, drink and entertainment every evening and a generous share of the spoils of victory. He had a cynical, but perhaps realistic, soldier's view of soldiers: feed their desires, and reward their greed. He talked about this many times in his family's language – the tongue of his homeland in the Ardennes. It had similarities with Norman, and I eventually came to understand it.

He also talked a good deal about Hugh de Payens and the Templars, and I realized that the King had a pragmatic approach to the merits of our Order. He knew that the Christian Holy Land had been won through the burning passion of the Great Crusaders and that if it was to survive, encircled by hordes of Muslims, it needed men like the Templars to give it backbone, both military and religious.

The Muslim leadership was constantly at odds with itself, riven by disputes about dogma. But if that ever changed, the Latin States would face a threat that could prove to be overwhelming.

We confronted the advancing Fatimid army at the oasis of Bir al-Abd, deep into Fatimid territory in Sinai. It was an inhospitable place – so much so that it made me wonder why anyone would want to fight over it. It seemed to be no more than an ocean of sand stretching to the horizon in the south, with only the occasional palm tree adding an isolated feature to the barren landscape. However, it was the major trading route between the Levant and the domains of Egypt and beyond, and so of strategic importance since antiquity.

King Baldwin organized his army in classical formation: three columns of infantry supported by archers, with his mounted knights in reserve to the rear. We were 4,000 in number: 3,000 infantry and archers, and 1,000 mounted knights. But the Fatimids were at least double that, creating a huge storm of dust as they approached. As the cloud enveloped them in swirls and waves, we could see their black war banners held aloft through the murk and hear their throbbing drumbeats drifting on the wind. Their infantry stamped their feet as they closed on us, adding to the deafening noise and making the ground shudder. It was intended to make their opponents tremble, but the King's army was composed of seasoned veterans, many of them sons of crusaders. As he ordered them to halt and stand their ground, I was impressed by their unflinching resolve – even in the face of such a formidable challenge.

The King checked the sun; it was directly overhead, making it difficult to see a hail of arrows. He immediately ordered several volleys of arrows to be fired into the Fatimids' ranks. Their infantry held firm. Within moments, it was on the move in a mass attack in a line several hundred yards wide.

Baldwin turned to me.

'Let's see what you Templars can do. I want the cavalry to attack between our columns of infantry. You're to join Eustace Grenier on the left flank in his vanguard. Go quickly, before the horde is upon us.'

Without pausing to think about how daunting my assignment was, I set off at a gallop with Eadmer close behind.

He called out to me.

'Don't get too far ahead when we charge! Make sure the squadrons are right behind you.'

'Stay close, Eadmer, this is my first cavalry charge.'

'Don't worry, I'll be right up your arse!'

When I arrived at the shoulder of Grenier, at the head of 500 battle-hardened knights, he looked at me and shouted his orders.

'You're a soldier of Christ! Lead the charge!'

With my lance couched, my sword held high – and Eadmer at my side with the crimson cross of the Templars' gonfalon taut in the breeze – I cried aloud to the men.

'*For God, the King and Jerusalem!*'

We were soon at full gallop, our heavy destriers streaming through the space between our columns of infantry and bearing down on the Fatimid front ranks, now only a hundred yards away, like a flood tide rushing towards the shore. Five hundred knights' pennons streamed in the air behind me, their myriad colours in stark contrast to the plain arid earth.

When we got close to the Fatimids, I could see the glistening curls of their oiled beards and the intricate twists and turns of their elaborate turbans. But, more than that, I could see the anxiety in their eyes. Even after a generation, the scale and power of the heavy European horse still struck terror in Muslim armies, and the solid line of men before me began to show gaps before a single blow had been struck. I could see Fatimid officers bellowing at their men to stand firm. Some took heed of them, but many did not, and we were able to flow through their lines like water through a breached dam.

The forlorn infantry beneath us were rich pickings, and we were able to thrust and cut like apprentice knights at a tilt yard. My mount skittled men before it like ninepins, and I had free rein to strike at will at those rushing to get away. There is nothing like the panic of defeat: men will tread on one another to reach safety and run aimlessly in any direction to avoid slaughter. I lost count of the number I slashed with my sword and impaled with my lance. It was like hunting defenceless creatures in a forest teeming with game. Their cries of anguish rang in my ears, and I could recall faces frozen in horror for years afterwards. But at the time, I did not hesitate or show an inkling of compassion. My warrior instincts had me in their iron grip.

We were soon through the ranks of infantry and heading towards the Fatimid cavalry, which had formed up in front of their general's command post. King Baldwin had ordered his infantry to advance, which would soon engulf the scattered pockets of Fatimids marooned behind us with neither unity nor discipline.

In one charge, the day had been won. The Muslim horns sounded the retreat, and the Fatimid general led his staff and entourage away at a canter. They were quickly followed by his cavalry, conceding the battle to the Christians once more. Rather than pursue them, the King sounded our recall. As he pointed out, we were far enough into Egypt and had created enough mayhem to quell the Fatimid challenge for at least a year. Our priority was the capture of Tyre – to complete Christian control of the entire Mediterranean coastline of the Holy Land.

We surveyed the battlefield and buried fewer than 200 Christian dead. On the other hand, Muslim bodies littered the ground like the leaves of autumn. The King sent a message to the Fatimid general, granting him permission to collect his fallen warriors. Carts soon appeared to carry them away. I counted over 1,200 corpses before dusk brought the gruesome task to an end for the day.

The King thanked me for the success of the charge, and Grenier slapped me on the back.

'I thought you would bring us an easy victory. The men believe your crimson cross heralds the courage of the Great Crusaders.'

The King ordered that we make camp a mile or so from the battlefield. As the army filed away, he turned to address me.

'Take your sergeant and ride up and down the column

with the Holy Cross. It will be the perfect end to a good day for the men.'

Despite my doubts about Hugh de Payens and our eminent Order, what followed in his name and that of my brother Templars was one of the most invigorating moments of my life. While I stood tall in my stirrups waving my sword in salute, with the setting sun blazing through it, Eadmer carried the Templar's crimson cross along the length of the Christian column. The cheers followed us like waves running along a beach and echoed all around us. At that moment, I realized that the Knights Templar were a force to be reckoned with in the Holy Land and that their influence may well extend way beyond its borders – even reaching back into Europe.

I had come through yet another challenging skirmish and was at last beginning to believe that my quest to write my own chapter in the illustrious history of my family might, after all, meet with success.

Three weeks later, we were back beneath the walls of Tyre, with the King freshly invigorated and determined to break the siege. News had also reached the defenders that the relief army from Egypt had been turned back, which must have weakened their resolve. Although Hugh de Payens' small force had been unable to stop the Emir from replenishing his supplies, he had been under siege for several months and morale within the city must have been running low.

Over the decades of their occupation, the Christians had brought in large numbers of pigs from Europe for plentiful supplies of pork and bacon, of which the Franks were particularly fond. Conversely, Muslims regard the pig as a filthy animal and loathe its presence, quite apart from finding it abhorrent as a food. The King ordered the collection and slaughter of dozens of pigs, and the army was fed roast pork for the coming days. However, the pigs' heads were spared the pot and instead hurled into the city by the basketful. Then, to compound the insult, after consuming pork for several days, he ordered his men to defecate into earthenware pots provided for the purpose. These too were launched on to the inhabitants of the city.

The King found the whole distasteful exercise amusing – in stark contrast to the revulsion that must have been felt behind Tyre's walls.

The catapults were then put to more conventional use and soon boulders, incendiaries and hot oil began to cascade from the skies. The Venetian ships also began to bombard the city, until missiles rained down on all sides. The barrage was relentless; a shift system was organized among the Christian sappers so that the aerial attacks continued all day and every night. For those trapped inside the city, sleep was almost impossible – especially for the citizens charged with extinguishing the many fires that were started by the flaming pitch. Despite the onslaught, there was no sign of capitulation from the besieged inhabitants.

But then, an unexpected development caught all of us unawares in late June 1124. I remember the date well because some of the men who still had hankerings after their old pagan traditions had just celebrated the Summer Solstice a few days earlier. It was about half an hour before dawn when the gates of the city suddenly opened to release a tumult of humanity. People of all ages ran in every direction. Many tried to run through our camp, some begged for mercy at our tents, and a few made for boats in the harbour to try to escape by sea. They were mainly civilians, but a few were armed and appeared to be from the Emir's garrison.

Within minutes, the city gates had been closed again and most of the escapees had been rounded up – a group of several thousand. There was no violence; these poor souls had simply had enough and had stormed Tyre's gates from the inside in a bid for freedom from the agony of the unremitting siege. They said that unrest was widespread – even among the Emir's men – and that disease had taken hold, killing dozens by the day.

The King immediately ordered that the runaways be quarantined, but within sight of the city. And then he made a shrewd decision: he ordered his cooks, stewards and healers to care for them. In full view of vantage points on the city walls, food was cooked and distributed, plentiful supplies of water were given out and even wine was made available for those who wanted it. The sick were treated, and sappers were stood down from their duties servicing the siege engines and preparing ammunition in order to erect shelters for the evacuees.

It took only two days for the King's generosity to work its magic inside the city. We could hear shouting and screaming from inside the walls, followed by the clash of weapons. Then, towards the end of the second afternoon, amidst much uproar and cheering, a large group of men appeared on the walls, just above the main gate. In the centre of the group, tied hand and foot, was a bloodied and beaten Emir of Tyre, al-Malik. The leader of the group then shouted down to us in good Norman, asking for food and water and safe passage to the Muslims of the east, rather than to Fatimid Egypt. He said that everyone in the garrison loyal to the Emir had been killed in fighting that had lasted for two days and that the Emir was now alone and defenceless.

Under instruction from the King, Hugh de Payens then walked forward and agreed to the citizens' requests. But he said it was conditional on the Emir being released.

Wild celebrations followed, both inside and outside the city. The next day, the Muslims of Tyre began their long walk to the east and a precarious future, while the Christian army entered their city – the last Muslim enclave in Palestine. But before the Muslims left, the King had his revenge for the blinding of the Armenians.

Al-Malik, already drenched in blood and only semiconscious, was dragged into the citadel's main square and tied to a column in the marketplace. A hot iron was prepared which Hugh de Payens brandished – with a relish unbecoming the Grand Master of a brotherhood of good men – before proceeding to take out the Emir's eyes. He was then cut down and made to kneel in front of the Grand Master, who raised his sword high above his head and cried: 'Go to your god to face his wrath and know that this is the punishment for anyone who defiles the children of the true God.' To my shame, our Grand Master then started to hack at the neck of the Emir until he had detached it from his body. It was an act a merciful executioner would have accomplished in one or two blows, but which Hugh de Payens took at least a dozen ham-fisted attempts to achieve.

Despite the brutality, the men of the army roared their approval – so much so that, in the weeks that followed, Jerusalem saw long queues of knights wanting to enlist as Knights Templar. I looked at the King, who had a troubled expression.

He had unleashed a beast in this man; I hoped he could contain it.

Dear Thibaud,

Another Sabbath today and the warmth of the sun is on our backs. Winter is nearly over, and I think the worst has passed.

I find it fascinating that over sixty years after the events Harold has described in so much detail, the same names and places are still part of the story of the Holy Land. More crusades, yet another Baldwin as King of Jerusalem. Cities fall and are retaken; it goes on and on. And we're only a few years away from the hundredth anniversary of the First Crusade.

Surely the great religions can live together? Do the Muslims not accept Christ as a great prophet? Could we not accept their prophet, Mohammed, in the same way?

But perhaps that's heresy. I crave your indulgence, my friend, for the musings of an old priest; don't tell your friends in the Vatican.

I enclose another bulletin for you. Harold's story continues, and his destiny takes him to far-flung places. He has an important pilgrimage to make, back to Hereward's mountain lair in the Peloponnese. His journey there will reaffirm his stubborn streak of Englishness — he is a tenacious young man! — and enable him to close the circle of his family's history.

Yours in God,
Gilbert

15. Aquitaine

When the dust of the desert began to settle, Eadmer and I began to talk once more about our future with the Order. Like me, he understood the life of a warrior, but when it became mixed with the passions of religious faith, he was at a loss to understand what was expected of him.

He was clear about our next move.

'Let us retrieve our purse in Antioch, travel to Aquitaine to see if you can claim your family inheritance, and then journey home to Norwich. You could buy an estate for your mother to retire to – and I could buy a farm and settle down.'

'Eadmer, I doubt that you will ever settle down. But if you do, I wager it won't be for many years yet.'

Our discussions about the future continued through the summer of 1124, a period that passed without incident, during which we spent most of our time training new recruits to the Order. Then, in August, we were called to the King's Great Hall in Jerusalem to meet with Hugh de Payens, the other founding members of the Order and a few of the recent senior recruits. The King presided over the meeting, but it was the Grand Master who did all the talking.

'Brothers, I have some excellent news. His Majesty King Baldwin II, Lord of Jerusalem, has agreed to join our Order as an honorary lay member. He will not take the same vows, but he has pledged his lifelong support to us and to our mission.'

There was applause from all the brothers. Ceremonial embraces were exchanged with the King before Hugh continued.

'I am also honoured to tell you that our Order has reached the second stage of its life – our coming of age. Where we were once a handful, we are now a legion. We cannot any longer rely on the generosity of the King's Exchequer; we must earn our own way in life. Godfrey will stay here to continue our work in the Holy Land, but I will travel to Rome to seek recognition from His Holiness and be granted the honour of being placed under his direct authority.'

I glanced at the King at that point and saw him move uneasily in his chair.

'The rest of you will travel throughout Europe to build our own Templar foundations and communities. We need land, we need money, we need weapons and armour – we need to be independent and in charge of our own destinies. Find benefactors; recruit lords and bishops to our cause; build churches, farms and granaries; train church-wrights, artisans and craftsmen who can create homes for our brothers to live in and chapels for them to worship in. We will function like the great monasteries – they will be our model.'

The Grand Master looked at us all with the intensity that was his mark. It was as if he was the Saviour himself sending his fishermen disciples to be 'fishers of men'.

'Do this in the name of our Brotherhood, The Poor Fellow-Soldiers of Christ of the Temple of Solomon. Amen.'

Eadmer and I had been given our passage out of the Holy Land – without having to confront our problems with the Order or examine our increasing misgivings over the behaviour of our leader.

We tried not to leave in too much haste. But within a few days we had made our way to Antioch where, in clear breach of our code, we retrieved our money from the moneylenders. We packed away our Templar's garb and sat in one of the city's many taverns in the lee of its walls and enjoyed a flask of Cypriot wine.

We were unsure how to deal with the task with which we had been charged – especially as the Grand Master expected that I would concentrate on spreading the Templar gospel to England. Given that we had already determined to travel to Aquitaine to visit my grandfather's family home in the Lot, we agreed that a decision about our future as Templars could wait for a while. We bought new clothes and armour – more befitting chivalrous warriors of some standing – and set sail for Narbonne, following in the footsteps of my family.

In Narbonne, we bought sturdy Norman destriers from a trader with stables in the shadow of the Cathedral of St Justus and St Pastor, then headed north and west via Carcassonne to Toulouse. It was late September and the first autumn rains had freshened Aquitaine's parched earth following a long hot Mediterranean summer. The fields were full of peasants harvesting the black grapes of the countless vineyards, and gathering the prune plums for which the region was renowned.

But there were also many abandoned farms and deserted villages, and we had frequent encounters with soldiers in full armour travelling along the roads. We soon learned that Toulouse and Poitiers had been at war for several years and that, after recent success, the Count of Toulouse had now turned his attention to a confrontation with Provence.

I thought about home. Although England had to live with the heavy hand of Norman rule, at least it was at peace. Life was far from pleasant for many, and the Normans were still harsh foreign rulers; nevertheless, they brought order and security, something I felt sure the good people of Aquitaine would relish in their current circumstances. I remained committed to the cause of England's freedom, but realized that any future struggle for the rightful heritage of our people would come at a high price. The Normans had been there too long; their fortifications were too powerful; their presence was permanent; and the outcome of any future fight for justice would have to involve an unlikely compromise that accommodated the Norman minority as well as the English majority. In some ways, I was relieved that any potential conflict seemed to be a distant prospect.

Toulouse was one of Europe's leading centres of money-lending and finance. Counts, kings and popes would raise money there, and traders would travel from all over the region to its thriving markets. The usurers were easy to find – mainly Jews or Lombards, they occupied both sides of the main street leading to the Cathedral of St Sernin.

Our promissory note bore the name 'Jakob il Ebreo di Siena'. It was dated and promised in the name of 'Edwin of Glastonbury' – my grandfather's standard-bearer and member of his extended family, who was killed in battle on the Great Crusade. Everyone in Toulouse seemed to know Jakob the Jew of Siena and we were soon sitting at his exchange table as he unfolded our note.

He did not speak for a long while. A man of some age, with a long white beard and shock of hair under his kippa hat and long robe, his brow furrowed deeper and deeper as he held the faded piece of vellum to the light.

When he finally spoke, his accent betrayed his roots in the County of Tuscany.

'This is a lot of geld, my friend. But you are not Edwin of Glastonbury. I remember him well; he was a fair young Englishman. Are you his son?'

'No, I am Harold of Hereford, the son of Sweyn of Bourne – a sworn brother of Edwin. He and my family had an estate near Cahors, at a place called St Cirq Lapopie. It originally belonged to my grandfather, Hereward of Bourne.'

'I know the estate well, and the famous English family who owned it. The estate has been sold several times since Edwin came to me and is now abandoned again . . .'

The old man paused, sensing an opportunity. His eyes widened.

'Perhaps you would like to buy it and return it to prosperity. You have more than enough money here.'

'Perhaps I will, but I think I would rather have the geld.'

Jacob the Jew handed the note back to me and passed a flask of wine across the table.

'Let me go and get you a price. Drink some wine. I will only take the smallest of commissions, just a token amount.'

I did some thinking: our money from Antioch was already substantial, and it made good sense to safeguard our assets in land rather than carry money around. Also, I relished the thought of persuading my mother to retire from her labours in Norwich and live in a place that had meant so much to her father and her extended family. I made an impulsive decision, but one that was very appealing.

Jacob was back within thirty minutes. The wily old fox looked stern for a moment, then broke into a smile.

'Listen, I will offer you a bargain. With the interest over the years, I owe you eleven pounds and sixteen shillings of silver. But I can get you the estate for seven bezants. So I will give you three bezants in gold and a pound of silver.'

'And the rest?'

'My commission, good sir.'

'You said a token!'

'It is a hard bargain, but I will add another six shillings.'

'I'm sure you will also take a commission on the sale of the estate, so you should give me eight.'

'It's robbery of a poor old Jew of course, but as you are a worthy knight bringing money to Aquitaine, I'll give you seven.'

I shook his hand.

I was never sure whether my impetuous investment was a bargain or a swindle, but it gave me a great sense of satisfaction to know that the home that had been so precious to my mother once more belonged to my family.

*

It took us over a week to reach St Cirq Lapopie, a place that my mother had described to me many times. She talked about the mighty River Lot meandering its way through a deep valley beneath high limestone crags. She told me about the rows upon rows of vines that yield the region's famous black wine, its acres of plum trees and its endless forests of truffle oaks and walnuts. When we had finished the long climb from the valley floor, I surveyed the landscape that my family had fallen in love with all those years ago. It was indeed idyllic.

Eadmer and I spent the rest of 1124 and the early months of the following year rebuilding the derelict farmhouse and recruiting local peasants to work the fields. We cleared the ground around the graves of the family plot and carved headstones for each of them. It was hard toil, but worth it, as the estate gradually began to regain the prosperity it must have enjoyed in its heyday.

I decided to give Eadmer a share of the estate in recognition of our friendship. My loyal companion seemed content, despite the fact that he was born to be a soldier. He seemed to mellow in the warm climate of the Lot and began to sing to himself and write his own ballads. He had a good voice and learned many tunes from the local itinerant troubadours of the area.

We lived well, enjoyed good hunting, entertained some of the local girls from time to time and slowly began to master the local language. Ultimately, the temptation to make the Lot a permanent home became more and more real. Spring came and we began to see the fruits of our efforts. The earth warmed and nature sprouted in abundance.

The following year produced an even better harvest; by May of 1126, the estate was thriving as it must have done years ago. But then I began to think about my mother – especially knowing that she was nearing seventy years of age. If she was going to enjoy some time in the Lot, I needed to return to Norwich to persuade her to leave her beloved cathedral and retire to Aquitaine.

So, at the end of May 1126, I appointed a good man as manager of the estate, and Eadmer and I began the long journey north to England.

When we reached London, we heard interesting news. King Henry Beauclerc's only surviving legitimate child, Matilda, who had been married off to Henry V, the Holy Roman Emperor, had just been widowed at the age of twenty-four. Although she remained childless, Henry had declared her his rightful successor. There was great excitement about the King's declaration among the English population, and dormant pride in the lineage of the old English kings resurfaced.

Although Matilda was the granddaughter of William the Conqueror, her mother was Edith of Scotland. Through her grandmother, Margaret of Scotland, she was a direct descendant of Edmund Ironside and the niece of Edgar the Atheling, the true Cerdician heir to the English throne. Given that King Henry was approaching sixty years of age, there was thus the real prospect of a monarch on the throne at Westminster whose blood was at least half English.

We hurried to Norwich. During the entire journey, I sensed for the first time the very real possibility that I might be able to make a contribution to England's future – just like my family before me. I had no clear vision of what form it would take, but the prospect was invigorating all the same.

My mood of euphoria evaporated as we approached Norwich. Instead of being busy with the traffic of traders, merchants and pilgrims, the road to Norwich suddenly became one long line of bedraggled humanity. And they were all moving away from the burgh.

'Scarlet fever,' was the short answer to our increasingly desperate questions. 'Norwich is a graveyard.'

My anxieties intensified as soon as we reached the cathedral precincts. Our small house was locked, and the few masons who were still working at the cathedral confirmed that the fever had taken my mother a few weeks earlier. I was handed her churchwright's tools and instruments and her drawings. I was also given a small handwritten note on vellum.

I took the note to the presbytery. I knew it would be a difficult message to read, and the presbytery was a special place for both of us. It was, after all, where she had helped me with personal doubts before my life's journey began. The script was a little shaky – I imagined her distressed with fever as she wrote – but it was written with all the elegance of a master calligrapher.

I fear I will not survive this fever; perhaps when I was younger, but not now.

You will soon be the only one of our Brethren left. I hear that Duke Robert still lives, God bless him. I hope his gaolers treat him with kindness, for he is a good man.

I think Prince Edgar too is still alive. If he is, go to him; you will learn much from him. He lives an isolated life high in the hills of the north, but the monks at Durham know where he is. He never had children, and he always looked on you as a son – especially after your father died. Remember to thank him for the inheritance he gave you.

I hope you are reading this safely back in Norwich and that the destiny you were seeking has revealed itself to you. Live long and be happy. I pray that you will be granted the chance to make a difference in this life.

Remember me.

With all my love,
Your Clandestine Mother,
E

I felt the saltiness of my tears before I realized they had been streaming down my face for several minutes. I looked up and squinted at the ceiling bosses way above my head. I saw the one that my mother had said was modelled on her. Although I could not see it in any detail, I recalled it distinctly: a lissom naked wench cavorting with the Devil. It was how she wanted to be remembered – full of energy and without any inhibition – and I resolved that this was, indeed, how I always would remember her.

16. Fugitive

My mother's letter had reminded me of the close ties of the Brethren and exhorted me to seek out Prince Edgar. And so, the next morning, we prepared to set off to the west to find the ancient road to York and beyond.

However, just before noon, horns and drums sounded the impending arrival of an important personage. Assuming it was the Earl or the Bishop, we carried on with our preparations. But moments later, voices started to be raised and amidst the hue and cry shouts could be heard.

'It's the King!'

'King Henry is here!'

As I turned round, I was astonished to see a vanguard of cavalry ride into the cathedral precincts. Behind them, flanked by Hugh Bigod, Earl of Norwich, and Everard of Calne, the new Bishop of Norwich, was Henry Beauclerc, King of England, followed by his resplendent retinue. He had aged a good deal since I had last seen him in Wales, over ten years earlier, but he still had the air of a supremely confident ruler and the easy manner of a man at the centre of attention every moment of his life.

We all bowed as the King passed, and we watched him dismount less than ten yards from us. He did not recognize me – indeed, I had not expected he would – but Hugh Bigod did see me and called me over.

'Harold, I am sorry to hear about your mother.'

'Thank you, my Lord.'

'You have grown, young man. And you're the colour of a blackamoor. Where have you been?'

'Many places, my Lord – Venice, Antioch, Jerusalem.'

'What is the medallion around your neck? It looks important.'

I looked at my feet uneasily.

'It is nothing, sire. I was given it by the Doge of Venice.'

'Really! And what does it signify?'

'Well, sire, I am a Knight Commander of Venice –'

At that point, Eadmer interrupted. He grinned from ear to ear as he spoke.

'Earl Hugh – if I may be so bold – my Lord Harold is too modest to mention his accomplishments, but I am not. Sir Harold saved the shipwrecked men of a Venetian warship, scaled the walls of Zadar, protected the Lady Livia Michele at the Battle of the Field of Blood, fought at the siege of Tyre and was personally commended by His Majesty, Baldwin II, King of Jerusalem.'

'Did he, indeed! It is Eadmer, is it not?'

'It is, my Lord.'

'How are you?'

'I am well, sire. Service with Sir Harold agrees with me.'

'I can see that . . . young Harold, a Knight Commander of Venice and such a long list of accomplishments. You have done well, Harold of . . . Forgive me, I mean, Sir Harold.'

'Thank you, my Lord.'

The Earl got down from his mount.

'What are your plans now?'

'We are going to go north. There is someone I would like to see.'

'Come with me. I'll introduce you to the King.'

I gulped a little as Hugh Bigod led me over to the King and told him about my family's background on the Great Crusade and my recent exploits. I addressed the King in Norman, which pleased him, and was sorely tempted to reveal all the details of my family's role in the English Revolt and our support for Henry's brother, Robert, at the Battle of Tinchebrai. But I thought better of it – there was no point condemning myself in the eyes of the King at the first meeting.

Then Hugh Bigod made an audacious suggestion.

'Sire, while you are here in Norwich, may I recommend Harold as a member of your bodyguard. He is a child of this burgh, much admired by its people.'

The King looked at me with a questioning frown.

'The Earl is encouraging me to add Englishmen to my bodyguard and retinue. He likes the English. I suppose I do as well, but most are a mystery to me. You speak excellent Norman. Where did you learn it so well?'

'It is a long story, sire. A very long story.'

'Is it? Very well – the Earl wants me to stay here for a month, God help me! You will have plenty of time to tell me your story.'

So, to Eadmer's consternation and to my surprise, I was unexpectedly a member of the hearthtroop of England's Norman ruler – a son of William the Bastard and a man against whom I had conspired only a few years earlier.

Eadmer was, as usual, blunt in his response.

'I thought we were heading north to find the true heir to the English throne. Yet now we're part of the personal bodyguard of our Norman King – the son of the Conqueror!'

'Well, I was not exactly in a position to refuse – especially after you'd told the Earl about our exploits on behalf of the Venetians. And remember, my grandfather was in the service of the Normans – and even William himself. And the King's brother, Duke Robert, is the other surviving member of the Brethren of the Blood of the Talisman.'

'And we're also Knights Templar! It's all too complicated for me – it's little wonder we're always in trouble!'

'Let's just keep our heads down while the King is in Norwich. We may hear something about his daughter, Matilda. If it's true that she has been declared his successor, then we will have a Cerdician queen on the throne.'

'But she is also a Norman!'

'Of course – but half a body of Cerdician blood is better than none at all. And not only that: her uncle is Prince Edgar, and she may allow him to return to court. She may even free Duke Robert.'

'But the King isn't dead yet . . .'

'No, my friend, but he will be one day!'

During our time with the King, we saw little of him. My main role was to present an English face to the people of Norwich as part of the King's retinue, which included stewards, apothecaries and physicians. While we helped the Earl and the Bishop restore normal life to the ravaged burgh of Norwich, the King spent most of his time hunting. But he was in good humour, and whenever he passed through the streets and along the roads, he smiled duti-fully and offered words of support and encouragement.

As for information about the Empress Matilda, we heard little. However, we did hear a good deal more about the problems the King had been having in Normandy.

Duke Robert's son, William Clito – a prodigious young man in his mid-twenties, his only child with the lovely Sybilla of Conversano – had already led two rebellions of disenchanted Norman lords against the King and each time had won the support of the King of France and the Count of Flanders. Clito's rebellions were the main rea-son why the King refused to release his father from captivity in Cardiff – in fact, many people thought it was surprising that the King had not had Robert executed in retaliation for Clito's behaviour.

Clito had a strong claim to the throne – especially among those Norman families that remained loyal to his father, Duke Robert. This claim had been strengthened significantly when King Henry's only legitimate son, Wil-liam Adelin, was drowned in the White Ship disaster in 1120.

The news about the activities of William Clito made me reflect on the sad circumstances of Duke Robert's imprisonment. Twenty years of incarceration must have been a living hell for Robert. Once Duke of mighty Nor-mandy, and a hero of the Great Crusade, he had spent the last decades of his life languishing in an austere and remote keep on the fringes of the kingdom. I thought long and hard about how I might be able to see him and at least take him some news of my mother and the exploits of his son. I hoped that my role as a knight with the King's bodyguard might offer at least the beginnings of an opportunity.

I could sense the King becoming impatient with his mission to Norwich during its third week. He had hunted almost every day and had clearly become bored with the surrounding countryside and its game. I recommended Foxley Wood to him, an area of ancient forest I knew well, about twenty miles north of Norwich on the road to Fakenham. I knew the hunting was good there and would offer the King fine sport. He decided to ride out, accompanied by his retinue. He enjoyed an excellent day's hunting, and stayed overnight.

After supper, the King called me over and asked me to tell him the story of my adventures in Venice and the Holy Land. I made the account as brief and as lively as possible, which he seemed to find interesting, and I then explained to him that my mother had been part of Edgar the Atheling's English contingent on the Great Crusade. I added that I was about to journey to the north to find him and inform him of my mother's death.

The King smiled at me.

'He's not easy to find. He lives at the ends of the earth – a desolate place called Ashgyll Force, in Northumbria. He was a good friend of my brother; I like to know where he is at all times, so that I can keep an eye on him.'

'Thank you, sire.'

'You can send him my greetings. He was very obliging to me in arranging my first marriage to his niece, Edith. And he helped draft my Coronation Charter.'

'It would be an honour, sire.'

Hugh Bigod then told the King more detail about my

mother and her work as a churchwright, which led to the usual complications about my 'real' mother, Adela, and her time fighting in the Great Crusade with my father. Yet again, I went through the contrived story that I had told so many times about Estrith and Adela and which of them was my birth mother. But as I did so, I could see Bishop Everard whispering in the King's ear. The new bishop was an unknown quantity to me. He was an English-born Norman of modest birth from Wiltshire; he had the look of a weasel about him and made me feel uneasy. I was right to be concerned. The Bishop had not gone hunting but had stayed in the camp, drinking mead, and had clearly consumed a large quantity of it.

The King's mood darkened as he spoke.

'My Lord Bishop tells me that he was your mother's confessor before her recent death.'

I glanced at Hugh Bigod, who looked worried.

'Apparently, the estimable Estrith, Abbess of Fécamp, was your birth mother after all. Not only that, she was a woman of . . . let's say . . . some spirit.'

'Sire, forgive me, I am at a disadvantage here. But whatever was said by Estrith on her deathbed should be between her and her Maker.'

Hugh Bigod came to my defence.

'I agree, sire – this is a private matter. The good woman, who saved many lives in the Holy Land, is not long in the ground.'

The King looked at Bishop Everard. Rather than relenting, the prelate just smirked.

'It is not a private matter if it involves a threat to the King himself.'

I began to look around, to see if I could locate Eadmer and our horses. He had also sensed danger and now caught my eye. He nodded in the direction of the trees to the west.

The Bishop continued.

'The title "Abbess of Fécamp" was given to her by the King's shamed brother, Robert, as a contrivance. She had never even been to the nunnery. Is it not also true that you were conceived out of wedlock in the desert and that the story you've just told us about the woman Adela is a lie?'

I had little option but to now speak the truth.

'My Lord King, my mother was a remarkable woman. She was ordained, but her passion was church architecture – and in order to pursue that, she hid behind her nun's habit. I make no apologies for that. Yes, I was conceived in the desert, in extremis, when my parents faced almost certain death. But it was in a tender and loving tryst with my noble father, Sweyn of Bourne. I make no apologies for that either.'

The Bishop was now warming to his devilment.

'Talking of your father, I have been making some inquiries. Is there not another family connection in Bourne? Your father was Sweyn of that village, but your mother, Estrith, was one of a pair of twins, the other being Gunnhild. Were they not Estrith and Gunnhild of Melfi?'

'They were, my Lord.'

I managed to remain courteous, but I could feel a great swell of rage rising in me. I was tempted to draw my sword and bring a painful end to the Bishop's tirade.

'Were they not the daughters of Hereward of Bourne,

the infamous outlaw – a man who had the temerity to challenge the King's father, our mighty lord, William, Conqueror of the English?'

The King's face blackened in fury. Hugh Bigod looked down at the ground in despair.

'There is more, my Lord King. This man's father fought with your brother against you at Tinchebrai. I am sure he is an infiltrator in your camp. There has been trouble in Norwich before – from the English masons, his friends. I would swear on the Bible that he was one of the conspirators.'

Hugh Bigod made one last attempt to defend me.

'That's nonsense! I recommended Harold –'

But the King raised his hand to stop the Earl in mid-sentence, and I saw him gesture to his constable on his right. I took my only chance and made a run for it. It was dusk and if I could make it to the trees, I had a chance. Chaos broke out behind me as men barked orders, swords were drawn from scabbards and horses were untethered. Eadmer was right in front of me and I followed him as he disappeared into the undergrowth.

Arrows imbedded themselves in trees all around us and I felt at least two cut through the air close to me. Our horses were only fifteen yards away. We covered the ground at breakneck speed before mounting in a single bound. But, as we did so, four mounted knights burst through the undergrowth and were soon on top of us, swords drawn.

Fortunately, my horse reared up in panic and stalled the Normans' charge, which bought me a few vital seconds to raise my axe. I caught my nearest adversary with a heavy blow into his left shoulder. His mail coat absorbed some of the blow, but I could feel my blade sink into the soft flesh beneath, which immediately began to spew blood through the mangled rings of his armour.

He stared at me with a look of surprise – shocked that I had been able to strike him so quickly. But his expression immediately changed to one of horror as the pain I had inflicted, delayed for an instant, told him how badly he was hurt. He began to turn his head to stare at his wound. But before he could complete the action, he fell from his mount and landed in a tangled heap on the ground.

Eadmer had managed to put ten yards between himself and our opponents. While I tried to find a way to extricate myself from the three surviving knights, an arrow from Eadmer's bow whistled past my horse's ear and hit one of them square in the chest. At that range, even with the protection of good-quality mail, the arrow must have embedded itself deeply into the man's body. He too hit the ground with a heavy thud.

One of the two remaining knights grabbed my reins, but a well-aimed blow from my axe took off his hand at the wrist, while Eadmer's fearsome charge in our direction persuaded the stricken man's comrade to lead his horse away rather than continue the skirmish.

We could hear more pursuers approaching at a gallop and so turned to make our escape. We knew Foxley Wood well and were easily able to outpace them.

Eadmer waited until we were out of immediate danger to state the obvious.

'You should listen to me sometimes!'

'I know. Perhaps next time . . .'

'I knew it would get us into trouble; now we are fugitives in our own land.'

Two days later, we were moving north on the ancient road to York at Falkingham. I had never been beyond the Trent before and was amazed at the difference between my home in East Anglia and the north.

Apart from the major roads and burghs, where there was a semblance of normality, the countryside was devoid of life; villages were derelict and fields were overgrown, slowly returning to wilderness. I had heard about King William's atrocities in the northern earldoms, and now here was the stark evidence before my eyes. Even on the main roads, people travelled warily and stories abounded of outlaws and brigands hiding in the wildwood beyond the reach of Norman law.

Thoughtfully, Eadmer waited a few days before raising the subject of what he had heard in Foxley Wood.

'I always knew Abbess Estrith was a remarkable woman and that your family had had many adventures. But I would never have guessed any of what I heard –'

'I find it hard to believe myself sometimes. At least there is now no need for secrecy any more.'

'How many more twists and turns are there?'

'A few, my friend.'

I smiled at my good and loyal companion.

He smiled back, but followed it with a typical rejoinder.

'I'm sure there are. And I'm sure they will get us into all kinds of trouble!'

I knew we had to reach Ashgyll Force quickly – I

gambled that the King would assume I did not have the audacity to travel to see Prince Edgar, having told him of my original destination. I soon realized the King had been right: Ashgyll Force was at the edge of the world, in one of the most godforsaken places I had ever seen. High in the Pennines, we followed the River Wear west from Durham, via the small hamlet of Wolsingham, and left any semblance of civilization at Frosterley, where a few intrepid miners still dug for the local marble. After their meagre cottages disappeared behind us, there was nothing but thick forest, eventually giving way to bleak windswept moorland. It was mid-summer, but the rain came down in swirling clouds – even a warm sunny day became swallowed in a dank gloom of mist within minutes.

In order to protect Prince Edgar, I left Eadmer with the horses about a mile away and approached Ashgyll Force in the middle of the night. It was important not to be seen – or to leave any evidence of our visit.

The Prince was asleep when I clambered into his chamber. I was careful not to alarm him. When he eventually woke with a jolt, I spoke softly to him.

'Prince Edgar, don't be concerned, I am Harold of Hereford.'

'You mean young Harry? Son of Estrith of Melfi and Sweyn of Bourne?'

'Indeed, sire.'

'Show yourself!'

'I cannot, my anonymity is important to me and to you. I need to tell you some things as a fellow member of the Brethren of the Blood and obtain your blessing for what

I have done and am about to do. My mother made me a full member of our Brethren when I came of age; she said you would be in agreement.'

'The monks of Durham brought me the news two days ago that your mother has died –'

'Scarlet fever; it devastated Norwich while I was away. She was a wonderful mentor to me and told me all about the Brethren and your lives together. She was content with her lot, and her work was everything to her. She took great pride in helping the great cathedral grow.'

'Did she give you the casket?'

'She did. That's why I'm here – to thank you for the endowment and the gift of land, and also to seek your permission. Duke Robert is still in Cardiff Castle and no one can see him. You and I are the only members of the Brethren at liberty, and I need your sanction . . .'

I was aware that I didn't have much time; I had vexed the King, who would surely be searching every shire in the land to hunt me down.

'I have decided to leave for Constantinople and the Peloponnese as soon as the winds are favourable. My mother told me where my grandfather's mountain eyrie is. I am going to see it, to spend some time and reflect there. I am sure he is long dead and buried, but I want to be sure he is properly in the ground. I am also going to see the Emperor, John Comnenus, to thank him for his father's very generous legacy. My mother told me he will give me the fabled Talisman of Truth and ask me to be its guardian.'

'You don't need my agreement for any of that.'

'I know, but my purpose in coming here is to tell you of a new Brotherhood . . .'

I recounted the oath I had sworn as a founder member of the Knights Templar, and told Prince Edgar of the men whose valour and virtue had attracted me to the Order.

'We wear the cross of Christ and are sworn to poverty, chastity, piety and obedience in the service of God and our fellow men. We are strong supporters of the Mos Militum, the code of chivalry that all knights should follow.'

'It sounds very worthy, but a little strict! I wish you every success.'

'Thank you. I confess, I have some doubts about my vocation to follow the code, but I hope to resolve them soon.'

I had one last question for the Prince: he had been there when my father died, and I needed to know that he had died bravely – a noble knight, just like my grand-father.

'He did; he took a lance intended for Duke Robert. Your father was a very brave man; it was my honour to know him.'

For about an hour, the Prince offered me his precious memories of my family, and as much wisdom from his life as he could. At the end, he gave me his blessing and one very important piece of advice.

'Wherever your destiny takes you and whatever it leads you to do, always remember your past and the legacy you have inherited. It will not only be your guide, it will also bring meaning to your life and to the lives of those who follow you. Your grandfather once told me that that was the message he had learned from the Talisman of Truth.

When the Emperor, John Comnenus, passes it on to you, I'm sure he will help you understand the wisdom of that message. Go carefully, Harold of Hereford.'

I left Prince Edgar's remote hall feeling rejuvenated. Although I had lost my mother and was a fugitive in my homeland, I felt that I had been handed my family's mantle of responsibility.

Eadmer was waiting patiently for me where I had left him.

'I don't like this place. It puts the fear of God into me.'

'I agree, it's not the most welcoming of places.'

'I feel I've had eyes on me since we arrived. Let's make haste to Durham.'

The sun was just cresting the hilltops as we rode downstream eastwards. Then Eadmer saw a figure silhouetted by the sun.

'Look, there!'

Standing alone, no more than fifteen yards away, was a motionless figure. He wore a simple grey robe of wool, tied at the waist. His long grey hair and beard almost obscured a heavy silver chain and amulet around his neck, while in his right hand he held a long oak staff topped by a ram's skull crowned by enormous horns. He stared at us, unmoving.

'He's a Celt; he looks like a Druid. Let's keep moving!'

I wished him a good morning in Celtic.

'*Bore da, syr.*'

After a moment, he offered us a slight nod of his head. We rode on, but when I looked back over my shoulder, he was gone.

Eadmer was relieved.

'I really don't like this place. They say the Celts will cut off your head and stick it on a pole.'

'I share your unease; I'll feel better when we've reached Wolsingham.'

Constantinople had to be my next port of call – and I intended wasting no time getting there.

We followed the River Wear all the way to Monkswearmouth, from where we found a succession of trading boats and worked our way down the east coast until we reached Wivenhoe in Essex. A busy port with regular trade to the Low Countries, we paid for passage on a ship bound for Antwerp.

As we had previously travelled to the south through the lands of the Franks and across the Alps, this time we decided to take a more easterly route. We journeyed through the Germanic lands of the Holy Roman Empire, a vast domain stretching from the cool North Sea to the warm Mediterranean. It contained a myriad of tribes and languages: some of its people were pale of skin and spoke tongues not unlike the Norse of my ancestors, while others were swarthy and had languages akin to the Veneto I had learned in Venice.

Rather than buy horses in Antwerp, we sailed north to the mouth of the Rhine and used its trading barges to travel upstream through Lotharingia and Swabia, joining the Neckar at Mannheim before travelling overland to Ulm, where we were able to join the Danube. Our progress was leisurely: the great cities of Vienna and Budapest alternated with remote forests and towering crags. We stopped several times to admire the different cultures and customs of the countless fiefdoms we passed through. Sometimes we stayed just a day or two, but on other occasions – in fascinating locations such as Linz, Bratislava and Belgrade – we stayed far longer.

The only constant was the boatmen – and their cargoes, an endless caravan of every conceivable form of artefact, chattel and merchandise. We saw sacks of grain and butts of wine, crates of timber and wool, tethered animals of every species, and human traffic by the score.

It was the turn of the year by the time we were disgorged into the Black Sea and another week before we were sailing through the Bosphorus, with the dome of the magnificent Hagia Sophia in sight.

17. Birthplace

Everything I had been told about Constantinople turned out to be true – except that not even the most redolent words could equal the breathtaking impact of the city's first impressions. The mighty walls – the largest in the known world, with nine major gates – were said to be big enough to allow an entire army to be positioned on them. Its palaces and churches were larger and grander than anywhere else. Its hippodrome could hold 100,000 people in a city that was said to house half a million people.

The city's greatest glory is the Hagia Sophia, the finest building in the world, a place where my grandmother, Torfida, had exchanged ideas with Christendom's most learned men, and which she had described as 'heaven on earth'. Said to be over 500 years old by the time she saw it, my mother said that the dome of the great church was a masterpiece of architecture, based on calculations Torfida understood and had explained to her, but ones that no mason she had ever met would attempt to replicate in stone.

After several days wondering at the sights of the city and enjoying its food and wine, we made our way to its north-west corner, to the Blachernae, the Emperor's private residence hard against and high above its impregnable walls – the place where I was born.

Cooled by fresh winds from the Golden Horn, the present emperor's father, Alexius I, had decided to move to the Blachernae during his reign to escape the heat and dust of the Great Palace in the centre of the city. Of course I had no recollection of the palace; as I stood outside its marbled entrance, an awestruck stranger from a distant land, it was hard to imagine that I had taken my first breaths inside its walls.

The entrance was guarded by two sentries who, from their appearance and armour, must have been Varangians, the legendary personal bodyguards to the Emperor. Exceptionally tall, the one fair and the other red-headed, they looked like battle-hardened Norse Berserkers or Saxon housecarls. Indeed, most recruits to the Guard hailed from northern Europe, including the few housecarls who had survived Senlac Ridge with King Harold. Eadmer nodded at the guards and spoke to them in English and then in Norse, but they ignored him – they were too disciplined to converse while on duty.

A bailiff and two young assistants sat under a canopy outside the gates, surrounded by a melee of supplicants trying to gain access to the palace. We stood in what vaguely resembled a queue as I practised my Greek. After half an hour, I was at the front of the line of people.

'I am Harold of Hereford, Knight Commander of Venice. I wish to have an audience with His Majesty, the Emperor, John Comnenus.'

The Byzantine Empire was notable for many things, one of which was its labyrinthine bureaucracy. The bailiff had not looked up during the entire time we had been there – he was busy instead taking a log of the visitors – but he did when I spoke to him, and with a supercilious grin on his face.

'You have to have a lawyer to petition here. And even then, no one has an audience with the Emperor. Go to your local lord.'

'My grandfather was Hereward of Bourne, known here as Godwin of Ely, Captain of the Varangian Guard under the Emperor Alexius.'

The bailiff stopped grinning and everyone around us fell silent.

'Godwin of Ely is well known here. What is your business at the Blachernae?'

'I was born here. My mother, Estrith, Abbess of Fécamp, and her companion, Adela of Bourne, came here from the Great Crusade in the Holy Land to be cared for by the Emperor's physicians during her confinement.'

'And why do you need to see Emperor John?'

'His Imperial Majesty has been caring for something that belongs to my family. I am now its guardian and I have come to collect it.'

The bailiff was now more courteous and listening closely to what I had to say.

'And may I know what this something is?'

'It is called the Talisman of Truth.'

'Come back tomorrow, Sir Knight. I will speak to one of the assistants to the Papias. He runs the Palace and may be able to speak to the Nobilissimus, who has the Emperor's ear. You are fortunate that the Emperor is here. He is fighting two wars at the moment – against the Hungarians to the north and the Serbs to the west – we hardly see him in the city.'

'Thank you. I appreciate your kindness.'

As Eadmer and I turned to leave, one of the Varangian

Guards who had been so steadfastly silent spoke to us in English.

'Sir, did you say you were the grandson of Godwin of Ely? And that he and Hereward of Bourne, leader of the English Revolt, were one and the same?'

'I did.'

The two Varangians beamed at one another.

'My grandfather was at Senlac Ridge with King Harold.'

'And my grandfather was a housecarl with Morcar, Earl of Northumbria. He fought at Stamford Bridge against the Norse. Our families have been here for two generations. There are many English families; we still speak English to one another.'

I was thrilled to meet men whose grandfathers would have known Hereward.

'It is an honour to meet men from such noble English families.'

'No, sir, the honour is ours. To meet the grandson of a legend – in fact, two legends! May we shake your hand? I can't wait to tell the garrison.'

There were smiles and handshakes all round.

I suddenly realized that a huge weight had lifted from my shoulders. Now that the secrecy surrounding my birth was no longer necessary – and the Norman King of England was aware of our family history – the true accounts of our deeds over three generations could be known to all and sundry, and take their rightful place in the proud story of our nation.

We were back at the gates of the Blachernae very early the next morning, but had to wait until the middle of the afternoon for an answer from the bailiff. This time, he was not only polite but he actually bowed before addressing me.

'Sir Harold, the Nobilissimus will escort you to the Emperor's Audience Room in one hour. The Varangians will take you into the palace.'

With that, the two Englishmen we had met yesterday appeared, thumped their chests with the closed fist of the Varangians' salute and strode through the gates ahead of us. Their long strides made us hurry, but I wanted to linger and admire the gleaming marble. I had seen marble before – as statues and high altars – but in the Blachernae the walls and floors were solid marble, as far as the eye could see, both outside and inside its sumptuous rooms. Carpets and tapestries the length of ten men were everywhere, as were gold, ivory, jade and polished wood of every hue.

In a room decorated from floor to ceiling with mosaics of past emperors, the Nobilissimus – a slight man with a wispy beard that led me to wonder whether he was a eunuch – greeted us with a nod of acknowledgement and beckoned to us to sit on a pair of gilded chairs.

'The Emperor will be here in a while. He leaves for the Hungarian campaign in the morning; there is much to do. He will not be able to give you more than fifteen minutes.'

With our Varangians standing guard, we were left to gaze at the astonishingly lifelike mosaics. Wine, fresh lemon juice, bowls of fruit and cool towels appeared from time to time – all brought with an unruffled reverence by young servants. They were dressed in fine silk cream-coloured smocks, pale-blue braccae trousers, tied at the waist and ankles with cords, and the delicate chamois-leather slippers worn by all the Emperor's household.

The refreshments were welcome and helped pass the time until the Emperor appeared. The low sun of an impending dusk filled the room with a golden light when the doors to John Comnenus' private apartments opened with a flourish.

Preceded by a pair of Varangians and followed by a host of stewards and servants, the most powerful man in Christendom drifted into the room in the long imperial purple robe of his office. With him was the other John about whom I had heard so much – John Azoukh, the handsome and beguiling Seljuk slave, adopted by the Emperor's father to be his lifelong companion.

While Azoukh, the slave by birth, looked every inch an emperor – with a profile that would grace any noble bust or coin of the realm – Comnenus, the Emperor by birth, was short, leathery-skinned, rather portly and some way short of handsome. Both were smiling from ear to ear as Eadmer and I sprang from our chairs.

We bowed deeply to our hosts.

John Comnenus, a man revered by his subjects and already held in even greater esteem than his illustrious father, grabbed me by the shoulders and pulled me upright.

'Harold of Hereford, what a pleasure to see you. I'm so sorry to have kept you waiting. Let me introduce Lord John Azoukh, my Grand Domestic, Commander in Chief of my armies.'

'My Lord Emperor, it is an honour to meet you. This is Eadmer, my sergeant-at-arms. I have heard so much about you and your father from my mother.'

'I was a little young at the time when your parents and their companions were here – a boy of eleven, perhaps twelve – but you are now the third generation of your famous family that I have met.'

'You flatter me, sire – especially coming from a Comneni Emperor, the most respected rulers in Christendom.'

'If I remember correctly, you were born here in the Blachernae ... something about a furtive birth, because your mother had taken Holy Orders?'

'Indeed, sire, it is a complicated story. But your father was very generous in allowing me to be born here in secret.'

'Come sit with me. I want to talk about the noble Godwin of Ely, as we know him – your grandfather, Hereward of Bourne. I will have to be brief, because my commanders are fretting about the readiness of the army.'

Despite the pressure on his time, John Comnenus sat for over forty minutes and described how, nine years earlier – which, bizarrely, was about the time I was setting sail for the Holy Land with the Lady Livia – he and John Azoukh had travelled to the Western Peloponnese to meet my grandfather.

'My father, Alexius, who had been Emperor for almost forty years, was dying, slowly and painfully. I was thirty years old, but my father thought I had led a sheltered life and lacked the wisdom and courage that came from struggle and adversity. He gave me an amulet that your grandfather had given to him when they became friends.'

'The Talisman of Truth, sire. I have heard so much about it.'

'My father told me that Godwin of Ely, who had served

as Captain of his Varangians for many years, was the most worthy man he had ever met and that I should hear his story and learn from it. So, armed with the amulet, Prince John and I went to meet him in his mountain lair, guided by the local priest. Your grandfather was very old – I think he said he was over eighty – but he still had the aura of a mighty warrior and the presence of a sage. He told us the story of his amazing life and held us enthralled for three days. He said he had been waiting for our visit and that it would draw his life to a fitting end. I was very moved by the whole experience, as was Prince John.'

'Yes, the Emperor is right. I will never forget our time with your grandfather – he was not only the greatest warrior Byzantium has ever had, he also possessed the wisdom of a seer. Wisdom and courage run in your family, you should be very proud.'

'My Lord Prince, you are very kind.'

The Emperor began to look at his stewards. Time was passing.

'Forgive me, but we must be on the road to the north early in the morning. So let me complete my account; I think it will give you great comfort. After your grandfather had finished his story, he died peacefully and contentedly, as if a great weight had been lifted from him. The final words he said to me were written down and have guided me throughout my reign.'

One of the Emperor's stewards handed him a scroll, which he began to read.

'"You have made a good beginning, my Prince. Your father is a great Emperor and an even better man. You seem to have many of his qualities. Follow his advice, live by his example, and you will become a worthy successor. Byzantium will flourish under your reign and you will leave a legacy that will be remembered for generations to come. But remember, you are only a man. Even Emperors are mortal. Lives – even great ones – soon become memories. Learn from the past, but live your life in the present, and hope that the future will benefit from what you do on earth. Remember, once your time is over, it has gone forever."

'We organized an honour guard for the funeral. Your grandfather was buried facing north-west, towards the England he talked about so fondly. Men of the Varangian Guard dug a deep grave, so that he would never be disturbed, and so that we could place in it all his precious belongings. The priest, a fine man called Leo of Methone, blessed each one as it was arranged around his body.

'Each of the Varangians present then took it in turns to cover the body with the parched earth of his beloved mountain, and Prince John placed a simple wreath of olive leaves on the grave. Afterwards, we ordered that everything on the hilltop be destroyed so that, in keeping with his oath to King William, no trace of his final resting place would ever be found. Leo of Methone then read an epitaph: "Here lies Godwin of Ely, known in a previous life as Hereward of Bourne. No nobler man has ever lived. May he rest in peace."'

I wept openly as the Emperor described my grandfather's resting place at the end of his life's long adventure. There were also tears in the eyes of the 'Two Johns of Constantinople', as they were popularly known. Each stepped forward and embraced me warmly.

The Emperor then beckoned to one of his stewards to step forward.

'We were going to bury this with your grandfather. But at the last moment, I changed my mind. Your grandfather sacrificed so much in its cause; I must have known that this day would come and someone would arrive to be its new guardian.'

The Emperor handed me a small pouch of soft leather. It was the Talisman.

My mother's detailed description of it came flooding back to me: 'Hanging from a heavy silver chain, it is a translucent stone the size of a quail's egg. Set in scrolls of silver, each of which is a filigree snake so finely worked that the oval eyes and forked tongues of the serpents can be seen in detail, the stone is yellow in colour and, at first glance, apart from its size and smoothness, seems unremarkable. But when held to the light, silhouetted in the baleful yellow glow of the stone is the face of Satan, the horned beast that has haunted men from the beginning of time. Close to the hideous face, trapped in the stone like the Devil's familiars, are a tiny spider and a group of small winged insects.' It was the most remarkable object; I felt overawed and unsure what to do with it.

The Emperor saw me hesitate and smiled at me.

'The Talisman of Truth has a new guardian. Why don't you wear it?'

It was the obvious thing to do. But such was its amazing pedigree, it hadn't occurred to me.

The Emperor took back the Talisman and, as I leaned forward, he placed it over my head, saying these words.

'Harold of Hereford, Guardian of the Talisman of

Truth, may it lead you to your destiny and a long and happy life.'

'Thank you, sire.'

'I have one final thought: before we left, I remember looking towards the north-west and saying to Prince John that I would like to go to England one day. Your grandfather had spoken very eloquently of the Wodewose of England's wildwoods. Would you like to go back to your grandfather's eyrie to see if the Wodewose protects his grave?'

'I would indeed, sire.'

'I will arrange for an escort for you – local men from the Peloponnesian theme. They will take you to the Governor of Messene, Basil of Nemea. He is a good man and will give you a guide to take you up the mountain. I hope Leo of Methone is still there. He will be able to tell you much more about your grandfather's life.'

'Sire, I am most grateful to you. Your kindness is more than generous.'

'Not at all. Thanks to your grandfather, I came to understand what courage and wisdom mean – and that they have to be earned.'

'Indeed, sire, my journey is only just beginning.'

'I'm sure it will be a successful one. When you get to your grandfather's resting place, the grave is not marked, but it is easy to find. You will see a small plateau in front of the rocks against which he built his shelter, and over by the lake a semi-circle of rocks breaking the ground, where we sat to hear his story. To the right of that, three strides away, is a hollow big enough for a man; that is where he lies. Give him my warmest greetings when you get there.'

'And mine', added John Azoukh.

'I will, sire.'

'One more thing, Harold of Hereford.'

The Emperor handed me a small casket.

'My father gave you a small dowry when you were a child. This is for your child – it is the least I can do for a family that has meant so much to my own family. When your child becomes the Guardian of the Talisman, he or she will need it. And remember, you and your family will always be welcome here.'

I knelt, kissed the imperial ring of John Comnenus, and bowed deeply to Prince John Azoukh.

As the two men left, I reflected that I had met earls, princes and doges, then kings and now an emperor. What next? I wondered as Eadmer and I were escorted out of the Blachernae.

John Comnenus had provided a small troop of Peloponnesian escorts – twelve good men, well armed and immaculately turned out – and we sailed for Messene, a port on the south coast of the Peloponnese.

My grandfather had chosen one of the most remote places in the Empire for his retirement refuge. He had led the Varangian Guard in a great victory against the Pechenegs at Levunium in 1091, after which he was garlanded through the streets of Constantinople. He was fifty-five years old by then and his many injuries, scars and broken bones were getting the better of his ageing body. His eyesight was not as keen as it once was, and his reactions were slowing. Alexius wanted to award Hereward a huge pension and vast estates in gratitude for his faithful service. He refused the offer, content with a modest casket of silver and a small plot of land in the western Peloponnese that was entirely virgin territory, almost all of which comprised Mount Foloi – a heavily wooded, rugged mountain with commanding views to the west and out to sea.

Some fifty miles north from Messene, it was both a picturesque and nostalgic journey. We crossed hills thick with forests of pine and deep river valleys that trickled water down to the sea in summer but were torrents in the winter. Of all the family shrines I had visited – whether the several in England or the family graves in the Lot – this was the last and most important.

When we arrived at the little church in the clearing at the foot of the mountain, it was just as my mother had described it: a plain stone chapel at the edge of a glade with small round windows, a solid oak door and a simple wooden hut behind the nave for the resident priest.

Governor Basil had given us a man who knew the mountains well. He told us that Leo of Methone was still in residence, but that he was now quite old and not as much in control of his faculties as he had once been. We called out for him. Our escort dismounted and began to scour the church and its surroundings for the priest.

After a few minutes, Leo appeared from the woods with his head covered in fine muslin. He was carrying several honeycombs, and muttering to himself.

'Honey – good for an old man's digestion!'

I walked up to him and offered my hand, but the old man walked straight past me.

'Good evening, Father. I am Harold of Hereford –'

I decided not to continue, as it was obvious that the old priest was unaware of my presence.

'Mixed with a little wine, makes me sleep.'

He then paused and walked away, back towards the woods he had come from, still gabbling at no one in particular.

'Pretty little bees, don't sting Father Leo. Pretty little bees . . .'

He was met by two local women, who took him tenderly by the arm and led him towards his simple wooden shelter. One of them looked as muddled as the old priest, while the other had the appearance of a witch, with long grey hair halfway down her back. She spoke bluntly to me.

'Don't mind him. He's a holy man, just a bit confused.'

'I understand. Please take good care of him. We are going to the top of Mount Foloi – we just thought we would tell Father Leo.'

'He won't mind. Help yourself, but it's a big climb. An old man from the far north used to live up there – a hermit, a man as big as a house, with scars on his scars. People say it's haunted. No one goes up there any more.'

'So I believe. We just want to survey the summit; the Governor may want to build a lookout there.'

'Suit yourself. But beware, these hills are sacred places; the oak forests over there are the home of centaurs and sprites. You should stay away from there, not even imperial troops can protect you from the mighty creatures. The sprites will lure you with pretty girls, but they belong to the centaurs who will hunt you down with arrows as long as a man.'

'What happened to the old hermit?'

'They say that a few years ago some imperial troops, like these men, came here and killed him because he was a necromancer who was riding with the centaurs and frightening the locals.'

Leaving the local women and a bewildered Leo of Methone in our wake, we made steady progress up Mount Foloi until, late in the day, we reached the flat top of the mountain. Everything that I had been told about my grandfather's special place was true. Even at dusk, far to the west, it was possible to see the sparkling iridescence of the Mediterranean. We seemed to be far above the clouds, and yet the air was only a little cooler than the boiling heat of the hot summer's day we had left lower down.

It was August 1127: how many scorching days like this did my grandfather endure? Perhaps he enjoyed them – after all, he had suffered far worse on his many campaigns for the Emperor. But what of the winter? At that height, abundant snows must have fallen on his modest shelter, and the nights must have been as cold as the frozen wastes of Hibernia. But he was used to that – he had survived winters in the icy Pennines and even led a campaign against William, Conqueror of the English, in the depths of one of England's harshest winters.

True to the Emperor's words, no trace of human occupation could be seen. The mountain looked as it must have done when Hereward first saw it: remote, tranquil and spellbindingly beautiful. If it was haunted, it was possessed by benign spirits. Perhaps the Wodewose, our Green Man of legend, did keep watch over England's fallen hero?

I could see all the places John Comnenus described and easily found the hollow where my grandfather's body lay. I approached it with some trepidation, like a pilgrim reaching his destination after years of steadfast travelling. We made camp and, while our escort busied themselves, I sat and stared at my grandfather's resting place.

I read John Comnenus' account of the words of advice he had been given by my grandfather: 'Lives – even great ones – soon become memories. Learn from the past, but live your life in the present, and hope that the future will benefit from what you do on earth. Remember, once your time is over, it has gone forever.'

I knew then what I had to do. I had completed my journeys in the footsteps of my family, now I had to return to England to find the path to my own destiny.

My dear Thibaud,

Spring is here in London — rejoice!

I don't think I could survive another winter like the one we have just had. Sadly, my health is not improving, and I'm feeling more and more lame.

Back to a man who knows more than most about the trials and tribulations of this earthly existence. I warn you, my friend, his account will spare no details in giving you the measure of Hugh de Payens, founder of the Knights Templars. As their Grand Master, he seems to encapsulate all that they have since become: superficially worthy and pious, but underneath dangerous zealots who obey no one but themselves. Use the information within these pages as you see fit to undermine the malign influence the Templars have within the Church; I certainly will.

Given the intimate details of the story at this point, I have made the decision to use only a single scribe for this part of Harold's story. I have chosen Father John; he is a good scribe and the finest of men. His discretion can be relied upon. With only one monk to write the account, I fear my pace has slowed down a little. But at least I have been getting a little more rest — I was often tempted to go on too long into the night by using the next scribe's stint with the quill. Mercifully, I am now getting some sleep.

But time is of the essence; onwards with my account.

Yours in God,
Gilbert

18. The White Tower

After leaving the Peloponnese and travelling via our safe haven at St Cirq Lapopie to check on the harvest, Eadmer and I reached England in March, 1128. All had been well on our estate and I travelled with a lightness of heart and sense of contentment, the like of which I had not experienced before. The bezants that John Comnenus had given me were sufficient to allow us to travel like lords and live luxurious lives, but, for the time being, we chose not to. We preferred to travel alone – in part, because I was still unsure about my sympathies for the values of the Knights Templar. I had neglected the task I had been charged with in Jerusalem and realized that one day there would have to be a reckoning. We were also renegades in England so when we arrived at Dover, we adopted new identities as mercenaries from Aquitaine – Robyn of Hode and his sergeant-at-arms, William of Scaerlette, names I borrowed from villages in the dukedom.

Eadmer was still composing ballads and his singing was improving all the time. Not only was his voice soothingly melodious, but his lyrics were usually thoughtful and sometimes amusing. Most of his songs were based on our adventures – usually with a good deal of poetic licence – and included the 'Ballad of the Lonely Knight of Venice' and the 'Ballad of the Siege of Tyre', in both of which

Eadmer, the doughty sergeant-at-arms, was at least as much of a hero as Hal, the worthy knight.

London was agog with stories when we arrived. King Henry had secured a marriage arrangement with Fulk, the Count of Anjou, for his widowed daughter, the Empress Matilda, to marry Fulk's son and heir, Geoffrey. Although he was only a boy of fifteen, he was handsome and virile and, it was assumed, would produce a son and heir to continue the Norman dynasty. An alliance with Anjou and Maine was also vital to the defence of the King's hold over Normandy – especially in view of the persistent threats from William Clito.

There had been many suitors for Matilda's hand. An empress in name, still only twenty-six years old, and the nominated heir to the throne of an ageing King of England, she was the most coveted prize in Europe. Besides all those inducements, she was also a woman of great beauty and charm and had a fine mind and ready wit. Princes and lords came from realms far and wide, but the King turned them all away. He knew what he wanted – a son that suited his purposes and an alliance with Normandy's strongest neighbour. So it was done.

London also brought us news of our friends, the Knights Templar. I was still a Templar – indeed, a founding member – but I had managed to put them to the back of my mind. I had a new purpose now, and it was not focused on the zealotry of the Templars.

Hugh de Payens had been in England for some time and had become the source of fascination. The Order had firmly established itself as the military guardians of the Christian States of the Holy Land. As Grand Master,

Hugh had acquired almost messianic status in the minds of many; young men from all over Europe were rushing to become 'Knights of Legend', as they were being hailed. The Order's wealth had become immense. They had been granted lands, and some lords had even left their entire estates to the Templars in their wills, believing it would earn them forgiveness for all their sins in the Kingdom of Heaven.

The Grand Master had been all over England and Scotland accepting grants of land and money and collecting recruits. He had been to see King Henry, who had given him a cartload of gold and silver, the like of which had not been seen since the days of the Danegeld. According to the local gossip, Hugh was still in London with his new recruits and a vast fortune, staying in the crypt of the small Saxon church All Hallows by the Tower.

Although I was reluctant, I knew it was an ideal opportunity to bring to an end my relationship with the Templars. I also knew it might be a task fraught with danger. Hugh was a powerful man, made even more so by the Pope at the recent Council of Troyes, where he had granted the Templars their own Religious Rule as a fully fledged Order in the eyes of God and the Church.

I sought Eadmer's opinion. He was typically blunt.

'Stay away from him; it's a thing of the past, from another place. We've moved on.'

'But we'll have to deal with it sooner or later. The Templars have reached every corner of Europe.'

'You see! You've asked me my view, but you've already made your mind up.'

'I have – but it's always good to have your advice.'

I smiled at my friend, and he responded in his imperturbable way.

'So, let's get on with it. What's the plan?'

All Hallows was surrounded by young men busy going about their duties. It looked as though the Templars were preparing to leave.

I approached a senior knight, notable by his Templar's cross on his sleeve.

'Sir Knight, I am looking for the Grand Master. Would you know where I can find him?'

'And who are you, sir? And what is your business?'

'I am Harold of Hereford.'

He looked startled and all within earshot stopped what they were doing.

'Do you mean, Harold of Hereford? One of the nine founders of our Order?'

'I do.'

He immediately drew his sword, as did those around him.

'Harold the Heretic! The Grand Master warned us we may find you in England.'

I quickly took my cloak and wrapped it round his blade, before pulling him towards me and placing him in a firm headlock with my forearm at his throat. Eadmer held the others at arm's length with his sword as I prodded my captive's neck with the tip of my seax.

'Templar training is obviously not what it was, my friend. Where is he?'

The knight struggled, so I pushed harder with my blade until blood began to flow.

'*Where is he?*'

'He's in the White Tower . . . as a guest of King Henry.'

'Thank you. Now tell your men we're leaving. They're to stay here, do you understand?'

He did as I demanded, and we backed away with the knight still at my mercy. After a few yards, I pushed him to the ground and we made a dash for it down to the wharves by the Thames. We lost our pursuers amidst the crowds and found a tavern to hide in on Ludgate Hill.

Eadmer was quick to make his point.

'That went well! Now the Master knows we're here . . . and he'll send all those young fanatics to look for us.'

'Yes, but we know where he is.'

'So?'

'We're going to have a parlay with him.'

'Do you mean "we"? Or do you mean, you will have a parlay with him?'

'Very well, *I* will have a parlay with him, but *you* will have to help get me in.'

'Into the White Tower?'

'Yes, of course.'

'But it's the most impregnable fortress in Europe!'

'We can get in. We'll need a few heavy arrows, some lightweight cord, a thick rope, a grappling hook, some pieces of leather and a few handfuls of raw wool.'

'Oh, is that all?'

'No – we'll also need a large amount of good fortune!'

It was possible to buy anything along the wharves of London, so it did not take long to find what we needed.

We approached the White Tower at dusk. It was the middle of April, but still very cold, and I prayed that the Tower's sentries would spend more time huddled by their braziers than patrolling the walls. The sky was heavy with thick clouds and the dark of the moon was almost upon us. By midnight, almost all London's torches and lanterns had been extinguished; only the guards' fires gave glimmers of light at the gates and on the walls of London's immense fortress.

It had not taken Eadmer long to work out the plan. We first covered the teeth of the grappling hook with wool and bound leather to deaden the noise. We waited for the sentry to finish his regular walk around the battlements. Then, with the lightweight cord attached to it, Eadmer shot his heavy arrow over the corner of the battlements. We attached the grappling hook to one end of our heavy rope and tied the other end to the lighter cord. While Eadmer stayed to guide the hook, I then ran round the corner to retrieve the arrow. I pulled the ropes over the battlements until the hook caught on the top of the wall. The easy bit was done.

It was a long climb – the White Tower was at least seventy-five feet tall. I had taken care to knot the heavy rope at one-yard intervals; even so, I was at the limit of my endurance when I reached the top of the battlements. I quickly pulled up the rope and hid it and its hook before sitting down in a stairwell to rest my arms.

I guessed that Hugh de Payens would have been allocated one of the royal chambers on the top floor of the tower, so I made my way down the spiral stairs towards the royal apartments. The whole floor was in darkness, save for one door, from the bottom of which spilled a thin shaft of light. There was a guard at the end of the corridor, his face lit by a small candle in the sconce above his head, but he seemed to be asleep. As I listened at the door, I could hear Hugh's distinctive voice in jovial conversation with at least one other. I counted the doors and decided to make my entrance through the chamber's window.

I returned to the battlements, waited for the sentry to pass, then secured the rope in a position where it could not be readily seen and lowered myself to Hugh's window. The wooden shutter was ajar, with only a woollen curtain across the opening. As I seated myself on the sill of the window to peer inside, laughter came from within. I could see wine goblets and the residue of a fine meal on a table in the middle of the room. There were also clothes, armour and weapons strewn across the floor. From where I was, I could not see the bed, but the voices coming from that direction were now uttering the unmistakable groans and squeals of lustful passion. At first, I thought I had caught the Grand Master of the Knights Templar with a couple of young girls. But then I realized that, although they were high-pitched, the voices were male.

I barely had time to reflect on the utter hypocrisy that allowed the Order to rail against the sin of sodomy, when its leader was himself a sodomite! As unpleasant as it might be to confront him in such circumstances, I had been presented with all I needed for my parlay with the Grand Master. I jumped down from the window as quietly as I could, kicked the weapons on the floor to one side and drew my sword.

'Good evening, Grand Master; I think you may be looking for me. So I thought I would come to you –'

Hugh jumped to his feet like a startled rabbit. The two

boys on his bed, perhaps twelve or thirteen years old, grabbed some clothes from the floor and ran to the corner of the room. Hugh was breathing heavily but made no attempt to cover his still erect manhood as he looked around the room for his sword.

'Harold of Hereford! What a strange way to renew our acquaintance.'

'All normal courtesies were suspended as soon as one of your Templars drew a sword on me.'

'Don't you mean, one of *our* Templars?'

'No, I don't – I have relinquished my oath. And so should you! Wine, fine food, the luxury of the royal apartments, buggering little boys – it doesn't seem much like the frugal life of a Templar to me.'

'Withdrawal from our Order is not permitted.'

Hugh was still erect; he seemed to be enjoying the confrontation. I threw him his shirt and leggings.

'Cover yourself, you charlatan!'

'Let me explain, these boys have been led astray. I am punishing them; they will not sin again when I have finished with them.'

He leered at me.

'They won't be able to walk for a month, let alone engage in buggery.'

'I should kill you where you stand, you bastard!'

I stepped forward and stuck the blade of my sword just below his Adam's apple.

'We are going to have a concordat – call it a treaty of peace, or whatever you like. You call off your dogs and publicly disown me as a Templar, and I will leave the way I came in. I will keep what I've seen tonight as our secret to guarantee your side of the agreement. You will make the announcement at All Hallows tomorrow, and it is to be posted on the church door. Oh, and these boys are to leave here two minutes after I do. I will wait outside the gates to see that they do.'

Hugh hesitated, trying to think of a way out of his dilemma. I pressed my sword harder into his neck.

'Answer me, you pig!'

He looked incandescent with anger, but eventually relented.

'Agreed . . . but watch your back, Harold of Hereford, in more ways than one. If ever we meet again, I will take great pleasure in punishing you like I've punished these naughty boys.'

He gave a nauseating thrust of his hips, like a rutting animal.

'Then I will kill you.'

I so wanted to kill him. But if I did, I would be a renegade from the Order and hunted for the rest of my life.

'Mark my words, Hugh de Payens, if I ever see you again, I will be the one doing the killing.'

I left the White Tower as I had entered it, but with a descent a lot less arduous than the ascent. We waited for the boys to scurry away from the tower gate before I turned to Eadmer.

'Let's find a tavern that is still open. I need a drink.'

When I explained to Eadmer what had happened, he was as appalled as I was. But he was not surprised.

'All fanatics have dark secrets. The more fanatical they are, the darker the secrets.'

My friend was becoming quite the philosopher.

Thankfully, Hugh de Payens' threat was an empty one. Although I saw many Templars over the years, as the Order steadily grew in importance, the Grand Master returned to Palestine shortly after our encounter. I never saw him again and, as far as I know, he never returned to Europe.

A few years later, I heard that he had died in Jerusalem; I thanked God at the time, and still do. But I remain deeply concerned that the Templars retain so much power in our world.

19. Anjou

Matilda's marriage to Geoffrey of Anjou was due to take place in Le Mans, capital of Maine, on 17 June 1128, so Eadmer and I prepared to cross the Channel once more. But our departure was delayed by an extraordinary blizzard.

It had already been a harsh winter and London's streets still had deep mounds of grimy snow piled along them. With faces made despondent by months of cold dark days, its inhabitants still shuffled about their business in heavy cloaks and thick leggings. Easter Day fell very late, on 22 April, a time of the year that ought to have brought warmth and the vibrancy of spring. But late in the afternoon, in what had been a clear sky with a waning moon clearly visible as the sun set, a huge wave of heavy grey clouds appeared over the fields beyond Shoreditch. The first snows fell at dusk, and by midnight a blizzard raged with winds so strong they created drifts as high as a house.

It snowed for three days under skies so murky that the daylight hardly penetrated. Easter services were postponed for a week, and it took the city at least that long to dig itself back to some semblance of normality. Some priests said it was a portentous omen about the wisdom of the proposed wedding. Many people believed them, thinking it a shame that King Henry's beautiful daughter was again going to be married off to a foreigner.

Our journey to Dover on roads more like cesspits than thoroughfares was tedious, with carts submerged to their axles blocking the route at regular intervals. We eventually reached Le Mans in late May. The wedding was much heralded in Maine and Anjou; their young count was not only marrying an English princess who was heir to her father's throne, but also a woman who was already an empress.

The nuptials were a dazzling occasion. Presided over by Bishops Guy of Ploermel and John of Sees, the cathedral of St Julien was full to the rafters with the aristocracy of northern Europe and even a few from more southerly climes. I had never seen a royal wedding before and was amazed at the endless rows of crowns and coronets and jewels sufficient to fill several wine butts. All the ladies wore fine silk, and there was enough ermine on the shoulders of the men to use up a whole season's supply. Eadmer was required to watch with the throng outside the cathedral, but my chevalier's garb and status as Knight Commander of Venice got me a position on the cathedral's upper gallery, from where I could look down on the ostentatious ceremony below.

King Henry gave every guest a present of silk or jewellery and, to a joyous reception by the citizens, money was scattered through the streets of the city. There was a repeat performance in Angers, capital of Anjou, four days later. It had been decided that the newly-weds would live in Angers for the time being, as Geoffrey's father had renounced his title, thus allowing Geoffrey to become Count of Anjou.

Empress Matilda looked radiant. She was a little taller than her new husband, who still had the frame of a boy.

Handsome though he was, he had no stubble on his chin and the gossip among the populace was that he was unlikely to be able to consummate the marriage without the patient help of his new wife. Rumours that Matilda's marriage to the Emperor Henry had not been a happy one, or that she was barren, were also widespread.

The closest I got to the Empress was a distance of just a few yards as, later, she progressed through the city's streets. She had removed her veil and I could see her gentle English complexion and fair locks, swept back from her face in a braided chignon. Her hair was long, the colour of flax, and her eyes were bright blue. For a moment, I was sure she looked straight at me and I bowed my head. She was the epitome of a Saxon queen of the past, a true Cerdician, a daughter of Wessex. I decided there and then that I would do all in my power to ensure that she would ascend the throne and renew England's royal heritage.

Only a month after the wedding, my hopes for her succession were strengthened significantly by news from southern Flanders. Still encouraged by Louis VI of France, William Clito had been campaigning in Flanders all summer to the great annoyance of his uncle, King Henry. In June, with his Norman knights and French allies, William defeated a major rival, Thierry of Alsace, at the Battle of Axspoele, south of Bruges. The victory brought fresh momentum to his cause, and he was joined by his father-in-law, Godfrey, Duke of Brabant. In July, their two armies besieged Aalst. But during the course of the siege, William was wounded in the arm in a scuffle with a foot soldier. The wound became gangrenous and he died, at the age of twenty-five, on 28 July 1128. He left no children and was survived only by his imprisoned father, the hapless Robert Curthose.

Sad though it was to hear of the death of Duke Robert's only son, his demise made Matilda's claim to the throne seem unassailable – as long as she had her father's support.

Although I was confident about Matilda's prospects, I was less so about my own ability to further her cause. The reality was that she was the heir to the throne, while I was not only a lowly knight but also a renegade. I needed a plan, but none was forthcoming. So I decided that we would find a house in Angers and bide our time.

At the very least, an announcement of a royal pregnancy and an imminent heir to the throne was expected by the end of the year, thus completing Matilda's credentials for succession.

By Christmas 1128, there was still no news and stories began to circulate in the city that all was not well with the marriage. Arguments could be heard echoing around the keep of the royal palace, and the gossip among those who knew servants of the royal couple claimed that Geoffrey hardly ever went to Matilda's chamber.

January 1129 was a bitterly cold month, with heavy snowfall at its end. Despite the inhospitable conditions, it emerged that Count Geoffrey had gone hunting with a large entourage of drunken friends, leaving behind a morose and angry wife.

I tried to think of a plan to bluff my way into the castle. Things were not going as I had hoped: Matilda was supposed to produce a grandson for the King and I feared that, if she did not, he might look elsewhere for a successor. After all, he did have at least two dozen illegitimate offspring, several of whom were powerful landowners with titles and rich admirers.

Eadmer could smell trouble brewing.

'Hal, you need to be careful; we don't want another situation like we had with Lady Livia.'

'On the contrary! That would be ideal – to be given the responsibility for Matilda's welfare. The problem is, how do we make that happen?'

'You're mad – as mad as a March hare! Stay well away. We're renegades and have crossed her father, who happens to be the King. He's hardly going to entrust her care to us.'

'Let's wait and see.'

'Have you forgotten, she's also got a husband? Who happens to be the Count of this realm.'

'Yes, but I think he's a husband in name only.'

Eadmer was right, the prospect of us being able to help Matilda's cause seemed remote.

But two days later, a tiny crack in the door of opportunity opened. It was very early, not yet light, when I felt Eadmer shaking me by the shoulders.

'She's gone, half an hour ago. One of the kitchen girls told me. The girl shared my bed last night and was going to work when a carriage and four horsemen sped through the palace gates, heading north.'

'How does she know it was Matilda?'

'She saw her. Her belongings were in another carriage. The word is, she's going home to England.'

'With only four escorts? That's not possible –'

'That's what the girl said.'

'Good! We need to get a move on.'

'Are you suggesting we follow her?'

'Of course, someone needs to keep an eye on her.'

'I knew trouble was in the air. I have a bad feeling about this –'

'Come on! There's no time to spare.'

We paid our debts in Angers, gathered our belongings and made haste northwards. By the middle of the following day, we were close behind them. I was tempted to make direct contact with Matilda. But I decided to keep them within sight, yet maintain a respectful distance. I guessed that she would be both upset and anxious and would be further unnerved by the sudden intrusion of a stranger.

Matilda's party made steady progress through Anjou and Maine. But as we crossed into Normandy, south of Sées, two of her escort – one a hefty sergeant, the other a tall sinewy knight with a broken nose and several scars – rode back to confront us.

'Name yourselves!'

'I am Robyn of Hode and this is William of Scaerlette. We are from Aquitaine.'

'Why are you following us?'

'We are not following you. We are travelling to England – we have business there.'

'Well, travel another way.'

'We will choose our own route –'

'I said, go another way.'

'And I said, we will suit ourselves.'

The hefty sergeant drew his sword. Eadmer immediately

responded in kind and made his intentions very clear to the knight.

'Put your sword away, or I'll take your arm off!'

I told Eadmer to sheathe his sword, and spoke softly to the knight.

'Tell the Empress Matilda that my father fought with her uncle, Edgar the Atheling, in the Great Crusade and that he and I are the last of a Brotherhood, the only other survivor of which is her uncle, Robert, Duke of Normandy.'

'The Empress Matilda? You are mistaken ... we are escorting one of the Empress's ladies-in-waiting.'

'I see. Well, tell her ladyship what I just told you.'

The knight looked at me questioningly.

'What did you say your name was?'

'I am Robyn of Hode.'

The knight paused for a moment, before yanking his reins and riding back to the carriage. He was not gone for long. Within minutes, he was cantering back towards us.

'Come with me.'

By the time we reached the carriage, it had been pulled over into a clearing and the Empress had stepped out, helped by her escort and a lady-in-waiting.

We dismounted and bowed respectfully.

'I hear you know my uncle, Prince Edgar?'

'I do, ma'am.'

'How is he?'

'He was well when I saw him last, ma'am.'

'Which was when?'

'Ma'am, two years ago – at his hall in Ashgyll, in Northumbria.'

'My uncle is dead. Sadly, he died over the winter. Are you sure you knew him?'

'Certain, ma'am. He was well, though very old, when I saw him –'

'What is this about a Brotherhood?'

'Ma'am, the Prince and your uncle, Robert, Duke of Normandy, were part of a small group of brothers-in-arms, which included my father and mother. They fought in the Great Crusade together; Duke Robert and I are now the only survivors.'

'But you are too young to have been part of the Crusade.'

'Quite so, ma'am. I am the next generation.'

'Not much of a brotherhood then! Just you and an old man incarcerated by my brother?'

'I agree . . . but it is an elite group, and the membership rules are very strict.'

Matilda realized I was being sarcastic. She smiled, which was a great relief – I felt I had broken the ice.

'And you are Robyn of Hode?'

'No, ma'am, that is a subterfuge. I am Harold of Hereford. I'm afraid I upset your father; Eadmer, my loyal friend and sergeant, and I are on the run from the King's men.'

'My father is easily upset. What did you do?'

'We had just joined the King's bodyguard at Norwich when a mischievous Bishop revealed several things about my past and accused me of being an infiltrator.'

'And were you?'

'No, ma'am. I have my opinions, but I mean the King no harm.'

'What was it about your past that annoyed the King so greatly?'

'A number of things, ma'am. But mainly that I had not revealed the fact that my father fought with Prince Edgar and Duke Robert at Tinchebrai.'

'Ah, I understand. Your father's choice of allegiance will not easily be forgotten by the King. But, to the matter in hand: why are you following me?'

'Well, it is a little delicate . . . May we talk in private?'

'No, we must press on. I want to get to Alençon before nightfall. Stay back with your man, we can talk in the morning.'

I bowed as she got back into her carriage.

She was charming and composed, beautiful and intriguing, and I knew then that I had made the right decision in committing my future to her cause.

We followed her to the outskirts of Alençon, where her escort pulled over next to an inn. She must have spent the night in her carriage because we did not see her again until the next morning, when we were summoned to see her. Dressed in clothes no finer than those worn by a merchant's wife, with neither jewellery nor regalia, she was sitting by the side of the road on a small stool eating a leg of cold chicken. It was an incongruous image for Europe's only empress, but one that did not detract from her beauty or allure.

'Good morning. What are you calling yourself this morning – Harold of Hereford or Robyn of Hode?'

'Good morning, Your Majesty. I trust you slept well. Please call me Hal.'

'I slept very badly – my carriage is a form of transport,

not a bed. But needs must . . . So, to my question of last night: why are you following me?'

'Ma'am, may we stretch our legs? And then I can explain.'

She nodded at the captain of her escort who, I assumed, was an Englishman – rather than one of her husband's men. The captain divested me of my weapons and walked a few paces behind us as the Empress and I strolled gently along the old road south from Alençon. He was tense and suspicious and watched my every move.

'Your Majesty, I have been in Angers for several months, waiting for news of you.'

'Why? Are you one of those sad men who follows women around?'

I was not fooled by the Empress's apparent levity. I knew I would have to choose my words carefully if I was to earn her trust and respect.

'No . . . well, yes . . . but only you, ma'am.'

'So you are a madman?'

'I hope not, ma'am; let me explain. My grandfather was Hereward of Bourne, the leader of the English Revolt in 1069. There was an English Brotherhood at Ely, and that tradition was carried on by my father, Sweyn of Bourne. As a little boy, he was rescued by Hereward and brought up by his family and friends. My mother, Estrith of Melfi, Hereward's daughter, was with him at the end of the Siege of Ely. She and my father formed a new brotherhood – the Brethren of the Blood of the Talisman – with Prince Edgar and Robert of Normandy.'

'A very interesting family . . . and a very laudable story. But what has your secret society got to do with me?'

'Well, the Brethren are committed to certain principles. They each swore an oath on the shrine to St Etheldreda at Ely: to fight for justice and freedom wherever they are denied, and to give their lives in pursuit of liberty.'

'I still don't see why all that means you have been prowling around Angers like a voyeur . . .'

'Although your uncle was Duke of Normandy and a true and faithful Norman, he sympathized with the claim of Prince Edgar, your English uncle, to the throne at Westminster. The Brethren believed that Norman rule in England was inherently unjust and unnecessarily harsh and would not be put right until a Cerdician monarch returned to the throne at Westminster –'

'And I have that Cerdician blood through my mother!'

'Yes, ma'am – you are a direct descendent from Edmund Ironside and all who preceded him.'

'So you are following me to protect me?'

'Yes, ma'am,' I fell to my knees and grasped her hand, 'and to declare my unwavering loyalty. Three generations of my family have fought for liberty. If you will have me, I would like to continue their courageous tradition by serving you and making sure that your father's wish that you become Queen is fulfilled.'

'That's quite a speech, Harold of Hereford. You may get to your feet. But you must know that I am also a Norman; my father is a Norman king.'

'Indeed, ma'am. At the beginning of the English Revolt, the Brotherhood opposed Duke William, your grandfather, believing he had unfairly seized the crown by force of arms at Senlac Ridge. But Hereward persuaded them to accept the inevitable, and instead they campaigned against the harshness of Norman rule. The English do not easily accept unjust regimes, which is why we believe a Cerdician queen would rule justly. Duke Robert understood that and was able to take the oath of the Brethren. I also carry this amulet, the Talisman of Truth – an object that has been worn by Caesars, kings and emperors. I am its guardian, the third generation of my family to be chosen.'

'Were you given it by your father?'

'No, ma'am, by John Comnenus, the Emperor of Byzantium.'

'I see, you certainly move in interesting circles for a mere knight. May I see the Talisman?'

I handed the amulet to her, but with a warning.

'Do not be alarmed, Your Majesty. It is not what it seems; it brings wisdom and insight.'

She examined it with some trepidation.

'It's like nothing I've ever seen before; one day you must explain it to me. You are an interesting man, Harold of Hereford. But how do you know I would rule fairly?'

'Because it is in your blood, Majesty; you are a Cerdician.'

'Is that not a sort of blind faith?'

'Indeed, it may appear so, ma'am. But remember, if your rule turned out to be harsh and unjust, the English people would resist you, just as they did your grandfather . . . and so would I.'

Matilda's face broke into a wonderful beaming smile.

'Well, you are certainly a man of conviction! I suppose you would now like to accompany me to London?'

'I am at your service, Your Majesty.'

'Very well, let us see how we get along. You may call me

"my Lady". England does not have an Emperor so, when I am Queen, I will be called "Queen Matilda, Lady of England and Normandy".'

'Very good, my Lady. May I ask why you are travelling with such a small escort?'

'No, you may not!'

I had taken a step too far and rebuked myself for being too bold. Matilda walked briskly back to her carriage. As she passed her captain, who continued to watch me like a hawk, she made the introductions.

'Captain Margam, Harold of Hereford will accompany us to London. He and his man will report to you. At any hint of disobedience or sign of mischief, get rid of them.'

'Very well, my Lady.'

Captain Margam looked at me with contempt as he returned my weapons. Then he leaned towards me and hissed a warning.

'You heard what my Lady Matilda said. But remember this, if I do have cause to get rid of you, you won't be in one piece when you go!'

A few years ago, a warning like that would have put the fear of God into me, but I had learned three important lessons over the previous twelve years. Firstly, most men can bark louder than they can bite. Secondly, the really dangerous men do not issue warnings. And thirdly, all men bleed – no matter how invincible they may seem – so always be the first to strike.

Eadmer had got the measure of Margam as well.

'He's a killer; watch your back. And I'll watch it too!'

The remainder of the journey across Normandy and the Channel to England was uneventful. I spent most of the time observing Matilda, who managed to remain dignified despite the uncomfortable circumstances. She was the daughter of the King of England and the widow of the Holy Roman Emperor – the two most powerful men in Europe whose two domains covered almost the whole of the continent – and was not accustomed to adversity. She was travelling with little or no protection and had none of the luxuries – such as numerous servants, frequent changes of clothes, hot water and portable commodes – that would have made the journey easier to bear.

She kept her temper and her humour, was prepared to relieve herself by the side of the road like everybody else and to remain unwashed rather than immerse herself in the filthy butts of water available at the roadside inns. She ate only what she was sure was edible, which often meant food had to be forsaken, and went without sleep for long periods.

Eadmer and I again adopted the pseudonyms Robyn of Hode and William of Scaerlette when we reached England. Choosing the path of caution, we stayed in the shadows at Westminster when Matilda went to see the King.

Fearing that Margam was very much the King's man – and likely to reveal our true identity to him – we were on our guard, with our horses ready to ride, during the entire stay.

20. Flight to Freedom

Fortunately, we did not have to wait in readiness at Westminster for long. Matilda's meeting with the King did not go well. As was true of most kings – especially Norman ones – he was used to being obeyed. For his daughter to depart her marriage bed, jeopardize a delicate treaty with a new ally and embarrass him in the eyes of Europe – all of this was a major misdemeanour. He was furious – shouting and bellowing along the corridors of Westminster – and, within a day, Matilda was back on the road to Dover. The King had given her a much bigger escort and entourage and a few more comforts than she had enjoyed when she left Angers.

We rejoined the end of the Empress's entourage south of Southwark. But within a hundred yards of doing so, Margam rode up to us with several men.

'I am arresting you in the name of King Henry! These men will take you back to Westminster to face his judgement.'

He turned to a sergeant and issued his curt instructions.

'Disarm them and bind them. Take their horses. They can walk, or be dragged.'

I looked at Eadmer.

He knew what he had to do and had his seax deep into the throat of the sergeant before the man could blink.

I raised my leg, knocking Margam clean out of his saddle.

Eadmer and I both kicked our mounts into a gallop. The road to Dover at Southwark was busy and the people, horses and carts using the highway helped our escape. We created confusion in our wake as we sped away, making it difficult for the posse of pursuers to catch us. As soon as the traffic thinned, we turned off the road, rode through the woods at Chislehurst and headed over the Downs to the coast in the hope of intercepting Matilda's escort before it left Dover.

We arrived at the port at about the same time as Matilda and her party. Her ship was waiting for her and I contemplated how we could make contact with her without alerting Margam and his men. I had discovered in London that Margam was a Welsh knight of the Lordship of Afan, in South Wales, a formidable warrior and not a man to be crossed.

I gambled that Matilda would stay at least one night in the comfort of Dover Castle before waiting for the tide and the right winds to make the crossing.

Gaining access to the castle was not difficult – my knight's pennon and the presence of both the Talisman and the Order of San Marco around my neck ensured that – but the difficulty was obtaining access to the royal chambers. Eadmer and I walked round and round the keep, but we could see no way of getting beyond the royal cordon – nor any way of approaching Matilda without being seen by Margam. There was just one, highly risky option: a message tied to an arrow shot through the window of her chamber. But even this assumed that we could ascertain in which chamber she would spend the night.

Eadmer had grave concerns.

'It's a shot of forty yards, at an acute angle, in the gloom. The window is less than a foot wide – and as soon as she goes in, her maid is going to close the shutter. You could easily hit her – or even the Empress! That shot's impossible –'

'But it's worth a try. Come on! I need to rehearse.'

We made an educated guess at the location of Matilda's chamber, based on the reasonable deduction that hers was the one with a double window. It was late January and cold, and we knew we had to make the shot before dusk – at which time, the shutters would be closed. There was a glow from the fireplace in the room and I could see shadows when anyone passed in front of it. I had blunted my arrow as much as I could and tied a piece of leather to its tip, but there was still a considerable risk that I would hit someone.

I waited until the shadows stopped moving.

I took aim; I only had one chance.

My note was scratched in charcoal on a piece of vellum purchased in haste that had cost a small fortune. The arrow clipped the arch of the window as it passed but went into the room. I thought I heard a shriek and hoped it was caused by shock and not by injury. My note read, in Latin:

My Lady,

I'm sure you know, but we were intercepted by Margam at Southwark and are now in even more trouble than before.

If you need our help, we are in the keep, in the corridor behind the stables.

Robyn

We waited for almost an hour, with horses saddled and a clear escape exit readily available. I began to think that our help was not required, or that the killing of Margam's sergeant had persuaded Matilda that we were not to be trusted. There was even the possibility that Margam was again about to ambush us.

At last, to our relief, through the darkness of the keep, three hooded figures moved stealthily towards us, one much larger than the other two. It was Matilda, a maid and a guard. I looked at the guard suspiciously.

'It's fine, you can trust him – he's a Swabian, one of the Emperor's finest.'

'My Lady, I'm sorry my message arrived a little melodramatically.'

'Melodramatically, indeed – you nearly speared my maid to the floor! But it was a fine shot. Where did you learn to use a bow like that?'

'I am an English knight, my Lady; we practise with a bow as soon as we can walk. We heard a scream – I hope it didn't alert your guards.'

'It did, but I told them it was a rat!'

Once again, I was impressed by Matilda's composure. And yet I couldn't help thinking that her lightness of tone was a clever way of masking her vulnerability.

'How are you, my Lady?'

'I am relieved you are here; we barely know one another, but I need help. The King has insisted that I return to Angers and apologize to my husband. He is livid with me for having tested his authority.'

'And what do you want to do?'

'I want to escape. When my first husband was alive, the

whole of Europe supplicated themselves at my feet. I was regent in Lombardy and in the lands of the Swiss – and even the Pope knelt before me when he needed to keep his Roman Bishopric safe.'

'Who can you trust?'

'Only Lothar here . . . and my maid, Greta. The rest are my father's men.'

'Where is Margam?'

'Drinking or whoring – possibly both. I don't trust him. He keeps an eye on me for my father, rather than protecting me.'

'So what is your plan?'

'Follow us across the Channel. We should rendezvous at the old Church of Our Lady in Beauvais. I know the priest there – he was my confessor in Mainz. Give him this ring, he will know it's from me. Wait for me there. I need to escape beyond the borders of Normandy and find refuge somewhere in the Empire, probably in Lombardy. Hal, you are my only hope, please be there!'

'Worry not, my Lady, I will be there. Will you need horses?'

'Yes – and supplies for a journey. Here is some money; please buy simple clothes for me and Greta.'

The three figures then scuttled across the keep as furtively as before and returned to the royal chambers.

We were in Beauvais as quickly as good horses and a worthy sea captain permitted, and there we waited patiently for Matilda.

Eadmer shared my concerns for the future.

'Margam has a lot of men who know how to handle

themselves. He'll alert every garrison in Normandy. Her husband will be looking for her as well, and he has many powerful friends from the Alps to the Mediterranean. She can't hide away forever.'

'I know, my friend, and to make matters worse a new Emperor has been elected in the Holy Roman Empire – Lothair, Duke of Saxony. He will have little sympathy for a fugitive wife.'

'It is going to be another pit of shit we're getting ourselves into!'

'I think you're right, but I also think she's worth it. She'll be a Cerdician queen one day, remember.'

'Not at this rate! If she doesn't go back to her husband and produce a grandson for the King, the crown will go to someone else.'

'You're right, of course. But first, let's see if she will tell us why she left Count Geoffrey. Then we can take it from there.'

During the third evening of our wait in Beauvais, the priest came to us with a message from Matilda: two hours before dawn, we were to be ready with the horses in the lee of the nave of the old church.

It was a cold night, and a bitter wind howled around the walls of the church as we huddled under our cloaks for shelter. Always anxious about ambush and betrayal, Eadmer circled the building several times but found only stray dogs and blasts of icy air.

'She needs to hurry! I'm freezing, and I'd much prefer a good head start in darkness.'

'Patience, Eadmer. She'll be here.'

A few minutes later, Lothar, Matilda's giant Swabian

bodyguard, appeared. He was alone, but questioned us in his heavy Germanic accent.

'Do you have everything ready?'

'Yes, all is prepared.'

'Wait, just two minutes; we are camped nearby.'

Three hooded figures appeared soon afterwards – as did the priest, who let us into the church. Matilda did not seem flustered and spoke with a calm authority.

'Good evening, Gentlemen. Did you bring clothes for us?'

'We did, my Lady.'

Eadmer handed the clothes to Greta, and both women went behind the altar to change.

When they emerged, Lothar handed me a casket and Matilda issued a firm order.

'That contains enough silver to take us across Europe several times. Now, let's ride!'

I felt justified in asking the obvious question.

'In which direction, my Lady?'

'South, of course. Let's go!'

South it was, day after day. Thankfully, both ladies could ride and we made excellent progress. We steered clear of large towns and cities. The women's modest clothing meant they were taken as yeoman's ladies and our anonymity remained intact. We camped in the open, despite the chill of winter. Matilda seemed not in the slightest perturbed by the cold air or the rain, as long as we made a good fire to bed down beside.

There was never a hint of any pursuers, and we were confident that we had left no trace or trail to follow. We veered west of Paris, passed Chartres, Orléans and Châteauroux, before reaching the High Limousin beyond Limoges, where we knew we could relax. There was snow on the ground, so we found a small village in the valley of the Charente and gave a farmer a piece of silver for the use of his hay barn for a few days.

While Eadmer and Lothar went hunting and Greta made up some bedding, I asked Matilda what her plan was. I had not raised the subject until that point, thinking it wise to let her get well away from Normandy. Feeling sure that she had a plan, I was impatient to hear it.

For the first time since we had left Beauvais, Matilda sounded hesitant and looked bewildered.

'Well, I suppose we should turn east soon . . . to head for Geneva and the Alps.'

'But, my Lady, it is midwinter and to the east is the high ground of the Massif. It may be wise to keep going south and cross into Lombardy along the Mediterranean.'

'As you wish; I would appreciate it very much if you took care of our journey.'

'With pleasure, my Lady. But what is our destination?'

'Well, Lombardy . . . or perhaps Savoy. I think I can rely on the Count there, Amadeus III. He is very ambitious and has always been an ally to me . . .'

'Are you not sure?'

She hesitated and suddenly looked vulnerable. There were tears in her eyes.

'To be honest, no, I'm not sure . . . I just need to get as far away from my father and my husband as I can.'

I felt that she was about to tell me the whole story, but

this was neither the time nor the place. An audacious –
even impudent – thought suddenly came to me.

'My Lady, you need time to think. I have a small estate
several days south of here. It is not an imperial palace –
nor, indeed, any kind of palace – but it is comfortable and
very private. You are welcome to spend as much time as
you like there.'

She looked at me with an expression that was a strange
mix of desperation and joy.

'It sounds perfect . . . I am so grateful to you. But it
could get you into trouble.'

'My Lady, I am already in a good deal of trouble. I don't
think it could get worse!'

The journey to the south would bring mixed emotions.
I was excited that one of the most important women in
Europe would be staying on my humble estate, but anxious that I was sinking deeper and deeper into a mire from
which there was no obvious escape. At times, my feelings
were almost childlike. The astonishing good fortune of
being able to play host to a beautiful empress made my
heart race. But it also galloped with fear: I was almost certainly pronouncing a death sentence on myself and
Eadmer. At times I had to pinch myself to be sure that
what was happening was indeed real and not a figment of
a storyteller's vivid imagination.

By the time we reached St Cirq Lapopie, Matilda was
smiling broadly and seemed happy – or as happy as her
circumstances would allow. The further south we had
travelled, the broader had become her smile and when she
saw how remote and peaceful the estate was, she beamed
from ear to ear. She had a wonderful smile – a smile that

seemed to light up her whole face and infused everyone around her with joy.

'You were right; it is wonderful. Thank you, Hal.'

'We need a name for you, my Lady. The locals will wonder who you are.'

'Of course! My family name is Maud – Greta and I can be your relatives from England.'

'Very well, Maud it is.'

I waited for almost two weeks before reminding Matilda of the realities of her circumstances. It was late in the afternoon; she was sitting at the top of the limestone crags at the back of the farmhouse, watching the full waters of the Lot flowing swiftly towards a rapidly setting sun.

'May I join you, my Lady?'

'Of course, Hal. Please call me Maud – my family name for my new family in the Lot.'

'Thank you.'

She smiled her distinctive, very uninhibited smile again. I was smitten by her presence and very proud that Maud was so happy in our humble abode. But I looked nervously towards the east, feeling anxious about the conversation I knew I had to have with her.

'The snows are melting on the Massif. It will be spring soon. You will like it here in the spring – it is very pretty.'

She sensed my anxiety and also knew perfectly well that her haven in the Lot was, at best, a temporary arcadia.

'But you don't think I should be here by then, do you?'

'Well, we need a plan. Your father will be angry – and so will your husband.'

'My husband will not give me a second thought. He's just a silly boy, petulant and spoiled. He has no conversation and no charm. He drives me mad!'

'That will change –'

'Perhaps . . . but there's no hint of hair on his face yet. And even less sign of virile manhood between his legs!'

'That will change as well.'

'I have no doubt! But my father expects a grandson, and I've told him there's no chance of that – unless the Angel Gabriel intervenes!'

'And what did he say?'

'He told me to use my feminine wiles to get him to perform. The typical response of a man! Hal, I had to get away. I begged the King to let me stay in London until Geoffrey is ready for a proper marriage, but he wouldn't hear of it. He was in a towering rage and threatened to put me in a nunnery.'

Despite the crisis we were in, I felt energized. Maud was confiding in me in forthright terms, like an old friend, and we were still able to enjoy our haven in the Lot – at least, for a while longer.

'You know I will do all I can to help. But we must get a message to the King, to tell him you're safe.'

'But how? Do you have a suggestion?'

'I do. We should send Lothar to Angers, and Eadmer to London, with messages from you.'

Tears started to form in her eyes.

'But I don't know what I want to say . . . I know that ultimately I must do my duty. I grew to like Henry; he was a good Emperor and a robust man. We never had children, but he knew what to do in the bedchamber and kept me content. But Geoffrey is not easy to like and certainly couldn't pleasure me as a woman. I began to look at the men at court . . .'

She paused and looked at me wistfully.

'Do you mind me talking like this? You see . . . I have no one else.'

'Of course not – I am no stranger to issues of the heart, and have experienced my own frustrations.'

'I'm sure you have. But I couldn't help noticing that there was no woman here, waiting for your return?'

'There have been girls here, but no one special. The one love of my life died in tragic circumstances. It took me a long time to recover from that . . .'

I suddenly felt a pang of pain from the past.

Maud gently asked the question I knew I would one day have to answer.

'Who was she?'

'Her name was Livia Michele, and she was a Princess of Venice. It is a long story; I'll tell you about it one day . . . But for now, we need to decide what you want to say in your messages.'

Maud was astute enough to recognize that there would be another time for intimate reminiscences. She gathered her thoughts and spoke with determination.

'I need time. I will return to London two years from now, in the spring of 1131, to see my father. He can summon Geoffrey to join me there – he will be eighteen by then and should have a beard on his face and a man's prick between his legs.'

I smiled at her crude turn of phrase, and she laughed out loud.

'What do you think?'

'I think two years is a long time, and the King will be furious! But if that's what you want, then that's what we will do. You must write it in your own hand and seal it. Lothar and Eadmer will deliver the messages, but they must not be captured. I fear they would be tortured to reveal your whereabouts.'

'So how do we get an answer to our messages?'

'Ah, that's easy – homing pigeons!'

'What are those?'

'The crusaders learned how to train pigeons from the Muslims; they have a postal service in many of their cities. Pigeonmen keep flocks in London, and I'm sure they will have them in Angers. All Lothar and Eadmer have to do is find a pigeonman and hire one of his birds in a basket. If he leaves the bird with your message outside the palace, the bird has a pouch on its leg for the reply. When released, it will always fly back to the pigeonman's home nest, where our men will be waiting. In that way, they can stay clear of capture.'

'How clever! But how do the birds know their way home?'

'I don't know – but they always fly home.'

'You are a resourceful man, Hal. What would I do without you?'

Matilda leaned over to me, kissed me warmly on the cheek, and then skipped back to the farmhouse like a young girl.

Eadmer was right; the situation was becoming yet more complicated. Not only had I devoted myself to Matilda's cause, but I knew then that I was in very real danger of falling in love with her.

The next day, while Matilda wrote her messages, I briefed Lothar and Eadmer on their tasks.

Lothar was dubious; he had never heard of carrier pigeons. But like the loyal man he was, he just accepted his task dutifully.

Eadmer was more belligerent.

'The King will be as angry as a snake in a sack. *Two years!* Is she mad? What are we going to do with her for two years? Don't answer that . . . I know what you'd like to do with her!'

'Don't tease me, Eadmer. She is our future Queen! There is no possibility of anything between us.'

'I'll wager good money that she'll be in your bed when I get back! I've seen the way she looks at you – and the way you look at her. But what concerns me now is a much more important point – my own safety. I'd better have a way out of London and a safe port to depart from. If the King delays his reply to Matilda's message, he could use the time to seal London and have the ports watched.'

'I know. I'm sorry I have to ask you to do this. Try to get a pigeonman outside the walls – perhaps in Southwark – and cross the Channel far to the west. Devon might be a good idea. And you could travel south through Brittany, even sail to Aquitaine from there. If the King puts out an alert in Normandy, and Geoffrey does the same in Maine and Anjou, an overland route might be dangerous.'

'I think you're right about the route; it's good advice. I'll be careful.'

I was relieved that Eadmer was taking my advice seriously. But then he started grinning at me.

'But what about my wager?'

'Enough! Take care and come home safely, old friend. I hope to see you again before the summer.'

Lothar and Eadmer left early the next morning. It would be a long and hazardous journey for them – and a long wait for Matilda and me. As I watched them wind their way down the track to the bottom of the valley, I thought about Eadmer's provocative wager.

In fact, I had been thinking about little else. I had spurned the advances of a beautiful aristocrat once before, and I did not intend making the same mistake again. I made the conscious decision that I would be guided by Matilda's feelings for me, rather than by mine for her.

If her feelings proved to be platonic, then so be it. But if they became amorous, then I would respond with as much passion as my mortal frame would lend me.

Dear Thibaud,

Another Sabbath has gone, and another service missed at St Paul's. I thought the warmth of spring would ease my aches and pains, but alas, no. My scriptorium is cool. I am now wheeled in there every day, as I find it almost impossible to walk.

Anyway, I digress; let us return to Harold of Hereford. This latest bulletin contains the most incendiary part of the tale — the morsel that must, beyond all others, be buried deep in the Vatican's vaults. I suspect the story of how baby Henry was sired will not prove to be the only example of its kind — whether within or outside the royal bedchamber. But enough of my treasonable musings! I suppose it is one of the few comforts when, at a great age and approaching God's judgement, one is only answerable to Him and inclined to say what one thinks.

And yet, my friend, I cannot help wondering: how do we judge Harold? You have heard countless confessions, as I have. I'm relieved that Harold has not yet asked for absolution in telling his tale, but would you grant it? Perhaps, at the end, we will know more upon which to judge him. I have already started to pray for his soul.

I am working without respite to complete Hal's story, much to the chagrin of my aides. I pray to Our Lord to give me the strength to complete my task, for my health is a worry to me. I fear I am in serious decline; pray for me.

Keep well, good friend.

Yours in God,
Gilbert

21. Heaven on Earth

The spring and early summer of 1129 in the Lot were hot and dry. There was no word from either Eadmer or Lothar, and St Cirq Lapopie had few visitors. Life on the estate continued harmoniously. I often looked out over the gorge and the river below, especially at sunset – just as my family must have done on so many occasions – and said to myself, 'This is Heaven on Earth.'

It was on such an evening in early May that Maud suddenly appeared behind me. She had been in a good mood all day, helping in the fields and playing with the children of the families on the estate. She no longer looked like an empress: she had the golden skin of the well-to-do wife of a landowner, who does not mind her complexion being darkened by the sun. Her hair had been bleached by the sun and her skin shone with the natural sheen of robust health. She was strikingly handsome before, but now I found her natural beauty more and more irresistible by the day.

When she spoke, her voice was tender and warm.

'When do you expect them back?'

'Lothar should be back by now. But Eadmer, not before the end of the month.'

'I hope they come back with news that my father has disowned me and that my husband wants the marriage annulled. Then I can stay here!'

My heart raced, and I found it hard to speak without my voice trembling. I probably should not have said it, but I just blurted the words out.

'Maud, that would be beyond my wildest dreams!'

Her face broke into one of her captivating smiles and she ran towards me with her arms outstretched.

'Oh, Hal, I'm so happy here. What more could a woman want!'

She threw her arms around my neck and kissed me passionately. In between hungry kisses, she gasped.

'It has been so long . . . I can't resist any longer . . . I've tried to remember my duty . . .'

I carried her inside the farmhouse and into her chamber, where Greta was tidying the room. When she saw us coming, she tried to curtsy but was so shocked that she only succeeded in falling over the bed. She excused herself and made a rapid exit.

Maud laughed out loud.

'See, Greta, he does want me . . . I think that will be all for tonight!'

Greta giggled and attempted another curtsy, but Maud kicked the door closed before she could execute it.

'So, my handsome Prince of the Lot, make this poor widow happy!'

We made love all night, only interrupted by a nocturnal dash down the hill to the river for a languorous bathe in its cool waters, after which we made love again on a small sandy inlet by the shore. Sleep brought a halt to our passion as, exhausted, we slumbered on the sand. We had run down the hill naked, so the chill of the night woke us, but not before dawn was glowing softly behind the Lot's towering crags to the east. We were both shivering from the cold and clambered back up the hill, teasing each other and laughing like young lovers who have just enjoyed their first tryst.

When we reached the farmhouse, the young milk-maids were on their way to the fields and got the shock of their lives as two naked figures bolted past them. Our encounter thus became the talk of the estate for weeks afterwards.

The month of May became one seamlessly blissful carnal interlude, where the long warm days just melded together in a haze of euphoria. Maud had an enchanting body, broad in the hips with strong shoulders. Her breasts were full, with large dark nipples, and she had a taut muscular backside – a faultless frame for the delightful activities in which we engaged and which devoured almost our entire time. Maud was ideally designed for raucous sex, and I could be as forceful as possible without fear of discomforting her – in fact, I was often the one overcome by fatigue. She was a woman of the world who had married an emperor at the age of twelve and lost her virginity only weeks afterwards. She was totally uninhibited and enjoyed sex more than any woman I had ever met. The Emperor had been sixteen years her senior, with vast experience from countless concubines, and had been a kind and thoughtful tutor in the bedchamber – an education from which I was now reaping the benefit.

By the beginning of June, we were living like man and wife and very much in love. Eadmer would have won his bet, had I accepted it.

St Cirq Lapopie was now an even more profound Heaven on Earth than before. But one evening after dinner – at the risk of breaking the spell of our enchanted time together – I raised with Maud what I thought was a crucial question.

'Darling, we are taking a big risk. You could get pregnant, and that could make things very complicated.'

She looked at me in horror. Tight-lipped and fighting to control her emotions, she pleaded with me.

'Don't spoil it . . . this is such a special time for us both . . . I don't want to think about anything else.'

'I don't want it to end either. But Lothar and Eadmer will be back soon – and they will bring the real world with them.'

'I don't care. The real world can go to Hell!'

I realized that the fantasy we were enjoying, no matter how much of a facade, was so precious to her. The time had not yet come to question it.

'I understand. I'm sorry, let's enjoy this for as long as we can.'

She smiled at me with relief, but her expression became thoughtful as she considered my original question.

'Hal, don't worry about babies. I am barren – I was married to the Emperor for over ten years, and there was never a hint of a pregnancy. But I know he had at least one bastard child with some mare from Lotharingia and there were rumours of several more.'

'But isn't it important that you produce a grandson for the King?'

'Yes – he told me in no uncertain terms that he wanted a grandson. But I no longer fear his displeasure. If I am barren and he finds a new successor, then I can come back to you and live out my days here.'

She smiled that smile again. Our first lovers' tiff was over.

But we were to have only a few more days of paradise in our illusory world before a tiny speck in the distance, in the valley of the Lot below, heralded Eadmer's return to St Cirq Lapopie.

When Eadmer reached the farmhouse, it was almost dusk. He looked gaunt and exhausted.

Maud joined me to greet him, and held my hand as we did so.

'Welcome back, good friend.'

'I'm glad to be back, believe me!'

He glanced down at our interlocking hands and whispered to me.

'I see I've won my wager –'

Maud heard his aside and interrupted before I could respond.

'Which was what?'

Eadmer looked a little timid, which was unusual.

'Well, my Lady . . . that you would be in his bed by the time I returned. I'm sorry, my Lady –'

'Well, you lose, he's in *my* bed!'

We all laughed together, and Maud took Eadmer by the arm.

'Let us eat! And have some wine to celebrate your safe return.'

Eadmer glanced at me. He looked concerned.

'What about Lothar? Is he not here? He had only half the distance to cover. He should be back by now.'

'It is worrying, my friend. I fear for him.'

After Eadmer had washed the dust of the road away, we sat with Greta to eat dinner and drink one of Cahors' better wines, a butt of which I kept for special occasions. Eadmer passed a small piece of vellum to Maud.

'Here is King Henry's response, my Lady. I hope it is the answer you want. It was not easy to get. I didn't trust the pigeonman – I was concerned that such men might operate under licence from the King, making it easy to track me down while I waited for the bird to return. So I bought all the man's birds and told him to disappear for a few days. I observed his loft from a distance, waiting for the return of my chosen bird. I was right to be cautious. The day after I left the pigeon with your message at the King's gate at Westminster, a squadron of his men arrived in Southwark and ransacked the pigeonman's little hovel. Mercifully, I was nowhere to be found! Two days later, my chosen pigeon appeared overhead. Sadly, I had to bring the poor bird down with an arrow, but the King's message was there, bound to its tiny leg.'

'You have done well, Eadmer. I am so very grateful to you.'

'Your father is frantic, my Lady. Every burgh in England is being scoured by his men – and it is the same in Normandy. Every ship leaving port along the length of the south coast of England is being searched. I had to buy passage on a Breton trader from Wareham, in Dorset. The ship's cargo was such that the captain preferred his crossing of the Channel to be as discreet as I hoped mine would be. I travelled a difficult route – using several ships through the western reaches of Brittany and Poitiers, and eventually down into Aquitaine – before reaching the Lot at Aiguillon. After that, it was familiar territory and home beckoned.'

Maud unravelled the note from the King, written on a minuscule piece of vellum. She was clearly agitated by its contents, and motioned to Greta to accompany her to her chamber.

'Hal, keep Eadmer company, he deserves several jugs of wine. Let's talk in the morning.'

She left her father's response on the table for me to read. I picked up the note and read the tiny but immaculate blackletter Latin.

Darling Maud,

You are a difficult child, but it was ever thus.

The summer of 1131 is agreed. I will ensure that Count Geoffrey is in London to greet you, but the months in between must be spent in Rouen. Your presence will keep Normandy happy, where there is still sympathy for your cousin, William Clito.

I want you in Rouen by Christmas Day, when I will be there for my crown wearing.

Wherever you are, you must now come home.

Your loving father,
Henry Beauclerc, Rex

That night was the first night we had not spent together since we became lovers. Maud wanted to be alone.

I desperately hoped it was just a temporary setback.

When Maud emerged quite late the next morning, she came to find me in the vineyard. She looked bleary-eyed and had clearly spent a sleepless night, but she looked and sounded determined.

'If you don't mind accompanying me, I would like to begin the journey to Rouen by the end of the month.'

'Of course, my Lady. Eadmer and I will make the preparations.'

She smiled wryly at my deliberate formality, then took me by the arm and laid her head on my shoulder.

'Hal, let's continue our little dream for a while. And then, when we get to Rouen, we shall see what mood my father is in . . . Perhaps I can find a way of making sure you stay close to me?'

'Is that a good idea for both of us – especially when your husband returns?'

'Let's cross that bridge when we come to it. The most difficult part will be handling my father. He's sure to remember you from your first encounter with him. And then there's the small matter of my escape . . . Also, he knows me well, and he will assume I have not been without companionship these past months.'

'You're right, we will be walking into a bear pit. But as long as we stay true to what we've learned here in St Cirq Lapopie, we can draw strength from one another.'

'I love you, Hal, and I always will. Please remember that, no matter what happens –'

'And I love you, my darling. I will always be at your side, come what may.'

Matilda had never told me she loved me before, and I was quick to respond by affirming my love for her – something I had wanted to do for a very long time.

It was a moment that changed my life. I had decided

some time ago that I would rally to her cause, now I knew I had to devote my life to her.

Eadmer helped me organize the estate for our departure, but he gulped hard when I told him we were due to rendezvous with the King in Rouen. His only comment was short and to the point.

'He'll cut your balls off and hang you from the nearest gibbet!'

Although I hoped his prediction would prove to be exaggerated, he was right. Of all our journeys, the one we were now preparing for was by far the most hazardous.

We were in Rouen before the worst of the winter of 1129 began. King Henry had sent orders that Matilda must be well taken care of in the ducal palace, and she arranged for me to be accommodated as a knight-escort of the royal household.

Rouen was busy; the city was storing the harvest and preparing itself for winter. Waiting for the arrival of the King was an anxious tedium, a calm before a raging storm. So as not to feed too much gossip, I only saw Matilda occasionally, although our arrival – as just a quartet without any escort or attendant paraphernalia, after months of absence – had already generated enough chatter to keep the busybodies happy for weeks. Fortunately, neither Eadmer nor Greta would ever reveal any of our secrets – so the surmise of the gossips remained no more than idle speculation.

However, the boredom of waiting for the King's arrival was relieved in a most unwelcome way about ten days after we had settled in Rouen.

Greta stopped me in the palace courtyard and ushered me to see Matilda in her chamber. Her mistress was lying face down on the bed in a state of considerable distress. Greta pushed me inside furtively and closed the door behind me.

Matilda rushed over and threw her arms around me.

'Hal, I'm at my wits' end. I think I'm with child!'

I started to speak. I must have looked bewildered, because Matilda voiced my thoughts.

'I know, I believed I was barren . . . but I've missed two months. There's either something wrong with me, or I'm pregnant. I've got all the other signs: I'm sick all the time and bad tempered with Greta. What are we going to do?'

'What do you want to do?'

'It's our child, I want to keep it.'

I tried to think quickly, but sensibly.

'Good, then we have to leave. When do you expect the King?'

'Any day now; the stewards are preparing everything.'

'We must leave before he arrives. We'll go to St Cirq Lapopie and make sure no one finds us.'

Looking relieved, she smiled at me.

'Oh, please . . . please stay with me tonight.'

'Of course, my darling. But first, let's tell Greta and Eadmer to prepare for the journey. You'll need to think of a reason for your swift departure.'

Although my night with Matilda was amorous enough, I did not sleep well – if our lives were not already beset by danger, our problems had just become much more ominous.

By late morning, all was ready for a rapid departure south-wards. Matilda had told the King's Chamberlain that she wanted to travel to Évreux to speak with Audin of Bayeux – the old bishop, famous for his wisdom and kindness. The Chamberlain was suspicious – especially when Matilda declined an escort – and made the obvious point that he would have to answer to the King if anything should happen to his daughter.

When we reached the gates of the palace, the Chamberlain was there with several of the garrison. He was still perturbed by Matilda's sudden decision to leave, just at the point when her father was expected to arrive. The Constable of the Palace then intervened, a senior member of the King's hierarchy in Normandy. The two men were on the horns of a dilemma: did they incur the ire of the Empress by preventing her from leaving, or the wrath of the King by allowing her to go?

It was obvious to me which decision they would make. I began to think of our options, the most obvious of which was a clandestine departure later that night.

I was about to whisper that thought to Matilda, when distant heralds sounded the approach of Henry Beauclerc, King of England. Eadmer looked at me, expecting a signal to make a run for it, but I shook my head. Matilda concurred with a frown and a shrug of her shoulders.

Our game was up.

The King was just as I remembered him – older of course, a little more rotund, but still formidable. He looked grim-faced. Perhaps he was tired from his journey, but his demeanour only added to my anxiety.

Matilda made a good fist of greeting her father with unbounded enthusiasm and rushed to his side. Henry looked at me only momentarily, without a flicker of emotion, as I tried to meet his glance with equanimity.

Eadmer was very anxious and forthright with his advice.

'We should ride like the wind. Let's leave now!'

'You go, my friend, and take care of St Cirq Lapopie. I'm staying with Matilda; I've made her a promise.'

'You're a love-struck fool. But as it's winter, and the Lot will be cold, I suppose I may as well stay here. And that makes me a bigger fool than you are!'

Matilda disappeared into the royal apartments with her father and his huge retinue – a host soon swollen by the entire nobility of Rouen, who rushed to the Palace to greet the King of England. He was a liege for whom they had much more affection in his guise as their Duke.

A celebratory feast began at dusk, and Eadmer and I retreated to a tavern to drink some of Normandy's infamous Calva – not the most elegant of brews, but one that could certainly leave its mark. Sadly, its potency solved none of my problems.

Should I not have stood my ground with the King? I was in love with Maud and she with me; was it not my duty to stay by her side and protect her? In my head, I knew that discretion was vital, but my heart screamed at me to burst in on the feast and declare my abiding love.

Would I ever see her again? It seemed unlikely.

We had only been in the tavern for an hour when the door burst open, and at least a dozen of the King's men set upon us with a vengeance. They wielded maces and staves and began raining blows on us.

Eadmer and I both managed to get to our feet and hurl ourselves at two of our assailants, knocking them to the floor. This reduced the odds a little, as we both managed to draw blood with our seaxes and relieve our opponents of their clubs.

A vicious exchange of blows ensued. Eadmer and I stood our ground amidst the confusion of a large group of men rapidly fleeing the tavern. But the sheer weight of numbers was too great for us to endure for long.

I saw Eadmer take a blow to the back of his neck before I suffered what I assumed was a similar fate. I felt a sickening crack to the side of my head and then nothing.

I did not even remember hitting the floor.

When I awoke, there was only a small speck of light high in the ceiling. I was sitting upright, devoid of clothes, with my arms chained to an iron ring in the wall above my head. I was confined in a small dungeon not much wider or longer than my own frame. I was in unbearable pain: the side of my head throbbed, my arms ached from being stretched upwards, and I was sitting in my own filth, which made my skin itch and burn.

I had no idea how long I had been there, but from my parched mouth and lips, and the severe pangs of my hunger, I assumed it had been several days. I could hear almost no noise – just the occasional sound of a door being slammed, or the faintest hint of human voices. I assumed I was in an oubliette, in the depths of Rouen's palace.

Horrifyingly, I knew that Norman custom meant that oubliettes were reserved for those who would never again see the light of day.

22. Hell on Earth

It was soon obvious in my stone tomb that I was not going to be fed, or even given water. I was enduring a long, painful and suffocating death sentence.

I thought of my beloved, the Empress Matilda, who had become my Maud of St Cirq Lapopie, and of Eadmer, who had always been at my side and had stayed in Rouen, knowing his fate was unlikely to be any better than mine. I thought of my family heritage and how my forebears would have dealt with such adversity.

Death can only have been a day or two away. As I slowly descended into delirium, whatever clarity of thought I could muster focused on how much I had achieved and whether I had made any contribution to my family's heritage.

To my shame, although I had enjoyed a brief but magical period of personal bliss with Maud – an adventure more enchanting than most men could dream of – I had fallen a long way short of continuing my family's struggle. That was an ambition that could only be achieved by ensuring Maud's succession – a hope that currently lay in ruins. Her succession required an heir – Geoffrey's child, not mine! My worst fears had become a terrifying reality.

The walls of my oppressive space seemed to close in on me; I was constantly on the brink of the terrifying panic of claustrophobia. My chest heaved against the confined space, but it was a futile struggle. I prayed for death to end the agony. I reached for the Talisman, but it was not there – even in my role as its guardian, I had failed. Not only was I about to suffer an excruciating death, it was also going to be an ignominious one. When my breathless terror finally subsided into unconsciousness, it was a relief. My pain and my shame were over.

But the Angel of Death did not come – or, if he did, he took pity on me and gave me a reprieve. Consciousness suddenly returned and I sensed that I was being hauled upwards. My arms felt as if they were being pulled from their sockets. I could hear voices, but they were muffled; I could see people, but they were only dark shapes. Then I was being dragged along a hard floor and up stone steps.

I heard a series of barked orders.

'Sluice him down! Feed him and get him dressed! He's to see the King – make sure he doesn't stink!'

The next time I opened my eyes, I felt less pain. I was no longer fettered, and I was lying on straw, fully clothed. The Talisman and my Venetian medallion were around my neck. I assumed water had been poured down my throat as the thirst that was previously unbearable was now tolerable. I could not move my arms, but the pain had been replaced by numbness. My head still throbbed – but no longer as if being smashed by a blacksmith's hammer, but rather as if held firmly in a mason's vice.

I was not in the oubliette any more. I was in a cell, in one of the castle's many dungeons, but at least I was one level above the forgotten place. I was in a room that was not much larger than my stone coffin, but at least I could turn around. I was in Purgatory, rather than in Hell. Later that day, nourishment appeared through a small flap in the door: a bowl of thin stew that was more a watery grease than a broth of solid meat and vegetables, a piece of hard stale bread and a jug of filthy water. To my ravenous eyes, the stew looked like the finest chef's soup. I ate as slowly as I could in an attempt to savour every mouthful and left not the smallest morsel. It gave me bucketing diarrhoea within minutes, but at least it was sustenance of sorts.

Two days later, I was dragged out of my cell, plunged into a butt of icy water and rubbed with vinegar, which burned my skin like the fires of Hades. I was covered in sores and assumed the vinegar was intended to remedy the infection, or kill whatever was biting me. These treatments continued for some time until my skin improved. I began to feel a little more comfortable, and the stew – although hardly a hearty diet – was at least putting a little flesh back on my bones.

The worst part of my captivity was the lack of human contact. When my skin improved, the vinegar regime stopped – and, with it, my only interaction with other people. The isolation gnawed at me, turning hours into years and weeks into an eternity. Although they were painful, I prayed for the vinegar treatments to return – at least then I saw my fellow man. Now my only glimpse of humanity was the fleeting digits of a right hand that slid my food into my cell every evening.

I had managed to create a pile of my own waste and keep it to a corner of my tiny world. But it loomed there like an ever-growing icon of my ultimate degradation, and it became a monument to my slowly decomposing existence.

The only thing that kept me alive was the thought that Matilda still needed me and that I could yet help guide England's future. I assumed that Eadmer had met a dreadful end, and I shed tears for him every day. He had always been with me, and the fact that he was no longer by my side could mean only one thing. I was to blame of course – as he always said, I was constantly getting him into trouble.

I lost track of time. Using the buckle of my belt, I started to scratch the passing of the days on a tally on the wall of my cell – but as I had not begun doing so at the beginning of my confinement, I had no accurate idea how long I had been there. The one thing I was sure of was that I had gone into confinement at the end of 1129 and that I had experienced one more winter since. After many hours of calculating, which I turned into a giant chronological riddle in my imagination, I estimated that it was the spring of 1131 by the time the door of my cell opened for the first time in many months.

When it did, I was reluctant to move. I had become a part of the room; everything else beyond my cramped space had become alien to me, and I was petrified of facing the outside world. Inexplicably, I feared the warmth of sunlight, the glare of vibrant colours. I dreaded the thought of smells other than the stench of my own putrefaction and I feared tactile experiences beyond the feel of the cold stone slabs of my harsh domain.

An hour later, barely recognizable as a human being, I was prostrate on the floor of King Henry's Great Hall. I felt like a prone midden rat, plucked from the cesspits of the city, displayed as one of the weekly count trapped by the vermin-catcher. The King, oblivious to my condition, cleared the room before addressing me as if I had just arrived at his court from a jolly hunt in the forest.

'Harold of Hereford, it has been a while since I last had the pleasure of your company.'

I was unable to respond coherently. The King continued, as if nothing was amiss.

'I think the last time was in Foxley Wood, when your duplicity was first revealed to me. Then you killed one of my men in Southwark, before abducting my daughter in Beauvais.'

I was able to lift myself on to my elbows only momentarily and then glance at the King before collapsing back to the floor.

'You are a subversive, like the rest of your family. Your clan seduced my brother Robert, with its oaths about freedom and righteousness, and he is still paying the price for his calumny. But all your family are now dead – or locked in dungeons, like you and Robert. Your dreams about the rebirth of a Saxon England are gone forever. I will see to that, you have my word.'

The King then bellowed at the top of his voice.

'*Bring Lady Matilda!*'

He looked at me and spat his command.

'Get to your feet! Your mistress approaches.'

I could not raise myself beyond my elbows, but I tried to respect her entrance as best I could, which I managed with no more than a lowering of my head. It was a weak gesture, little better than the ungainly nod of a drunk in a tavern.

Matilda walked in with her face hidden by a veil. I could not see her expression, but I could hear her heartfelt sobs. The King motioned to her to sit next to him.

'Hail the next Queen of England. Bow to her! You, a filthy yard dog, who has the gall to fuck an empress!'

Matilda cowered, convulsed with spasms of grief.

'The child of your foul coupling is no more. You came to her like a fiend in the night, for which you ought to have died. But she has pleaded that you be shown mercy.'

The King extended his hand to Matilda in a gesture of warmth.

'I have consulted my seers here in Rouen and spoken to the Archbishop. All agree that the fecund seed of this rampant goat may have been the spur your fertility needed. Their wise judgement and your pleadings for him have saved his life.'

He turned back to me.

'Your bestial tupping of my daughter has done me a great service. She told me about that strange amulet around your neck and all those ancient English legends about the Wodewose. She says you and your family have the powers of soothsayers. When I told my seers about you and showed them the amulet, they said that you have been able to conjure powerful forces to make Matilda fertile.

'God help me for doubting my seers, but for my part, I think you just fucked the blockage out of her! The child is no more. But thanks to your little amulet and your big magician's wand of a prick, Matilda is fertile after all. Her husband will soon arrive in Rouen to seed the furrow you have ploughed for him. Then I will have my heir.'

Still delirious from my ordeal, I was only half aware of what was being said. Matilda abandoned her place by her father and, despite my appalling condition, sat beside me, cradling my head in her arms to reassure me. She began to repeat the gist of the King's diatribe, but with less invective, before he cut her short.

'*Enough!* Harold of Hereford, I am about to make you an offer no man could refuse – especially one in your current predicament. I assumed, entombed in my oubliette, you would die. Matilda begged me every day to release you, and eventually I relented and had you put in a dungeon. When you still didn't die, I took it as an omen that I should think again, and I consulted the seers.

'Matilda's husband returns within the week. The resumption of the marriage must continue in the eyes of the world. The recent hiatus must be seen as no more than that – the succession to my throne depends on it. I have given you a vacant title and some landholdings. I have many illegitimate children; you will become one of them and be quoted in the registers as the Earl of Huntingdon. In the first instance, you will stay in your home in Aquitaine until the time is right for you to return to Normandy. By then, young Geoffrey should have given me a legitimate heir of the royal blood. If, in the meantime, there is any hint that your seed has come within a mile of my daughter's loins, you will be a dead man. Once Geoffrey's task has been performed, I care not in the slightest if my daughter takes you to her chamber as often as she likes – as long as no ill-begotten child results. And remember this, as my acknowledged bastard child, Matilda becomes your half-sister and any offspring you produce would be seen as the rotten progeny of an incestuous coupling.'

The King pushed back his chair and stood. In my disordered state, he seemed to have twice the dimensions of his earthly form.

'You can have five minutes together now. After that, you may not see one another until Geoffrey of Anjou's pips are firmly planted in my daughter's belly.'

The King began to leave, but with one parting comment.

'You are a lucky man, Harold of Hereford, now Earl of Huntingdon. The planets must have been in a rare alignment when you were born! Hold tight to that amulet – it has saved your life.'

The King left with a flourish and I heard the door of the Great Hall slam shut behind him. I tried to speak but was incoherent.

Maud embraced me.

'My darling Hal, I've missed you so much. But you're alive! That's the most important thing. You will be safe now. My father will give you an escort to take you to St Cirq Lapopie, and I have arranged for Eadmer to meet you a few miles south of the city.'

I shook my head in disbelief.

'Eadmer is fine; they didn't guard him as closely as you. He escaped not long after you were captured. He's been living in the forest ever since, but he's well. Greta takes messages to him. When you are better, send word to me and I will arrange for you to come back to Rouen. I'm sure to be pregnant by then –'

I shook my head again, this time as violently as I could manage, and croaked a strangled, 'No!'

'We have no choice. It was your life in exchange for an heir. But more importantly, we can be together for the rest of our lives. It's a small price to pay – and England's future depends on it.'

Tears started to run down my cheeks.

'Don't cry, my beloved. He was going to banish you forever. Then he realized that he would do better to retain my loyalty by allowing me to see you. Not only that, but I suggested that if you happened to be one of his many bastard children, he could keep a close eye on you. I remembered the story about Estrith being your real mother, after all, and thought how easy it would have been for her to have been one of his secret conquests. He needs me and he knows he has to keep me content. He's sixty-three years old and his grandson isn't born yet; I will be Queen Regent for many years before the child is old enough to succeed.'

Maud was smiling, trying to muster my strength with her determination. I began to realize that she had created a very shrewd resolution to an apparently insoluble dilemma. I managed one brief question.

'The baby?'

'They took it. Oh, Hal . . . I fought with all my strength, but they took it away from me. They tried pennyroyal and all sorts of potions. But it was strong like you, and wouldn't die.'

Maud started to sob.

'Eventually, they used the instruments on me and pulled the little mite from my body. They hurt me so dreadfully, Hal . . . but not as much as they hurt you.'

She kissed me. I could taste her tears and feel her chest heave. But she soon recovered her composure.

'Now we know what we have to do, and then we can be together. Soon I will be the first Queen of England and Duchess of Normandy – and you will be a noble earl and my secret lover. It's worth waiting for! Go home to St Cirq Lapopie, get well and thank God for that prodigious seed of yours – it has solved all our problems.'

Despite all that had happened, and the fact that her duty would now force her to produce children with a man she did not care for, she appeared to be resigned to her fate. Although I hated the thought of another man in her bed trying to impregnate her, I realized that she expected me to have as much resolve as she had and to join her in thanking God for the only salvation that circumstances permitted.

Our five minutes together had passed and the King's Constable appeared with several men to take me to a chamber in the royal apartments. My weapons and armour were there waiting for me, together with the coronet and ermine of an earl of the realm.

I had become a bastard to earn them, but a lucky bastard all the same.

After several days of recovery, I was able to begin yet another journey to the south. I was given a small escort of cavalry, a steward and a groom. The life of an earl had some obvious advantages!

As promised by Maud, Eadmer was waiting some fifteen miles south of the city, at the ancient Pont de l'Arche on the Seine. He was a sight for sore eyes, and his first remark brought a smile to my face.

'You've looked better, Hal. Let's get you home to the

Lot and see if we can make you resemble a human being again.'

'Thank you, Eadmer, it's good to see you. Remember, you're addressing an earl now – so show due deference.'

'Yes, Your Earlship! How did you swing that one? One minute you're a dead man. The next, you're the Earl of Huntingdon! But you were better looking as plain Harold than you are now!'

I spent the greater part of the journey to St Cirq Lapopie listening to Eadmer's exhaustive account of his dramatic escape from the clutches of the King's executioners. I also heard many times the several new ballads he had written while idling away his time in the forest. He said he was going to compose a new one called 'The Ballad of Robyn of Hode', which began:

> To Hereward, a grandson, Harold by name,
> To the Empress, a lover, one Robyn of Hode.
> And to England an earl, Lord of Huntingdon's shire,
> A knight for all men and all maids to desire.

He also had news of Lothar, Maud's faithful bodyguard. Apparently, he had been captured trying to get her message to Count Geoffrey. Despite many days of torture, he had refused to reveal her whereabouts. Death was his only saviour. Thankfully, that finally came to him and ended his suffering. Maud found it difficult to bear the news – especially as the detail of it was told to her with cruel relish by Count Geoffrey.

During Eadmer's time in the forest, Greta had brought him food and regular news about my captivity. She had also been given Maud's permission to disclose the full story of her pregnancy and subsequent ordeal. He was full of praise for Maud's fortitude and told me that she had been vital to his escape by distracting his guards.

As usual, he was both forthright and sardonic in his reflections.

'I always encouraged you to get on with it and get her into your bed. As a reward, you've now ended up as an earl. You see, you should listen to me more often!'

It was good to have Eadmer at my side again. After a few days, I decided to give him a dose of his own medicine.

'So, what about young Greta? She's a handsome Teutonic lass, broad in the beam, strong in the shoulders, flat-bellied . . . She'd make you a happy man!'

He was unusually coy in his response, which made me probe further.

'I see . . . so after emptying the bread basket she'd brought you, you rewarded her by filling hers!'

He avoided a direct answer – which I took as an admission that my inference was accurate – before he changed the subject.

'You must be feeling better, Hal. Let's get you home to the Lot before you start getting frisky again.'

At least for the rest of the journey, I had found Eadmer's Achilles' heel. I smiled at the thought that I could return to it whenever I needed entertainment.

St Cirq Lapopie was a fine sight when it first came into view. Although Maud was not there to share it with me, I could still relish the fond memories it brought me. After my recent incarceration, thankfully, it was once again a haven of refuge and a symbol of hope for the future.

I tried not to think about Maud trying to conceive with her feckless husband, but only of the past, our joyous time together, and of the future when, God willing, we would be together again.

By the winter of 1131, I was fully recovered from my ordeal in King Henry's dungeon. Growing impatience now began to become the dominant feature of my mood.

During the spring of 1132, by which time there was still no word of a pregnancy for Maud, my impatience turned into exasperation. The only saving grace was that I found myself preoccupied with the many tasks demanded by the estate. But eventually, even these were no longer a respite for my frustrations.

I had bedded several of the local girls, in search of some distraction, but the shallowness of these encounters only added to the problem. Eadmer was doing the same despite, for the first time, admitting his love for Greta – like me, all he wanted was to be with his beloved again. We were like chivalrous young knights, revelling in our love for our ladies, and did not mind admitting it to one another, often over too many flagons of Cahors' best vintages.

We hoped that Maud and Greta were in Rouen, where at least their Norman kin could keep an eye on them. But we feared that they may be in Le Mans or Angers, among Geoffrey's kin – a thought that only added to our woes.

Then, in May, a rider arrived at St Cirq Lapopie. He wore the clothes of a merchant, but was heavily armed.

He said almost nothing, other than to ask for me by name, before handing me a folded vellum note closed with a distinctive seal: 'Matilda, Emperatrix Romanum'.

It contained only a simple message: 'Venire mox, pons Yssoir, Le Mans'. So, fortified by optimism, we headed north-west to respond to Maud's summons: 'Come soon, Yssoir Bridge at Le Mans'.

At the end of May, we tethered our horses and waited on the west bank of the River Sarthe in the lee of the ancient walls of the Presbytery of Our Lady of Le Mans. We could see the ancient Roman walls of Le Mans on the opposite back, with the ornate roof of the Cathedral of St Julien towering above them. Later that day, a plainly dressed rider crossed the old bridge and waited for some time before returning to the city. He did the same thing the next morning, leading us to conclude that he was a messenger from Maud.

When he came back in the afternoon, I greeted him.

'Who do you seek, friend? I am Harold, Earl of Huntingdon.'

He responded curtly.

'Wait here for further messages, my Lord.'

The following afternoon, the messenger reappeared with another short instruction.

'My Lord, the Empress sends her greetings. Go to a small lake in the middle of the Forest of Loudon. Travel for ten miles eastwards from the city, on the old road to Orléans, and you will come to a crossroads. Go south for two miles towards a village called La Raterie, where you will see the lake through the trees on your right. Be there tomorrow night.'

I could not wait to see Maud, to hear her news. But more importantly, after what had seemed like an eternity, I longed just to cast eyes on her beautiful face once again.

23. Loudon Mere

It was almost June, and a warm sunny evening in the Forest of Loudon. The lake was just like a fenland mere – a series of shallow ponds amidst marshland, thick with undergrowth and populated by waterfowl of all kinds. As the sun went down, the reeds and tall marsh grasses became silhouetted against the glistening gold of the water. The vivid reds and yellows of the marsh orchids and water irises faded in the encroaching darkness. It reminded me of some of the mysterious and romantic places in the Fens and Broads of my home.

With darkness fully settled, we could see the light of a couple of lanterns to the west, on the far side of the mere. It was the dark of the moon, and not easy to make our way over wet ground that would have been impossible to cross in winter. But then one of the lanterns moved towards us – it was held by Maud's messenger, who guided us to a makeshift camp.

There were two royal carriages, drawn up around a large camp fire. Hidden in the trees was an escort of just two guards, with a picket-line of horses. With Greta behind her in the shadows, Maud stood close to the fire, the flames of which danced provocatively on the smooth silk of her midnight-blue kirtle, highlighting the delights of her womanly form. The cord at her waist rested on the ample hips I had come to know so well, its tassels hanging down to the heart of her femininity. She looked as enchanting as ever.

She ran towards me, with tears of joy in her eyes, and rushed into my arms.

'Hal, I can't believe you're here. It's been so long! You are looking wonderful, my handsome Earl of Huntingdon!'

'So are you, my delectable Empress of Rome!'

Out of the corner of my eye, I saw Greta and Eadmer embrace.

'I assume you know about those two lovebirds?'

'I do, indeed! Isn't it wonderful? Greta tells me he's a beast in the bedchamber. What is it with you English – are you all stallions?'

'Just the men! The women make the best brood mares, though. Especially one I know well – England's finest mount.'

'Well, good sir, we must be the perfect breeding pair then?'

'Indeed we are, Ma'am.'

I couldn't help laughing at Maud's earthy humour, but our banter was short-lived. I needed to ask her some questions.

'Your messenger and your other escort – are they Count Geoffrey's men?'

'No, they're Lotharingians – my men. They know what happened to Lothar. They're his brothers, totally loyal to me. When Geoffrey insisted that we live in Le Mans, I asked my father if I could have my own people. He readily agreed, not wanting to leave his daughter defenceless in her husband's domain. I don't think he likes him any more than I do.'

Then I came to the vital question – the one to which I dreaded hearing the answer.

'So does your message mean you're pregnant?'

She pulled away from me, suddenly tense.

'Walk with me, darling Hal . . . It has been a nightmare. Do you mind if I give you the unsavoury details? They are tiresome and unpleasant, but important.'

She suddenly adopted the guise of an empress who had been regent of a sovereign domain: authoritative and precise.

'Geoffrey is a man now, but he still acts like a child. He is passionate about his hunting, about his feasting and drinking, and about the many whores I'm sure he keeps. That is where he is now – hunting to the north, with a coterie of young girls in his entourage. He comes to me from time to time and fumbles around. Sometimes he manages a proper union, but it's like copulating with a cold fish – there is no excitement for me. If he is planting his seed, nothing is sprouting in my belly. He has no problem tupping other women, but I think he only likes young girls – I fear he sees me as his mother!'

I held her as tightly as I could. I knew that what she was telling me was hard enough for me to hear, but even more humiliating for her.

'In fact, his mother died young – she and I would be about the same age. I'm convinced that, for Geoffrey, getting into bed with me is like getting into bed with her . . . I'm sorry to have to share these sordid facts with you.'

I now understood that Maud's message had been sent, not because she was pregnant, but because she was not.

She continued her formal explanation.

'I keep telling Geoffrey about his responsibilities. I have reminded him that I went to him with a dowry that would buy a kingdom and that his part of the bargain was to do what most men cannot stop themselves doing – to sire a child. But he's oblivious to reason and has got neither the will nor the wherewithal to fulfil the arrangement. More importantly, he's threatening to destroy our dream.'

Realizing the truth behind our encounter, I looked her in the eye.

'So I'm here as a stud bull?'

She looked vulnerable again, losing the imperious tone, and pleaded with me.

'Is that such a bad thing?'

An image came into my head of Maud snuggling up to me and pressing herself into my loins. I suddenly began to question the diabolical covenant we had struck with her father.

'It's not the most romantic of circumstances –'

'I know, my darling, but the pact with the Devil has been made. We have no option, if we are to have a life together. And wouldn't you prefer your seed in my belly than his?'

'But what kind of life would it bring us and the child – furtive and illicit? He would be a bastard, like me!'

'Do you think I don't know that! But there are only two other options. We could abandon one another and live separate lives, or we could retreat to St Cirq Lapopie and give up the throne. Do you want either of those?'

It was hard to accept, but she was right. I was desperate to share my life with Maud, even on a compromised basis. And if she were to give up the throne in exchange for a life of humble pleasures in the Lot, what would become of England's destiny? What would become of the hopes and dreams that my family had fought for so relentlessly, for over sixty years?

My mind began to accept the strength of Maud's logic, just as my body began to warm to her presence. My scruples about the wholesomeness of the pact with the King were waning, just as my lascivious feelings for his daughter were waxing.

She led me to her carriage, which had been arranged like a bed, and pulled me down on to the straw mattress covering its floor. She pressed herself against me, whispering in my ear.

'I need you so much; I hunger for you. Let's give life to the next King of England . . .'

The hours that followed became a blur of wild passion. Dawn came and went, and the heat of the day made the confined space of the carriage as hot as a furnace. The sweat poured from us, but the heat only heightened our hunger, our bodies slithering in their own sap. Our hair was matted to our heads, and our juices mingled as nature intended. If ever a mating was intended to produce robust offspring, this was it.

We stopped only for food and wine at midday, which Greta had dutifully left at the door of the carriage, and continued our feast of love well into the evening. By the time we had satisfied one another, my loins ached and Maud's naked limbs were curled around me in blissful exhaustion.

Sleep was the next delight, with sweet dreams that lasted until dawn, when the gentle sounds of the mere heralded the next day. Maud was still sleeping soundly, but outside Eadmer and Greta had got the fire going and were heating yesterday's bread and stirring fresh oatmeal. The loyal Lotharingians, taking it in turns to watch over us, were still standing sentinel, and the rising sun was making the dew glisten like a gossamer blanket.

The amorous assignation continued for three days – just as intense, and just as exhausting – until Maud called a halt, declaring that she feared her husband would shortly return to Le Mans. It was a bitter parting for all of us – made worse by the knowledge that in order for Maud's ploy to work, she must soon take her husband to her bed to make sense of the pretence we were trying to create.

I understood, but I felt sad and not a little sordid. I rested my head on her shoulder as we said our goodbyes. She knew it was hard for me to bear.

'I know, my darling. Believe me, it will take all my resolve to do what I have to do, but you know it's what I must do. There can be no suspicions of anything amiss. Let's only think about the next time we can be together. Be at the bridge in three weeks' time. I'll send word.'

We had one more similarly passionate rendezvous at Loudon Mere. But at our third meeting, on a beautiful day in August, her mood was less ardent, though no less animated.

Maud did not run into my arms; she walked at a gentle pace, and looked reserved.

'Darling Hal, it's wonderful to see you, but I'm afraid something has happened. I cannot stay for our tryst . . .'

I stretched out my arms, sensing her discomfort.

'That's fine, my darling. The important thing is to be able to see you, however briefly –'

Then I saw Greta trying to hold back a giggle, which made Maud scream with delight.

'I'm pregnant! It must have been that first time we were together. I can't believe it's finally happened.'

Greta cried and Eadmer slapped me on the back. I felt tears running down my face. I could not find the right words, but just kept saying how happy I was.

Maud adopted her imperious guise again to describe the next stage of our devious plan.

'Darling, I must return to Rouen now. Apart from wanting to give my father the news in person, it takes me away from Geoffrey, who is mightily relieved that he has delivered his side of the bargain. I am going to take to my bed and live in a shaded room. Nothing must happen to this child! I'm going to eat like a horse and grow as fat as a pig.'

Eventually, I took on the role of the authoritative new father.

'Eadmer and I will return to St Cirq Lapopie. We cannot be near Rouen until the child is born. As soon as the time is right, and your father sanctions my return, I will be with you as fast as is humanly possible.'

This time, it was a bitter-sweet parting. We were both excited that the first part of our pact with the King had been accomplished, and in a far more satisfying way than we had dreamed of. But we were also anxious that the future was fraught with so many dangers.

Nevertheless, the deed had been done. And there was no turning back.

Another phase of my life was about to begin. Eadmer's question summed it up, in his typically succinct way, on our long journey back to St Cirq Lapopie.

'What does it feel like to have sired a future King of England?'

I did not answer. I just smiled, but inside I had mixed feelings. There was joy at the thought of what it meant in terms of my family's journey, disappointment that the truth of our place in the royal lineage must never be known, and anxiety that Maud and I had woven a web of deceit which, no matter how worthy our intentions, may have serious consequences for all of us.

I touched the Talisman around my neck and wondered what all those who had worn it would think about its present guardian. Indeed, in the light of Maud's momentous announcement, I was momentarily arrogant enough to contemplate the thought that I might be the rightful recipient of the Talisman, rather than its guardian.

Maud gave birth to a son on 5 March 1133, in Le Mans. Although Maud resisted it, Geoffrey had insisted that she return to Maine for the birth, rather than have the child delivered in Rouen. Maud had agreed, in the end – simply to keep Geoffrey happy.

A hefty and vigorous baby, with a shock of red hair, he was named Henry, after his grandfather. He was heir to a vast domain that encompassed not only England and Normandy, but also vast stretches of western France including Maine and Anjou. The King was particularly delighted about the red hair, which was so reminiscent of his own father's famous mane, the great patriarch of the

Norman dynasty, William, Conqueror of the English. He ordered that, at his expense, celebrations be held throughout his realms.

The King, true to his word, allowed me to return to Rouen in the summer of 1133, where I met young Henry, my handsome son, for the first time. I also met Geoffrey, Count of Anjou, who had adopted the name 'Plantagenet' to reflect his love of hunting – derived from the Latin for a sprig of broom, *Planta genista*, which he liked to wear in his hunting cap. And so Henry, my son, became 'Henry Plantagenet' – a good name, I thought.

I could see why Maud disliked her husband – he was frivolous, often drunk and loud – but men took to him. They enjoyed his merry company and relished joining him in his debauchery and womanizing. Maud introduced me to the Count during one of the King's banquets. She was uncomfortable, and I found it hard to contain my hostility towards him. Fortunately, he barely acknowledged me, being already the worse for drink and far too preoccupied with the nubile young ladies of the court. His aloofness was a relief, as it meant I only had to exchange the minimum of courtesies with him.

He was handsome, athletic looking and full of self-confidence. He was still only twenty years old – fifteen years my junior – and I reflected on how immature I had been at the same age. As I looked at him, I couldn't help wondering how he would react if he knew I was cuckolding him. Perhaps he would not care, such was the light-hearted way in which he approached life.

He soon returned to Le Mans, allowing me to spend as much time as I liked with Maud and baby Henry. It became a very happy time; Eadmer and Greta were also able to be together, and we enjoyed life as a cheerful quintet. Not surprisingly, it was not long before Greta announced her own pregnancy, which brought more elation for all of us.

Eadmer then made a heartfelt request: he wanted his child to be born in England.

Maud jumped at the opportunity.

'My father wants me to go to England as soon as Henry is weaned, so that he can show him off to his magnates. He's already made them swear oaths, promising to be loyal to me as Queen. Now that Henry has been born, he wants them to swear again. And he wants me to be there when they do – the fact that I have a son will make it so much easier for them. We can travel with my father. I will speak to him directly.'

Maud had no difficulty in persuading her father to allow me to travel with her. She could do no wrong in his eyes; she had given him the grandson he thought he was never going to have. The King and Maud had come to an understanding with Count Geoffrey: she would travel to Le Mans twice a year and spend a month with him on each occasion. For the rest of the time, they were both free to live their own lives.

It was not a perfect future for Maud, Henry and me. But for ten months of the year, it was as good as circumstances would allow.

Henry Beauclerc, King of England, called a Christmas Court at Westminster for the end of 1133. His daughter, Matilda, now revered as the 'Lady of the English', took pride of place beside him. In her arms was the young

Henry, a future ruler of the realm. Significantly, not only was the boy a true Norman, he was also a true Englishman – a child able to unite the whole of the realm.

All the leading magnates of England were at Westminster. They came from far and wide to kiss the forehead of the King's grandson and kneel at the feet of Matilda to swear their unwavering loyalty to her.

There had been no occasion as grand as this for a generation. The monks sang and the echoes rang around the nave of the mighty cathedral built by King Edward, the last Cerdician King of England. Set against the bland cream stone of the nave were the rich colours of the gonfalons and pennons of the lords and knights of the realm, mixed with the rich silks of their ladies. The crowds outside the cathedral cheered with a fervour they had not shown since King Harold had assumed the throne in 1066 in his vain attempt to keep England's shores secure.

As an earl of the realm, I stood less than ten yards away from the anointing of Maud as future Queen of England, and our son as her successor. I felt immensely proud of both of them. I thought about my family: my great grandfather, the Old Man of the Wildwood, who began our saga; my grandfather Hereward and grandmother Torfida, who fought to the death against King William; my father and mother and their friends, who found a way to keep England's dream alive.

What would they think now, knowing that their descendant would, one day, be King of their ancient realm?

My eyes filled with tears, as did those of many in the cathedral – Norman and English alike. I looked around at the high and mighty of the realm. Inspired by the pomp and ceremony of the occasion, I dared to imagine the future.

Perhaps, I thought, when Maud becomes Matilda, Queen of England, Englishman and Norman will be as one after almost seventy years of bitterness?

I glanced at Maud.

She smiled warmly at me; she was happy.

Our plan was working.

24. Death of a King

While the King returned to Normandy, we spent the rest of 1133 touring Maud's future kingdom. She was hailed wherever she went. Not only did her reputation as the beautiful Empress go before her, but her adopted title – Lady of the English – reminded the people of her noble Cerdician pedigree. She was one of them. And with her was Henry, who was also one of them.

In November, Maud fell pregnant again and we returned to Rouen for the confinement. Greta gave birth to a daughter in March of the following year. To her parents' delight, Gretchen was a happy little bundle of blonde hair and pink skin.

At the end of May 1134, Maud went into labour. She was worried, as there had not been a conjugal visit to Geoffrey at the right time, and so it was announced that the arrival was premature. In any event, her husband seemed not in the slightest bit interested and made no attempt to travel to Rouen for the birth.

However, the date of the child's conception became the least of Maud's worries. The baby was breech and the labour protracted. The midwives struggled and Maud went through hell for many hours. When the child did arrive, Maud bled profusely and was severely torn. She lost consciousness – which, at least, was a relief from the pain – and the midwives called for the King's physicians, who rushed to her bedside.

All sorts of remedies were administered, but there was no sign of her regaining consciousness. The doctors claimed her body was going into a deep sleep to recover, but I had my doubts. Greta slept on the floor by her bed and acted as wet nurse to the child – a sweet blond-haired boy who Maud had decided should be called Geoffrey, after her husband.

Her loyal Lotharingians, Otto and Berenger, stood guard at her door with instructions from me that no one was to pass.

When Maud eventually came round, she had a high fever; it was obvious that she had become infected. She was soon delirious, and urgent messages were sent to the King and to Count Geoffrey. The King was hunting nearby and soon arrived, but Geoffrey was in Anjou, a journey of several days. Her condition deteriorated and her prospects looked grim. The physicians predicted that she would not survive beyond another day.

When the King arrived, he sent for Hugh, Archbishop of Rouen, who administered the last rites on the evening of 17 June 1134. The priests told me that this day was the feast day of St Botolph – an English saint who had helped bring Christianity to the Gauls and whose remains are revered in the crypt of Ely Cathedral – and suggested that I should pray to him.

I took the link to Ely as a propitious sign. After everyone else had left, instead of praying – which I left to Greta and Eadmer – I placed the Talisman around Maud's neck. Its legend said that it had been worn by kings and emperors and had helped them find wisdom and truth, so there could be no better person than Maud to wear it. My recent passing fancy that, perhaps, I was its next recipient had long since vanished; it had been just an idle thought.

Harold of England had been the last King to wear the Talisman. I begged the Fates, the Wodewose and the spirits of my family to succour my conviction that it was now being worn by England's next Queen. Although Maud was desperately ill, I knew at that moment she would recover – I do not know how I knew, but I did.

It took several weeks to overcome the fever, followed by several months of recuperation, but by the end of 1134, Maud was restored to us in glowing health. Not only that, but our quartet of friends now had three babies to care for.

Count Geoffrey did appear in the late summer to see his son and namesake, and immediately gave him the title Count of Nantes. He was kind to Maud and brought her some beautiful jewellery from Provence. He was even courteous to me.

'Earl Harold, I am grateful to you for the care and devotion you show to our family. Empress Matilda speaks very highly of you.'

'It is not in the slightest a burden, Count Geoffrey. She is my half-sister, and the King has made it my duty to protect her at all times. What more honourable task could a man ask for?'

'Quite so! But tell me, what is that strange amulet she now wears around her neck? I've never seen anything like it.'

'It is the Talisman of Truth, a family treasure said to be centuries old.'

'Is it a lucky charm?'

'It has sometimes been regarded as such, but it's more a symbol of hope, like a crucifix.'

'Isn't that blasphemy?'

'Some might consider it so, but the Talisman is older than the Cross – and probably means much the same thing.'

'That is blasphemy. Does the Empress believe that?'

'I'm sure not. She just wears it because I have asked her to; I believe it helps protect her.'

'So, it *is* a lucky charm?'

'If you like . . .'

Geoffrey shuffled off, clearly bemused. I thought about what I had just said and it dawned on me that I was beginning to talk like a seer. God help my soul!

We did not see Geoffrey again into the winter of 1134. The cold months passed slowly; the weather was typically harsh, and people hibernated as usual. Henry, Geoffrey and Gretchen grew at a pace – and Maud and Greta spoiled them, as mothers tend to do.

We received very sad news at the beginning of 1135. Word arrived from England that Robert Curthose, the firstborn son of King William – who, as Duke of Normandy, had befriended Edgar the Atheling and my family – had died in Cardiff Castle at the age of eighty-one. He had been incarcerated at King Henry's pleasure for almost thirty years. I had often thought about him: a hero of the Great Crusade, a just ruler and a good man, but a broken one after the loss of his wife, Sybilla. His remaining years must have been an interminable purgatory.

His death meant that I was the last survivor of the

Brethren of the Blood of the Talisman – and the final link to the Brotherhood of Ely. It was the end of an era and reinforced what I already knew: the outcome of what had been fought for since 1066 could only be determined by me. I now had my own small family and a group of loyal friends – as had my father and grandfather – and through Maud and baby Henry, I had the chance to bring the long journey to a happy conclusion.

The burden was great, but the task was simple: ensure Maud and Henry's succession.

Towards the end of November, Maud lifted my sombre mood with the best possible news.

'I'm pregnant again, Hal – number three. It seems I can't stop conceiving!'

'Wonderful news, my darling, another summer baby. What shall we call it?'

While Maud thought about names, I came to an unwelcome realization.

'William, if it's a boy, and Maud, if it's a girl –'

'Maud, I hate to dampen the occasion . . . but this time, we can't contrive for there to be any chance that the child is Geoffrey's.'

Maud did not share my concern.

'He won't care – and neither will my father. The terms of the marriage settlement were fulfilled long ago. As long as they both think young Henry and baby Geoffrey are his, then they won't care about a third child. Two legitimate heirs are plenty.'

Maud seemed content, so I chose to put the question of the baby's parentage out of my head. I knew it would add some spice to my next meeting with Count Geoffrey – but I had faced worse prospects!

The King continued to enjoy good health, sharing his time evenly between Normandy and England. He had repeated the oath-taking ritual once more, and all the magnates of both realms had sworn their loyalty to Matilda for a third time. They must have regarded the whole exercise as irksome, but they did it without overt complaint.

But all was not well in King Henry's domain. He had always been a strict ruler, but he could be excessively cruel and had made enemies – especially among the lords on the periphery of his domains, who were often courted by his enemies.

When he was a young man in Rouen – during the Dukedom of his eldest brother, Robert – there was a revolt among the burgesses of the city, which Henry crushed ruthlessly. Many young hotheads were cut down in the streets by Henry's cavalry. When their leader, Conan, son of Pilatus, was caught, Henry had him dragged to the top of the tallest tower of the city's walls. Then, with the young man begging for mercy, Henry threw him from the top – laughing as he did so. Conan was very popular, and the incident was never forgotten by the townspeople.

In 1119, in a dispute over the lordship of Breteuil in Normandy, Henry sent a hostage, a boy called Ralph Harenc, to his rival, Eustace of Breteuil – his own son-in-law, the husband of his illegitimate daughter Juliana – to try to secure his loyalty. Henry held Eustace's daughters, his own granddaughters, as hostages in exchange. When Eustace blinded the boy Ralph and sent him back, Henry was so angry that he agreed to Ralph's request for revenge by allowing the two little girls to be blinded and have the tips of their noses cut off.

Mass executions and mutilations were not uncommon. Many people said that although there was peace throughout most of Henry's reign, it came at a high price – one that was all too reminiscent of the draconian rule of his father, William the Bastard, Conqueror of the English.

Memories were long among those the King had wronged and among those who thought that siring more than two dozen illegitimate children and giving them all land and titles were both an affront to God and an outrage to those who paid him taxes and tithes. Henry was in his sixty-seventh year, and those with scores to settle knew that he could not live forever.

The old stag was nearing his end, and the young bucks were circling.

The King had spent almost the whole of 1135 marauding around the fringes of his realm, reminding any doubters of his power. He had prowled around Wales and the West of England with a large force, inviting challenges from the Welsh Princes, or from his own lords. He had made a point of inviting himself to the castles and fortifications of those he knew had an axe to grind, insisting on the laws of hospitality for himself and his retinue, making any troublesome nobles fawn at his feet, or challenge him. No challenges had been forthcoming, but the resentment had grown.

He had then turned his attention to Normandy – especially the south, where the French King, 'Fat' Louis VI, was constantly trying to win the allegiance of the local lords. Henry had taken control of the castles at Alençon, Almenêches and Argentan, and had then moved north to the border with Flanders. After another show of force, he had taken a break to indulge his third greatest passion, after power and women – the thrill of the hunt.

On Friday 29 November – only a few days after Maud realized she was pregnant – the King went hunting in the Forest of Lyons at St Denis and returned to the castle to a dish of lampreys, another of his many passions. He was violently ill in the night and died on Sunday evening, the first day of December 1135. It was a day that became etched in the memory of all Normans as the day when the last of the three mighty Norman Kings of England died.

The King had insisted that his body be taken to England, to be buried beneath the altar of Reading Abbey, his own foundation. It had been built, as he decreed: 'for the salvation of my soul, and the souls of King William, my father, and of King William, my brother, and Queen Edith, my wife, and all my ancestors and successors'.

The gruesome task of preparing the King's body for such a journey fell to a local embalmer, who was greatly honoured to be given the responsibility. He removed the brains, eyes and intestines, which were buried in an urn at one of Henry's favourite churches, Notre Dame du Pré at Emendreville, before scoring the rest of the body with deep cuts to allow salt to penetrate deep into the flesh. The body was then sewn into ox hides and placed on a bier for the long journey by land and sea.

Unfortunately, the innocent embalmer had not been told that the King had ordered that when his task was complete, he was to be executed and his corpse dealt with in the same grisly manner.

Maud and I were in Rouen when we heard the news of her father's death. But before we could make arrangements to accompany her father's body to England, word arrived by courier that trouble had flared in the south. Scores were being settled and willful vengeance was replacing the rule of law. As Maud was now the titular Duchess of the realm, she decided it was her duty to ride south to impose her authority.

I disagreed with her decision.

'Send your husband to the south. Make use of him – make him your regent in Normandy if needs be – but you must make England your priority. That's what your uncle did when your grandfather died, and that's what your father did when your uncle died.'

'My priority is here. What would they think of me in Normandy if I hurried away to England when the south is in uproar?'

She made a strong case, but I knew how important it was to get to Westminster to claim the throne and the loyalty of London, and to secure the Treasury at Winchester.

'Maud, England is the biggest prize – your birthright.'

'Both England and Normandy are my birthright!'

She looked at me sternly. For the first time, she was speaking not as Maud, my lover, but as Matilda, my Queen.

I did not feel cowed by her comment, but I respected it. I looked at the Talisman around her neck. It caught the light streaming in through the window of Rouen's ducal palace, and I knew that a new chapter in my life had begun.

'To the south it is! I will tell the Constable to prepare the garrison.'

'Good, and tell him that you will command the garrison.'

'Very well, Your Grace.'

I used her title without mockery. Our lives had changed.

My dear Thibaud,

Thank you for the latest information from Rome. I also appreciate your prayers for my health.

I believe Our Lord is listening to you; I am feeling much better. You obviously have His ear. I fear He ignores me — I hope it doesn't mean I have too much time in Purgatory to come.

Anyway, back to Harold and his compelling tale. So, the old King is dead. I remember his reign; we were all terrified of him, but I suppose he brought peace and prosperity. It is strange to think that we now live in the reign of his namesake and grandson all these years later. But although this Henry is just as firm in his rule, he is a much better man.

We now approach the events that shook England to its foundations. Even though it was half a lifetime ago, the memories were still vivid for me even before I heard Harold's story.

It was difficult to hear it all again: so much ambition; so much greed; so much suffering. I confess, Harold's words made me weep at the loss of so many of England's finest young men.

Yours in God,
Gilbert

25. Betrayal

Events moved at a frightening pace over the next few weeks, but not in the direction we had planned.

The first omen of problems ahead came immediately. When I went to Henry de Pomeroy, the Constable at Rouen, to mobilize the garrison, he was polite but unhelpful.

'I can give you three hundred men, but no more.'

'But the Duchess orders it —'

'I'm sorry, Earl Harold, but she is not the anointed Duchess yet.'

'But it was the King's wish — and oaths have been sworn.'

A tall dignified man, an old warrior and a man of honour, he looked uncomfortable.

'Take the squadrons I've offered you. I shouldn't even offer those, because whoever becomes Duke will not be happy.'

'Explain yourself, man!'

'I leave for Lisieux in the morning. All the lords of Normandy are meeting there to discuss the succession.'

'Then we will go with you.'

'That may not be wise.'

'Then we will make it "wise".'

'The Empress Matilda is not invited. She will not find any support.'

'And what of the oaths to the King?'

'The King is dead.'

'Will the twelve squadrons you're offering be loyal to her?'

'I don't know. Things are moving too quickly for me. There is fighting all over the Dukedom – it's just like when old King William died. An iron glove has no power if there's no fist in it. I'm an old campaigner, and this is a young man's game. I'm sorry.'

I rushed back to Maud.

'You have been betrayed. There is to be a council in Lisieux to choose a new duke.'

'But not a new duchess?'

'No, the magnates are renouncing their oaths.'

'Then we must put a stop to it, impose my authority!'

'We have no men. Hugh de Pomeroy will give us three hundred, but he's reluctant even to do that. There's mayhem everywhere. Let's go to the coast and escort your father's body home to England. That will confirm the succession.'

She looked furious for a moment, and I realized I had not calculated the effect of my words. But she soon rallied and accepted the changed circumstances.

'Agreed. It seems I am now required to admit that you were right after all!'

We travelled with only a small retinue: one groom, two stewards and two maids. Maud had made Greta a lady-in-waiting, so had her own maid in addition. Besides Eadmer and myself, our only armed men were Otto and Berenger. It was not the sort of entourage we had expected to accompany us on our first journey through Normandy after King Henry's death.

The King's funeral cortège, accompanied by several of Normandy's leaders, had reached Caen, but there were no favourable winds in the Channel for the crossing. The body, which by then was the source of odours and discharges foul enough to turn a man's stomach, was kept in the choir of the Cathedral of St Étienne. By the time the winds turned, several weeks had passed, Christmas had come and gone, and none of Normandy's worthies was prepared to make the crossing with the rotting corpse.

But Matilda did not hesitate.

'I will take my father's body home.'

She turned to the monks of St Étienne.

'Will you help me?'

'We will, Your Grace.'

They were the first and only men to refer to Maud as their Duchess.

'Thank you, we leave on tomorrow's tide.'

It was not a journey any of us was looking forward to. The Channel north of Caen was at its widest; it would be a long crossing. However, later that evening, catastrophic news arrived, which not only dealt a hammer blow to Maud's already damaged chances of becoming the Duchess of Normandy, but also to the likelihood of her becoming Queen of England.

It arrived in the form of a breathless monk in the service of William of Corbeil, Archbishop of Canterbury. He had a personal message for Hugh of Amiens – Archbishop of Rouen and the man in charge of the King's funeral bier. Hugh summoned us to St Étienne to hear the monk's message.

Stephen of Blois, Maud's cousin – the son of Maud's

elder sister, Adela – had happened to be in Boulogne when the King died and, within days, had crossed the Channel with a small retinue of knights. He was in London only two days later and immediately agreed to grant it commune status to match many of the large trading capitals of Europe. He also offered guarantees of trade with Boulogne and other cities in Flanders, and thus won the support of all London's burghers and merchants. He toured the strongholds of the Norman lords and made them profuse promises. He reminded them of his grandfather, King William, who he resembled, and a wave of support for him spread far and wide. As in Normandy, lawlessness had broken out as soon as news reached England of the King's death, and Stephen promised to restore order.

Maud turned to me.

'This is not possible! Am I not the King's daughter, his chosen heir?'

'He has done what William Rufus did to Duke Robert, and what your father did when Rufus died – he has made haste to England to grab the crown.'

But the young monk's news got even worse. Having won over London, Stephen had gone to Winchester to the Royal Treasury. There, the King's key-holders – Roger, Bishop of Salisbury, and William Pont de l'Arche – had bowed to Stephen and handed him the keys.

Maud was shaking with anger.

'It is an outrage! This has been planned in advance, long before my father's death.'

The last part of the monk's account was the most difficult to bear, as it involved the man who had been kind to me in Norwich when I was a boy – Hugh Bigod, Earl of Norwich. He had sworn an oath, with several others, that he had been with the King during the weekend of his death in Lyons St Denis and that, with death approaching, the King had changed his mind about the succession. He had decided that his nephew, Stephen of Blois, should be his heir, not his daughter, Matilda.

Maud erupted in fury.

'It is a conspiracy! It's all lies; Hugh Bigod wasn't even in Normandy!'

The Archbishop tried to calm Maud.

'Ma'am, please, your father rests close by. Please be seated.'

Maud sat down reluctantly to hear the monk finish his message. He delivered it like an announcement from the pulpit.

'The oath taken by Hugh Bigod convinced the nobles of the land that King Henry had chosen Stephen of Blois as his successor. On Sunday the 22nd of December 1135, the Archbishop of Canterbury crowned Stephen of Blois King of England and Duke of Normandy at Westminster Abbey.'

I thought about the good people of England. Although Stephen may well have won over the Norman lords and bishops, and indeed the prosperous English merchants, the ordinary downtrodden peasants, yeomen and artisans of England must have been heartbroken. Their 'Lady of the English', the great-granddaughter of Edmund Ironside, had been supplanted by a man whose odious Norman blood was diluted not by pure English blood, but by the blood of a clan from a land even more alien than Normandy. I thought about the people of Bourne, the young masons of Norwich, and all those who had hoped for a new dawn for England.

It was a wretched day for all of us.

The monk bowed to us all and made his exit, leaving us feeling that we had been struck by a thunderbolt. Maud was livid, her face white with fury.

'Let's talk.'

Eadmer, Greta and I followed her into the cloister of St Étienne.

'They poisoned him! Lampreys, the easiest thing in the world to poison. Why did Stephen just happen to be in Boulogne, two domains away from his home in Blois? And Hugh Bigod's part in this conspiracy is beyond belief.'

Maud was adamant, and I had to admit that her construction of events was credible. Her father's death had been very sudden, and he had been making more and more enemies.

'Maud, I know this is a body blow, but we must think carefully and develop a plan.'

'I already have a plan; we sail for England with my father's body in the morning. My conniving cousin will want to come to the interment, and there I will confront him.'

'With what, my darling?'

I took her into my arms. She was rigid with anger.

'I must have some supporters!'

'You do, but we have to prepare – and prepare carefully – because the only way we can win the throne now is by force of arms. That means civil war. We can't go to England now. At best, Stephen will force us to come straight back. At worst, he could send you to some godforsaken castle under lock and key – just as your father did to your uncle, Robert Curthose. You are with child, we can't go to war with you in this condition. But that gives us time – and time is what we need.'

'Stephen didn't wait –'

'But that was when the throne was vacant; for him, it was vital that he acted quickly. Now he has the throne, so we have to act slowly and carefully to build our resources, then act decisively when the time is right.'

'So, what do you suggest we do?'

'We have to go to Le Mans, and plan from there.'

'Back to my husband?'

'It's the only place where you'll be safe.'

Maud was quiet and thoughtful on the way back. When we reached Argentan, a massive donjon on the border of Normandy and Anjou, she decided that she would like to retreat behind its huge walls, rather than continue to Le Mans.

'I know the Lord here, Fulk of Falaise; he's a good man. His loyalty is to the local people – he has no strong allegiance to either Normandy or Anjou.'

I could sense that Maud wanted to withdraw from the problems she faced, at least for a while, and concentrate on her unborn child – a child that Geoffrey would know was not his. It was probably a wise decision, as it soon became apparent that Count Geoffrey was creating mayhem further south. He had begun his own war on the southern border of Normandy, laying siege to cities that he thought should be part of his realm. Maud immediately sent a messenger to request a rendezvous at Argentan.

Fulk of Falaise was a good host, and we spent the

winter and spring of 1136 biding our time with him. But we were not idle: messengers constantly went to and fro in all directions, as we tried to garner support for Maud's cause in both England and Normandy.

Count Geoffrey did not appear until the end of July 1136, about a week after Maud had given birth to our third child. It was another boy, who we named William – not a fair child this time, but a dark-skinned brunette like me. We had had three boys, each of whom seemed to represent our tribal pedigrees: a red-headed Viking-Norman, a fair-haired Saxon and a tawny Celt.

We now had a good idea who might support Maud's cause – and it was a growing number. Every time Stephen asserted his authority and imposed his rule in either England or Normandy, he made new enemies. His was an unenviable task, but we were the beneficiaries.

In England, there were willing supporters among the barons of the south-west, East Anglia and parts of the north. The Welsh Princes could be persuaded with money and concessions, as could King David of Scotland – who was Maud's uncle and coveted the north of England, as did all his kin.

Most importantly, we had received a coded but supportive message from the most powerful man beyond Stephen's inner circle: Robert Earl of Gloucester, Maud's half-brother and King Henry's eldest son. He had been sired with Nest, the beautiful daughter of Rhys ap Tewdwr, the King of Deheubarth. Such were Robert's stature and regard that, were it not for his illegitimacy, he would be unopposed as England's king.

His message was succinct.

Dearest Sister,

Hold fast, timing is everything.

Your loyal brother,
Robert

In Normandy, the chaos after King Henry's death was even greater than the disorder in England, and was made much worse by Count Geoffrey's non-stop campaigning. Stephen had ignored the province since his dash to grab the English crown, an act that had won him no friends in the Duchy. Although Count Geoffrey's harassments were winning us as many enemies as friends, the instability was constantly undermining Stephen's authority.

When Maud had recovered from the birth – a delivery far less traumatic than the arrival of her second son – she called a council of war with Geoffrey. It was not the most prodigious gathering of warriors ever assembled.

Geoffrey had arrived with a small but formidable group of supporters: William Talvas, Count of Ponthieu; William, Duke of Aquitaine; Geoffrey of Vendôme; and William, son of the Count of Nevers. Nevertheless, despite the lack of warriors, Maud possessed the most important element of all in the conflict to come: her bloodline. In young Henry, now three years old and prolific in every way, she had the future King her father had always wanted and thus her rightful claim to be Queen Regent.

Significantly, all the nobles present – including the powerful Duke of Aquitaine – treated Maud with the deference appropriate to a ruling monarch.

Maud began the meeting in her most authoritative style.

'My Lords, I am grateful to you for joining me today. Let me also thank my good friend Fulk, Lord of Falaise, for his generosity here at Argentan, where we have been very happy these past months. As you know, Stephen of Blois has usurped my rightful inheritance, as decreed by my father, but he will not enjoy the fruits of his treason for long. Now that I am delivered of my child, my campaign will begin in earnest. I have not been idle. I will now hand over to the Earl of Huntingdon – an experienced soldier and veteran of campaigns for the Doge of Venice and in the Holy Land – who, as you know, was entrusted with my safety by my father, King Henry, may he rest in peace.'

I could sense some surprise in the room, and I felt not a little trepidation myself. But this moment had to arrive sooner or later, and I was prepared.

'My Lords, I'm pleased to announce that His Royal Highness, King David of Scotland is preparing a force at this moment for an invasion of the north of England. That will be the opening of our campaign in England. In Normandy, my Lady Matilda requests that Count Geoffrey launches a similar campaign into the heart of Normandy. My Lady wishes to participate in the campaign in Normandy in order to show her commitment to the cause. In a second stage, my Lady would then travel to England to become the figurehead of a rising against Count Stephen. Our information is that many lords will rush to her colours as soon as she sets foot on English soil.'

After I finished, there was a brief but ominous silence.

There was obvious consternation in the room: who was I to be speaking to such men?

But then Count Geoffrey got to his feet. He looked around at the assembly and then smiled broadly at his supporters, clearly relishing the prospect of what lay ahead.

'Very well, it sounds like a sound strategy to me. When do we begin?'

I rose to respond, feeling a welcome surge of relief.

'King David is unlikely to be ready for some time – perhaps even a year – but there is no reason why our Norman campaign can't begin as soon as your forces are ready.'

'I agree. We will go to our lands, get the harvests in and gather our forces for a campaign towards the end of September. Are you with us, Gentlemen?'

There was unanimous consensus around the room.

Maud was ecstatic after the meeting.

'Hal, you were impressive; that can't have been easy for you.'

'It wasn't, but you were at your best too – Empress, Queen, Duchess, *Magnus Princeps*. We owe a debt of gratitude to your husband; he was more than generous.'

'Indeed, he was. But he knows the reality of the situation; he wants to be Regent in Normandy, and he can only achieve that through me. He will not rock the boat.'

There was a gleam in Maud's eye that I had not seen for a while. We both knew that we still had a long way to go, but we had taken the first steps.

Just as I was about to leave Maud's chamber, Greta appeared with news that Count Geoffrey would like to see us. Even though the conversation was certain to be a difficult one, we had no choice but to agree.

Geoffrey conducted the discussion without rancour – a reflection of his increasing maturity and the pragmatism with which he approached his wife's campaign.

'I thought it best that the three of us speak together – to avoid any misunderstanding, or bad blood.'

He walked over to the window and stared out towards the town of Argentan below. He had grown taller and filled out since the early days of his marriage to Maud; he now looked every inch the noble warrior.

'We can only win this fight together, so we must have an understanding.'

I glanced at Maud, who was looking pensive. She started to walk over towards Geoffrey, but he put his hand up to stop her. Then he drew a deep breath.

'Of course, you humiliated me as a boy when you ran home to your father . . .'

He paused. These were traumatic memories for him.

'But you came back. I am thankful for that –'

He stopped abruptly and flashed a despairing look at Maud.

'I was too young. Perhaps it could work now, but it's too late – you are now with your lover, the "noble" Earl of Huntingdon.'

He turned to me; there was no doubting the scorn in his eyes.

'What a wicked web you have woven.'

Maud interrupted before I could speak.

'Don't blame Hal, blame me! It wasn't easy for me, either. Like you, I was a pawn in my father's game.'

Geoffrey's face softened. He understood Maud's position only too well.

'We are all pawns in our fathers' games. But I have no reason for bitterness – I have my two sons, and Henry will one day be King of England and Duke of Normandy. Through me, he will rule lands that will extend his realm far to the west and south. His will be a realm to rival the Holy Roman Empire. I will do everything I can to keep him safe until that day dawns.'

He looked at me – but this time, if not with warmth, at least with less hostility.

'I surmise that the new baby is yours; I'm glad he will be called William, it is a good name. But we must, for everybody's sake, treat the three boys exactly the same, as if they are all mine. There must be no doubt about the integrity of our family's heritage. Do you agree?'

'I do.'

Maud grabbed Geoffrey's arm.

'We must hold firm, all three of us – for the sake of the boys and for a future Anglo-Norman domain.'

Maud and Geoffrey embraced warmly. I offered him my hand, which he accepted before bidding us farewell.

'Until September. I entrust the boys to your care; look after them.'

Maud and I slumped into our chairs after he left. She had tears in her eyes as she spoke.

'He's right; we have woven a wicked web. Will God ever forgive us?'

'For which sin? For our adultery, and for conceiving Henry and little Geoffrey? Or for letting your husband think he is their father?'

My stark summary was too much for Maud, who collapsed in convulsions of anguish.

'I am a wicked woman, God will never forgive me.'

I cradled her in my arms and rocked her like an infant.

'God will judge you at the end of your journey, not halfway through. Wait until we reach the end of the road before judging yourself.'

I too felt pangs of guilt for my selfish duplicity. It had been easier when Geoffrey was a callow youth. But now he was a man who had developed many admirable qualities, and he was also a crucial ally. I looked at the Talisman around Maud's neck. Our journey still had a long way to go before we reached the end. I hoped that our actions, although sinful and selfish, may prove to be vindicated – at least, to us.

26. Battle of the Standard

Count Geoffrey launched his campaign in Normandy on 21 September 1136. Maud was in the vanguard of the army whenever it was safe, looking magnificent in her long flowing cape of red velvet. Underneath her cape she wore a red leather jerkin, with cavalry leggings and boots. Over a plain white silk wimple and veil she fixed a small gold ducal coronet, which we acquired from the monks at Mont St Michel. Although she had neither armour nor weapons, she carried a jewel-encrusted mace, which she held aloft through every village, town and city we entered.

I was very proud of her. She looked like the warriors of fable: the great Zenobia, Queen of Palmyra, or the legendary Boudicca, Queen of the Iceni. She inspired confidence in our men, and she commanded respect everywhere we went.

Our army was small but mobile: 80 knights, 150 cavalry, 100 archers and crossbowmen, and 200 infantry. Geoffrey's strategy was simple. He relied on speed of movement, swiftness of action and maximum disruption. It was not the most wholesome form of warfare; intimidation until submission was the main objective. This involved wholesale looting and burning, with harsh reprisals for anyone who resisted.

When a fortification fell, its lord had to either declare a humiliating surrender and accept Duchess Matilda as his liege lady, or face execution, the destruction of his castle and the sequestration of his land and property. Few resisted. But when they did, Geoffrey did not hesitate to act ruthlessly.

The campaigning continued throughout the winter of 1136 and into the spring of 1137. Eventually, the harassment achieved its objective. In March 1137, Stephen brought an army across the Channel, landing at Saint-Vaast-la-Hougue on the Cotentin Peninsular, from where he marched south. It was a large force, made up mainly of Flemish mercenaries, and it was rumoured that he had almost emptied his treasury to pay for them. His objective was simple: to intercept our army and put an end to our challenge to his throne.

The battle never came. Stephen had some success in the Cotentin, but his Flemish mercenaries soon became difficult to control. A dispute over a butt of wine led to a mass brawl and fighting broke out wholesale between the Flemish and English contingents. Then, with morale plummeting, the bloody flux infected Stephen's army and he had to order his entire force to retreat. As one witness put it – in explicit detail – the army left in its wake a trail of diarrhoea across the Norman countryside as wide as a tilt yard.

Stephen turned back towards home and, with his tail between his legs, embarked for England, furious and frustrated. The first part of our plan had been successful. Geoffrey could now be left to take Normandy in hand, while Maud and I could return to Argentan to plan our campaign in England.

*

The year 1138 offered renewed optimism for our cause. King David of Scotland intensified his punitive raids into the north of England, letting loose his more ferocious highland kinsmen on the wretched English burghs and monasteries. Maud was upset to hear of some of the brutality and desecration being committed in her name and sent messages to her uncle pleading for moderation. But she had asked him to release his dogs of war and, once off the leash, they were difficult to control.

In the spring, Robert of Gloucester played his decisive opening gambit. With Stephen humiliated in Normandy and King David causing unrest in the north, he instigated challenges to Stephen among several lords along the Welsh Marches and in the south-west. Stephen took the bait and headed west with a large force. Castles were besieged and surrendered as the King went round the country putting out the fires of dissent. Earl Robert's tactic was working perfectly. Although the violence was only minor, and the dissent little more than token, the impression created throughout the realm was that King Stephen's authority was under serious threat.

After weeks of campaigning, Robert waited until Stephen and his supporters had reached the point of exhaustion before sending a messenger to him. The King was resting at Hereford when Robert's message was delivered. It was stark and succinct.

To Stephen of Blois,

I renounce your possession of the throne of our English realm and to that of our kin in Normandy. You sit in Westminster and

Stephen responded angrily, as it was hoped he would do, and began to harass the supporters of Earl Robert in the West Country. He committed several acts of brutality – in particular, after his capture of Shrewsbury Castle. Its lord, William FitzAlan, managed to escape with his family. But his lieutenant, a courageous knight called Arnulf de Hesdin, was hanged on a gibbet along with a hundred of the garrison. It was an act that increased opposition to Stephen's rule, rather than reduced it.

When we heard news of Robert's declaration, we sent word to King David in Dunfermline, asking him to cross the border with the biggest army he could muster, which he did at the beginning of June. His part of the plan was to take possession of the north as far as the Ribble in the west and the Humber in the east, which he would hold as part of his pact with Maud. With Geoffrey holding Normandy, we would take and hold England, with both King David and Geoffrey declaring their loyalty to Maud as 'Lady of the English, Empress of the North'.

The next three months were an agonizing time as we waited for news from King David. Our strategy was to move to Caen. Count Geoffrey had sent a personal retinue of twenty knights and a hundred men-at-arms to act as Maud's personal bodyguard for a Channel crossing, and to escort her to a rendezvous with Earl Robert.

The castle at Caen had been built by King William, Maud's grandfather, and was said to be the most formidable fortress in the realm. The Constable made the ducal apartments available to us and, for the first time, Maud began to feel like a sovereign again. The men that Geoffrey had sent were seasoned campaigners and we made preparations to be ready to sail to England as soon as we heard positive news from across the Channel.

The messenger arrived with the much-anticipated news at the beginning of the second week of September. He was a tall and distinguished man, dressed in a russet-red Celtic leine. He spoke clearly, in excellent English.

Maud sat back in her ducal chair, still wearing her warrior's garb, impatient to hear what the herald had to say as he rolled out a beige vellum document.

'His Majesty, David, Lord of the Isles, Prince of the Galwegians and Cumbrians and King of Alba, sends his felicitations to his niece, Matilda, Lady of the English. His Majesty's army, twenty-six-thousand-strong, entered Northumbria in June 1138 and proceeded south. King David was acclaimed by all who saw him and where there was resistance from Norman lords and their garrisons, it was overcome with ease.

'A major battle was fought in Yorkshire, outside the walls of Clitheroe Castle on the estate of Robert de Lacey, Lord of Bowland, where the forces of Stephen of Blois were comprehensively routed. A few of the English army escaped to the west along the River Ribble to Preston. But most scattered to the east to seek refuge beyond Pen Hill in the forests of Burnley and Trawden, where they were hunted down in their hundreds.'

I smiled at the name of 'Clitheroe Castle', and wondered if it had been built on the spot that my grandfather once used as a base when he began The English Revolt against the Conqueror in 1069. We had called it 'Clitheroe Mound' in our family stories, but almost seventy years had passed – more than enough time for the Normans to have fortified the hilltop position. I began to feel a rising tide of nostalgia and optimism.

But the euphoria was soon dispelled by the rest of the messenger's account.

'When Stephen of Blois heard the account of the Battle of Clitheroe, he despatched a large force northwards under the command of Bernard de Balliol, William Peveral and Robert de Ferrers, which was joined by the armies of the Norman lords of the north, led by Thurstan, Archbishop of York. On the 22nd of August, King David's army gave battle to the Norman horde at Cowton Moor, near Northallerton in Yorkshire. Thurstan raised a standard at the commencement of the battle – a ship's mast with a silver pyx on its top containing a consecrated Host.

'King David regarded this as a desecration and instructed his army to fight for "The Standard" in the name of Scotland and of God. The Norman-English forces were well organized, and their archers inflicted many casualties, causing panic in the Scottish ranks. The Galwegians on King David's right attempted a reckless charge against the centre of the English lines and were cut down by wave after wave of quarrels and arrows, creating terror in the Scottish ranks.

'Witnesses said that Galwegian dead lay on the ground in piles as high as a man and that their bodies had as many arrows in them as sticklebacks have spines. Try as he might, His Majesty King David was unable to rally his men and he had to order a retreat. Our losses were great – almost ten thousand brave souls. The King instructs me to confer his regrets, but reassures you that he still has a significant force at his disposal. He intends to stay in Carlisle for the winter, where he will await your further instructions.'

Maud stood and left the Great Hall of Caen Castle, devastated and indignant. When I caught up with her in her chamber, she was white with anger.

'What was my uncle doing? It sounds like a shambles. Stephen wasn't even there, but still David managed to suffer an ignominious defeat! What do we do now?'

I felt devastated too, but I reassured Maud that it was merely a setback.

'Let's wait for the advice of Earl Robert. The key is still getting you on to English soil – but only when the time is right.'

She looked me in the eye. Her expression changed from anger to despair. I could see tears forming.

'It has been nearly three years. Will we ever get to England?'

'Yes, my darling, of course we will.'

'Don't you sometimes wish we were at St Cirq Lapopie, away from all this? Just you, me and our boys –'

'All the time. But our die is cast; we can't hide in the Lot when Henry is heir to your throne, and Geoffrey and William next in line of succession behind him. We could never find peace.'

'Hal, please help me to be strong.'

I took her into my arms and held her as tightly as I could.

'Darling Maud, you have the strength of ten men; there's no obstacle we can't overcome together.'

Matters deteriorated even more at the end of 1138, when news arrived in Caen that Pope Innocent II had sent Alberic, Cardinal Bishop of Ostia, to Carlisle to negotiate a settlement between Stephen and King David. It took him three days of rancorous argument, but at its end, David agreed to withdraw north of the Tweed for the winter and to cease his raids. David's son, Henry, was made Earl of Northumbria, with effective control of the north of England, for as long as he acknowledged Stephen as his lord.

As Maud was quick to point out when we heard the news, this effectively isolated her uncle from the coming conflict and removed one of her most important allies. It was bad news heaped upon bad news, and it prompted me to suggest a change of plan to Maud.

'I think I should take Eadmer and a few good men and go to England to see Earl Robert. Lothar and Berenger, and the rest of your bodyguard, can stay with you. I'll send word as soon as possible for you to set sail. I fear things are stalling, because we're too far away.'

Maud was enthusiastic about the idea – if anything, a little too enthusiastic.

'You're right of course! But I should come too –'

'No, my darling, not yet; you will be too conspicuous. The ranks of your bodyguard are too big to land secretly, and too small to pose a serious threat.'

'Then we'll travel as a small group, like we used to.'

'It's an attractive idea, but when you next land on England's shore, it should be to a fanfare announcing the arrival of the future Queen. Let us see out the winter here in Caen and watch our boys grow, and I will travel to England in the spring.'

Maud agreed, albeit reluctantly, and we spent the long winter months in front of the colossal fireplaces of Caen Castle. We listened to Eadmer's long repertoire of ballads and enjoyed a voice that he had perfected to match any I had heard. We all agreed that our favourite was 'The Ballad of Robyn of Hode', to which he had added new lines about the 'fair lady Maud' and 'The arrow that rescued a fair damsel / Captive in the wicked King's castle'.

It was a cold winter, as they had been in recent years, and we had few visitors until spring arrived in March. Eadmer and I recruited four redoubtable men-at-arms and, in May 1139, we sailed for England's south coast, once again adopting our pseudonyms 'Robyn of Hode' and 'William of Scaerlette', which Eadmer had shortened to 'Will' so that it scanned better in his ballads.

It was a reluctant parting from Maud and the boys. Her words to me were simple, insisting that I return soon. She placed the Talisman over my neck, making me promise that I would wear it at all times while in England.

'To keep you safe, my darling.'

'It is not a lucky charm, Maud.'

'It is for me; it brought you to me.'

She embraced me passionately, then pushed me away and turned hurriedly to hide her tears.

As for the boys, Henry had just celebrated his sixth birthday and Geoffrey was approaching his fourth, so they were much more voluble – excited by the preparations for my departure, and clamouring for presents on my return. Young William was not yet three and oblivious to it all.

Maud and I, knowing that the truth of their paternity must be kept from them, realized that one day we would find it difficult to explain my constant presence in the household and the permanent absence of their father. For the time being, I had taken on the role of 'Uncle Hal' – their mother's guardian, as designated by their grandfather – but it was not easy, especially at farewells like this one.

Our first port of call was Devizes, where Roger, Bishop of Salisbury, had just completed a castle of palatial quality to rival any in the land. Lord Chancellor under King Henry, he was one of the most powerful men in the country, and clever and ambitious in equal measure. Although Earl Robert had stressed in his messages that he could be trusted only as far as his own self-interest would permit, Roger was known to be a supporter of Maud's claim to the throne.

Devizes was indeed a castle of imposing proportions, and Roger was no less prodigious – either in girth or presence. His garrison of men was well armed and looked like a formidable fighting force. His private apartments were more like those of a king or a duke: the floors were covered with large rugs and the walls with tapestries of equal scale; his high table gleamed with silver plate; and a huge gold crucifix on an oak pole stood against one wall.

He greeted us warmly, but with some suspicion.

'Gentlemen, you wished to see me. I am Roger, Bishop of Salisbury, and this is my prior, Roger of Caen.'

The Bishop was a man as round as he was tall, while his prior was as thin as a quill and with the bearing of a man of letters. Both men were scrutinizing us carefully. The Bishop smiled, but with the false grin of an inquisitor.

'The names Hode and Scaerlette are not familiar to me; they sound neither English nor Norman.'

'They are from Aquitaine, my Lord Bishop.'

'I see. And yet, you sound English?'

'I am English. But before we go further, may I ask you a telling question?'

'You may ask, but I can't promise to answer.'

'I hear you are loyal to the Empress, the Lady of the English?'

The old Bishop hesitated.

'That is a discourteous question for a complete stranger to ask.'

He was right. I decided I should avoid needless prevarication, and make a clean breast of it.

'You are right; I apologize. My real name is Harold of Hereford, made Earl of Huntingdon by King Henry Beauclerc; I am Commander of the forces of Empress Matilda. For obvious reasons, when travelling in England I use a name from my home in Aquitaine. This is the commission appointing me, with her seal.'

I handed him my roll of vellum, which he studied carefully before handing it to his Prior. He was still sceptical, so I outlined my background – in particular that King Henry had acknowledged me as his bastard son before ennobling me as an earl. He knew both the Earl and Bishop of Norwich and had heard of my mother and her work on the cathedral. He seemed reassured and ordered that wine and cold cuts be served.

'I am relieved that you appear to be who you say you are. Stephen is suspicious of everyone; these are dangerous times. Yes, I do believe that the Empress's claim is stronger than Stephen's. The squabbling among the lords is getting worse, Normandy is in turmoil and Stephen has given Northumbria to Henry of the Scots, despite routing them in battle. Even his supporters think he is losing all respect. How can I be of service to you?'

'I need a true assessment of the sympathies of England's magnates, both temporal and spiritual.'

The Bishop paused. I was reminded of Earl Robert's warning about the man's strong streak of self-interest and imagined him to be calculating how he could profit from the answer to my question.

'Stephen has called the royal court to gather at Oxford, a burgh that is growing in importance, on the feast of the Nativity of St John the Baptist, on the 24th of June. Tell me, are you known here in England?'

'Hardly – and not at all as the Earl of Huntingdon.'

'Good, then if you and your man would like to adopt your Aquitaine names, you could join my retinue. It is the first court Stephen has called for some time and will be a perfect opportunity to test the mood in the realm.'

'Thank you, Bishop Roger. That is very generous of you.'

'But we should be careful. I hear that Stephen doubts my loyalty and may challenge me. Also, we should check at Oxford, but I think Stephen granted the Earldom of Huntingdon to Henry of the Scots, as part of the settlement brokered by Cardinal Alberic. But it wouldn't be the first time a title has been granted twice!'

The Bishop gave us lavish chambers to reflect my rank as an earl of the realm, and we waited as his retinue prepared for the journey. We had a long time to kick our heels, as the court's date was another three weeks away.

Early the next day, as I enjoyed the fresh air of an English summer morning, the Prior approached me as I crossed the castle bailey.

'Good morning, Earl Harold.'

'Good morning, Prior Roger.'

He had the same expression as the Bishop had sported the day before – the disingenuous grin of the interrogator.

'Tell me, my Lord – if I may be so bold. Your mother, Estrith, Abbess of Fécamp, was one of King Henry's many mistresses?'

I sensed danger. He was asking a question to which I felt certain he already knew the answer, so I avoided falling into his trap.

'Why do you ask?'

'Before I answer that, I need to know your real purpose here.'

His expression was no longer a false smile, more an accusatory frown.

'My purpose is as I described it to you yesterday – nothing more, nothing less.'

'I see. I did not mention it to the Bishop last night, as I preferred to have this conversation with you first, but unless you are frank with me, I will have to express my concerns to him.'

'And your concerns are?'

'Well, my understanding, from an impeccable source, is that Harold of Hereford, son of Estrith of Bourne, later the Abbess of Fécamp, was conceived in the deserts of the Holy Land during the Great Crusade and that his father was the knight, Sweyn of Bourne.'

I was rooted to the spot, astonished that this stranger should know such intimate details about my life.

'You need to explain yourself, Prior Roger. Where did you get that information?'

'From a fellow member of a Brethren of which you must be the only survivor.'

I made a guess, clutching at a remote possibility.

'Were you confessor to Robert Curthose in Cardiff?'

'No, but that is a good surmise. I wasn't exactly confessor to another man – but I was scribe to the man who was his confessor and chronicler.'

I knew then who it must be.

'Prince Edgar?'

'Yes, indeed. I was a scribe to William of Malmesbury before I came to Gloucester. In the winter of 1126, he and I travelled to Northumbria – to a godforsaken place called Ashgyll Force – to meet Edgar the Atheling. Abbot William persuaded the Prince to give us an account of his life, and it was my responsibility to commit it to vellum when we returned. It was a fulsome account, running to hundreds of pages, and – if I may say so – a most remarkable story.'

'Well, Prior, then you know exactly who I am and the history of my family.'

'I do. And also, from its description, I recognize the amulet around your neck. It is the Talisman of Truth. I also know that you visited the Prince just before we did.'

'Very well, Prior, you have caught me in a lie. I am not King Henry's illegitimate son, but I *am* the Earl of Huntingdon, anointed by the old King, and I do command the forces of Empress Matilda. The reasons for the falsehood are convoluted, and it is very important that you are not privy to them. Do you understand?'

'I understand very well – and I suspect I will sleep easier in my bed if I remain ignorant of the circumstances to which you have alluded.'

'Indeed.'

'Now that we have dealt with that, may I interest you in a little excursion to Malmesbury? We have time before we must depart for Oxford, and there is a man there who would be delighted to meet you.'

After arranging with Bishop Roger to meet him in Oxford, Eadmer and I and our four men-at-arms travelled to Malmesbury with Prior Roger.

An ancient but small burgh, with the towering edifice of Malmesbury Abbey at its centre, its modest scale disguised its importance in the ecclesiastical world. Not only did the Abbey house the most important library in Europe – other than the Vatican Library in Rome – but it was also home to England's most learned sage, the historian William of Malmesbury.

Looking exactly as you would expect a wise man to look – tall, slightly stooped, benign in countenance, eccentric in his mannerisms – he greeted us at the door of his scriptorium as if we were old friends. His eyesight was poor; he fumbled around a little before seating himself and asking us to do the same.

We spent the rest of the day, and well into the evening, exchanging stories and reminiscing about the life and times of England – and, in particular, the role my family had played in those events.

Eventually, he began to tire.

'I must retire to my chamber. It is late.'

'Thank you for your time, Abbot William.'

'Not at all. Thank you, Earl Harold, I know so much about your family and now I've met another generation. They would be very proud of you, as would Prince Edgar.'

He got up to leave, but paused and looked at me with a despairing expression.

'I am pleased that you came, but I know that your presence here in England is because you hope to promote the Empress Matilda's cause. In that respect, I am sad. I think her cause is just, but the pursuit of her right to rule means civil war.'

England's finest mind shuffled off to his bed looking disconsolate, leaving me to ponder the truth of what he had said. He was right: a war was coming. In fact, it had already begun – in Normandy and in Northumbria – and now it was about to be unleashed in England's heartland.

Early the next morning, as we were about to leave for

Oxford, Roger of Caen joined us for the journey, but under his arm, he carried a large wooden casket with a heavy bronze clasp.

'Abbot William would like you to have this.'

'He is very generous; it is a beautiful chest.'

'Yes, but what is inside is even more noteworthy.'

I peered in. It contained a thick manuscript, beautifully written in Latin, in blackletter script, with the title '*De Vita Edgar, Princeps Anglia*'.

'It is the story of the Prince – and of your mother and father and all their brethren – as told to us by him at Ashgyll. Keep it safe.'

I was overwhelmed.

'I would like to thank Abbot William in person.'

'There is no need; he is sleeping. He is happy that you should keep it. With a war coming, it should not be made public – it is safer with you. Now, let us go to Oxford.'

Over the next few days, I read Roger of Caen's beautifully crafted account – almost without pause for sleep or food. It was a revelation. I was profoundly moved as all my mother's stories and memories were once more brought to life in vivid detail. When I had finished, I placed my other precious pieces of vellum in the casket: John Comnenus' record of my grandfather's words of wisdom to him, the last thing my grandfather had said; and my mother's letter, written to me on her deathbed.

I handed the casket to Eadmer.

'We must guard this with our lives.'

Dear Thibaud,

It is glorious summer here; Fulham has never looked better and the river is full of people bathing and frolicking. Young lovers come to lie by its banks in the late evening.

I forbid my monks to spy on them, but many defy me. I'm too old to be tempted myself, but I do remember the time when I might have had a brief peek! Ah, to be young again . . .

We are coming to the part of Hal's story in which I make an appearance. I hope you will not judge me too harshly when I confess that I am proud of the small role I played in helping our young hero fulfil his destiny. Harold of course did not need to remind me of our fateful encounter in Gloucester, when he came to me in 1139, just after I had been installed as Abbot. But, for the sake of completeness, and so that future generations may read the full story of this noble young man's deeds, I have decided that I will include the details here. I have indulged myself in a little of my storyteller's imagination and described the encounter in the words Harold might have used. I hope you forgive me, but it seemed the right thing to do.

You are in my prayers every day. I pray for your health and happiness and I also pray that you are able to bring your great wisdom to the Holy See.

Yours in God,
Gilbert

27. The Good Abbot, Gilbert

We arrived at Oxford in the middle of June. What then followed changed all our lives.

The burgh was in chaos. There were men and horses everywhere; it was a sultry day and tempers were frayed. There were too few beds and only about half the stables needed – either Stephen's royal household had miscalculated, or the lords and bishops had brought far bigger entourages than had been agreed.

Our host, Bishop Roger, had brought a retinue of more than thirty assorted bodies, most of them armed. If he was typical, there could well have been over 500 visitors to the modest burgh. He introduced us as Englishmen who had been raised in Aquitaine, and said that we were now in his retinue as professional soldiers. Thankfully, no eyebrows were raised by our presence and we moved around unnoticed.

A certain calm descended in the afternoon as men filled the taverns and forgot their frustrations, leaving the stewards to try to sort out the sleeping arrangements. Stephen's Royal Chamberlain, aware that the King was due to arrive that evening, convened a meeting of all the stewards in order to resolve the problems with the accommodation. But rather than produce a solution, it created chaos.

The Chamberlain began the meeting by producing a list of those magnates who were required to give up their planned lodgings in Oxford and move to whatever could be found in the villages around the burgh. In most cases, that was little more than a barn, cowshed or open field. The indignation among those on the list bordered on fury. Word spread like wildfire and soon reached the taverns, where jests became taunts, banter became brawls, and fisticuffs became sword fights.

Eadmer and I were with Bishop Roger's Constable and some of his senior knights when our tavern suddenly turned from a merry haunt into a gladiator's arena. Our neighbours, the men of Earl Alan of Richmond – a Marcher earl from Northumbria who, up to that point, had been quietly drinking ale – suddenly made straight for us, swords drawn. Their attack seemed premeditated, rather than provoked by the general melee.

Roger's Constable bellowed at a group of his knights.

'Get the Bishop back to Devizes! Don't hesitate, and don't let any man stop you!'

We were outnumbered, three or four to one, and Roger's Constable was cut down by almost the first blow. Eadmer gathered our men in a close circle around us and tugged at my cloak.

'Let's get out! This is an ambush.'

He was right. We turned to fight our way towards the rear of the tavern. There were men and weapons every-where – so many and so much, that it was difficult to strike a blow. Even so, seaxes were doing damage and maces were being wielded overhead. The tavern's whores were caught in the scrimmage, all shrieking in horror, and many were cut down.

We managed to reach the rear door of the tavern,

where we tried to join the many who were pouring out like water from a pump. I saw a knight about to club Eadmer with his mace and ran him through with my sword.

Almost at the same instant, I felt the searing pain of several blades. A blow to my shoulder pushed me into the heavy timber of the tavern doorway. I remember my head striking the door jamb, then nothing else for some hours.

When I came round, my men-at-arms had laid me out on one of the tables in what appeared to be a refectory. I was covered in blood from a gash to my forehead, and had suffered deep wounds to my side, shoulder and thigh, which physicians were already binding with bandages, making no sound as they did so.

When I looked around me, I saw a figure standing in the shadows, dressed in the black habit of the Benedictine's monastic order and wearing an Abbot's crucifix. In my confused state, I pieced together a jigsaw of memories from the tavern in Oxford, and realized that Eadmer must have managed to get me away to the sanctuary of a nearby abbey. I struggled to raise myself upright, and bellowed at the hooded figure.

'Away with you, priest, I have no need of you!'

The Abbot did not appear shocked by what he probably assumed was the anger-laden fear of a dying man. His reply was gentle.

'As you wish, I will be nearby if you need me. I am Gilbert Foliot, Abbot here at Gloucester.'

'Forgive me, Abbot . . .'

I winced in pain and began to falter.

'Perhaps we could talk a little . . .'

I could not finish the sentence and fell back. My head hit the hard oak of the table with a thump. Stunned and incapable of further speech, I listened to the Abbot and his infirmerer discussing the extent of my injuries.

'Abbot, he has lost much blood, I doubt that he will survive the night.'

'Do what you can. What's his name?'

'We don't know; he would not give us his name, and neither will his men.'

I heard the Abbot ask his Prior to give me the extreme unction of Christ's sacrament, and then his footsteps started to recede as he turned to leave the refectory. But as he reached the door, the Prior summoned him back.

'Abbot, look at the amulet he is wearing – I've never seen anything like it. It must be an evil charm!'

The Prior seemed very agitated by it, but the Abbot replied with a calm authority.

'It is certainly unusual. I have tucked it under his jerkin; give him extreme unction and we will ask him about the amulet in the morning. If he lives that long . . .'

The Abbot's words were obscured by the fog of unconsciousness that threatened to claim me, when all hell suddenly broke loose in the Abbey. First it was the thunder of the hooves of a large force of cavalry, then the hurried footsteps and clanging of armour of a significant body of men, followed by orders being barked and the door of the Abbey being thumped impatiently, demanding admittance.

The Abbot swiftly issued his commands to the Prior.

'Draw the screens around our wounded visitor. The law of sanctuary requires us to protect him, whoever he may be – and however he may have acquired his injuries. Then prepare to open the door and greet our guests.'

'But, Abbot, there are a lot of men out there –'

'Open the door!'

The Prior did as he was bid, and I heard the unmistakable sounds of at least a dozen fully armed and breathless men pouring through the entrance. Hidden behind the screens, feeling as weak as a baby, my safety depended on the Abbot's ability to contain the violent intent of the intruders.

'We seek a knight and his band of brigands! They have committed mayhem and murder at King Stephen's court at Oxford.'

'Sir Knight, I realize you are on important business, but is it not courteous to begin with formal introductions? I am Gilbert, Abbot of Gloucester, and this is Prior Anselm. And you are?'

'I am Waleran, a Knight of Northumbria. I serve my Lord Alan, Earl of Richmond. He and his men have been attacked in full view of the King by a group of thugs in the service of the Bishop of Salisbury.'

I was aware that everything hinged on the Abbot's reply. Was he a supporter of the Empress Matilda's claim to King Stephen's throne?

'I know Roger of Salisbury well. I'm sure his men would not commit a heinous crime anywhere, let alone at the King's court.'

'Abbot, I must apologize for contradicting you, but that is the case. And the men responsible were only an hour or so ahead of us as we approached your Abbey. Are they taking shelter here? At least one of them is wounded.'

Again, I had no idea how the Abbot would respond. If he denied that I was here, and with my men's horses still outside, he risked aiding and abetting men who seemed to be beyond the law. Andy yet, my instincts suggested that he too was a supporter of Matilda and that the identity of his nameless guest interested him – an identity made even more intriguing by the peculiar amulet I wore around my neck, and which had so alarmed the Prior.

'We have had no visitors here tonight, wounded or otherwise.'

Waleran was clearly unconvinced by the Abbot's denial.

'I need to search the Abbey.'

'Do you doubt my word?'

'It is my duty to hunt this man down. He may have gained entry without your knowledge.'

I knew the game was up: the Abbot could only deny entry to Waleran and his men based on an obstinate sense of territoriality, or because he had something to hide. As he had already denied that the man being sought was in the Abbey, his obstinacy was likely to cost him dear.

Then I was thrown a lifeline; one of the knight's men appeared at the door.

'Sir, their horses have been found tethered at the quayside by the river.'

I heard Waleran's impatience in his voice.

'Thank you, Abbot Gilbert. I am sorry to have troubled you at this hour; it looks like the villains have made off by boat.'

He then turned, shouted new orders to his men and was gone.

After a moment of silence, I heard the Abbot reflect calmly.

'Clever, they must have secured their horses by the river before doubling back to the Abbey. Our guests are clearly used to the need for making clandestine contingencies.'

To the amazement of the Abbot – and to my intense relief – his anonymous visitor did not die in the night.

When the Abbot came to see me after morning prayers, I was very weak and pale, but still breathing. He sat with me for a while and offered some silent prayers for my recovery, all the time unaware of the identity of his mysterious visitor.

After a while, I felt able to open my eyes. I laboured to speak in a low voice.

'Is it morning, Abbot?'

'It is.'

I winced in pain as I tried to adjust my position.

'I need to piss.'

'There is a pot here.'

'Pissing in pots is for old men.'

I tried to get up, but fell back, this time with a heartfelt grimace. The Abbot helped me to sit up and use the piss pot.

'Not very dignified for an abbot.'

'I've done worse. But when you need a shite, I'll summon my infirmerer; that's part of his job.'

'My prospects do not seem too good at the moment.'

'You have lost a lot of blood. Rest is the only cure.'

'I cannot rest. There are things I must do.'

'May I know your name?'

'You may not. I know it seems ill-mannered, but I have my reasons.'

'Would you like to purge your soul? It may be wise.'

'You mean a spiritual shite? I suppose that's your job. You may well be right, Abbot, and I thank you for the thoughtful offer. But although my sins may be legion and my need for divine cleansing greater than most, I am not quite ready to die.'

'A young knight, Waleran of Northumbria, was here last night, looking for you and accusing you of murder in the name of Roger of Salisbury.'

'He is right in part; I killed a man at Oxford, but it was not murder. There was a fight, and men die in fights. We acted not in the cause of Roger of Salisbury, but in the name of Empress Matilda. I heard you tell the knight that I wasn't here. I am grateful, Abbot, but why did you lie on my behalf?'

'I don't know, but my instincts suggested I should protect you.'

'You have good instincts, Abbot Gilbert. I am in your debt.'

'You can repay me.'

'How?'

'Tell me who you are, and tell me about your amulet.'

'I cannot give you my name but I can give you a clue. Coincidentally, my grandfather escaped to a new life from Gloucester quay a very long time ago. You will know his name. As for the amulet, it is the Talisman of Truth. I am its guardian, as were three previous generations of my family.'

'Your answer only begs more questions. I have a distant

recollection of a "Talisman of Truth". Tell me more – at least, your grandfather's name.'

'That would be unwise. I've said as much as I can, I'm sorry I can't say more.'

It was time to stir myself; I shouted to my men, who were waiting outside the door, as loudly as my condition allowed.

'Eadmer, get the men organized, and saddle the horses! We're leaving.'

I needed help to get to my horse. Three of my sturdy men-at-arms appeared and helped me towards the door. I was still in great pain and perspiring profusely. It was hard to disguise my discomfort as my men almost dragged me to the doorway. I looked at the infirmerer and his assistant, who were both looking on anxiously.

The shook their heads in unison.

'Good knight, stay here for a while. You are giving yourself a death sentence by attempting to move.'

I stopped momentarily and turned to face Abbot Gilbert. I set my jaw firmly, determined to take my leave with all due courtesy.

'I will always be grateful to you for what you did last night. My men will leave you a purse of silver to help with your work on the Abbey.'

'Thank you, all contributions to support our important work here are gratefully received.'

'You know that I am a supporter of the Empress Matilda –'

'Are we not all fond of the late King Henry's beautiful daughter?'

'That's not an answer. A war is coming, and you know

403

what the conflict will be about. So I ask you now: do you support the Empress in her claim for England's crown?'

I saw the Abbot hesitate at first, before deciding to respond candidly.

'I have always thought that Matilda has a stronger claim to England. Indeed, her father, Henry Beauclerc, declared that he wished her to succeed him.'

'I am grateful for your honesty, Abbot. You will be gratified to know that she will soon have her chance. Say nothing of this, or of my presence here. If you give me your word on that, and if circumstances permit, I promise to return one day. You can hear my confession – not that it will do me much good.'

'You have my word.'

'I hear you also oppose the power of the Knights Templar?'

'I do, their influence has gone too far and their power is much too great. Their Grand Master now stands equal to cardinals and princes.'

'Good men in the Church are rare – especially among the Norman hierarchy.'

The events of the previous night had proved that Abbot Gilbert was one such good man.

I knew now what I must do, and summoned Eadmer to bring the casket that had been entrusted to me by William of Malmesbury. He handed me the heavy wooden casket, locked by a large bronze clasp.

'Please keep this with your reliquary. I trust this to you as a man of God; it needs to be protected on hallowed ground and far from the grasp of the Templars. Please don't let me down.'

'I will guard it as you wish. It will be safe with me. But you will understand if I say I am reluctant to take on such a responsibility for an anonymous man?'

I could prevaricate no longer. I adjusted my stance, with a frown of discomfort, and gave the Abbot the best answer I could muster.

'You have done me a great service – and to England and its future Queen. You have put your trust in me; I think now I must trust you. I am Harold of Hereford, my father was Sweyn of Bourne, loyal servant to Edgar the Atheling and Duke Robert of Normandy. My grandfather was Hereward of Bourne, who fought with King Harold at Stamford Bridge and on Senlac Ridge and then led the defenders against William the Conqueror at the Siege of Ely.'

The Abbot was stunned for a moment. Searching for words, he made a shallow bow.

'We are honoured to have you here in Gloucester.'

With that, our conversation was at an end.

Supported on either side by my men, I shuffled away, relying on Eadmer to supervise our departure from the Abbey.

I feared the spectre of death would soon have its way with me. But whatever lay ahead, I had fulfilled my promise to William of Malmesbury to guard his casket. Thanks to the intervention of Abbot Gilbert, it would now be locked safely in the crypt with the other relics of Gloucester Abbey.

28. Landfall at Last

The days after my visit to Gloucester were difficult for me and for England. My wounds were severe and I needed rest, but England's wounds were then only mild; there would be much worse to come.

Eadmer got me away in a small boat down the River Severn – just as my grandfather had escaped when he was an outlaw – and we made landfall at the mouth of the River Brue in Somerset. We lost ourselves deep into the hinterland, in search of a place for me to recuperate. In the middle of the wilderness of Somerset's marshland, we met Juliano – a large and jovial Cistercian monk from Navarre. He was on his way from Glastonbury to a new Cistercian foundation called Forde Abbey, at Thorncombe.

It was a perfect destination for us. Hidden in thick woodland on the western edge of the Dorset Downs, but only a short distance from the ancient Fosse Way between Lincoln and Exeter, it offered a refuge from the turmoil engulfing England. The monks, mainly Iberians from Navarre and Castille, had only just begun to speak English and kept to themselves as much as they could. There was a foundation of nuns nearby, headed by Abbess Alicia, a very fetching Galician woman, and I always thought there was more to her friendship with Juliano than a shared love of the Church's catechism.

It was several weeks before the earnest young Cistercians got me back on my feet. It was a frustrating time, but I had to be patient while I recovered. I tried to find contentment within the tranquillity of England's meadows and forests, but it was difficult, knowing that events were moving rapidly and that Maud was still waiting for news in Normandy. Eadmer would help me walk around the villages nearby. I found a perfect perch for reflection, high on a hill above the village of Wynsham, from where I had fine views of forests and meadows all the way to the sea at Lyme Bay.

Juliano was a fine host; all he asked in return for his hospitality was help in learning English, a service I was delighted to render. He learned quickly and was soon fluent – especially when he learned to speak at a normal English pace, rather than in the excitable babble of his native Castiliano.

Eadmer managed to get a message to Earl Robert at Gloucester, asking him to send it on to Caen. It simply reassured Maud that I was well, and urged her to remain in a state of readiness.

By late August 1139, I had regained my strength. After thanking Juliano and his monks, and donating a pouch of silver for an altar cross to grace their new chapel, Eadmer and I rode to Robert of Gloucester's impressive fortification at Bristol. Bounded by the River Avon on one side, moated on the other three sides, and fortified by a huge curtain wall and towering keep, it was one of England's most secure citadels.

Earl Robert greeted us warmly when we arrived at Bristol.

'My Lord Huntingdon, I have the pleasure of meeting you at last – another half-brother. What a prodigious father we had!'

'Indeed, Lord Robert; and I am delighted to meet the elder statesman of our family.'

'Yes, but our family is a matriarchy, is it not? Surely Matilda is mother to us all.'

'Well said, sir.'

'Let's dispense with formalities. I hear you go by the name Hal. Please call me Robert. Come and sit, I have important news.'

I took to Robert immediately. He was a tall man, fair in complexion, but with a warrior's build. He was welcoming to Eadmer and had a casual rapport with all around him, especially his soldiers. We sat in front of the fireplace of his Great Hall, which, even in August, roared as it consumed several logs as big as a man's thigh. Like my mother's great cathedral at Norwich, the Normans' mighty stone keeps never seemed to be warm.

'Hal, Stephen has made a grave mistake. The time for us to strike is coming soon. The brawl at Oxford, where you were wounded, was instigated by him. He has become mistrustful of everyone – especially of the bishops and, in particular, of Roger of Salisbury. He thinks everyone is plotting against him. The Earl of Richmond's men provoked the melee at Oxford, and several were killed. But Stephen laid the blame on Bishop Roger's men – and in particular on you, the Earl of Huntingdon, posing under a pseudonym, one Robyn of Hode. So, after me, you are the most hunted man in England!'

'I regard it as a position of great privilege.'

'So you should! Stephen has had Roger of Salisbury arrested, along with two of his nephews – Alexander, Bishop of Lincoln, and Nigel, Bishop of Ely. He has taken their palaces and holdings into his own Exchequer. But it was a serious mistake: there is uproar, and even Stephen's own brother, Henry of Blois, Bishop of Winchester, has called him to account. Henry convened an ecclesiastical council at Winchester, to which he summoned Stephen to justify what Henry called "an act of barbarity against the Church". Stephen was humiliated in public and has lost all credibility among the earls.'

'Then Maud must come to England immediately.'

'Agreed! You must go to her at once; but we have to be careful. The journey from Bristol is too far by sea, and Stephen still controls the ports in the south, bar one.'

'Which is?'

'Arundel, which is held by Adeliza, King Henry's widow, our stepmother. She is now married to William d'Aubigny, and both are loyal to our sister. Adeliza is particularly annoyed that King Henry's wish that Matilda should be Queen was ignored by those who were supposedly loyal to him.'

'I will leave for Normandy immediately.'

'Good, when you set sail, get word to me here in Bristol and I will wreak havoc in the West Country sufficient to persuade Stephen to mount a campaign down here and deflect his attention from the south coast. Again, when you arrive in Arundel, send word and I will rally our supporters and gather our army.'

*

Maud was overjoyed at the news when we were reunited in Caen. Count Geoffrey provided a small contingent of knights and seemed delighted that, unhindered by his wife's presence in the Dukedom, he would soon have free rein as Lord of Normandy. Our children – Henry, Geoffrey and William – together with Eadmer and Greta's daughter Gretchen and her newly arrived sister, Ursula, were left in the unstinting care of Fulk of Falaise, at Argentan.

We all set sail for England. These were happy days during which our quartet of brothers-in-arms revived the spirit of our clandestine encounters in the Forest of Loudon and resumed our adventure.

Empress Matilda, Lady of the English, made landfall on the banks of the River Arun on 30 September 1139, eight years after she had last set foot on English soil. Adeliza was there to meet us and had called out her entire garrison to create a processional route fit for the Queen. Cheering wildly and shouting 'God Bless you, Queen Matilda, Lady of the English!' the people of the burgh lined our route as we made our way up to the castle.

Maud looked radiant and wore the small ducal coronet she had used in Normandy. She was in her thirty-eighth year, the mother of three children, but she still looked like a girl in her twenties – exactly as I remembered her when we first fell in love at St Cirq Lapopie. Indeed, our subsequent nights together – in a very private chamber that Adeliza made available to Maud in Arundel's colossal gateway – were also wonderfully reminiscent of our time together in the Lot.

I chose a particular moment carefully. It was early one

morning, and the cold air of autumn was already bringing a chill to the ground. I awoke to find Maud, covered only by her cloak, standing by the arched window of our chamber. The sun had just brought its golden glow to the morning mists over the burgh and the meadows beyond. She was staring at her realm, her England.

I took the Talisman and, once again feeling honoured to be its guardian, placed it around her neck.

'There you are, my Lady of the English, the Talisman of Truth for our new Queen. It looks right on you. Come back to bed. I would like to pay homage to my liege as her loyal servant.'

She smiled her incomparable smile and turned to kiss me.

'I will rule well here, I promise. I will bring the best of my Norman blood and the best of my English heritage. But you have to promise to keep feeding me with that powerful seed in your loins – I have my appetite back again!'

At first, we assumed that it was Robert's army that approached Arundel in early October, but it was Stephen's force. He had received news of our landing at Arundel while he was besieging Corfe Castle in Dorset, refuge to one of the growing number of his enemies. England's usurper King did not lack resolve, nor did he lack the ability to act decisively. Within ten days, Stephen's formidable army had moved far more quickly than Robert's, had isolated Arundel, and had begun preparations for a siege. We were trapped with only our own small force and Arundel's modest garrison for protection.

The next morning, Stephen asked for a parlay to be convened within the hour. We had no choice but to agree, and so Maud and I rode out to meet her cousin – the man she had not met since he swore his oath of loyalty to her in Rouen eleven years earlier. Adeliza insisted on accompanying us, as did her husband and several members of Arundel's retinue. Eadmer was by my side, while Otto and Berenger flanked Maud. Stephen was accompanied by several senior supporters, notably his brother, Bishop Henry, who now seemed to be reconciled with a man whose position as King he had seriously undermined just three months ago.

Inevitably, the atmosphere was icy; Stephen spoke first, smiling broadly at his stepmother.

'Queen Adeliza, thank you for playing host to my cousin; and my thanks to your husband.'

When he turned to Maud, his smile became more forced.

'Welcome to my realm, Cousin Matilda. You know my brother – Henry, Bishop of Winchester.'

Maud remained calm, despite the provocative greeting.

'This is Harold – the Earl of Huntingdon and Commander of my personal retinue.'

'Ah, yes, the Earl of Huntingdon. Or are you using your commoner's name today?'

'I am using my real name – unlike you, who is passing himself off as the King of England!'

The forced smile on Stephen's face became a sneer.

'Well, well, cousin. He's got a vicious tongue, has he not? No wonder he spends his time brawling in taverns.'

Maud, none too pleased with my outburst, decided to intervene.

'Cousin Stephen, let us come to the point; your illegal reign here is no longer tenable.'

'How so? I think it is my army – England's army – that surrounds you, an uninvited guest in my domain.'

'Stephen, let me be clear. You know that you no longer command the respect of your lords and that the bishops have gone so far as to admonish you in public. I will grant you safe passage to Blois and will honour a treaty bringing peace to Blois and Normandy.'

Stephen grinned.

'So, even though I have you surrounded here at Arundel, you expect me to relinquish my throne to you and sail away to Blois? I think you have taken leave of your senses.'

'My army, with Earl Robert of Gloucester at its head, is massing in the west at this moment.'

'Then they're in the wrong place, aren't they? We're in the south, and this is Sussex.'

He laughed loudly, a hearty guffaw, and those around him did the same.

'Cousin Matilda, I will give you two choices: submit to me now, and I will escort you to your ships for a safe return to Normandy; or stay here and feel my wrath. I am the King here in England, and you challenge my authority; that I cannot tolerate.'

Adeliza was growing increasingly irritated by the exchange.

'Don't be foolish, Stephen. I am the Dowager Queen of England; Matilda is Dowager Empress of the Holy Roman Empire. You cannot do us harm here. If you do, your already tenuous grip on power will be loosened completely.'

Adeliza had brought Stephen up sharply. He looked across at his brother, Henry, whose expression suggested that he thought Adeliza's argument could not be gainsaid. Stephen, clearly disconcerted, adjusted his position in his saddle.

'Very well, I will grant you and your retinue safe passage to Earl Robert. But understand this: thereafter, whenever our forces meet, battle will follow, with no allowance for your feminine status, or Adeliza's eminence as dowager of the realm. Matilda, if you want to rule like a king, you will be treated like a king. But take my advice, be content as Dowager Empress and Countess of Anjou. England is mine.'

Stephen rode off, leaving Maud crestfallen; her dream, although not yet destroyed, had been dealt a severe blow.

I tried to console her, but it was a bitter disappointment for all of us. We chose to eschew any pretence of a regal progress to Bristol. Leaving her elegant clothes and regal accoutrements behind, to follow by carriage, Maud joined Greta in wearing the thick leggings of a knight as we rode at a canter westwards across the Downs. Had events turned out differently, it would have been an exhilarating ride, but in our present circumstances it became a necessary chore.

On the high ground of the Downs and across Salisbury Plain, England seemed serenely beautiful and at peace, but in the burghs and villages there was turmoil everywhere. Lord fought lord, and arguments were settled by the sword; instead of nurturing the souls of men, the clergy seized land and chattels at will. Many poor people hid in the forests. Villains roamed freely, pillaging as they pleased. The many fortifications built to bring Norman law to the realm closed their gates and provisioned themselves for the coming winter – not just to protect themselves against the seasonal winter, but also against the winter of lawlessness that was engulfing the land. Farms were robbed of their beasts and crops, barns were emptied, granaries raided. Those left outside the walls of the fortresses were abandoned to starvation and destitution. England was in a state of anarchy.

Earl Robert's castle at Bristol was a welcoming sight. Camped all around was a significant body of men – perhaps as many as 6,000 – and we all began to feel much more optimistic. Earl Robert had been able to gather the majority of Maud's supporters in one place, but that task had made it impossible to get to Arundel in time to thwart Stephen's advance. He and his fellow supporters were shamefaced about it when we arrived, but were nevertheless relieved to see that Maud had made it to Bristol without their aid.

Maud called a council of war within an hour of our arrival. Gratifyingly, her supporters were a formidable gathering. Apart from Earl Robert, the most respected soldier in the land, there was Miles, High Sheriff of Gloucester – a man of honour who had loyally served Maud's father all his life – and Brien FitzCount, the illegitimate son of the Count of Brittany, a brilliant military tactician and commander of cavalry. Although there were many other lords present, those three were our High Command.

Maud's address to her supporters began solemnly, but ended with a rousing call to arms.

'My Lords, at long last I am with you! England is in chaos and our army is ready to strike to put an end to Stephen's misrule. But do not underestimate him; he is brave and moves his army at lightning speed. We must be strong and decisive. No more lady's finery for me until I'm Queen; I ride with my army in cavalry breeches like the rest of you. Together we will free England from its reign of terror and put King Henry's chosen successor where she belongs.'

Raucous cheering echoed around Bristol's walls as Maud finished her rallying call. She asked me for my sword and raised it high above her head, creating even more enthusiastic support.

We spent the rest of 1139 campaigning in the west until, one by one, all the major fortifications west of Salisbury were loyal to Maud: Worcester, Trowbridge, Dunster, Gloucester, Devizes and Malmesbury, all were persuaded to become part of our growing domain.

In November, Roger, Bishop of Salisbury, died – as a direct result, it was said, of his treatment at the hands of Stephen. This further reinforced the clergy's distaste for his rule.

The year 1140 saw a war of attrition unfold as Stephen struck back at every gain we had made in the previous year. Prompted by thuggery, bribery and blackmail, loyalties among the nobles wavered. Few battles were fought; Stephen's tactics relied on a show of force, followed by threats or promises, then capitulation.

Vital resources of men and money started to become diminished for both protagonists. Treasuries were emptied on both sides of the Channel; heavy debts and obligations were incurred.

The gravediggers were exhausted and the moneylenders became rich. Everyone else suffered – especially the poor and the peasants, who died in their droves. In many parts of the land, the suffering populace endured a return to the death and destruction of the Great Conquest by William and his marauding army. Even those who were relatively secure in their walled fortresses, able to live off the resources they had plundered, had to live in a climate of terror.

It became a stalemate – not a temporary hiatus, but one that lasted for months – during which the suffering and anguish of the people continued unabated. Whole burghs were burned to the ground and homeless families littered the roadsides as they evacuated their meagre shelters to find refuge in the wildwood. Whole communities, some numbered in their thousands, scratched a living from the forest. Torture and mutilation were commonplace. Knotted ropes were used to slowly squeeze people's heads until their skulls shattered. Others were crushed in what became known as 'torture chambers'. Small iron boxes were made, into which victims would be placed before heavy stones were piled on top of the box to suffocate them. Iron collars, clamped around a victim's throat and chained high up on a wall, were used to bring a lingering death as, bound at the wrists, the prisoner could neither sit nor lie down, being denied sleep or rest. Eventually the poor unfortunate choked to death, unable to hold their weight any longer.

Priests prayed, and masses were said to bring an end to the misery. But to no avail; the torment continued.

Stephen's brother, Bishop Henry, tried to negotiate a

treaty of peace at the end of the year and even crossed the Channel to discuss it with Maud's husband – who was now in complete control in Normandy – and with the French King, Louis VII. Maud was prepared to accept a negotiated settlement to put an end to the suffering, but Stephen refused.

By the autumn of 1140, Robert had agreed that Maud should have her own court at his castle at Gloucester, and we had been living there for several months. Eadmer and Greta, our loyal companions, were with us, as always; she had started to accompany him in his ballads, bringing a sweet female pitch to his lyrics. Eadmer's singing became well known among the army and many men could, in moments of happiness or melancholy, be heard singing them – especially the best-known one, 'The Ballad of Robyn of Hode'.

But winter was beckoning, with no prospect of a respite from the agony.

Maud had had enough.

'Hal, I can't bear it any more. The two armies are exhausted, our coffers are almost empty, and the people are dying like flies.'

I felt the same, but knew I had to encourage her to keep going.

'We've come too far, my darling. If we capitulate now, Stephen's vengeance will know no limit. The suffering will be even worse.'

'But don't you think the price being paid by the people of England is too high already?'

'You're right, it is a terrible price. But our cause is just, and we have to see it through.'

'Is that what your father and grandfather would have done?'

'Of course! And your father and grandfather too. Remember, our grandfathers fought over this land more than seventy years ago. The fight still goes on.'

'But I am a woman. I'm not sure I have the stomach any more.'

'Yes, you do. You're every bit as strong as Stephen. And don't forget that my mother and grandmother, as well as the brave Adela, were also part of the fight. Adela became a Knight of Islam and fought alongside my father.'

'I know in my heart that you're right, Hal. I can accept the campaigning and the days in the saddle, the terrible food and the makeshift latrines. But it's the people's faces I can't cope with: sunken cheeks, hollow eyes, the vacant look of hunger. I can barely look them in the eye, because they know I'm to blame.'

'You're not to blame, your cousin is the guilty party. And one day, when the suffering is over, the people of England will thank you for delivering them from his disastrous rule.'

'Oh, Hal, I pray you're right.'

29. Battle of Lincoln

Several councils of war were called at the end of 1140, where it was agreed that the fight against King Stephen must go on. Count Geoffrey sent vital resources of money, food and weapons from Normandy to fuel his wife's cause.

As there was little chance of breaking the deadlock of strike and counter-strike in the west of England, we turned our attentions to the east, where we already had the support of the two nephews of Roger of Salisbury. There had been several risings against Stephen in the east, each of which he suppressed.

But at the end of 1140, at our instigation, Ranulf, Earl of Chester – the most powerful lord in the north, and more inclined to Maud than to Stephen – attacked and captured the castle at Lincoln.

It was a ruse designed to bring Stephen to the burgh, where we would ambush him.

Stephen responded to our provocation as we knew he would and, with typical speed, descended on Lincoln on Twelfth Night, 1141. We were well prepared and left Gloucester for Lincoln as soon as the trap was set. Maud had developed a fever, accompanied by a hacking cough, and I insisted that she stay behind to be nursed by Greta, guarded by Otto and Berenger. She was reluctant to stay, but a forced march on horseback across 120 miles of open country in the middle of winter was out of the question.

Her parting words to me were a reflection of the two things that she meant to me, as my lover and my sworn liege.

'Bring me my crown, if you can. But come back safely, if you can't. If I may not have an empire in England, then we've always got our empire at St Cirq Lapopie.'

In the west, the winter had been wet, with significant snow; in Lincoln the ground was dry, but hard from weeks of frost. It reminded me of Norwich – pleasant enough on most days, but when the wind blew from the east, it was a cold and miserable place.

Stephen had not brought a large force to Lincoln. Its garrison was not formidable, and it was a long way away from the heartland where most of England's conflict was occurring. The burgh's castle was of significant proportions, reworked on an original Roman fortress. In order to join our ambush, Ranulf had ensured that Lincoln was well supplied and secure before he slipped out of its ancient Newport Arch – from where, in another age, Rome's legions had marched to conquer the distant north.

He left his wife, Maud of Gloucester – the daughter of our loyal friend, Robert of Gloucester – to reject Stephen's demands to relinquish the castle, which she did resolutely. By the time our force arrived, Stephen was in the midst of constructing his siege engines and organizing his assault teams. We caught him completely unawares and outnumbered. But to his credit, he chose to stand his ground – as a man of courage, retreat was anathema to him.

He had lived all his life with the slur of cowardice. During the Great Crusade, forty years earlier, his father, Count Stephen II, had fled in panic to his home in Blois during the appalling Siege of Antioch. Such was the disgrace that his mother, the formidable Adela – the daughter of William, Conqueror of the English – forced him to return to the Holy Land two years later to try to redeem himself. Sadly, he was killed at the Second Battle of Ramla.

We camped on the south side of the Fosse Dyke, west of Brayford Pool on the River Witham, and plotted our strategy for the next morning. Miles of Gloucester would take the left flank to the north, leading his own men and reinforced by Welsh mercenaries. Ranulf of Chester would take the right flank, to the south, also supported by the Welsh. Robert of Gloucester, Brien FitzCount and I would lead the centre, with our most formidable group of men, an elite force of knights supported by archers and infantry. In all, we numbered close to 1,800 men, far superior to Stephen's force of 1,200.

The night brought a fierce storm; the ferocious winds played havoc with our tents, and the hard ground was softened to heavy mud by torrential rain. Stephen would have to fight on foot, penned in by the walls of the castle at his back. With the River Witham to the south, his only viable escape route would be to his right, heading north along Ermine Street to the Humber.

Sunday 2 February 1141 did not start well for Stephen, as the monks who came out to hear the confessions of our men were eager to tell us. He had attended mass in St Mary's Cathedral at dawn and, according to tradition as King of the realm, had carried the lighted candle for the service. But the candle broke and fell to the floor, extinguishing the flame. Even worse, during the service a pyx containing the Host fell from its fastening above the altar and broke on impact, scattering its contents at the priest's feet. The audience gasped and crossed themselves; all agreed that it was a very bad omen for Stephen.

Rain was still falling as we rode across Fosse Dyke. Our mounted knights kept their torsos dry; not so our foot soldiers, who had to wade across the swollen dyke submerged up to their shoulders. Stephen's men were not much better off. They had been formed up for almost an hour and stood in the pouring rain, sinking up to their ankles in freezing mud.

We formed up close to Stephen's lines, close enough to hear one of Stephen's supporters, Baldwin FitzGilbert, rallying his men for battle. Although they were outnumbered, they were led by seasoned warriors in the best Norman tradition. Besides FitzGilbert, Stephen's left flank was commanded by William of Aumale and William of Ypres, who brought Flemish troops to the fray. His right flank was taken by Hugh Bigod, Earl of Norwich, once my mentor, who had since perjured himself by swearing that King Henry had changed his mind about the succession. Stephen held the centre with his senior men: William Warenne, Earl of Surrey; Simon de Senlis, Earl of Northumberland; Waleran, Earl of Worcester; and Alan of Penthièvre, Earl of Richmond, who had been our ambusher at Stephen's court at Oxford.

Robert of Gloucester had asked me the night before if I would speak for Maud before the battle. I was not daunted by the challenge; I knew it was my duty. My grandfather had made his famous speech at Ely when the Brotherhood faced King William's squadrons for the final battle, so I knew it was also my destiny.

I knew what should be said and rode in front of our line confidently. I was also fortified by the Talisman, which Maud had insisted I take with me. It had been worn by so many brave men: Macbeth at Lumphanan, Harold at Senlac Ridge, Hereward at Ely and Alexius Comnenus at Levunium. It was easy to feel inspired by it.

Eadmer acted as my standard-bearer and held aloft my gonfalon. I had had it made in Gloucester, displaying the colours – gules, sable and gold – that my grandfather fought under at Ely. I had also created a new shield: two gules lions rampant on a golden field, bordered by a tierce in sable. Maud had suggested the design, and I felt very proud to carry it. I had commissioned replicas of my grandfather's helmet and sword to replace the ones I had lost while serving the Doge of Venice; I could feel the helmet's nose guard resting gently on my face, and I gripped the pommel of my sword firmly.

I stood high in my stirrups to speak, as Eadmer led my mount backwards and forwards along the line. The ground was flat, and my voice carried far and wide.

'Soldiers of England, warriors from Wales, fighting men of Normandy! We stand together today to right a terrible wrong. This land is in agony. Its people are suffering and dying in their thousands; its ruler is a usurper. Old King Henry's wish that the throne should go to the Empress Matilda, our Lady of the English, is known to every soul in the realm. Opposite you are men of evil. They are men who have stolen a crown, men who have perjured themselves before God and before their kin, and men who have killed, tortured and maimed to further their own cause. We can end their savagery here today.'

I raised my sword high above my head and filled the sky with my voice.

'For Matilda, Lady of the English, a daughter of the royal families of every Celt, Englishman and Norman! A Queen for all our lands!'

A great roar echoed across the battlefield and travelled all the way up the hill to Lincoln itself. The speeches were over, the battlelines set. I felt certain that, by the end of the day, England would have a new ruler.

Eadmer was the first to congratulate me on my rousing speech, but in his own distinct way.

'Well done, Hal. I think you've just written a new ballad for me!'

Robert was also very complimentary.

'Quite the orator, Earl Harold. If that doesn't win us the day, nothing will!'

Robert ordered his herald to sound the advance. The Battle of Lincoln had begun.

We dismounted most of our knights, so that they could fight on foot, and left only a few cavalry in reserve. The mud was deep and progress was difficult, especially in trying to maintain close formation. I called for several volleys from our archers at the rear, aimed specifically at Stephen's flanks, where his less committed Breton and Flemish mercenaries stood. The arrows plummeted to earth like hailstones; men covered their heads with their shields, but many arrows hit their targets, cutting into exposed legs, arms and feet. They were not fatal wounds, but they put men out of action and spread fear in the ranks.

As we advanced, it was clear that our numbers were significantly greater than Stephen's. I could see the anxiety roll through his army like a wave. Sergeants began to bellow orders, commanders tried to steady their men.

Robert turned to me and shouted.

'I am going to commit our left and right flanks!'

'I agree – they should attack at a run, while we go on slowly. Stephen's flanks are crumbling.'

Robert sent orders to Miles and Ranulf to charge, and I ordered more volleys of arrows to precede them.

'Robert, I propose we divide the cavalry to attack those who desert the field. I will send most to Ermine Street, and some to cover those who try to cross the river.'

'Yes, do it, my friend!'

The Welsh on our left and right hurled themselves forward like packs of hunting dogs. They made no attempt to keep formation, but just ran like banshees, screaming obscenities at the enemy. They attacked bravely, like a barbarian horde. Against resolute opponents it could have proved disastrous, but Stephen's flanks were already beaten.

The front ranks of Breton and Flemish soldiers turned as the Welsh closed on them, running into those behind, so that when the Welsh horde struck, their lines were in disarray and easy prey for the ferocious Celts. The knights loyal to Miles and Ranulf were close behind the Welsh vanguard. When they lent their disciplined cohorts to the melee, the whole of Stephen's forces on the left and right streamed from the field. It soon became a stampede, but one met by our cavalry, who started to cut into the fleeing men at will.

A slaughter ensued; all Stephen's previously brave and loyal senior men deserted him and galloped away, leaving him to stand alone at the front of his knights. Our advance had taken us within fifty yards of him. Robert and I were at the front of our men; by then, we were sinking up to our knees in mud.

I turned to Robert.

'He faces annihilation; we should offer him surrender.'

'I agree.'

But before we could call a halt to our advance, Stephen let out a mighty cry and ran towards us waving his sword in great arcs to encourage his followers. We were hit by a wave of sound as the whole of his central column rushed towards us in a frenzy.

Robert and I had no choice but to respond in the same vein. The two columns of men, at least ten deep, closed on one another at alarming speed. Our column was 600 strong; Stephen's contained perhaps 100 fewer. His desperate tactic was both brave and his only possible salvation. His one chance was to break through our centre like a battering ram and destroy our High Command.

The clash of sword on shield was deafening, the screams of dying men terrifying. The hand-to-hand fighting was ferocious; men swung their weapons wildly, often hitting friend and foe alike. It was difficult to find room to use tried and tested training techniques, the pressure of men from behind making such discipline impossible. The only effective method was to move forward like a Roman legionary, deploying the shield as a bludgeon, and using the sword to make short stabbing thrusts.

When men fell, they were trampled underfoot by wave after wave of the massed ranks moving forward. The mud changed colour from brown to a bloody purple, with countless distorted bodies protruding from the mire like broken dolls. I looked up as often as I could to see that our line was gradually eating up the ground towards the walls of the castle, leaving no space into which Stephen could retreat.

I felt no fear. I had been in too many battles; I was hardened to warfare and, like all seasoned warriors, I relished the primordial thrill of combat. There was always anxiety before an encounter and afterwards always reflection, usually tinged with regrets. But during the heat of battle there was only the crude thrill of warfare, and pride in the supreme skills of the professional soldier. Many men fell before me and I despatched them without mercy. There was no other way. In battle, there is no room for sympathy – a moment's hesitation could cost you your life.

I caught sight of Stephen several times, no more than five yards away. He had lost his sword, but was wielding an English battle-axe to awesome effect. I saw him turn towards the western gate of the city and lead away those close to him. The weight of their numbers managed to force the gate open and more than a hundred men poured into Lincoln's narrow streets. But they were unable to close the gate behind them, and we followed them into the burgh.

The fighting spread to all corners as Stephen's men

tried to find an escape route. Now civilians were caught up in the maelstrom, and the cries of women and children were added to the cacophony of battle. Fires broke out and smoke started to fill the air. Many of our troops, including the Welsh mercenaries, flooded into the burgh and began looting.

Robert tried to issue the order to desist. But it was to no avail; bloodlust had taken over.

Eadmer saw Stephen first. He was surrounded by fewer and fewer knights, and was trying to lead his men up the steep ground towards the cathedral and the main gate of the castle.

Robert of Gloucester had taken a heavy blow to his side and sank to his knees. He grabbed for my hauberk and entreated me urgently.

'Go after him! He won't get into the castle, he'll go for the cathedral. Don't let him reach it – we don't want blood spilled on consecrated ground.'

With Eadmer at my shoulder and a posse of knights behind me, I headed up the hill. We had to battle our way through several ranks of Stephen's knights, but Eadmer and I had developed a powerful close-quarters battle technique. We soon reached the small plateau in the shadow of the great western front of the cathedral. Stephen was on top of a mounting block, circled by a dozen knights. It looked as if he had chosen his ground for a final redoubt.

Held by his giant bearded standard-bearer, and flying proudly above him, was his war banner – a golden manticore with a hunting bow. His azure shield with argent bend signified his home in Blois, while to honour his wife's county he flew the gonfalon of Boulogne – three roundels in gules on a field of gold.

He was breathing heavily. His armour and cloak were dripping with blood – as were his face and beard – though none of it seemed to be his own. The ground around him began to clear as people rushed towards the cathedral for sanctuary. I ordered several knights to place a cordon around the area to make sure none of our marauding Welsh troops made a crazed dash for Stephen.

I stepped towards him, my knights a pace behind. Eadmer whispered to me as we walked.

'Be very careful. This is a proud brave man, and he's about to lose a kingdom.'

Stephen caught my eye, and put out his hand to calm his men.

I called out to him.

'Stephen of Blois, I am Harold, Earl of Huntingdon! On behalf of the Empress Matilda, I offer you quarter.'

Enraged by the fighting, his chest was heaving with anger and exertion. He cried out in an anguished voice.

'I am Stephen, King of England, Duke of Normandy and Count of Boulogne! And you, sir, are a traitor! My sources tell me that you are also my cousin's tup, and that you are cuckolding the Count of Anjou.'

I tried to remain calm.

'I offer you quarter and the mercy of Matilda for the last time.'

Stephen still sounded desperate, like a man in a bear trap.

'You are a knave! I believe you claim to be the bastard son of King Henry Beauclerc. But Hugh Bigod, Earl of

Norwich, tells me that your family name is Harold of Hereford and that the King once ordered your arrest for the murder of one of his men.'

'Attempting to provoke me will change nothing. Will you surrender or not?'

'Not even to an earl, and certainly not to the likes of you!'

Stephen jumped down from the mounting block and hurled himself across the ten yards that separated us. He held his axe two-handed, high above his head, poised to strike me as soon as I came within range. He was so overcome by his emotions, he was oblivious to danger. But it was a futile attack; he was exhausted and outnumbered.

When he got within striking distance, he unleashed a fearsome lunge at my helmet, but I easily parried it with my shield. I hit him in the face with the gauntlet of my right hand, which was firmly coiled around the pommel of my sword, knocking him to the ground. This time the blood on his face was his own; his nose was split and there was a deep gash to his cheek.

He tried to get up, but I put my foot on his chest while Eadmer put his foot on his axe. Stephen's knights moved to come to his aid, but did so half-heartedly. They were surrounded, their brave retreat over.

Stephen continued to struggle on the ground and had to be restrained by several knights. His taunts and insults were endless, and he tried to break free at every opportunity. Eventually, we had to bind and hood him and tie him on to the back of a cart, but still he cursed and strained at his ropes.

I ordered that he be treated with respect and asked

Miles of Gloucester to take him in hand so that Eadmer and I could assess the situation on the battlefield and in Lincoln. I suddenly realized that it was still raining heavily; I could now hear the rain lashing the ground and the wind swirling around the tall towers of the cathedral.

The battlefield was strewn with bodies; fresh puddles of rainwater had filled the hollows we had made and blood was beginning to seep into them, turning them into pools of crimson. I could see some men still moving in agony, or breathing their last. Our men were already among the corpses, collecting weapons; the scavengers from the burgh were robbing the dead of anything they could find.

'Eadmer, I want burial parties organized immediately. All the dead are to be buried – friend or foe. And get rid of those ghouls robbing the dead.'

The burgh was in chaos; fires were still burning, and there were still the harrowing screams of rape and looting to be heard.

'Find the senior burgesses and the Dean of the cathedral; we have to help them restore order.'

I thought back to my reflections in Aquitaine many years previously about the price people have to pay in pursuit of a cause. Even if a cause is worthy and just, a war on its behalf unleashes the beast in us and, once free, it's almost impossible to get the rampant creature back into its cage.

England had lost the peace and security of its rigid Norman rule; the Normans were now fighting among themselves. But one of them was a woman who was so precious to me, and who carried the English blood that I also cared so much about.

I just hoped that the price so many were paying was worth it.

It took us several days to complete our tasks in Lincoln, and another week to march back to Gloucester with our quarry. Stephen was still being awkward and Earl Robert, feeling sore from his wound, lost patience with him and had him put in chains. When Stephen continued to abuse the Earl, he had him gagged, made him go barefoot, dressed him in sackcloth and had his head and beard shaved like a common criminal. Stephen still shouted abuse when his gag was removed, so Robert made him walk at the back of his cart, which in winter, and without shoes, was a painful experience. Still he would not be cowed and slowly earned the grudging respect of his guards and the whole army.

When we reached Gloucester, Maud had organized a guard of honour to greet us. She summoned Miles, Brien, Ranulf and Robert to congratulate them, and she thanked her High Command for all that had been achieved. After this, she asked that Stephen be brought before her.

When he arrived, she was visibly shaken by his chains and filthy appearance, but she chose to say nothing in front of him.

It was Stephen who spoke first.

'Cousin Matilda, I can't say I'm delighted to see you. But were circumstances different, I would of course be thrilled –'

Robert, still infuriated with his behaviour, rounded on him.

'Behave yourself, man! You are defeated, and you're in the presence of your future Queen. Show some dignity!'

'Don't talk to me about dignity, Robert of Gloucester! What do traitors know of dignity?'

Maud commanded them both to be quiet.

'Enough! I will not have men bickering like boys in a nursery! Stephen, you treated me well when you came to Arundel. I will make you the same offer now: safe passage to your brother, Theobald, in Blois, if you relinquish the throne to me. Otherwise, you will languish here – not to "feel my wrath", as you so elegantly put it to me at Arundel, but at my pleasure. You will be confined, as Robert Curthose was by my father, for the rest of your life.'

Stephen started to laugh.

'That is an empty threat. My supporters still hold the Treasury at Winchester, and all the earldoms east of Oxford. London will not turn against me. Make the threat again when you're Queen.'

He continued to jeer and taunt as Maud ordered him to be taken away. As soon as he had gone, she turned to Earl Robert.

'Please, take him to Bristol, I don't want him here. But hear me clearly: I want him to be well treated. I want him fed and clothed appropriately and confined in a secure chamber befitting his status, with a garderobe, not in a filthy dungeon. He is to be given a fire, candles, books and vellum – and servants, as necessary.'

Maud sounded like a monarch, as was her birthright. But Robert began to argue.

'Matilda –'

434

'That is my name when we are together as friends, in private. This is a matter of the realm; my title is "ma'am".'

Robert bristled, but he knew Maud was right.

'Very well, ma'am. But if I may, perhaps I can make a plea regarding the defence of the realm?'

'Of course.'

'Order his execution, ma'am –'

'I won't hear of it!'

'While he lives, he's a threat. As he said, there are Winchester and London to win. And then you have to be crowned by Theodore of Bec, Archbishop of Canterbury, if your coronation is to be recognized by the English magnates – and he's Stephen's man.'

'Stephen's man! He'll turn to me when he knows he has to. I will not have my cousin executed, and be accused of cold-blooded murder.'

'He has committed treason! He usurped your throne and, as you have said, probably had your father poisoned. He deserves to die.'

'Would you say that of my father? He also grabbed the throne when Rufus died. I'm content that I now have the crown within my grasp. Let Stephen fester in Bristol for a while.'

Then Maud made a statement that took me by surprise, though it was probably a wise thing to say to her closest supporters.

'I hear my relationship with Hal is the subject of much speculation, and that Stephen made lewd accusations about our friendship at Lincoln. Let me say this to all of you in private; it is a state of affairs that I am happy is known to those close to me. But after I have made the position clear, it need no longer be the subject of rumour and innuendo. Count Geoffrey and I have lived apart for many years. Hal has become my closest friend and taken my children under his wing, as well as taking charge of my own happiness and welfare. I would like it to be known that I am very happy with that arrangement.'

The others nodded their understanding.

I smiled at her carefully chosen words. My clandestine life was no longer a secret — at least, not from those close to Maud — which meant I could have a more honest relationship with our children. The dilemma of their paternity remained — an issue that would have to be dealt with at some point in the future — but for now, I was content with Maud's declaration and impatient to complete her capture of the throne.

Fulham Palace, 29 September 1187

Dear Thibaud,

It is the feast of St Michael and All Angels today and I managed to make it to St Paul's to say mass. I have been feeling better these past few days; the mild weather has helped. Today is Saturday, but I don't think I will return to St Paul's tomorrow; that will be too much for my present state of health. We will have a quiet mass here, and invite the local clergy to celebrate it with us. One must tend one's flock!

We are drawing near to the end of Harold's story. You will find it fascinating to hear how easily fortunes change; there is much intrigue and plotting, and it saddens me to see so many actions that are motivated by greed and avarice. I fear this is a salutary lesson for us all.

I'm afraid that as I approach the end of this tale, my output is slowing down. Apart from rare excursions like today, I am now almost bedridden and not much use to my flock. The autumn is already beginning to bite hard. I think this may be the last time I will see those glorious autumn colours.

My only incentive now is to complete what I have started. Please pray to God that I am able to do so.

Yours in God,
Gilbert

30. Treachery

Leaving Stephen under Earl Robert's watchful eye in Bristol, I escorted Maud to Winchester to negotiate with Henry, Bishop of Winchester. As Stephen's younger brother, the holder of the keys to the Royal Treasury, the Pope's legate in England and the most powerful cleric in the land, he was vital to our cause.

We met him on 2 March 1141, the Feast of St Chad of Mercia, as he duly reminded us when we met. It was a tense encounter, held in a meadow outside the village of Wherwell, ten miles north of the burgh. Ever the pragmatist, Henry wanted to be Maud's primary link to the ecclesiastical establishment of England, a position that would grant him immense power – even more than he had already. He also insisted that he be installed at Canterbury when the time was right.

Maud bristled openly; she was very reluctant to concede, arguing that he was dictating terms to her. But I persuaded her to acquiesce, for the time being.

It was a hard bargain but, in return, Bishop Henry gave her a ceremonial welcome into Winchester the next day, swore his allegiance to her in public, opened up the Royal Treasury and handed her the keys. She was also given the royal crown known as 'Edward's Crown', worn by her forebears reaching back to her ancestor, King Edward. It incorporated jewels set in the ancient crown of Alfred the Great, eight generations earlier in England's royal lineage.

Maud was now halfway to the throne: she had Stephen under guard, and the Treasury was hers. She still needed the support of London, and a coronation at Westminster. But it seemed that her destiny, and mine, would be fulfilled.

In addition, I received an unexpected windfall at Winchester. When King Henry had made me an earl in Rouen – in an agreement that seemed to have been sealed a lifetime ago – he granted me lands in the north, in Barnsdale and Loxley Chase, and a large hunting forest called Sherwood, south of Worksop. To my amazement, the dutiful clerks in the King's Exchequer had been diligently collecting the income from my holdings. The Pipe Rolls for the last ten years recorded that I was owed almost 200 pounds of silver – not quite enough to pay the ransom on a king's head, but enough to live for many years with all the trappings of wealth.

Maud agreed that the silver should go to Fulk of Falaise in Argentan – to be kept as a discreet nest egg for the future – and Otto and Berenger were immediately despatched to ensure its safe delivery.

We moved to Oxford, while Bishop Henry called a Great Council of the Church at Winchester to debate the succession. At the Great Council, Henry delivered on his promise. In front of the entire ecclesiastical hierarchy of the kingdom, he issued a declaration.

While I should love my mortal brother, he has won nothing but hatred, and therefore, I should esteem far more highly the cause of my immortal father. Our kingdom cannot stumble along without a ruler and therefore we choose as Lady of England and Normandy the daughter of a King who brought us peace, and we promise her faith and support.

They were powerful words. As soon as we heard the news, we set out for London. At Wilton we were welcomed by Theobald of Bec, Archbishop of Canterbury, and a huge gathering of cheering crowds. There were also rapturous welcomes at Reading and St Albans, and every day messages arrived from magnates all over the land declaring their loyalty to 'Matilda, Lady of the English'. It was a blissful time, during which we were carried along on a wave of euphoria.

Maud was dressed in the clothes she had worn on her march through Normandy and looked like a fairy-tale queen. Her red velvet cape gleamed in the bright sunlight and her winning smile could easily be seen through the fine white silk veil draped from her wimple. A pristine cream kirtle hugged her womanly figure, bringing gasps of admiration from the crowd. She rode side-saddle and waved regally to the hundreds who had come out to see her pass. I had returned the Talisman to her and it sat neatly between her breasts; every now and then it caught a beam of sunlight and flashed like a beacon, signalling a new beginning for our beloved homeland. I thought back to the story my mother had told me many times about the moment when a beam of light had illuminated the Talisman in the Chapel of St Etheldreda after the end of the Siege of Ely – a moment that had saved my grandfather's life. He would have been a very proud man if he could have witnessed the scenes that greeted us – as would everyone else in my family, and all those who had died for England's cause.

At St Albans we had met with several of the burgesses of London, who outlined their plans for a ceremonial procession into the burgh through the ancient gate at Aldgate. The route would take us past King William's mighty tower and on to Westminster via Ludgate.

Maud's entry into London was a memorable occasion. England had never had a reigning Queen before, and I knew of none in any other land. But the people of London – Norman and Englishman alike – cheered and cried out their approval. Perhaps the ruling Normans, always realists, accepted her through shrewd calculation. But for the downtrodden English, she was seen as their saviour – the embodiment of the brave King Harold and all their Cerdician kings stretching back to Alfred the Great.

When she later entered the Great Hall of Westminster, all the clerks and officials of government were lined up to greet her. To one side stood the monarch's private household, all hoping to be renewed in the roles they had held for Stephen. There were also more than two dozen nobles from all corners of the realm. Everyone present was warm in their welcome and fulsome in their praise.

But almost all also had a pressing need, an axe to grind, or a bargain they would like to strike.

*

Maud's work as Queen began early the next morning. It was not a new experience for her – she had acted as regent for her first husband – but the volume of business to be dealt with was colossal. Stephen had been an absentee King for years and the anarchy across the realm had suspended efficient government in all but a few centres of royal power. All suppliants were impatient, and the years of turmoil had created a widespread mood of antagonism and bickering.

By dusk, Maud was exhausted. But the business of the day was still not over; a deputation of burgesses from London were due to dine with the Queen that evening. Maud invited me to join them for supper.

The gathering of the rich and powerful of London did not go well. The burgesses were overtly humble to the point of being obsequious, and Maud charmed them as only she could, but they soon raised the serious business they wished to discuss. Crucially, they wanted Maud to acknowledge Stephen's decision to grant London commune status and to reaffirm the tax concessions that went with it.

Maud trod carefully, but she was firm with them.

'Gentlemen, I appreciate that no one likes to pay tax, but the Treasury at Winchester is bare. Stephen tried to win popularity by giving concessions while, at the same time, he spent all his reserves laying siege to his opponents and paying an army of mercenaries to fight his battles. My priority is to bring peace and to refill the coffers of the kingdom.'

The burgesses' main spokesman was a merchant called Osbert Eightpence. His name and his appearance suggested he was an Englishman, but in fact he was the son of a Norman from Rouen, who had changed his name from 'Huitdeniers'. Nevertheless, his cleverness and his silky tongue were not in doubt.

'Ma'am, we understand the task you face. Perhaps if you were to put your financial affairs in the hands of your Chamberlain, it would relieve you of a great burden? We could then discuss the matter with him.'

It was not clear whether he meant the insult calculatingly, or perhaps he had not realized how condescending he was being, but the effect was the same. I tried to catch Maud's eye, but I was too late. She nodded in the direction of her Chamberlain, who was sitting close to her at the huge oak table of Westminster's Great Hall.

'Sir, my financial affairs are already in the hands of my Chamberlain. He is here with me; you know him well. If you're suggesting that finance is a matter better dealt with by a man, then you do not know me.'

'Forgive me, ma'am, I was not suggesting anything of the sort, merely offering you a solution to the dilemma you face. Would it not be wiser for you to concentrate on showing yourself to your subjects across the realm? They love you dearly, and thus you may bring unity to us all as Lady of the English.'

He was playing her like a fish, and he had her hooked. I managed to catch her eye, but it was to no avail.

'So you suggest I parade around the realm like a court jester? And while I'm making an exhibition of myself, you run London and get richer than you are already, while the kingdom is on its knees!'

Osbert backed away and bowed. He appeared to be

chastened, but I am sure he knew he had won an important victory. Maud then made matters much worse.

'Gentlemen, I am revoking London's status as a commune. You will pay the same taxes as everybody else.'

Maud pushed back her chair and stood bolt upright. It was the signal for the end of the meeting; the richest commoners in England trudged away muttering to themselves.

Later that night, I tried to reason with her.

'You are not their Queen yet. Treat them like your subjects when they *are* your subjects, but not until then.'

'So now you are telling me what to do!'

'I am giving you advice.'

'That's what that spineless little merchant was trying to do! The burgesses are trying to extract the maximum benefit for themselves before I'm crowned. But if I concede, I'll never rule this land as a woman. I am my father's daughter and the granddaughter of William the Bastard. He wouldn't have stood for it, and neither will I!'

In many ways I agreed with her. But I could sense dangerous times ahead; we were in unknown territory, and danger was part of our chosen path.

For the next few weeks, earls supplicated themselves, seeking more land, barons sought earldoms, knights begged for baronies, and countless others came to make demands or bring offers of 'advice'. Maud grew tired of it all, saying often, 'If I'm kind to someone, it proves that a woman doesn't have the fortitude to rule. If I'm firm with somebody, I'm a harridan, arrogant and not worthy of my sex!'

444

I felt so sorry for her; she was trapped by her womanhood. Fate had made her Empress and Queen – but her peers wanted her to be a consort, not a monarch.

One evening, when she was feeling particularly overwhelmed, she speculated with me on possible solutions.

'Would they accept Geoffrey as Regent?'

'I doubt it; he would need at least a little Norman or English blood.'

'What about you?'

I smiled at her.

'You mean, rule together? Wouldn't that be wonderful! But it must remain a dream. I am a commoner, my title is a contrivance, and there are too many skeletons hidden away. I am content that young Henry will rule this kingdom after us. In the meantime, you must stay strong; I will do all I can to help you.'

In late May 1141, Bishop Henry appeared at Westminster with Stephen's wife, Countess Mathilde of Boulogne. They had two petitions. Firstly, that Stephen be released into Henry's custody at Winchester. And secondly, that Stephen and Mathilde's eldest son, Eustace, a boy of twelve – almost four years older than our son Henry – be recognized as Maud's legitimate heir.

Maud behaved impeccably towards Mathilde and was as polite as she could be in hearing both petitions. But instead of buying time until the coronation by saying she would think about them, she refused the first on the grounds that Stephen had proved he could not be trusted, and the second on the basis that Henry was her heir and that she intended to remove Eustace from the line of succession altogether. Needless to say, neither Henry nor Mathilde was overjoyed at the outcome.

Both suggestions were of course preposterous, but they were clearly part of a plan that seemed to be well orchestrated and deliberate. Although I did not reveal my worst fears to Maud, I despatched Otto and Berenger to Bristol with a note for Earl Robert. The message was simple, saying that he would soon receive an invitation to the coronation. However, I directed him to come as soon as possible and bring a body of men with him to protect the Queen against any dissenters.

Earl Robert appeared in the middle of June with a large corps of knights, which took Matilda by surprise.

'Why so many men?'

Robert was very diplomatic.

'I couldn't keep them away; they all want to see you crowned.'

When I explained my fears to Robert, he concurred.

'I heard in Oxford that Stephen's wife, Mathilde, is raising a substantial body of men to attack London from her base in Kent. There is a conspiracy afoot. I'm sure Bishop Henry is involved, as well as William of Ypres – who deserted the field at Lincoln.'

'If he's involved, that means Flemish mercenaries. But where are they getting the money from?'

Robert smiled at me, as if to say, 'Aren't you being a bit naive?'

Then I realized.

'The rich men of London!'

'Well done. Their loyalty to the Queen cannot be

guaranteed – I fear they would easily betray her, if it would turn a profit for them.'

'I'll post my own guards to keep an eye on the royal guards.'

'Good idea! I'm very pleased that Maud has you by her side. Keep her safe these coming days.'

I embraced Robert and thanked him. Although we were not in fact brothers, we had become close allies in Maud's cause and both knew we would give our lives to defend her.

On 24 June, late in the afternoon, we were preparing for a grand banquet at Westminster. It was to be a feast to celebrate two vital breakthroughs. Firstly, the Archbishop of Canterbury had agreed a date for the coronation, on Saturday 26 July, and preparations were well under way. Secondly, a grand regal procession was to take place through the streets of London on the following day, 25 June, when the date of the coronation would be announced.

News of the Archbishop's agreement had come as an unexpected surprise to Robert and me – and even more so, the procession organized by London's burgesses. But they were pleasant surprises, and all Maud's supporters had gathered to enjoy an evening of rejoicing. Miles of Gloucester had arrived, as had Brien FitzCount and Ranulf of Chester.

All of Maud's royal household and officials – who seemed to have warmed to her diligence and thoughtfulness – were invited, and all appeared to have fully accepted her succession. The fact that she did not suffer fools was not, in their eyes, a weakness – in fact, quite the reverse. Also, her honesty and fairness in judgement were a refreshing change from the partiality and nepotism that had been typical of the recent past.

The Great Hall at the Palace of Westminster was beginning to fill with guests when alarm bells were heard to ring. They were the distant bells of London, drifting across Lambeth Moor and the nearby Thames. I hoped the bells signalled a domestic issue, such as a fire. But almost immediately messengers came running in to announce that a large force, led by William of Ypres and Stephen's wife, the Countess Mathilde, had laid waste to a vast swathe of Kent and had entered London across Stephen's new bridge from Southwark.

Within minutes, we had more news. The church bells were ringing the alarm as far west as St Clement Danes in the Strand, and an armed mob was pouring out of London at Ludgate, burning and looting as it went.

Robert and I agreed that he would rush his men to Charing at the end of the Strand and hold the mob there, while I got Maud away to Oxford, where we would rendezvous in two days' time.

It was a near-run thing. I summoned a small escort of only a dozen knights. Maud and Greta barely had enough time to change their clothes. As Otto and Berenger helped the ladies on to their mounts, Eadmer grabbed the royal seals, the keys to the Treasury and King Edward's crown, while I ran to the gates of the palace to check the situation up the hill at Charing. Robert had formed up his knights to block the road, but men armed with an array of weapons were already streaming through the fields on either side to outflank them. The mob seemed to be hundreds strong, if not thousands. Miles, Ranulf, Brien and their escorts formed another cordon at the gates of the palace, but the crowds just washed around them like waves over pebbles on the seashore.

With Otto and Berenger flanking the women, Eadmer took the rear and I led the vanguard as we rode through the west gate of the palace with only minutes to spare. We kept close to the river, but even before we reached the Manor of Neate – within a stone's throw from the palace – we could hear the frenzied cries of the mob and the dreadful sounds of the wanton destruction behind us.

We rode most of the night and were safely inside the walls of Oxford Castle late the following afternoon. As soon as Robert joined us, we tried to make sense of what had happened. Miles and Ranulf had rushed back to their castles, but Miles sent word – based on rumours he had heard while at Westminster – that it was a plot which had been many weeks in the hatching.

Robert sat Maud down and gave her his interpretation.

'Bishop Henry has changed horses again. After Winchester, when he thought you could be easily manipulated, he was happy to endorse you. But after you denied him and Mathilde their petitions, he changed his mind. London turned against you as soon as you stood up to them – again, they thought you would be a malleable Dowager Queen for many years until Henry was of an age.

'Much the same applies to the earls and landowners. They don't mind a queen, as long as she doesn't act like a king. That mob from London had been worked into a frenzy; purses of silver and free barrels of ale would have been at the back of that. I wager that every ne'er-do-well in the burgh would have been recruited. I saw stevedores with billhooks, young farmers wielding pitchforks, and even apprentice masons brandishing their mallets.'

Robert had voiced what was now obvious to all of us.

Maud did not seem angry or disappointed – rather, she remained determined.

'Well, whether they like it or not, this Queen is going to fight like a king for what is right. How quickly can we gather an army?'

'To what end?'

'To march on Winchester.'

'Is that wise?'

'It may not be. But I intend to make Bishop Henry pay for his duplicity!'

Robert looked at me, clearly concerned. He was no doubt hoping that I would advise Maud to be cautious.

'Maud, it may be wise to go back to Gloucester and assess the situation from there –'

'I know it's a risk. But if we can snare Henry and put him where Stephen is, it will send a clear message that I will not be denied.'

Maud's strategy was bold; it was dangerous, but it could be a vital blow. Henry's duplicity was there for all to see. Maud had every right to challenge him.

Robert nodded his approval.

Maud smiled at us both.

'Thank you, Gentlemen; let's go and snatch victory from the jaws of defeat!'

Robert, who was always up for a fight, quickly warmed to the idea.

'I will ride to Bristol and bring more men. I will also send word for Ranulf, Miles and Brien to join us. Let us agree to meet at Andover on the fourth Sunday in July.'

31. Winchester in Flames

Maud donned her campaigning clothes for the attack on Winchester, which we launched on 31 July 1141. She rode out at the front of the column, her hair flowing in the wind. She refused armour, but wore a thick leather jerkin similar to the ones used by archers. Under the jerkin she had a heavy woollen smock and wore cavalrymen's leggings and boots. Otto and Berenger flanked her and had strict instructions to get her to the rear of the column at the first hint of danger.

She was a great inspiration to the men, and I tried to think of a precedent. I could come up with only one warrior queen in our history – a figure from the distant past that my mother had told me about – Queen Boudicca, widow of Prasutagus, King of the Iceni, one of the ancient tribes who had fought the Romans.

Robert, Brien, Miles, Ranulf and I rode behind her in line abreast, leading over 100 knights and almost 1,000 infantry and archers. Eadmer carried my colours and Robert's standard-bearer held Maud's new colours. She had chosen them as monarch, a variation on mine: three golden lions rampant, one each for England, Normandy and Anjou, on a gules field. Her colours symbolized everything about her.

We had three objectives at Winchester: the burgh, where the Treasury was located; the old castle, to the west within the burgh's walls; and Bishop Henry's new castle, Wolvesey, on the eastern side of the settlement. When we arrived from the west, we found the city gates open and were able to ride in with ease. But as we did so, we saw that Bishop Henry had broken into the Royal Treasury and emptied it. He and his entourage had then escaped to the east, leaving his garrison to defend his episcopal castle. It was a well-built fortification, and we prepared for a long siege.

The castellan of the old fortress, built in the time of Maud's grandfather, readily opened its gates to us, and we made it our base for the assault on Wolvesey. I also asked Eadmer to organize patrols to see if they could track down Bishop Henry.

Two days later, early in the morning, we woke with the smell of acrid smoke in our nostrils and the sound of anguished screams in our ears. Maud and I reached the window of our chamber together. We looked out over Winchester and all we could see were plumes of black smoke rising from the burgh, peppered with spits of bright flame.

Eadmer started to bang on the door.

'*Hurry!* Henry's men are burning the burgh. They slunk out of the castle under cover of darkness, throwing flaming brands everywhere.'

It was a frightening scene. People were running in all directions, some already consumed by flames ignited by the intense heat. Buildings close to those already ablaze seemed to burst into flame spontaneously, giving the unfortunate people in the streets between them no chance of escape from the inferno.

Thankfully, we were safe behind the stone perimeter of our fortified position, but most of the burgh of Winchester was destroyed; all that remained intact were the two stone-built fortresses and the cathedral.

People started to leave before dusk that day; by the afternoon of the next day, the burgh was a deserted and charred shell.

It was a callous act; Bishop Henry had ordered the burning of his own burgh. But it was also astute. He had denied us shelter for the army, provisions for men and horses, and entertainment in the taverns and whorehouses.

I called an urgent meeting of our High Command.

'If we make camp outside the walls of the burgh, we will have no protection from attack. If we choose to stay within the walls, we will have to begin to clear the ground immediately.'

There was a consensus: we had to camp within the walls and continue the siege of Wolvesey. We began the task in earnest, but it was a frustrating process. All we could do was proceed with the tactics of attrition.

We sealed the fortress and began the long patient wait of siege warfare.

Two weeks later, with the siege still in its early days, Eadmer's sentries, still searching for Bishop Henry, reported that the roads around Winchester were blockaded by the men of Mathilde and William of Ypres.

I immediately despatched Eadmer.

'I need a full report. Go around the blockades, I need to know what Mathilde and William are up to.'

It took Eadmer two days to complete his reconnaissance. When he returned, he brought unwelcome news. I called everyone together to hear his report.

'Ma'am, the Countess of Boulogne is camped at Stoke on the Itchen with an army led by William of Ypres. They are mainly Bretons, with Flemish mercenaries. But there are also several squadrons of the London militia who, I am ashamed to say, are mainly Englishmen. I estimate two hundred knights and at least two thousand infantry, including archers and crossbowmen. Henry of Blois, Bishop of Winchester, is with Countess Mathilde.'

Brien FitzCount could contain himself no longer at the mention of Bishop Henry's name.

'What a bastard! He has a remarkable gift for discovering that his duty always points in the same direction as his self-interest!'

Even in the midst of the gloomy news, we could not fail but smile at Brien's sardonic turn of phrase.

Eadmer finished his report with two more pieces of grim news.

'All the roads are closed, nothing can get in or out of Winchester. And their army is beginning to break camp – they will be on the march tomorrow.'

Earl Robert stood and began to pace the floor.

'How far away is Stoke?'

'Eight miles, my Lord.'

'Well, it seems we're snared in our own trap. We can't get an army the size of ours inside this bailey and then feed them. And we can't hold the burgh's wooden ramparts, most of which have been damaged by the flames, against an army the size of Mathilde's. We've also got to think of Henry's garrison inside Wolvesey; they will be an additional problem.'

He looked at me, almost plaintively. I nodded, signalling that I concurred with the only obvious solution. He spoke on behalf of us both.

'Ma'am, you must get out tonight under cover of darkness – you, Greta and your Lotharingians. Earl Harold will get you away with Eadmer, just the six of you. Take some horses, but no regal trappings. I will hold the fortress here to give you time to get away. Hopefully you will be secure in the west by the time they realize you've gone. Ranulf, I suggest you take your men north to Chester, break through the blockade; we'll need your men for another day. Brien, you should do the same. Go to your castle at Wallingford; it is our most eastern outpost. If you can hold it, it will remain a thorn in Mathilde's side. Miles, you and your men will stay here with me.'

'Of course, my Lord. It will be an honour.'

Maud stood; her hopes and dreams were in tatters. She took several deep breaths before addressing us.

'My Lords, I am grateful to you all. The last few weeks have not gone well for us. Stephen is still being financed from Flanders, and I suspect he also receives support from the King of France. Now it seems the London merchants are lending him their silver too. But I will not give in; with your support, I will fight on.'

She kissed and embraced each of us, then beckoned to Greta.

I issued final instructions before the ladies took their leave.

'Greta, we depart at midnight. You must prepare only

two bags each. Eadmer, you are to look after King Edward's crown and the great seals. You can leave the keys; the Treasury has already been ransacked.'

Once again, I thought about our cause. Maud's success was under serious threat and the once proud burgh of Winchester, old King Edward's favourite place, was a charred cinder, its people destitute.

They were paying a high price, as was England.

We rode all night, finding some rest at John FitzGilbert's castle at Luggershall, then on to Devizes and finally to Gloucester, where Greta and Maud collapsed in total exhaustion.

Ten days later, Miles of Gloucester appeared. He was alive, but was in a sorry state – he had lost his armour and his weapons, he was naked from the waist up, and his horse was spent. Eadmer and I helped him into the Great Hall, gave him a cloak and seated him in front of the fire. We gave him food and a flagon of wine. He waited for Maud to arrive, before giving us his account.

'I'm afraid I had a difficult journey back, ma'am, so please forgive my appearance. I became separated from my knights and was pursued all the way across Salisbury Plain. I had to go to ground to get away. Winchester was a rout. When William and Mathilde's army appeared, they swept over the walls of the burgh like a tidal bore. We had to abandon our position and attempt a fighting retreat to the north-west. We made a stand at Stockbridge and held our ground for a while. In the midst of their onslaught, an old friend rode into our lines. David, King of Scotland, had been on his way to support you at Winchester with two hundred knights. To his immense credit, when he heard of our plight, instead of returning home, he rode to our aid. His men bought us some time, but we were still overwhelmed.

'We formed a final redoubt, but it was futile; men fell in droves until I counted our number as only a few dozen. King David managed to get away with a bodyguard of knights. My Captain put me on a horse before he was cut down, but I don't think Earl Robert made it. The last time I saw him, he was surrounded by Flemish knights; I fear the worst.'

Maud sat by Miles and cradled his head in her lap. It was a touching moment. She summoned the stewards.

'Take this brave man to his chamber!'

That evening, Maud and I had a heart to heart. She sat on my knee in front of the fire, looking forlorn. When she spoke, her question was candid.

'Is our game over, my darling?'

'Not quite. You've still got Stephen cooped up in Bristol. As long as you have him, the game is still on.'

'But we are in retreat and our position looks bleak. My chance has gone; we have suffered enough, the people have suffered enough. I want to rule a strong and peaceful land, but England is in ruins.'

'I admit that our situation is not ideal, but we've come so far. Don't abandon hope yet.'

'I don't feel as strong as you. Help me, Hal. Lend me some of your courage.'

'You are the strongest woman I've ever met; you don't need to borrow anything from me. While you live and the boys live, your cause – and that of England – is still alive.'

458

'Thank you, Hal. I love you very much.'

I carried her to our bed, where she eventually fell asleep, leaving me to reflect on our future.

It was true, we were still in the game, but the odds were swinging against us. I knew that Maud missed the boys more and more with every passing day. At least there was one small crumb of comfort: we had been about to send word to Argentan for them to be brought to Westminster for Maud's coronation. But thankfully, that never happened; recent events would have been impossible to bear, had they been with us. I started to drift off to sleep and, as I did so, I longed to be in St Cirq Lapopie with our boys.

At the beginning of October, our refuge in the Lot became even more appealing. To our astonishment, an envoy appeared at Gloucester with a message from Mathilde of Boulogne. It was short and to the point.

The forces of King Stephen of England have in their custody Robert, Earl of Gloucester, captured at Stockbridge during a rebellion against his lawful King.

We propose an exchange of prisoners.

Queen Mathilde will offer herself at Bristol as hostage in exchange for the release of her husband, Stephen, our sovereign King. After the release of Stephen, and when he reaches Winchester, Earl Robert will be released, subject to his son, William, being taken as hostage.

When Earl Robert reaches Bristol, Queen Mathilde will be released, as will Earl Robert's son in Winchester.

It was an elaborate but clever exchange. It spelled disaster for our cause, but it was a dark cloud with a silver lining: we had assumed Robert had been killed, but this meant he was alive. Maud and I discussed Mathilde's offer and brought Miles into our confidence.

Miles, ever loyal, gave a response typical of a faithful supporter.

'Do not accept, ma'am. Stephen's incarceration means you are within touching distance of the throne. If you let him go, the throne recedes into the far distance, and will remain beyond your grasp. Robert knows that; he would not want you to give up the throne on his behalf.'

Maud turned to me.

'Hal?'

'I agree with Miles. Mathilde can't execute Robert for two reasons. Firstly, he is universally admired. But secondly, and more importantly, she would be giving you the ideal premise for ordering the execution of her husband. Robert will bear imprisonment on your behalf.'

'But they will torture him.'

'No, and for the same reasons.'

Miles then introduced an argument that had been made before.

'You could of course grasp the initiative, and do away with Stephen first. Robert has made the point already. The throne would be yours. You would be the only possible successor.'

'But Stephen has a son —'

'Not old enough. And his blood is not close enough.'

'It would be a death sentence for Robert.'

'It would be of course. But winning a civil war is not without pain and sacrifice; Robert knows that.'

'I need time to think. Let us discuss this tomorrow.'

It was a difficult night for both of us. On the one hand, we both knew that relinquishing Stephen would make it unlikely that Maud would ever be Queen. On the other hand, Robert was not only Maud's kin, but also a loyal supporter and a close friend.

We lay in bed together, wide awake until late into the night. I was as desperate as Maud was for her to be crowned, but there had to be a limit to ambition.

Maud placed her hand around the Talisman.

'You brought this amulet to me. Isn't it supposed to tell me what to do?'

'No, you know that's not its purpose. It doesn't bestow wisdom; it merely reminds us of the value of wisdom.'

'Well, I understand the value of wisdom, but I'm lacking it at the moment. What do you think, Hal? What would your grandfather, the mighty Hereward, have done?'

'I wish I knew. He was certainly prepared to lay down his life in support of Edgar the Atheling, to thwart your grandfather. But this is different: you would be making a sacrifice of someone else's life for your own benefit.'

'So it would be noble of someone to lay down his life for me; but it would be ignoble of me to ask it of another.'

'Well put, my darling. I thought you said you lacked wisdom?'

'It's your Talisman; it's very clever. I will send the courier back to Mathilde in the morning, agreeing to the exchange.'

I loved Maud so much; she was brave and strong, but

she was also a woman of great integrity. England would have been a better place with her as Queen – but not at any price.

We travelled to Bristol for the exchange. Stephen and Maud spoke few words before he was released. Some mutual respect had been established – much more than had existed before – but both knew that their conflicting ambitions could never be reconciled.

The complicated exchange of prisoners was completed by the end of October 1141, and the civil war returned to a stalemate.

Stephen was anointed as King of England once more in an elaborate ceremony at Canterbury on Christmas Day – amidst, it was said, great rejoicing – but by then, we had developed a new strategy.

When Earl Robert had returned to us, he roundly condemned us for a serious error of judgement. Of course we should have sacrificed him! He would not have executed Stephen; he would have let him escape, and then arranged for him to meet a grisly end somewhere in the wildwood. Either way, we were wrong to have given him up. Nevertheless, Robert was happy to see his home and family again and to resume our cause – as we were to see him.

We immediately began to plan Maud's new strategy. She was the main instigator of it, and it was both simple and clever. She acknowledged that Westminster and the earldoms of the south-east would be beyond her control for as long as Stephen lived. Therefore, regardless of the legitimacy of his claim, she conceded – at least, in private to us – that he was, de facto, King of England. However, Geoffrey held Blois in his own name and also held Normandy – de facto, like Stephen's hold on Westminster. Moreover, Ranulf held sway over most of the north-west, and King David controlled the northern borders as well as his own Scottish domain. Significantly, our own base of power was extensive: from Devon and Cornwall into Wales; northwards to meet Ranulf's lands at Chester; and west as far as Oxford and Wallingford, less than fifty miles from London.

Although Stephen held a domain of great wealth and power, our sphere of influence was at least as great, if not more so. Our plan was to hold the south-west, a domain not unlike the ancient Kingdom of Wessex, which Maud would rule as her own.

And so it came to pass. We built bigger and stronger fortresses, raised taxes, issued coinage and created a system of government like any other. The disappointments of 1141 began to recede, and by the summer of 1142 Maud began to relish the role of monarch in her own western domain.

But there was also a longer-term goal. Our son, Henry Plantagenet, would reach his majority in March 1151 – less than nine years away. Our kingdom in the west would be the foundation stone of an empire we still hoped he would inherit.

We soon established a safe route from Argentan – via Caen to Wareham in Dorset, and then on to Bristol – so that our boys could make regular trips to England. As they got older, we hoped these visits would become longer and that eventually England would become their home.

Young Geoffrey was made Count of Nantes by his father, and little William was named Count of Poitou, but their elder brother's potential inheritance was still the glittering prize and the focus of our burning ambition.

In an attempt to signal our resolve to Stephen, we moved our seat of government to Oxford in August of 1142.

It was a bold move and it tempted fate.

32. Into the Perilous Night

Maud liked Oxford. It was a compact burgh and she felt comfortable walking its streets and talking to its people. Their local English dialect was a little difficult to follow, but it had a lilting harmony to it. Most importantly, its castle was formidable and she felt safe there.

Unfortunately, in September 1142, Stephen's spies discovered our secret route via Wareham. In a lightning attack, he overran the garrison and destroyed the town. As soon as he realized that young Henry had been visiting England, he raised a large force of mercenaries and marched on Oxford. As usual, he moved quickly and effectively and soon had the burgh surrounded. He took his men across the Isis and stormed into the town. He showed no mercy. Within minutes, every building was ablaze. People ran for safety and many tried to swim across the river, both east and west. We could only watch from the castle's tall tower as Stephen made the poor people of Oxford feel his wrath.

We were trapped.

Earl Robert and Miles of Gloucester were in Normandy trying to persuade Count Geoffrey to send us more money and men, and Brien FitzCount's garrison at Wallingford was too small to relieve us. Thankfully, we were well provisioned and had supplies to see us through the winter.

Stephen seemed prepared for a long siege and began to build wooden billets for his men. He also started to create two large earthen mounds close to our walls, the purpose of which was obvious. Come the following spring, he would build powerful catapults on the top of these hillocks and batter us into submission.

Maud had escaped Stephen's clutches before; now she needed another miracle.

Three months passed, and Christmastide was imminent. We had introduced strict rationing and firm discipline within the castle. We had managed to keep disease to a minimum, and found space to bury the dead in the castle keep, but morale was the biggest threat. With a determined opponent camped outside in vastly superior numbers, hell-bent on bringing the castle to its knees, there seemed to be no salvation – except of course for Maud to surrender herself. With this in mind, I became as watchful inside our walls as I was beyond them. It also made me realize that if, somehow, we could spirit her away – as we had done before – we could live to fight another day.

Oxford castle was surrounded by a deep moat, fed by the Isis, which made our fortress strong. But this also made escape more difficult; in the icy depths of winter, the moat became a bridge instead of a barrier. I saw the potential late one evening as I was watching a fox begin its nocturnal prowl. It appeared through the undergrowth beside the moat and paused by the water's edge, as it had done many times before. But then it proceeded to walk across the thick ice that had recently formed there.

The next morning, I gathered up Eadmer, Otto and Berenger and took them to Maud's chamber, where she was being attended by Greta.

'I think we have an escape route. It is not without risk, but it is imperative that we are away from here long before Stephen begins to hurl his missiles at our walls. We have to use the winter weather to our advantage. We'll wait for deep snow and the dark of the moon, then camouflage ourselves so as to be lost in the blanket of snow. Using the frozen moat, we can walk away.'

Eadmer was sceptical.

'And how do we get out of the castle without being seen?'

'Down a rope! You and Otto will go first. Berenger and I will then lower Maud and Greta down to you. We'll follow, and then throw the ropes back over the wall. We'll make for Eynsham – it's only five miles away – where we are sure to find horses. We'll be deep in the Cotswolds before anyone notices we're gone.'

Eadmer responded with his usual sarcasm.

'Well, that sounds straightforward enough! Tell me, how do we get past Stephen's sentries?'

'We'll follow the course of the river, and go through the water meadows; the sentries won't have their braziers above frozen water.'

'Of course, how simple! And the camouflage?'

'Long cloaks with hoods, soaked in limewash.'

Eadmer's expression changed. No longer sceptical, he began to smile. He looked at Maud, who nodded her approval.

'Good, then we wait for the next heavy snowfall.

Otto, Berenger, please prepare the cloaks and three stout ropes. We will need a few purses of silver, two lanterns and a little bread and water. The next dark of the moon is the week after Christmas. Let us all pray for a blizzard.'

It duly began to snow late on 28 December, the Sabbath, and did not relent for two days. By the morning of 30 December, the snow was a foot and a half deep with drifts piled up as tall as a man against anything that thwarted the wind. The landscape looked like a frozen sea, with waves held stationary in time. There was no wind, and the sky was heavy and grey; the night would be as black as Hell.

We went about our business as normal during the day and ate together as usual. Then, just after midnight, we made our way to the north-west wall of the castle and lowered our ropes. We were careful not to alert our own sentries, and maintained a strict silence.

I had left a note for the Castellan – a good man worthy of at least an explanation – asking him for forty-eight hours in which to make good our escape, before he surrendered the garrison to Stephen. I explained the reasons for our flight, asked for his understanding and wished him well.

Maud also left Edward's Crown and the royal seals of state in her chamber. Having decided that the throne at Westminster was a lost cause, she had no need of them and would commission her own regalia in Bristol for her new realm in the west.

The limewash made our cloaks very heavy, but that was

the only hindrance to our descent down the ropes. When we reached the frozen moat, it was almost impossible to see where we were going, even in the white landscape. But the limewash rendered us almost invisible – certainly beyond twenty yards.

Noise was our biggest enemy; the night was still, and even the slightest sound carried far into the distance. Our feet crunched the deep snow and the icy conditions made twigs and even fallen leaves brittle. Animals scurried from us and waterfowl took flight. These were probably sounds that seemed normal to Stephen's sentries and thus aided our escape. But to us, it seemed as if we were waking the dead.

We paused many times to hear if we had been discovered and to let the creatures of the night settle again. The biggest temptation – especially when we had covered a hundred yards or so – was to make a run for it. But that would have been catastrophic.

When we reached a point just short of where I guessed the sentries would be, I sent Eadmer ahead to see if he could locate them. The last thing we needed at that point was to stumble into Stephen's men in the gloom.

I looked at Maud and Greta; they looked petrified in both senses of the word. I found a piece of solid ground a few feet away, and the four of us huddled together to keep warm while we waited for Eadmer's return. Over thirty minutes passed and I began to be concerned; my main worry was that he had been unable to find his way back in the dark.

At last he appeared, breathing heavily. With hand signals, he told us that the sentries were only thirty yards apart.

He then had to whisper the most important information.

'The only way past them, even with our cloaks, is to walk along the frozen Isis; the gap between the sentries is more like fifty yards there. If we are any closer to them than that, the light from their braziers will reveal us.'

We all nodded that we understood.

'Lead the way, Eadmer. But first, we must even out our weight. Stay two yards apart, in single file, and maintain complete silence from now on.'

It was a perilous trek. We could trace the course of the river because the snow was flat and even, and there was a complete absence of vegetation. We were walking through thick snow, which gave a firm footing, but every step produced a murmur from the ice below, as it cracked and moved to adjust to the pressure of our weight. Eadmer led, and I placed myself between Maud and Greta. Otto and Berenger, both huge men, brought up the rear, creating even more disconcerting creaks and groans from the fragile ice sheet.

Several times Eadmer halted us, making us freeze like statues. But we could not stop our hearts, which thumped like blacksmiths' hammers. In such moments, it was easy to imagine us being given away by the deafening rhythm of six heartbeats, echoing across the water meadows like a peel of cathedral bells.

When we were almost midway between the sentries to our left and right, Eadmer signalled to us to kneel and move forward on our hands and knees. We could see the braziers easily, and the flickering shadows of the sentries. I prayed that they were cold and miserable and had eyes only for the fire.

Putting our hands on the ice made its squeaks even more noticeable. It also meant that our chins were brushing the top of the snow, adding hugely to our discomfort. Every time I looked at Greta and Maud, I could see them shaking themselves like dogs, trying to remove the loose snow which had by then invaded every layer of our clothing.

Eventually, after what seemed like an eternity, but was probably no more than two hours since we had left the castle, the sentries' fires were long gone and our position was hidden by trees on either side of the Isis.

I spoke softly, my voice sounding strange to my ears after our prolonged silence.

'Well done, everyone. Otto, light the lantern. Eadmer, take out your lodestone; Eynsham is to the northwest.'

Maud's almost miraculous escape from Oxford convinced her supporters and many throughout England that she had, after all, a divine right to the throne. Although Stephen continued to attack for several years, Maud's New Wessex held firm. Henry Plantagenet made more frequent visits to our western domain and was tutored in the arts of war by Earl Robert and myself in Bristol. Geoffrey's control of Normandy meant that young Henry's intellect could be schooled by the most learned men in Rouen. By the time he was sprouting stubble on his chin, he had the strength of an ox and the mind of an ecclesiastical scholar.

With piercing grey eyes, a fresh freckly complexion and a russet-red mane, he was said to be a living likeness of his great-grandfather, William the Conqueror. But of course, I recognized in him his paternal great-grandfather, Hereward of Bourne. Either way, it was a prodigious pedigree. Barrel-chested, with powerful forearms, he was a born warrior. But he was also charming and considerate, and was well liked by all who knew him.

Maud and I were immensely proud of him, such that any sense of loss regarding the throne of Westminster diminished each time we saw him. Our only concern was for our other two sons; we strove as hard as we could to ensure that, as Geoffrey of Poitou and William of Nantes, they had their own destinies and domains on the borders of Normandy.

Although England's civil war continued throughout the 1140s, it became less damaging and destructive. Maud and I found relative contentment; we had established a new headquarters at Devizes and enjoyed its tranquil setting. As each year passed, Stephen's position became weaker: he had lost Normandy for good, and he knew that Henry Plantagenet was rapidly approaching the age when he could challenge him for his English crown.

The march of time was becoming ever more prominent in our lives. Stephen was approaching his fiftieth birthday, and Maud and I were not getting any younger. The moment was approaching when the next generation would be dictating affairs.

One by one, our loyal followers were no more. The Christmas of 1143 was not a happy one: our loyal friend, Miles of Gloucester, now the Earl of Hereford, was killed by a stray arrow in a hunting accident in the Forest of Dean. Four years later, our dear kinsman, Robert, Earl of Gloucester, the bravest of the brave, developed a fever in his castle at Bristol from which he never recovered.

His funeral proved to be a watershed for Maud.

Before the service, the irrepressible Brien FitzCount announced that he would be retreating from the trials of being a castellan and a soldier. He intended to pursue a life of contemplation with the Benedictines of the Priory of the Holy Trinity at Wallingford.

During the service for Robert's interment at St James' Priory in Bristol, which was his own foundation, Maud hid her tears behind her veil. But she recovered her composure sufficiently to deliver a moving valediction to her half-brother, her friend and her most steadfast supporter.

'This realm has produced no braver man. No Saxon, Celt or Norman was a better warrior. All praise to a mighty Englishman, a son of a proud Norman family!'

Maud's words seemed to reflect a new England – a land where both Englishman and Norman could be proud of their heritage. As she delivered her eulogy, I hoped it would herald a better England: Maud's England, an England ruled by our son, Henry Plantagenet.

We returned to Devizes, where Maud gradually recovered from her grief at the loss of Robert. As the Christmas of

1147 approached, she asked me to walk with her in the meadows of the burgh. Such walks revealed so much about Maud. She knew everyone we passed by name, and the mutual warmth between her and the local people was touchingly sincere.

But on that day, she was in a pensive mood.

'Hal, let's spend the winter making sure our castles are in the hands of strong men with well-armed garrisons. Then, when we are sure that Henry's legacy is safe, let's return to Argentan and spend as much time as we can with the boys before we lose them to their destinies. We can take them to St Cirq Lapopie and show them our little piece of Heaven.'

I could sense Maud's mixed emotions. She was weary of the interminable struggle against Stephen, but optimistic about Henry's future. I was sorely tempted by the prospect of returning to St Cirq Lapopie and felt much the same as she did.

'Henry is England's future and we have the chance to help him become a King we can be proud of, a King every Norman, Celt and Englishman would be honoured to call their Lord.'

'Hal, I am so fortunate to have found you. I was captivated from the moment I saw you on the road from Anjou. The circumstances should have told me that you were a madman, intent on doing me harm. But I knew straight away that you could be my saviour. My time with Geoffrey had been so awful as a pawn of his and my father's ambitions, but in you I found someone who cared only for me and my future.'

'We have both been lucky. For me it has been a

remarkable journey, the most important part of which was to fall in love with you. We will have many more years together, let's relish everything we have shared together and everything yet to come.'

Epilogue

Fulham Palace, 31 October 1187

Dear Thibaud,

I am sorry to have taken so long to deliver this final chapter, my friend, but I have only been able to dictate in short interludes. I am finding it difficult to breathe, a terrifying ordeal to endure.

Pray for a sudden death when your time beckons.

Also, there has been another distraction. Following the death of King Henry Beauclerc, our lord of many years, we have a new ruler, Richard, called Lionheart; a propitious name for a young man we all hope will become a fine monarch. What's more, for reasons you will of course now know, it is news that would make our storyteller very happy. Richard was crowned here at Westminster a month ago, to great rejoicing, for he is of noble Norman descent, but also carries the blood of old England, not only through his maternal grandmother, Edith of Scotland, but also, as you now know, through Harold of Hereford, his covert grandfather.

Harold will now be re-united with his beloved Maud in Heaven; they will both be very contented.

I so wish I could have delivered this account to you in person, but God in his infinite wisdom had other plans. It is All Hallows' Eve, such a melancholy time. But how appropriate! Next year they will be able to honour me on this night.

Well, I have written what I needed to write; the saga is

complete. *Accompanying this epistle is the precious casket and its contents that William of Malmesbury entrusted to Harold. I have kept it secure in the abbey vaults since Harold, in turn, entrusted it to me at our first meeting, nearly half a century ago. The last time I saw him, he was at pains to ask that the casket and his account should be kept together for posterity's sake, so it seems appropriate that it should be deposited in the Vatican Vaults with his manuscript. You know how important it is, as it precedes our account and gives our story its crucial beginning.*

Harold's story is now recorded for posterity. His remarkable family is not only blessed with an illustrious past, but also a fascinating future. As for the Church, the scandalous early history of the Knights Templar contained in these pages is vitally important. Many have suspected it. But now we have the testament of one of the Nine Founders to verify the hypocrisy behind their high moral virtues, and the immorality of the wicked and duplicitous Hugh de Payens. I know you will use the testimony wisely.

Below are Harold's parting words to me in 1176. Over the past ten years, I have replayed our final conversation in my head many times, but now I must commit it to vellum. As an old man, I have gained much comfort and solace from my memories – and especially from my memories of this remarkable man. I will see him in my mind's eye once more as his story draws to a close.

'So Maud and I left for Argentan in the spring of 1148. It was a great relief; we could watch our boys grow into men and live in peace. St Cirq Lapopie continued to be our secret place, and we spent many happy days there. Eadmer and Greta lived there permanently, as did Otto and Berenger when they became too old to be Maud's bodyguards. They both married local girls and

478

started their own families. I was proud to be part of a community at St Cirq Lapopie that was not unlike the one my grandfather had founded; that made me very happy.'

'But surely that is not the end of your story? This is 1176, over twenty-five years later!'

'There is nothing more for me to tell you. The rest is Henry Plantagenet's story – and you know that as well as anyone.'

'And thanks to you, I now know much more. Did you ever tell him that you were his father?'

'No, I was sorely tempted – and Maud said she would be happy for me to tell him when he came of age – but I decided it was a dangerous piece of information, both for him and for England. I decided that I would remain his uncle and guardian; that sufficed. The most important thing was to watch him grow and to be his mentor.'

'And you and Maud continued to be happy?'

'Yes, indeed. She never returned to England. When Henry was crowned King Henry II in 1154, Maud was over fifty years old and did not want to cross the Channel. By then, we rarely went to St Cirq Lapopie; it was too far for her. She was sad not to be in Westminster Abbey, but I was there to see our son crowned and I reported back to her with every detail. By then, Henry had married the indomitable Eleanor of Aquitaine, a woman his equal in every respect and someone I am privileged to call my daughter-in-law. Thus Henry took the titles King of England, Duke of Normandy, Duke of Aquitaine and Count of Anjou.'

'And now, Henry has added Ireland and Scotland to his empire.'

'Yes, my grandfather always said that both Scotland and Ireland would eventually come to be ruled from Westminster. Thankfully, Henry rules wisely and I am proud that the great

Anglo-Norman empire Maud and I dreamed of has come to pass. Henry's domain extends from the Highlands of Scotland in the north to the Pyrenees in the south, and from Flanders in the east to Kerry in the west.'

'He has been a good King.'

'I'm pleased that you think so. I'm proud of him. Normans still dominate this land – that will last many lifetimes – but, thanks to Henry, this is a fairer land for Norman and Englishman. He has curtailed the excesses of the earls and barons, introduced courts to administer justice and fair trials by twelve lawful men, and put an end to the excesses of the Church.'

'You lost Maud in 1167, I think.'

'I did; we were very happy until the end. There were sad times of course – especially as we watched Henry struggle to keep his vast empire together, or when he and Eleanor squabbled. We also lost Geoffrey and little William very early: Geoffrey was only twenty-four when he died, and William just twenty-seven.

'Maud became quite frail, but she never lost that smile – the one that could melt my heart even from her deathbed. We spent her final years in Rouen, at the Priory of Notre Dame du Pré, a foundation tied to her endowment at the Benedictine Abbey, at Bec. She found tranquillity there and spent her time caring for the sick, as well as helping the monks with their pastoral work. It was the monks of Bec who stood around her as she died, singing gently as she went to meet her Maker. As she breathed her last, she squeezed my hand and I leaned forward so that I could hear her. She whispered faintly just six words: "Our son is King of England." I wept only briefly; it was not a moment for tormented anguish, more a time to reflect on the life of a remarkable woman.'

'She was indeed an extraordinary woman. But she was also

fortunate to have met you, Harold of Hereford. Thank you for allowing me to hear your story.'

'You are very kind, Abbot. But it is a story that had to be told – and it could only be told to you, Gilbert Foliot. I hope it has not been too onerous.'

'It has been a privilege; I will make sure it is written down and committed to the archives.'

'But not in my lifetime, good Bishop, nor in the lifetime of my son.'

'Of course not. When it is written, I will find a way of getting it into the Vatican Vaults; they have a library there that is almost a thousand years old.'

'I am very grateful to you. But let me add a couple of things before we are done.'

'Which are?'

'Firstly, the inscription on Maud's tomb: "Great by Birth, Greater by Marriage, Greatest in Her Offspring. Here lies the Daughter, Wife and Mother of Henry." And secondly, the thing that gave her the most satisfaction at the end of her life: the name Henry often used, which was "Henry FitzEmpress". There was no greater comfort she could have had at the end of her life.'

'And how have you spent the years since Maud's death?'

'Mostly at St Cirq Lapopie – especially in the last few years, when it has been harder to travel. The estate thrives; we have a monastery and a community of over a hundred souls. My old friends have all gone now, buried in the family plot there, but their families keep me young and take care of me.'

'That reminds me: do you want me to regard your account as your testament before God?'

'Yes, I suppose I do – although my family has never been particularly religious.'

'No, indeed; I remember all that Old Religion heresy and the Wodewose nonsense! But we must let God be the judge of that. As far as my authority as a Bishop of Christ extends, I will grant you absolution subject to the following penance. You are to make a pilgrimage: you must go to the tomb of St Etheldreda at Ely; she will be pleased to hear your prayers.'

I blessed Harold of Hereford and, as I did so, I remembered one small point of detail to complete the story.

'What became of the Talisman of Truth? Did you give it to Henry?'

He put his hand into the neck of his smock and pulled out his Venetian medallion together with the fabled amulet.

'He wore it on his early expeditions to England, before he became King. But by the time he was crowned, he already understood all it had to say to him. So now I am its guardian again.'

'And what will you do with it? Should it not go into the Vatican Vaults where it belongs?'

'No, Gilbert, it disappeared into the vaults of the Monastery of Monte Cassino for decades. I don't want it lost again. Besides, it still has work to do. After I have done the penance you have been kind enough to give me, I am going to give it to a man who will be King one day; he may need it. He is only nineteen but is currently in Aquitaine, putting down revolts for his father. His exploits have already earned him a legendary name.'

'May I ask who he is?'

'Richard, Duke of Aquitaine, "The Lionheart", my grandson. He and his ancient "great-uncle" are going to have a conversation about chivalry, brotherhoods and amulets.'

Thus ended my conversation with the remarkable Harold of Hereford.

He strode back across the courtyard of my Palace in Fulham, just as purposefully as when he had arrived all those weeks ago. I never saw him again, nor did I hear any reports of his death. But he must have died by now; I assume he's buried at St Cirq Lapopie with his friends and family. Or perhaps he found a mountain eyrie, or a lair in the wildwoods, like his father and grandfather before him?

He was not the most godly of men. In fact, I suspect that deep down he was a heathen — closer to his pagan myths of seers and amulets than to our Lord God. But he was a good man, all the same. When he had gone, I found the most beautiful silver crucifix by my bed. It had an inscription on the back in English: 'Heaven Awaits, Gentle Scribe.'

My dear friend, I hope that you continue to bring your wisdom to the Holy See for many years to come. I will pray for that until my dying breath.

Pray for my soul.

Yours in God,
Gilbert

Codicil

Eminence,

May I introduce myself; I am Father John, scribe to my Lord, Gilbert Foliot.

I thought you would want to know that Bishop Foliot died in his sleep two days ago, on Friday 13 November. His end was peaceful. Although his breathing became difficult, he bore it with his usual stoicism.

He was a great man of the Church here in England, much loved and much admired. His knowledge, as you will know, was immense and his gift for words beyond equal. He acted at all times with diligence and integrity. He won universal admiration within the Church for his wisdom and piety.

I am proud to say that I am one of his protégés here at Lambeth, and I pray every day that I can become half the man he was.

Before he died, he asked me to let you know that he had recently heard some news about Harold of Hereford, but that he could not verify it. It seems that Harold did his penance, as the Bishop had asked him, and that he had then travelled to Aquitaine to see Duke Richard. The bearer of the news, a trader from Bordeaux, said that Harold was still alive some time later, but was not sure of the year. No word has been heard of him since.

485

Typically, Bishop Gilbert was thrilled to hear the news; such was his thirst for knowledge.

We will miss him.

A mass will be said for him every day here at Fulham until the festival of Christmas. He asked in particular that we remember you in our prayers and commended us to pray for all the important work you do for the Church.

Yours in God,
John

Postscript

Henry II, Henry Plantagenet (5 March 1133 – 6 July 1189), ruled England for over thirty-five years, from 25 October 1154 until his death in 1189.

After his mother, Empress Matilda, left England in 1148, the young Henry continued her struggle for succession to the English throne. Shortly after he married Eleanor of Aquitaine in 1152, he invaded England with a large army. His rival, King Stephen, lost his own son, Eustace, to a sudden illness in 1153, leaving the possibility of a compromise between the King and young Henry. This was enshrined in the Treaty of Wallingford, agreed shortly after Eustace's death: Stephen would retain the throne until his death, whereafter he would be succeeded by Henry.

King Stephen died on 25 October 1154, at Dover. He was buried at Faversham Abbey alongside his son, Eustace, and his wife, Mathilde.

Henry Plantagenet ruled a vast empire. He is regarded as one of the most significant figures of the Middle Ages and one of England's greatest monarchs. He and Eleanor had eight children – five boys, three of whom became kings, and three girls, two of whom became queens – and he had at least three illegitimate offspring. Their marriage was, at best, fraught; Eleanor eventually plotted on behalf of her sons against Henry, for which she was placed under house arrest for fifteen years until Henry's death. She was released by her son Richard, who was crowned Richard I of England on 3 September 1189.

Eleanor acted as regent in England while her son, Richard the Lionheart, went on the Third Crusade. She lived into the reign of her youngest son, King John. She outlived all her children, except John and Eleanor, Queen of Castile. She died on 1 April 1204, at the age of eighty-two.

Thibaud de Vermandois was elected Pope in December 1189, but refused the honour in favour of Paolo Scolari, who became Pope Clement III. De Vermandois died the following year, on 8 November 1188, just over a year after his old friend, Gilbert Foliot.

John Comnenus, Emperor of Byzantium, died on 18 April 1143, at the age of fifty-five. He was succeeded by his son, Manuel Comnenus, who ruled for the next thirty-seven years. John's tenure, and that of his son, continued the work of the founder of the Comneni dynasty, John's father, Alexius. The period of the Comneni dynasty is very highly regarded in the history of Byzantium.

John Comnenus' lifelong companion, John Azoukh, died in 1150. By then, although born a slave, he had been fully integrated into the Byzantine hierarchy.

The Knights Templar continued to be a major force in the affairs of the Catholic Church for many years. They remained vital to the defence of the Holy Land, using the vast resources and manpower they had available to them in Europe.

At its peak, the Order consisted of 20,000 members, 2,000

of which were knights. But they were always surrounded by controversy. Rumours about the Templars' secret initiation ceremony and ascetic lifestyle created mistrust.

In 1307, King Philip IV of France, deeply in debt to the Order, had many of the Order's members arrested. They were tortured into giving false confessions, and burned at the stake. Under pressure from King Philip, Pope Clement V disbanded the Order in 1312.

Their abrupt disappearance gave rise to speculation and legends, which have kept the Templar mystique alive to the modern day.

The earliest printed version of 'The Ballad of Robyn of Hode' appeared sometime after 1492, called a 'Gest of Robyn Hode'. It was a printed version of a ballad which, like many similar songs, told of the derring-do of heroes, of outlaws fighting for the oppressed and of wrongs being righted.

The earliest handwritten ballad is 'Robin Hood and the Monk', preserved in manuscript form at Cambridge University. It was written shortly after 1450 and it contains many of the elements still associated with the legend. There are almost thirty surviving medieval ballads referring to Robyn of Hode. The origins of the ballads are a mystery, just as there are numerous theories about the characters portrayed in them. The stories they tell may simply be legends. However, it is widely accepted that Robin Hood and his fellow outlaws reflect the deeds of various 'outlaws' of the eleventh and twelfth centuries – including Hereward of Bourne, those who fought with him and those who continued his fight against tyranny.

Acknowledgements

To all those who have made this possible – dear friends, loving family, dedicated professionals – I will always be grateful.

With much love and grateful thanks.

Glossary

Antioch, Siege of

The capture of the great fortress of Antioch was vital to the success of the First Crusade – without control of Antioch, the crusaders could not have moved on to Jerusalem. The siege lasted for seven and a half months, and conditions for the crusaders were often worse than those inside the city. Located in the valley of the Orontes, in mountainous country, the city itself was on the valley floor, with the almost impregnable citadel high in the mountains above. Antioch finally fell on 9 February 1098.

Apoplexy

Apoplexy was the word used for centuries to describe sudden loss of consciousness and death. Strokes and heart attacks will often have been described as apoplexy in the past.

Arrouaisian monks

The Abbey of Arrouaise was the centre of a form of the Augustinian monastic rule, the Arrouaisian Order, which was popular among the founders of abbeys during the 1130s. It had developed into a community which adopted the task of providing a service to travellers through the great Forest of Arrouaise in Artois, Flanders.

Artuqid

The Artuqid dynasty was a Turkmen dynasty that ruled in Eastern Anatolia, Northern Syria and Northern Iraq in the eleventh and twelfth centuries.

Atabeg

Atabeg, Atabek or Atabey, the equivalent of a prince, is an hereditary title of nobility of Turkic origin, indicating the lord of a region or province, usually subordinate to a monarch.

Atheling

The Anglo-Saxon name for the heir to the throne. Interestingly, the name 'Clito' – as in William Clito, the son of Robert, Duke of Normandy, and claimant to the English throne – was a Latin version of the same thing. The Germanic form was 'Adelin' – as in William Adelin, the son of King Henry I (Beauclerc) and heir to the throne, who drowned in 1120.

Attar of roses

Attar of Roses, or rose oil, is a fragrant oil distilled from fresh petals of the rose family. Rose oils are a valuable ingredient of fine perfumes, liqueurs, scenting ointments and toilet preparations.

Berserkers

Berserkers were Norse warriors who are reported in Old Norse literature to have fought in a nearly uncontrollable trance-like fury, a characteristic which later gave rise to the English word 'berserk'.

Bezant

A gold coin from the Byzantine Empire.

Blackletter

Blackletter, also known as Gothic script, Gothic minuscule, was a script used throughout Western Europe from approximately 1100 to well into the seventeenth century. It continued to be used in the German language until the twentieth century. Blackletter is sometimes called Old English, but it is not to be confused with the Old English language, despite the popular, though mistaken, belief that the language was written with blackletter. The Old English (or Anglo-Saxon) language predates blackletter by many centuries, and was itself written in the insular script.

Bloody flux

Bloody flux is the old name for dysentery, an inflammatory disorder of the intestine, especially of the colon, caused by viral, bacterial or parasitic infestations. It results in severe diarrhoea containing mucus and/or blood in the faeces, with fever and abdominal pain. If left untreated, dysentery is often fatal.

Braccae

Braccae is the Latin term for trousers, but now refers to a style of pants. The Romans first encountered this style of clothing among peoples who they called Gauls. Braccae were typically made with a drawstring, and tended to reach from just above the knee at the shortest to the ankles at the longest, with length generally increasing in tribes living further north. When the Romans first encountered the braccae, they thought them to be effeminate; Roman men typically wore tunics, which were one-piece outfits terminating at or above the knee. However, braccae eventually became popular among Roman legionaries stationed in cooler climates to the north of southern Italy. Eventually they became fashionable in late Roman times and into the Eastern Empire of Byzantium.

Bucentaur

The bucentaur was the state galley of the Doges of Venice. It was used every year on Ascension Day up to 1798 to take the Doge out to the Adriatic Sea to perform the 'Marriage of the Sea' – a ceremony that symbolically wedded Venice to the sea. The last and most magnificent of the historic bucentaurs made its maiden voyage in 1729 in the reign of Doge Alvise III Sebastiano Mocenigo. Depicted in paintings by Canaletto and Francesco Guardi, the ship was 115 feet long and more than 26 feet high. A two-deck floating palace, its main salon had a seating capacity of 90. The Doge's throne was in the stern, and the prow bore a figurehead representing Justice with sword and scales. The barge was propelled by 168 oarsmen, and another 40 sailors were required to man it. The ship was destroyed in 1798 on Napoleon's orders to symbolize his victory in conquering Venice.

Burgh

The Saxon name for a town or city.

Cappa robe

A long-sleeved, ankle-length ecclesiastical robe, tied at the waist by a corded belt. Usually made from cotton or wool, for Templars it would have had a slit at the front and rear so that it could be worn on horseback. In battle, the cappa would have been worn over a full-body hauberk of chain mail.

Carucate

The carucate was a unit of assessment for tax used in most Danelaw counties of England, and is found in the Domesday Book. The carucate was based on the area a plough team of eight oxen could till in a single annual season. It was subdivided into oxgangs, or 'bovates', based on the area a single ox might till in the same period, which thus represented one eighth of a carucate; and it was analogous to a 'hide', a unit of tax assessment used outside the Danelaw counties. The tax levied on each carucate came to be known as 'carucage'.

Castellan

A castellan was the governor or captain of a castle. The word stems from the Latin *castellanus*, derived from *castellum* (castle). Also known as a constable, governor of the castle or captain.

Catapult

Castles, fortresses and fortified walled cities were the main form of defence in the Middle Ages and a variety of catapult devices were used against them. As well as attempting to breach the walls, missiles and incendiaries could be hurled inside, or early forms of biological warfare deployed, such as diseased carcasses, putrid garbage or excrement. The most widely used catapults were the following:

Ballista

Similar to a giant crossbow and designed to work through torsion. Giant arrows were used as ammunition, made from wood and with an iron tip.

Couillard

See 'trebuchet'

Mangonel

These machines were designed to throw heavy projectiles from a bowl-shaped bucket at the end of an arm. With a range of up to 1,300 feet they were relatively simple to construct, and wheels were added to increase mobility.

Onager

Mangonels are sometimes referred to as 'onagers'. Onager catapults initially launched projectiles from a sling, which was later changed to a bowl-shaped bucket.

Springald

The springald's design was similar to that of the ballista, effectively a crossbow propelled by tension. The springald's frame was more compact, allowing for use inside tighter confines, such as the inside of a castle or tower.

Trebuchet

Trebuchets were probably the most powerful catapult employed in the Middle Ages. The most commonly used ammunition was stones, but the most effective involved fire, such as firebrands and the infamous 'Greek fire'. Trebuchets came in two different designs: traction, which were powered by people; and counterpoise, where the people were replaced with a weight on the short end of an arm. A simplified trebuchet was known as a 'couillard', where the trebuchet's single counterweight was split, swinging on either side of a central support post.

Cerdic/Cerdician

The dynastic name of the kings of Wessex, who ultimately became Kings of England, from Egbert, King of Wessex in 820, to Edward the Confessor's death in 1066. The only exceptions were the three Danish kings, Cnut and his sons Harold Harefoot and Harthcnut, between 1016 and 1042. The name reputedly derives from Cerdic, a prince of the West Saxons from *circa* 600, who was an ancestor of Egbert, the first King of England.

Chemise

A simple garment worn next to the skin to protect clothing from sweat and body oils, the precursor to the modern shirt. The chemise seems to have developed from the Roman *tunica* and first became popular in Europe in the Middle Ages. Women wore a shift or chemise under their gown or robe. Men wore a chemise with their trousers or braies, and covered the chemise with garments such as a doublet or robe.

Chignon

A female hairstyle that can be traced back to antiquity, where the hair is swept back from a central parting and tied in a loosely folded bun at the back of the head.

Churchwright

A church builder or architect.

Cloth of gold

Cloth of gold is a fabric woven with a gold-wrapped or spun weft. In most cases, the core yarn is silk wrapped with a band or strip of high-content gold. In rarer instances, fine linen and wool are used as the core. It is mentioned on both Roman headstones for women and in the Book of Psalms as a fabric befitting a princess. The Ancient Greek reference to the Golden Fleece is thought to be a reference to gold cloth. Cloth of gold has been popular for ecclesiastical use for many centuries.

Constable

Historically, the title comes from the Latin *stabuli* (count of the stables) and originated from the Eastern Roman Empire. Originally, the constable was the officer responsible for keeping the horses of a lord or monarch. The title was imported to the monarchies of medieval Europe, and in many countries developed into a high military rank and great officer of state, for example, the Constable of France.

Cordwainer

A cordwainer is a shoemaker/cobbler who makes fine soft leather shoes and boots. The word is derived from *cordwain* or *cordovan*, the leather produced in Córdoba, Spain. Historically, there was a distinction between a cordwainer, who made shoes and boots out of the finest leathers, and a cobbler, who repaired them.

Corselet (corselette)

Now an item of female underwear, the corselet was originally a piece of armour, covering the torso, made of leather or mail – chain or lamellar. The origin of the English word comes from *cors*, an Old French word meaning 'bodice'.

Crusades

The Crusades were a series of religious wars first initiated by Pope Urban II in 1095 with the goal of restoring Christian access to the holy places in Jerusalem. Jerusalem was and is a sacred city and symbol of all three major Abrahamic faiths (Judaism, Christianity and Islam). The Byzantine emperor, Alexius I, feared that all Asia Minor would be overrun by Muslims and called on western Christian leaders and the papacy to come to the aid of Constantinople by undertaking a pilgrimage or a Crusade that would free Jerusalem from Muslim rule. The main series of Crusades, primarily against Muslims in the Levant, occurred between 1095 and 1291. Historians have given many of the earlier Crusades numbers. After some early successes, the later Crusades failed and the crusaders were defeated and forced to return home.

Several hundred thousand soldiers became crusaders by taking vows and the Pope granted them plenary indulgences. Their emblem was the cross — the term 'crusade' is derived from the French term for taking up the cross. Many were from the domains of northern France and called themselves 'Franks', which became the common term used by Muslims.

The First Crusade (1095–99) was The 'Great' Crusade that finally captured Jerusalem in 1099 and led to the establishment of the Christian States of the Holy Land. The Second Crusade (1147–9) was called by various clerics, particularly by Bernard of Clairvaux. French and Southern German armies, under the Kings Louis VII and Conrad III respectively, marched to Jerusalem in 1147, but they failed to win any major victories and launched a failed siege of Damascus.

The Third Crusade (1187–92) was the most famous of the crusades. The Muslims had long fought among themselves, but were finally united by the Sultan Saladin. Following his victory at the Battle of

Hattin in 1187, where he easily overwhelmed the disunited crusaders, he captured all of their holdings except a few coastal cities. Saladin's victories shocked Europe. Pope Gregory VIII issued a papal bull proposing a Third Crusade. Emperor Frederick I Barbarossa of Germany, King Philip II Augustus of France, and King Richard the Lion-Hearted of England responded. Frederick died en route and few of his men reached the Holy Land. The other two armies arrived but were beset by political quarrels. King Philip feigned illness and returned to France, there scheming to win back the Duchy of Normandy from Richard's control.

In 1191, Richard captured the island of Cyprus from the Byzantines, who had aligned themselves with Saladin, and the island became used as a crusader base for centuries to come. After a long siege, Richard recaptured the city of Acre and placed the entire Muslim garrison under captivity; they were then executed after a series of failed negotiations. The crusader army headed south along the Mediterranean coast. They defeated the Muslims near Arsuf, recaptured the port city of Jaffa, and were in sight of Jerusalem. However, Richard did not believe he would be able to hold Jerusalem once it was captured, as the majority of crusaders would then return to Europe, and the Crusade ended without the taking of the city. Richard left the following year after negotiating a treaty with Saladin. The treaty allowed trade for merchants and for unarmed Christian pilgrims to make pilgrimages, but the city remained under Muslim control.

Curfew

The word 'curfew' comes from the French phrase *couvre-feu* (cover the fire). It was used to order the extinguishing of all lamps, candles and fires. The purpose was to guard against accidental fires overnight in towns and cities that were mainly built of wood and thatch. It was soon adapted to get people off the streets in times of unrest or danger.

The word was later adopted into Middle English as 'curfeu', which later became the modern 'curfew'.

Denaro

The 'silver penny' of Venetian currency of the time, a descendant of the Roman Denarius.

Destrier

A Norman warhorse, often called the Great Horse. The Normans had four designations of horse: a destrier (for use in battle); a palfrey (a good riding horse); a rouney (an ordinary riding horse); and a sumpter (a packhorse). Modern shire breeds like the Percheron and Suffolk Punch may descend from destriers, but they may not have been as large as today's shire horses. In fact, a destrier was probably not a breed, just the name for a horse bred and trained for war.

Eunuch

A eunuch is a person who, by the common definition of the term, has been castrated early enough in his life for this change to have major hormonal consequences. Less commonly, in translations of ancient texts, 'eunuch' may refer to a man who is not castrated but who is impotent, celibate or otherwise not inclined to marry and procreate. Castration was carried out on the soon-to-be eunuch without his consent in order that he might perform a specific social function; this was common in many societies. The practice was also well established in Europe among the Greeks and Romans, although their role as court functionaries did not arise until Byzantine times.

In the late period of the Roman Empire, after the adoption of the oriental royal court model by the Emperors Diocletian and Constantine, Emperors were surrounded by eunuchs for such functions as bathing, hair cutting, dressing, and many bureaucratic functions – in effect acting as a shield between the Emperor and physical contact with his administrators. Eunuchs were believed loyal and indispensable and enjoyed great influence in the imperial court. At the Byzantine imperial court, there were a great number of eunuchs employed in domestic and administrative functions, actually organized as a separate hierarchy, following a parallel career of their own. Archieunuchs, each in charge of a group of eunuchs, were among the principal officers in Constantinople, under the emperors. Under Justinian in the sixth century, the eunuch Narses functioned as a successful general in a number of campaigns.

Extreme unction

The anointing of the sick or dying carried out in extremis as part of the last rite of passage. The last rites traditionally include three elements: penance, unction (anointing) and receiving the Eucharist (Christ's sacrament) in order to prepare the dying person for the next life.

Fitz

A prefix to patronymic surnames of Anglo-Norman origin. This usage derives from the Norman *fiz* or *filz* (son of) which was coupled with the name of the father (for example, FitzGilbert, meaning 'son of Gilbert') as in the Scandinavian tradition of adding *-son* behind the father's name, and the Gaelic traditions: 'Mac' and 'O'.

Futuwwa

An Arabic term that has similarities with chivalry and virtue. It was also a name of ethical urban organizations or 'guilds' in medieval Muslim realms that emphasized honesty, peacefulness, gentleness, generosity, hospitality and avoidance of complaint in life. In modern-day dialects of Arabic (for example, in Egypt) the term is sometimes used for youths who do quasi-chivalrous acts such as helping others resist intimidation by rival groups.

Garderobe

The term garderobe describes a place where clothes and other items are stored, and also a medieval toilet. In European public places, a garderobe denotes the cloakroom, wardrobe, alcove or an armoire. In a medieval castle or other building, a garderobe was usually a simple hole discharging to the outside leading to a cesspit or into the moat, depending on the structure of the building. Such toilets were often placed inside a small chamber, leading by association to the use of the term garderobe to describe them.

Geld

Another word for money in Dutch and German (*gelt* in Yiddish), in medieval England it meant tax, or tribute or a ransom – as in Danegeld.

Golden Horn

The Golden Horn is an inlet of the Bosphorus to the east of the city of Constantinople (Istanbul) forming a natural harbour that has sheltered ships for thousands of years. It is a scimitar-shaped estuary that joins the Bosphorus just at the point where that strait enters the Sea of Marmara, thus forming a peninsula, the tip of which is 'Old Istanbul' (ancient Constantinople).

Gonfalon

A small tailed flag or banner, flown from the top of a lance or pole to indicate lordly status, common throughout Europe. It would carry the colours, crest or heraldry of its owner.

Grand Domestic

The title of *Megas Domestikos*, or the Grand Domestic in English, was given to the commander-in-chief of the Byzantine land army. Its exact origin is somewhat unclear; it is first mentioned in the ninth century, and derives from the *domestikos* of the *scholai*, with the epithet *megas* added to connote the supreme authority of its holder. Both titles appear to have co-existed for a time, until the *Megas Domestikos* fully replaced the earlier office by the mid-eleventh century. In the Comnenian period, in an echo of the tenth-century arrangements, the *Megas Domestikos* would command the entire field army of the Empire.

Greek fire

The secret weapon of the Byzantine emperors. A sort of ancient napalm, it was invented by a Syrian engineer, a refugee from Baalbek, in the Egyptian city of Heliopolis in 673 AD. The mix of ingredients, a closely guarded secret, was reputedly handed down from emperor to emperor. It has remained a secret to this day, but was thought to be a combination of pitch, sulphur, tree resin, quicklime and bitumen. The key ingredient may well have been magnesium, which would explain why the 'fire' would burn under water. Varieties of it began to be used by other navies, most using pitch. The 'fire' was often poured into wooden barrels or clay pots before being lit and hurled at the enemy.

Hauberk

A chain-mail 'coat', worn like a long pullover down below the groin. Hauberks for the infantry were slightly shorter so that the men could run in them, and were only split at the sides. Cavalry hauberks extended to the knee and were split front and back. The mail could extend into a hood (ventail), like a balaclava, but had a flap in front of the throat and chin that could be dropped for comfort when not in the midst of battle. Three kinds of mail were used and were progressively more expensive: ordinary ring mail, scale mail and lamellar mail (when overlapping individual plates were fastened together by leather thongs).

Hearthtroop

The elite bodyguard of kings, princes and lords of the ninth, tenth and eleventh centuries.

Heraldic terms

Azure: blue
  Bend: diagonal stripe like a sash
  Field: background of a shield, usually consisting of colours or
    metals (tinctures) or symbolic vair
  Gold (or): yellow
  Gules: red
  Roundel: sphere
  Sable: black
  Tierce: A third part of a shield (background), usually a band down
    the left-hand side
  Vair: variegated furs (ermine, squirrel, etc)

Housecarls

The elite troops of the Anglo-Saxon kings, following their establishment by King Cnut in 1016, in the Danish tradition. Cnut brought his own personal troops to supplement the English fyrd (citizen army) when he succeeded to the throne following the death of Edmund Ironside.

Jihad

Jihad is a religious duty of Muslims. In Arabic, the word translates as a noun meaning 'struggle'. Jihad appears 41 times in the Quran and frequently as the expression 'striving in the way of God'. A person engaged in jihad is called a mujahid; the plural is mujahideen. Jihad is an important religious duty for Muslims. A minority among the Sunni scholars sometimes refer to this duty as the sixth pillar of Islam, though it occupies no such official status. In Shi'a Islam, however, Jihad is one of the Ten Practices of the Religion. In western societies the term jihad is often translated by non-Muslims as 'holy war'. Muslim authors tend to reject such an approach, stressing non-militant connotations of the word.

Kipchak bow

A recurve-style bow used throughout Asia Minor in the Middle Ages. Like a Turkish bow, it got its name from the Kipchak tribe who, as the Golden Horde, ruled the western part of the Mongol Empire until the thirteenth century.

Kirtle

A kirtle is a long tunic-like dress worn by women in the Middle Ages into the baroque period. The kirtle was typically worn over a chemise or smock and under a formal outer garment or gown.

Lamprey

Sometimes also called lamprey eels, lampreys are an eel-like order of jawless vertebrates, characterized by a toothed, funnel-like sucking mouth. The common name 'lamprey' is derived from *lampetra*, which translated from Latin means 'stone licker' (*lambere* 'to lick' + *petra* 'stone').

Leine

The leine is a unisex smock of Celtic peoples, not unlike a Roman toga. The word means 'shirt' and early descriptions from the fifth to the twelfth centuries talk of a long smock-like linen garment, ankle-length or knee-length, either sleeveless or with straight sleeves.

Levunium, Battle of

A decisive battle on 29 April 1091, when the Byzantine Emperor Alexius I defeated the army of his rivals, the Pechenegs, a semi-nomadic people from the Central Asian Steppes, thus removing their long-term threat to the Empire.

Lodestone

A lodestone is a naturally magnetized piece of the mineral magnetite. Ancient people first discovered the property of magnetism in lodestone. Pieces of lodestone, suspended so they could turn, were the first magnetic compasses and their importance to early navigation is indicated by the name lodestone, which in Middle English means 'course stone' or 'leading stone'. One of the first references to lodestone's magnetic properties is by Greek philosopher Thales of Miletus who, in the sixth century BC, is credited by the Ancient Greeks with discovering lodestone's attraction to iron and other lodestones.

Lumphanan, Battle of

Lumphanan is a village twenty-five miles from Aberdeen in Scotland and is the site of a battle in 1057, where Malcolm III of Scotland defeated Macbeth of Scotland.

Manticore

A Persian legendary creature similar to the Egyptian sphinx (which is female). It has the body of a (male) red or golden lion, a human head with three rows of sharp teeth and a trumpet-like voice. Other aspects of the creature vary from story to story. It may be horned, winged, or both. The tail is that of either a dragon or a scorpion, and it may shoot poisonous spines or arrows. Sometimes it is portrayed as a hunter armed with a bow. It may have come into European mythology in Roman times or as a result of the First Crusade.

Mantle

A mantle (from *mantellum*, the Latin term for a cloak) is a long, loose cape-like cloak for outdoor protection worn by men and women from the twelfth to the sixteenth century.

Midden

A domestic waste and sewage dump for a village or burgh. A word of Scandinavian origin, it is still in use in Scotland and the English Pennines.

Mos Militum

A code of knightly ethics, loosely based on the ancient noble tradition of the Roman aristocracy and the influence of Islamic ethics, such as those of the Futuwwa, which appeared in the late eleventh century and formed the basis of the values of the Age of Chivalry.

Nobilissimus

From the Latin *nobilissimus* (most noble). Originally a title given to close relatives of the Emperor, during the Comneni period the title was awarded to officials and foreign dignitaries.

Oubliette

From the French, meaning 'forgotten place' it was a form of dungeon which was accessible only from a hole in a high ceiling. The word comes from the same root as the French *oublier* (to forget), as it was used for those prisoners that captors wished to forget.

Outremer

From the French *outre-mer* (overseas), it was a generic name given to the Crusader States established after the First Crusade: the County of Edessa, the Principality of Antioch, the County of Tripoli and especially the Kingdom of Jerusalem. The name equates to the 'Levant' of the Renaissance. The term was, in general, used to refer to any land 'overseas'; for example, Louis IV of France was called Louis d'Outremer as he was raised in England. The modern term outre-mer (spelled with a hyphen) is used for the overseas departments and territories of France (*Départements d'outre-mer*).

Papias

The great concierge of the imperial palaces of Byzantium, responsible for the opening and closing of the palace gates each day.

Pectoral cross

A pectoral cross or pectorale, from the Latin *pectoralis* (of the chest) is a cross that is worn on the chest, usually suspended from the neck by a cord or chain. In ancient times pectoral crosses were worn by both clergy and laity, but during the Middle Ages the pectoral cross came to be indicative of high ecclesiastical status and only worn by bishops and abbots. Unlike abbots, abbesses did not carry a crozier, but were allowed to wear pectoral crosses.

Pennon

A small streamer-like flag, flown at the top of a knight's lance to signify his status. It would have a combination of one, two or three colours to identify him, his origins or the lord he served.

Pennyroyal

Pennyroyal is a plant in the mint family *Lamiaceae*. The leaves of the European pennyroyal *Mentha pulegium* (also called Squaw Mint, Mosquito Plant and Pudding Grass) exhibit a very strong fragrance similar to spearmint when crushed. Pennyroyal is a traditional culinary herb, folk remedy and abortifacient (a substance that induces abortion).

Phrygian cap

The Phrygian cap is a soft conical cap with the top pulled forward, associated in antiquity with the inhabitants of Phrygia, a region of central Anatolia. In the Roman Empire, it came to signify freedom and the pursuit of liberty, probably through a confusion with the pileus, the felt cap of emancipated slaves of ancient Rome. The Phrygian cap is sometimes called a liberty cap.

Pike

A pike is a pole weapon. It is a long, sometimes very long (even up to five metres and beyond) thrusting spear used extensively by infantry. Unlike many similar weapons, the pike is not intended to be thrown, but is a defensive weapon, especially against cavalry. Pikes were used by the armies of Philip of Macedon and Alexander the Great and regularly in European warfare from the early Middle Ages until around 1700, wielded by foot soldiers deployed in close order. They were also common in the armies of Asia.

Pipe Rolls

Sometimes called the Great Rolls, they are a collection of financial records maintained by the English Exchequer or Treasury. The earliest date from the twelfth century, and the series extends, mostly complete, from then until 1833. They form the oldest continuous series of records kept by the English government, covering a span of about 700 years.

Pugio

Shorter than the gladius – the standard heavy, stocky sword of the Roman army – the pugio was a side-arm, a weapon of last resort, a tool of assassination and often a highly decorated status symbol for senior army officers and members of the equestrian class.

Putrid fever

One of the many names – others include slow/camp/ship/jail fever (it flourishes in overcrowded human environments) – for epidemic typhus. The name comes from the Greek *typhos* (hazy), describing the state of mind of those affected. Symptoms include severe headache, a sustained high fever, cough, rash, severe muscle pain, chills, falling blood pressure, stupor, sensitivity to light, as well as delirium. During the second year of the Peloponnesian War (430 BC) Athens suffered a devastating epidemic, known as the 'Plague of Athens', which killed, among others, Pericles. The plague returned twice more, in 429 BC and in the winter of 427/6 BC. Epidemic typhus is thought to have been the cause in each case.

Pyx

A pyx or pix, from the Latin *pyxis* (box-wood receptacle) is a small round container used in the Catholic, Old Catholic and Anglican

Churches to carry the consecrated Host (Eucharist) to the sick or to those otherwise unable to come to a church in order to receive Holy Communion.

Qaadi

Also known as qadi, qaadee, qazi, kazi or kadi, is a judge ruling in accordance with Islamic religious law (sharia) appointed by the ruler of a Muslim country. Because Islam makes no distinction between religious and secular domains, qadis traditionally have jurisdiction over all legal matters involving Muslims. The judgement of a qadi must be based on the prevailing consensus of the Islamic scholars.

Quarrel

A quarrel or bolt is the term for the ammunition used in a crossbow. The name is derived from the French *carré* (square), referring to the fact that they typically have square heads. Although their length varies, they are shorter than longbow arrows.

Reliquary

A reliquary is a container for relics. These may be the physical remains of saints, for example, bones, pieces of clothing, or some object associated with saints or other religious figures. Often elaborately carved wooden boxes with decorated or gem-encrusted clasps, or made from brass or even gold, they can be among the most precious artefacts of the Middle Ages.

Seax

A short, stabbing sword, sometimes as short as a dagger. Seax is an Old English term for 'knife'. The term is used particularly for the fighting knife typical of the Germanic peoples and especially the Saxons, whose tribal name derives from the weapon during the Early Middle Ages. In heraldry, the seax is a curved sword with a notched blade, appearing, for example, in the coats of arms of Essex and the former Middlesex.

Senlac Ridge, Battle of

The original name for what is now known as the Battle of Hastings in 1066 between the Norman army of William, Duke of Normandy, and the English army of Harold, King of England. Victory for William led to a Norman dynasty on the English throne and a dramatic new course for English and British history. A few miles north of Hastings on England's south coast, Senlac Ridge was originally known in English as Santlache (Sandy Stream), which the Normans changed into Sanguelac (Blood Lake) and which was then shortened to Senlac. Senlac Ridge, also called Senlac Hill, was approximately 275 feet (84 metres) above sea level, before the top of the ridge was levelled off to create Battle Abbey.

Siege of Ely

The Siege of Ely was the last redoubt of the English Revolt against Norman Rule in 1069. By 1071 only a small number of survivors, led by Hereward of Bourne (who later became better known as Hereward the Wake), were besieged by King William at Ely, which was then an island in reality as well as in name. William's siege was successful in the autumn of 1071. Most of the defenders were killed, while a few survivors are thought to have escaped into the fens or the wildwood; all became legends.

Succubae

In folklore traced back to medieval legend, a succubus (plural, succubae or succubi) is a female demon or supernatural being appearing in dreams who takes the form of a human woman in order to seduce men, usually through sexual intercourse. The male counterpart is the incubus. Religious traditions hold that repeated intercourse with a succubus may result in the deterioration of health, or even death. In modern fictional representations, a succubus may or may not appear in dreams and is often depicted as a highly attractive seductress or enchantress; whereas, in the past, succubi were generally depicted as frightening and demonic.

Thegn

A local village chieftain of Anglo-Saxon England. Not a great land-owner or a titled aristocrat but the head of a village. Thus, thegns formed the backbone to the organization of Anglo-Saxon life. While serving with the army, usually as part of their service to the earl of their province, they formed a large part of the king's elite fighting force, the housecarls.

Theme

The Byzantine Empire was organized into military districts or themes, which reflected different nationalities within the Empire. Themes were responsible for generating their own regiments for the Emperor's army. In turn, retired soldiers were granted lands in the military theme from which they served. By the end of the eleventh century, there were 38 themes in the Byzantine Empire, each composed of between 4,000 and 6,000 men, giving a standing army of approximately 200,000 men.

Trireme

Originally an Ancient Greek galley with three rows of oars, each above the other. A vessel of war on which the oarsmen's strength could produce a ramming speed of significant impact. Although twelfth-century Mediterranean ships resembled triremes, they were not often used for ramming; the oarsmen's main job was speed and manoeuvrability, especially when the wind was adverse, or in calm conditions. Despite this, medieval galleys resembled ancient triremes in design, with a prominent beak at the bow instead of a figurehead.

Turcopoles

From the Greek, meaning 'sons of Turks', they were locally recruited mounted archers employed by the Christian states of the Eastern Mediterranean. The crusaders first encountered Turcopoles in the Byzantine army during the First Crusade. These auxiliaries were the children of mixed Greek and Turkish parentage and were at least nominally Christian, although some may have been practising Muslims. The Turcopoles served as light cavalry providing skirmishers, scouts and mounted archers, and sometimes rode as a second line in a charge, to back up the Frankish knights and sergeants.

Varangian Guard

The elite bodyguard of the emperors of Byzantium for several hundred years. They were extremely well-paid mercenaries who also shared in the booty of the Emperor's victories, thus the Guard could attract the finest warriors. Most were drawn from Scandinavia and were often referred to as the 'Axemen of the North'. Their loyalty was legendary, as was their ferocity. It is thought many of Harold of England's surviving housecarls joined the Guard after Senlac Ridge in 1066.

Veneto

Veneto, Venetian or Venetan is a Romance language spoken as a native language by over two million people, mostly in the Veneto region of Italy, where almost all of the five million inhabitants can understand it. The language is called *vèneto* or *vènet* in Venetian, *veneto* in Italian; the variant spoken in Venice is called *venexiàn/venesiàn* or *veneziano*, respectively. Although referred to as an Italian dialect, even by its speakers, it is in fact a separate language, not a variety or derivative of Italian. Instead, Venetian differs in grammar, phonetics and vocabulary. Venetian has little in common with the Gallo-Italic languages of north-western Italy.

Ventail

See 'hauberk'.

Wimple

A garment worn around the neck and chin, which usually covers the head. Its use developed among women in early medieval Europe. At many stages of medieval culture it was thought to be unseemly for a married woman to show her hair. A wimple might be elaborately starched, and creased and folded in prescribed ways, or supported on a wire or wicker frame (cornette).

Genealogies

The English Monarchy from the House of Wessex to the Plantagenets

The Twelfth-Century Doges of Venice

The Comneni Emperors of Byzantium

The Twelfth-Century Princes of Antioch

The Twelfth-Century Kings of Jerusalem

The Twelfth-Century Holy Roman Emperors

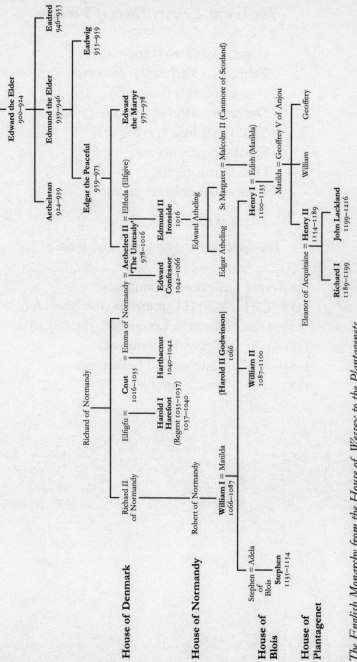

The English Monarchy from the House of Wessex to the Plantagenets

The Twelfth-Century Doges of Venice

Ordelafo Faliero (1102–1117)
Domenico Michele (1117–1130)
Pietro Polani (1130–1148)
Domenico Morosini (1148–1156)
Vital II Michele (1156–1172)
Sebastiano Ziani (1172–1178)
Orio Mastropiero (1178–1192)
Enrico Dandolo (1192–1205)

The Comneni Emperors of Byzantium

1081–1118   Alexius I Comnenus
1118–1143   John II Comnenus (the Beautiful)
1143–1180   Manuel I Comnenus (the Great)
1180–1183   Alexius II Comnenus
1183–1185   Andronicus I Comnenus
1185–1195   Isaac Comnenus

1098–1111	Bohemond I
	(Tancred, Prince of Galilee, regent,
	1100–1103; 1105–1112)
1111–1130	Bohemond II
	(Roger of Salerno, regent, 1112–1119)
	(Baldwin II of Jerusalem, regent,
	1119–1126; 1130–1131)
1130–1136	Constance
	(Fulk of Jerusalem, regent, 1131–1136)
1136–1149	Raymond of Poitiers (by marriage)
	(Baldwin III of Jerusalem, regent,
	1149–1153)
1153–1160	Raynald of Châtillon (by marriage)
	(Aimery of Limoges, Patriarch of Antioch,
	regent, 1160–1163)
1163–1201	Bohemond III
	(Raymond of Tripoli, regent, 1193–1194)

The Twelfth-Century Kings of Jerusalem

1099–1100	Godfrey (Protector of the Holy Sepulchre)
1100–1118	Baldwin I
1118–1131	Baldwin II
1131–1153	Melisende (with Fulk of Anjou until 1143; with Baldwin III from 1143)
1131–1143	Fulk of Anjou (with Melisende)
1143–1162	Baldwin III (with Melisende until 1153)
1162–1174	Amalric I
1174–1185	Baldwin IV the Leprous (with Baldwin V from 1183)
1183–1186	Baldwin V (with Baldwin IV until 1185)
1186–1190	Sybilla (with Guy Lusignan)

The Twelfth-Century Holy Roman Emperors

Salian Dynasty
1086–1125 (elected 1099) Henry V

Supplinburger Dynasty
1075–1137 (elected 1125) Lothair III

Staufen Dynasty
1122–1190 (elected 1152) Frederick I (Barbarossa)
1165–1197 (elected 1169) Henry VI

Welf Dynasty
1176–1218 (elected 1198) Otto IV

Maps

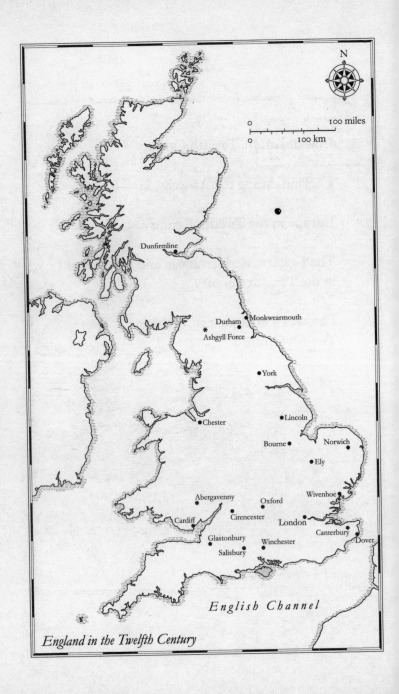

N

100 miles

100 km

Dunfirmline

Durham • Monkwearmouth
* Ashgyll Force

• York

• Lincoln
• Chester

Bourne • • Norwich

• Ely

Abergavenny • Wivenhoe
Oxford •
Cardiff • Cirencester • London
Glastonbury • • Canterbury
Winchester Dover
Salisbury

English Channel

England in the Twelfth Century

Land under Stephen's control around 1140

Land under Matilda's control around 1140

N

Carlisle

Battle of the Standard

Clitheroe

Lincoln

Gloucester

Oxford

St Albans

Malmesbury

Wallingford

London

Bristol

Reading

Devizes

Wilton

Winchester

Forde Abbey

Wareham

Arundel

50 miles

100 km

English Channel

England During the Anarchy 1135–1153

Europe in the Twelfth Century

Antwerp

R. Rhine

Rouen

Mannheim

R. Neckar

Paris

Ulm

Dijon

Montreux

Geneva · Martigny

Aosta

Ven

The Eastern Mediterranean and The Holy Land in the Twelfth Century

N

Genoa

Venice

Senj

Zadar

Vis

Rome

Messene

o   200 miles

o   200 km

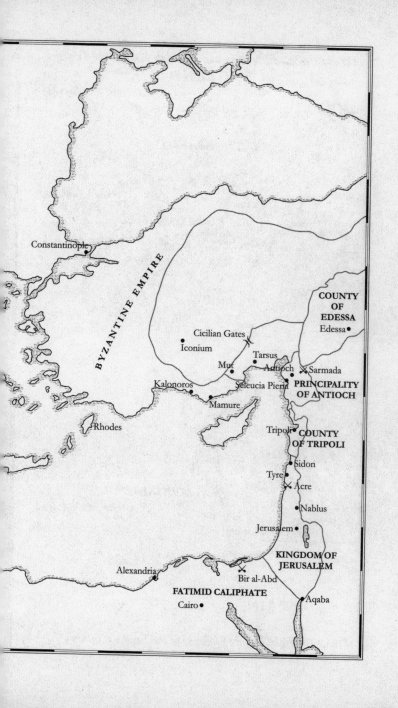

Constantinople

BYZANTINE EMPIRE

COUNTY
OF
EDESSA
Edessa

Cicilian Gates

Iconium

Tarsus

Mut

Antioch

Sarmada

Kalonoros

Seleucia Pieria

PRINCIPALITY
OF ANTIOCH

Mamure

Rhodes

Tripoli

COUNTY
OF TRIPOLI

Sidon

Tyre

Acre

Nablus

Jerusalem

KINGDOM OF
JERUSALEM

Alexandria

Bir al-Abd

FATIMID CALIPHATE

Cairo

Aqaba

France, Normandy and Aquitaine in the Twelfth Century